HALF THE CHILD

A Novel

William J. McGee

For Kathy—
It's the small things!
Bill McG

www.HalfTheChild.com

Book Layout © 2017 BookDesignTemplates.com

Half the Child/ William J. McGee. -- 1st ed.
ISBN 978-0-6921453-4-0

*This book, at last, is
for those who knew me first*

*My brothers and sisters—
Bobby, Judy, Kathy, Richie, Mike,
Janice, Patty, Margie, John, and Nancy*

And my parents—Florence and Robert

"Nick was startled. He had not even noticed the boy was awake. He looked at him sitting beside him on the seat. He had felt quite alone but this boy had been with him. He wondered for how long."
—*ERNEST HEMINGWAY, "FATHERS AND SONS"*

"The past is never dead. It's not even past."
—*WILLIAM FAULKNER*

"Dad cracked a joke, all the kids laughed
But I couldn't hear 'em all the way in first class"
—*KANYE WEST*

"What fresh hell can this be?"
—*DOROTHY PARKER*

CONTENTS

BOOK ONE

It's a summer of colors, especially primary colors. The life of a two-and-a-half-year-old is packaged with redder reds, bluer blues, yellower yellows. No mauves or fuchsias or taupes. Toddlerhood is the first critical lock in the canal of capitalism, when lifelong brand loyalties are forged, so the designers, packagers, architects, and marketers all possess the same palette. On *Thomas & Friends* DVDs, Thomas the Tank Engine is blue, James is red, and Molly is yellow. Shading will come later.

Ben becomes obsessed with colors this summer. They help him codify his world. When I call to say I'm coming by to pick him up, he asks, "In the *blue* station wagon?" Within hours my bicep will be red from playing Punch Buggy, a game in which time and again I prove exceptionally myopic to Volkswagens.

Two hours past nap time he cries hysterically when the red boat at Adventureland is sealed with masking tape because a seat belt strap has broken. I point out, quite impotently, that the orange boat is just as good.

He calls broccoli *green trees*, and cauliflower *white trees*. And when I ask about a friend from the park, he says, "Alex with the *brown* shirt?"

On another night he watches me researching a paper for graduate school and then suddenly asks why the letters in Google—a word he cannot even read—are blue-red-yellow-blue-green-red. I acknowledge I don't know, but together we soon learn why.

When I play my Beatles CDs in the car, Ben asks why the submarine is yellow.

We spend the summer at zoos and My Gyms and piers and amusement parks and beaches. I try to chat earnestly—usually without success—on purple wooden benches alongside snack bars, or on long lines for tram rides. Hey, buddy. Wanna talk?

I stand outside holding his tiny Reeboks while he somersaults into rooms filled with colored plastic balls.

*   *   *   *

By Memorial Day, I've finally conceded. For the last time, I call to ask her out for dinner, hopes fading even as I punch in her number. Within hours of that frosty response, I reluctantly take off my wedding ring, and remove all photos of her from my wallet. I drop off the tennis racket her stepbrother loaned me. There are two portraits of us in the bedroom, and I replace one with yet another image of Ben and the other with a sketch of the LGA tower. I edit my social media pages and eliminate any references to relationships. I realize there's a snapshot of her magnetized to the refrigerator, so I swap it for one of George Carlin.

*   *   *   *

I'm working arrivals and speaking to a Delta 737—inbound from Atlanta, of course—and I've lost him momentarily over Rockland County. When that happens, it's a scary, sick few seconds, and then he's back and you can feel your heart beating again. I see him on the screen now. It's the second time this guy has descended an extra thousand feet beyond what I told him.

"Delta two-four-niner, I say again, sir...flight level one *seven* and maintain. That's one *seven*."

He's prompt in responding: "LaGuardia, Delta two-four-nine. Copy your last."

Sure, now you do. This is just one of those guys you have to stay glued to, all the way to the deck. Of course, I've got plenty of other guys to worry about too, but this one I'm giving a little something extra.

Now I feel it.

There's a tickling sort of throbbing on my right thigh and I can see the faint outline of light underneath the fabric of my pants. We've got to shut off all cell phones and other civilian toys up here, as the constant Safety Management Systems alerts remind us. But Ben is with my mother, so I've kept it on mute.

I look carefully to my left and then my right and then slowly over my shoulder. Then I slip out the Nokia and rest it right in my crotch. I see *718* and I know it's my mother. I wait and wait for the voicemail. Delta 249 is still putzing around up near the Tappan Zee Bridge. And no beep for a completed message from my mother.

"JetBlue five-five-zero, correct. Hold and maintain, sir."

My mother's been speaking for *at least* two full minutes. I pass off Frontier 52 to ground control. They were supposed to just stay home today, maybe go to the park. Nothing further than a few blocks away. Shit. Delta 249 is drifting below 17,000 again. There are only two streets to cross between her house and the park. And I think the new guy, just transferred in from Dulles, he keeps looking at me.

Finally there's the silent beep and the light flashes.

1 message

Now it really gets tricky, but I manage to slowly, *slowly* punch in my password, which is *NIMAJNEB*. Shit! I hit a nine instead of a six for the second N. An Air-India heavy bound for JFK looks like he's going to cross right into my space, so I watch him. And I'm still watching Delta 249. I start punching my password again. The Dulles guy definitely is looking over.

"Delta two-four-niner, correct, sir. Descend and maintain."

Now I've really got to watch this guy. Two more letters on the password. That electronic woman on the phone—that familiar voice, it's as if we all know her, she should narrate the saga of the 21st Century for us all, tell us of births and deaths—she notifies me I have one new message. I punch for it. Then I take the offensive and stare at the Dulles guy. He turns away quick. Screw you, buddy. Virginia horse country ain't LaGarbage. Another Delta, this one a 757, gets handed to me. Then it's my mother's voice. I take one quick look around and—screw it—I listen.

She knows I'm at work and she knows it's busy and she doesn't want to bother me but she knows I leave the answering machine thing on my phone when I'm working so she knows it's okay to leave a message and she and Ben are back from the park and he played in the sprinklers but now he's pooped and he fell asleep on the sofa and she doesn't want to wake him to go to the store because she doesn't really have anything in so how about on my way over to her place I stop off at Hunan Gardens. And don't forget beef-on-a-stick for Benjy.

I sigh.

"Delta two-four-niner, LaGuardia. Need you to continue descending, sir."

In the old days, when I walked into this room, everything else ceased to exist. Even in the married years, she ceased to exist too.

That was before Ben. He changed all the rules. And I realize this isn't the first time lately my son has distracted me from my life-and-death work high up in this tower.

*   *   *   *

It's a summer spent talking with professionals. Two marriage counselors, one child psychologist, three attorneys, two mediators, one accountant, one certified social worker. Trained professionals all. The offices are lined with laminated Ivy League degrees, curlicued certificates, Albany-issued licenses.

I'm living in the now-quiet one-bedroom apartment in Queens. She and Ben are just a few blocks away, with her parents. And when he's with me, I find we often stay overnight with my mom in the old row house where I slept as a child and where my sister Katie comes to play with her favorite nephew. The professionals all have offices in Manhattan. This is somber business—not for outer-borough types.

Currently we're separated but not yet divorced and have no formal or even informal visitation schedule in place. I just pick up Ben whenever my shifts allow. My strongest supporters think I'm deluded, but most mornings I wake up hoping this whole thing can be put back together, primarily because I'm not even absolutely clear why she left.

What I don't know is soon the time Ben and I spend together will be micromanaged not to the day or even the hour, but to the minute. (*The Father shall return the Child to the Mother on the second and fourth Wednesdays of the month by 7:45 p.m. Eastern Daylight Time.*) What I also don't know is these agreements will become more, not less, restrictive as the years pass. I'll learn "two weekends a month" is not the same as "every other weekend."

And now at work I rap on the cubicle of my union rep. Is there a time limit on the counseling from the Employee Assistance Program? So could it cover legal advice, too? Can you break down my monthly Aetna HealthFund deductions—you know, how much for me and just one dependent?

I'm back working five-day shifts again, which at congested LaGarbage in the summer feels like ten days. My ears hum for hours afterward, and I jerk spasmodically in odd settings. She always said I spoke to inbound aircraft in my sleep.

I've been granted a leave for graduate school, so some weeks I'm only in the tower three days. But ever since she dropped those words—"We've got to talk"—I'm thinking I'll have to postpone grad school. I can't work and spend time with Ben and still go to NYU, so school may wait. Even though I already waited six years, while she got to finish graduate school ahead of me.

Aside from any sentence including the term *testicular*, I think the worst four words a man can hear are: "We've got to talk."

Drinks after work in Astoria with other controllers. Asking the same rhetorical questions. Over and over. Sometimes forgetting I'm not going home to my wife and son.

*   *   *   *

I'm drying off Ben after 45 minutes in the tub. His blond hair looks dark since it's wet and combed over and his face is flushed and his skin is still clammy and he smells terrific and he's tired but he's smiling and he's got that happy-little-kid-who-just-took-a-bath look no amount of money can buy to make your heart soar any higher.

"Daddy, make me a bundle," he asks. "A *blue* bundle."

I'm tired, but I can't refuse. I take the large bath towel, more soggy than fluffy now, and start wrapping it around him, mummy style, until the only flesh that peeks through is his head. He's already giggling. I lift the whole package by securing leverage just above his knees so he doesn't top heavily bend over into himself like one of those balloon men dancing outside car washes, and he stiffly leans against me as we walk to our bedroom. But I make a tactical error.

"Ha!" I laugh. "You're trapped. The Good Guys' leader...no way to escape!"

He's laughing too. That little head sways back, and is propelled forward so quickly I can't even respond before it cracks into that patch of forehead just above the bridge of my nose. When I shout, he cries.

Later, after he's untrussed and two bath towels have soaked up the A-Positive pouring from both nostrils, it takes all my energy to smile, so Ben knows Daddy's still standing even after the Liverpool Kiss of all Liverpool Kisses.

He holds Dog and asks why the blood is red on my face but brown on the towels. We ponder that too.

*   *   *   *

I live in the present. I'm on break but I haven't left my station, and I stare for long minutes without blinking. It's the rare day Runway 22 is in use for departures, and I watch as aluminum meets that mix of nitrogen and oxygen and each time—every time—the eye is deceived and the pressurized vessel somehow manages to lift and then it grows smaller and smaller still, that old *New Yorker* cover not so funny now to anyone up high like me, staring past Flushing and the Bronx and Connecticut and this blue ball itself.

I live in the present, but there are many things I don't know, so I'm continually learning and forgetting, learning and forgetting. Among the things I don't know is that my life, which has never been worse, is going to get much worse, and much worse still, and even much worse after that. I don't know fundamental truths will be exposed as lies, allegiances will shift, dormant veracity will form new foundations.

I don't know that later I will say if I had known all the things I had not known at this time, I would have killed myself, perhaps on this very day, this rarest of days, a Runway 22 departures day. I'm one more pressurized vessel, with external pressure fighting pressure from within.

And so I find myself staring at those pressurized tubes ascending and descending on the horizon as if they always had and always will and I continually ask, but who are we? We pretend we inhabit emotions one at a time—that sensations patiently approach us like faceless ninjas who bounce on the balls of their feet, dutifully waiting their turn to attack the bloated hero in a cheap action movie. A Psych seminar I've signed up for is unironically titled Understanding Grief and the instructor addresses the Five Stages as if they are Mount Rushmore-like in their chiseled separation, as if denial and bargaining can't cohabitate, or anger and acceptance never overlap. As if we are one person, rather than thousands, and with tens of thousands more to come.

Are we still the same person when at our worst? Or at our best? Do we split the difference? Or we're all that—and more? Less?

I've read that biologically our cells completely regenerate every seven years. But do our eternal truths remorph as well? What of the moments when we shout *I HATE YOU! I HATE YOU!* Who are we then? And who are we when we whisper love and devotion? When time unfolds in ways we never had the ability to foresee, do dead feelings coalesce into lies? How are we to know when the truths of now will calcify into the lies of then?

Is nothing we feel truly *certain*? Ever?

Why do we attribute individuals with qualities—bravery, fidelity, devotion—as if such qualities are unchanging? We can be brave on Tuesday, and cowardly on Wednesday, and brave again on Friday. We can keep vows, and keep them, and keep them, and keep them—and then not keep them. We can be devoted. Until we are not.

I'm old enough to have written essays for school on a typewriter, and that ancient device gave me a permanent record of the changes, the edits, the tweaks. The pages were filled with scratch-outs, cross-outs, inserts, subtractions, additions, improvements, detractions, and of course the gloppiness of Wite-Out. But a record nonetheless. Now the ever virginal tabula rasa of my MacBook Pro screen reflects all too accurately how I record internal sentiments, but I record them only in the now, my heart blinking like a cursor. I have no past feelings, and there are none to come—just *this* urge, this pang, this pull, escape, infatuation, panic, horror, devotion.

When I was a kid we always had station wagons, and sometimes I sat looking out the rear and sometimes I sat in the forward-facing second seat, and now I wonder which view was more accurate—where I've been or where I'm going. Both vistas can turn hazy, like the horizon I can barely see past the Whitestone Bridge towers.

Annabelle, my mentor when I was a Psych major, told me I should keep a journal, that writing about my feelings will bring lucidity and maybe—dare to hope?—even transcendence.

So here it is.

Professionally, I've always wanted to do two things: speak to airplanes and study the human mind. But I find my own mind keeps shifting, and shifting so quickly I have no memories, just memories of memories, photocopies with ever fading pixels, the instantaneous impressions upon which they first formed continually rubbed raw. These sands keep dribbling and flowing, even though after 34 years one would think they should have solidified.

My break is over and I literally shake myself, as if a canine were about to speak to 737s and A320s. It gets darker, and more pressurized vessels appear on the horizon.

I find all my deepest feelings can teeter or realign or cement or crumble. I've moved through Shakespeare's ages, and while I was once a schoolboy and once a soldier and once a lover, I know one truth. I may or may not continue to be a husband. But I am and always will remain a father.

*   *   *   *

It's a summer spent thinking of past summers.

Through the dog days of 2010 she did everything right. She continued taking yoga classes into her ninth month. Alcohol, smoking, and drugs weren't even issues. She ate so correctly other women loathed her for gaining only 11 pounds in giving birth to a six-pound, one-ounce infant; I joked I gained her baby weight in sympathy. In fact, when we brought Ben home the old couple next door thought we'd adopted.

But while she was carrying, despite all precautions, she still got nervous whenever anyone discussed the pregnancy. More than nervous. What I thought was a superstition became a phobia and then a religion. She was so afraid of losing that baby she refused to speak to it, or even of it.

I spared her a needle by testing for Tay-Sachs myself, but she was hardly relieved when it came back negative. My mother and sisters wanted to throw her a shower, but the thought paralyzed her with fear; I told my family baby showers weren't a Jewish thing. When I'd stare in rapt adoration at the sonogram she'd bite her lower lip and turn away.

And so it was up to me to communicate not wisely but too well with the pulsing, squirming, kicking life. At night I'd rub her stomach and press my lips close. At first I didn't know what to say. Finally I started singing, and it became ritual. My family's been here since the Potato Famine That Wasn't a Potato Famine Thanks to the British, more than five generations. Yet somehow I fell into Irish lull-

abies. Or what I considered Irish lullabies. *Too-Ra-Loo-Ra-Loo-Ral.*
Brown-Eyed Girl.

A limb of some kind would poke at her abdomen, and I'd sing
right into the flesh until the movement abated.

In Dublin's fair city, where the girls are so pretty, I first set
my eyes on...sweet Molly Malone.

Then it was five a.m. on a Wednesday morning in December,
and Four Ones Car Service (*718-441-1111*) screeched up. The driver
couldn't have been calmer. We do this for a living, he explained quietly as we zipped through the Queens-Midtown Tunnel. We held hands
for more than 12 hours in an anteroom while she crunched ice chips.
They gave us a clicker and we found Turner Classic Movies. I remember *High Noon* came on at noon. No drugs for her, not so much
as Advil. I worked my phone in the hallway.

By six p.m., it was happening, and I smiled through my Lenox
Hill Hospital mask as I positioned myself. I was his first sight and his
first sound. I snipped the cord and stayed close as the nurse weighed
and Apgarred him.

Hey, buddy. It's me. Dublin's fair city. *Me.* Where the girls
are so pretty. He stopped crying when I held him.

After I made all the calls my battery would allow, I found
them both in a double room. She smiled nervously for the first time,
and strands of her loose red hair fell across white skin. He nestled with
his eyes closed. She softly whispered a Richard Rodgers tune in his
ear: Ten minutes ago I met you...

I left them finally, and walked until I found the 6 train. Amazingly, the world was functioning pretty much as it had the day before.
I boarded the subway and sat. Club-bound teenagers were innocently

jostling and making noise. I tried reading a Claritin ad, but the tears brimmed over too quickly.

I imagined quite a few more decades like this, and it didn't seem at all bad. In fact, I can't admit this out loud, but it would still seem good to me.

*   *   *   *

It's the FAA's Annual Picnic, and I take Ben. He sits in my lap during tug-of-war.

*   *   *   *

So this is just to keep the record straight. Because I guess it's necessary.

I grew up in Queens, and I'm the middle in an Irish brood of six. Not *a* middle, *the* middle. Cause there's five now. My father Tom met my mother Eileen late and he was pushing 40 when I came along after the Bicentennial. I'm stuck in the pack. The oldest is Tommy and the youngest Kevin. And I've got two sisters, Kerry and Katie. My sister Elizabeth, who came right before me, died when I was young.

It was Catholic grammar school and Catholic high school. Then at Queens College I ran into a little difficulty I try not to forget. The five-year plan, but my Gap Year wasn't spent in Venice or interning for a family friend in the Senate; I worked construction in Long Island City and wondered whether or not life was worth living without anti-depressants. Drinking with illegals that flooded into Sunnyside and tore up their return tickets on Aer Lingus. Sleeping with Delia, a divorced mom 15 years older than I who loved 10,000 Maniacs, and getting stoned to *Hey Jack Kerouac*. After a while QC looked damn good. It took an extra year, but I pursued dual studies for a degree in Psychology with a minor in Meteorology, of all things.

But I actually did have a plan. See, in the summers we rented bungalows in Rockaway, even after Rockaway turned to shit, and then turned back again. Of course, last year Hurricane Sandy introduced new waves of shit. But for me, Rockaway wasn't about the beach or boardwalk; it was the final approach to JFK. Especially Runway 4L, right over our heads. I became an aviation geek drooling over L1011s before I walked upright. In fact, I spent a good chunk of my childhood unintentionally high on Testors glue from slapping together model planes. I started talking to aircraft, and now I still do.

I went straight from QC into the Air Force, and made it into controller school. Then I spent time at MacDill near Tampa, and another year in Dover, Delaware, before they finally stationed me at Naval Air Station Keflavik in Iceland. Up there I drank too much and for the first time slept with women I didn't know by name. When I got out, my FAA paperwork was filed. I did civilian training down at the Mike Monroney Aeronautical Center in Oklahoma City. After Oak City, I spent a few years in the tower at Stewart, in upstate Newburgh. I was at LaGuardia before I was 30. Some of the shortest runways coupled with some of the most crowded airspace, all resting on Flushing landfill. I soon found out why they call it LaGarbage. And in the Greatest Nation on Earth we're still using Korean War-era radar and slips of paper to track airplanes.

Only thing is, I had a secret. Sure, I always liked talking to planes. But I also wanted to learn more about the people talking to planes. That's why my major was Psychology. I'd plotted it out: put in a few years, apply for a grant, earn a paid leave, attend graduate school, and study the challenges of high-stress work. A specialist, an expert, a go-to guy. Even the FAA liked it. And it was scary how perfectly everything went. Right until the day I met her.

Stewart is near West Point, just off the Thruway, and she came to spend the day. She was researching her master's thesis and some wingnut in Regional Public Affairs greenlighted her, without worrying if she was al Qaeda. She had long red hair and wore a gray two-piece suit, a little too tight maybe, and carried a battered soft-sided briefcase with one broken handle. This will sound insane, but that broken handle helped me fall in love with her. Her field was Cognitive Psychology and she had this whacked idea of analyzing controllers—both on and off the job—to determine the philosophical and social leanings of those in high-suicide rate professions.

I became the off-the-job subject.

That was in 2007. We married in 2008.

Ben was born on December 1st, 2010.

She walked out one month before Ben's second birthday.

*   *   *   *

It's a summer of diners.

My parents have de facto separated, but only because complications from his bypass surgery have kept my father in the VA Hospital in Fort Hamilton indefinitely. It's generally understood by everyone he'll die there someday. My mom now lives alone in our old house and each of us local kids regularly drives her out to Brooklyn for non-conjugal visits. Although when it's Katie's turn she walks my mom to the downstairs lobby but doesn't go up; instead she sits in her car, the car with the bumper sticker: *IT'S NEVER OKAY TO HIT A CHILD.*

And so a chronically leaky heart valve and the GI Bill of Rights have combined to overrule the Church of Rome and do what my parents never would have done on their own, which is serenely live out their days under separate roofs.

He's allowed out for quick jaunts so about once a month I bring Ben and we fetch him for a trip to the diner. Actually, it's Ben's idea since he can't get enough of Grandpa Tom. The meals usually give me agita, but if Ben wants to maintain relations with any of his paternal relatives, I'll make it happen.

We swing into the winding driveway and see he's already waiting on a bench with other vets who clearly served in Korea or maybe even the Big One. He's wearing a Yankees *2000 World Champions* cap not because he cares about the fortunes of any given baseball team but because he knows I'm a Mets fan and wants to give me yet another dig, in a lifetime of giving me digs. And I'm not paranoid; the Bronx Freaking Bombers won 27 World Series but he only commemorates the one against the team from Flushing? In many of my key relationships, I could swear rulebooks were handed out I didn't receive. Most times I don't even know the goals.

I toot the horn and Ben lights up at the old man shuffling to the station wagon, dragging a large shopping bag. He sticks his head through the rear window and grabs Ben above his kneecap. "Hey, Ish Kabibble!" he cries as Ben giggles. "You're pulling my leg!"

As he settles into the death seat, I put out my hand but he immediately chuckles. "Still driving this piece of shit, huh?"

I look at my watch while they babble.

Her name was Shi'anna Wilkins of Far Rockaway. And because of Shi'anna, my father is one of the most decorated men to ever serve in the New York City Fire Department, an organization synonymous with uncommon bravery. It was a two-alarm that almost immediately became a four-alarm in the low-income projects along the waterfront. Four residents died, dozens were treated for smoke inhalation, and five different members of Engine 181 were recognized for gallantry above and beyond the call. But my father...well, his obituary will contain the name Shi'anna Wilkins. In 1987 Lieutenant Thomas J. Mullen was the sole recipient of the department's highest honor for valor, the James Gordon Bennett Medal.

Shi'anna was only four years old, and her stepmother's charred corpse was later found in the bathtub. My father entered the apartment with three others, and all four were pushed out by a vicious pocket of roaring flame. He reentered, and was struck on the shoulder by a falling cabinet that broke his left arm and sent him back out into the hallway. Then he charged in a third time, clomping through three rooms before finding Shi'anna cowering in the kitchen, and using his unbroken arm he carried her out through what *The New York Times* later termed "a virtual wall of fire" to what had been the living room. By then he had second-degree burns on his arms and neck, and parts of his gear were melting onto his flesh. He carried Shi'anna to an emergency stairwell and *up* three more floors, despite additional burns received when they ascended onto the flaming roof. With one good arm, he lifted her to outstretched hands dangling from an overloaded

NYPD helicopter, and then waited another agonizing 12 minutes for his own rescue from a roof that was quickly imploding.

For years my parents' bedroom was plastered with framed copies of the *Daily News* and *New York Post*.

BRAVEST SAVES TOT IN R'AWAY

4 DEAD; 1 RESCUE BY F.D. ANGEL

QUEENS BLAZE HERO—"NO BIG DEAL"

SHI'ANNA KIN: THANKS, FDNY

Months later, Mayor Koch invited the Mullens to Gracie Mansion; my brother Tommy was in the Marine Corps, but the rest of us were dressed like Easter, and little Kevin wore a plastic FDNY hat in a snapshot that made the tabloids. For years Katie and I laughed about it because you could see only the left arm of my leisure suit and her right leg in white tights.

ED LAUDS BRAVEST, FINEST

HIZZONER: BRAVEST OF THE BRAVEST

I was nine years old and tremendously proud that day. In fact, I remain tremendously proud today. Even though later I would feel somewhat lightheaded at the party in the Catholic War Veterans hall when I heard my father and others from his engine company—still in dress uniforms but with ties loosened and shirts unbuttoned—refer to the Wilkins family in such odd terms. Words not even in use in the Northeast in the 1980s: *darkie, pickaninny, cottonpicker*. At best, my father would refer to Shi'anna as the colored girl, and we all knew whom he meant. Because of his injuries, he was placed on restricted duty after the hospital, so life for him became demarcated—Before the Colored Girl and After the Colored Girl.

We're early birds so the joint is fairly empty and they give us a corner booth, which is terrific. These days I'm conscious of Ben causing a fuss, and I don't want him kicking someone's seat or flinging juice at unsuspecting Uber drivers. I get them both settled, wondering which of them requires more maintenance.

The waitress leans in. "Can I get all you gentlemen a beer to start off with?"

Ben giggles and my father laughs so hard you can see the gap from his missing tooth; he lost it falling down a fire escape when it separated from the wall of a burning bodega. Once again, I'm the odd and awkward and restless member of this trio, just like always. I may be in the middle chronologically, but with my father and son I always feel not centered but distant.

The waitress tweaks Ben's chin and winks. He smiles shyly, never sure how to respond to the wisecracking, heart-of-gold types. And she looks like she's balanced hot plates on her forearms since Ebbets Field was still open. "How bout a milk instead?"

Ben nods and I order a Pepsi. My father does the same, even though I heard his doctor advised cutting out sugar. But I'm not my father's keeper.

I set up Ben with crayons and show him the connect-the-dots diagram on the kids menu. Ben lights up, even though it's a basic ROYGBIV box of only eight colors; we contrast purple and violet. My father watches us—I can feel his gaze—and then pipes up. "What's going on with the lawyers?"

I stare directly at him, raising my eyebrows, silently sending signals that aren't received. "Let's talk later…"

"Oh. You don't wanna talk in front of him, right?"

I sigh. "Looks like it's gonna be a fire truck," I tell Ben. I think of The Nut House, the nickname for the engine company in Rockaway where my father spent the most pleasurable hours of his life, away from his family. And where he was decorated for conspicuous heroism on three separate occasions. Thrice, as they say.

For the record: After 9/11, I was just as awed by the city's firefighters as millions of others were globally. Awed, but not surprised. In a country where heroism is cheapened and the mantle of *hero* is unjustly bestowed upon shortstops and people reading off teleprompters, the nation's collective subconscious was shocked by genuine selflessness. Simply put, most people run *out* of burning buildings, not *into* them.

But then politicians and media conglomerates stepped in, and firefighters became très chic. A guy at my Archbishop McCarthy Memorial High School reunion told me that clear through 2002 he was still getting laid by different unknown women when he reported in Park Slope, so he started showing up on his off days. And not the usual Seagrave Annies my father's crew cavorted with at picnics in Jacob Riis Park—these were marketing VPs and television producers and magazine fact-checkers, women with advanced degrees who read off Kindles in Town Cars. Women who wear pantyhose to work. Women who usually covered their ears and turned away when fire trucks raced by. It was a crazy time, when families from Wyoming wore FDNY baseball caps in Disney World, families that wouldn't step foot in Corona or Bed-Stuy unless sponsored by a reality show.

At the height of it Katie and I were sometimes heretics, committing treason by sarcasm and flirting with sacrilege by secretly mocking the new-found fans. Mocking the bravery or mocking the sacrifice or mocking the loss or mocking the widows and orphans? No, *never*, not once. Mocking the editorials and the talk show hosts, babbling about men they'd never met and had no desire to meet. *We* had met them, and we knew them well, dozens and dozens, the fallen as well as survivors. We knew them as heroes. But some of them were flawed heroes—like my father. Thankfully, there's a new generation of men and women transforming the culture, bringing diversity where once it was stifled. I've seen it for myself with friends from the neighborhood and high school. My father's workforce is finally giving way, just as my father's parenting ways are as dead as the lame sitcoms and commercials that pretend dads still can't change a diaper.

But Katie and I couldn't help recounting the FDNY parades we grew up attending in Broad Channel. The float with firemen in black face eating oversized slices of watermelon. The gay wedding parody with a hairy-backed, 260-pound hook-and-ladder driver named Rolf wearing a white mini-skirt. The Puerto Rican Day "tribute" that consisted of 23 firefighters all pretending to sleep on one king-sized mattress. The "hanging" of a dummy made to resemble Al Sharpton.

Finally my mother overheard Katie and me discussing Frankie Fratelli, a veteran fireman who escaped the North Tower. We recalled how he had once worn a four-foot tall white Afro wig at a Christmas party while handing out gifts as David Dinkins, the city's first African-American mayor. Eileen blasted her two adult children as if we were Ben's age. We didn't bother defending ourselves. If studying meteorology taught me anything, it's that contradictions are a vital component in the workings of the universe.

The waitress mistakenly thinks we're in no hurry, so I signal her. After I explain Ben wants applesauce and a side of peas and carrots and a plate of spaghetti completely dry, she mock-argues with the boy. That's right—no butter, no sauce, no oil, no nothing. Not even a *dab* of sauce? Not even a dab. Ben shakes his head emphatically. I order a western omelet with well-done home fries and a bagel; ever since Iceland, I often eat breakfast at dinnertime. My father wants chicken Francese with fries and buttered peas, not exactly key components of a cardio patient's regimen, and he opts for the full dinner.

Even though we're in a corner, I realize it's not very spacious; there's more booth than table. And it quickly fills up with ice waters, Pepsis, milk, my father's navy bean soup, sour pickles, coleslaw, ketchup, a large basket of rolls, butter, salad, and dressing. And now we learn what's in the large brown shopping bag.

"Hey, Charlie, I got something for ya."

The boy's eyes brighten as he crumbles crackers. "What?"

"You tell me, Mikey."

"He's Benjy," I say. "I'm Mikey."

"Hey, I thought you were Bacciagalupe," he tells Ben.

The bag is huge, and as he swings it toward Ben's corner it hits my left ear and knocks one of the ice waters into the basket of bread. I jump up fast and throw napkins at the spill, but the old man's intent on delivering his package.

"Watch it!" I snap. "Lemme get this!"

I hate that once again my temper is flaring. He ignores me and shoves the bag toward Ben, who struggles with the transfer. But it's way too large and gives way, slamming into a salad dressing, which mercifully is capped, though it manages to knock over my Pepsi.

"Shit!" I cry out. Once again, I paw at napkins, even as Ben allows the bag to collapse onto the seat beside him. The Pepsi sops across my half-eaten pickle and I collect the soggy mess.

"A car!" Ben cries. The sharp corners are digging into the bag at odd angles.

"Hold on!" I yell at Ben.

My son glances at me, wide-eyed.

"Damnit," I mutter, throwing more napkins.

Ben looks at me. "It's...*brown!*"

"Okay. You can play with it later. When we get home."

The lower lip trembles and I feel internal organs constrict. "I wanna see!"

"Later..."

Now both eyes are filling. He glares at me. "You're mean!"

My father chuckles. "Your old man's a spoilsport, Gitchigomee." I contemplate chicken Francese dripping from my father's earlobes but say nothing.

I speak quietly: "It's too big to open in here, buddy." My primary goal is to avert drama.

"I just wanna *see...*"

I reach in and retrieve a large brown Hummer with wireless controls allowing it to accelerate, reverse, turn, brake. The diagram indicating lights and horns makes it clear a power source is needed.

"Where'd you get this?" I ask without looking up.

He's working the navy beans. "Ah, guy comes round once a week. Little Chinaman. S'got all sorts of crap."

I flip to the side: *Requires (4) C-sized batteries.*

"It needs batteries," I tell him. "Did you bring any?"

He shakes his head, crumbling Saltines. Now I notice the left tit on his golf shirt: *Lava Dogs*. The nickname of his old outfit, the 1st Battalion 3rd Marines. A dig at my time in the Air Force, what he called the wussy branch?

"Daddy?"

"Needs batteries, buddy. But we don't have *any*..."

Ben starts crying. "Get them, Daddy!"

"You mean, now? Before my omelet?"

As I speak the swinging door opens and I know instinctively those plates are ours.

"We can't get batteries now, buddy. After dinner."

Ben lets out a wail and then slides Huggies-first onto the floor beneath the table.

"Hey!" the waitress says, plopping down plates. "Wasn't there three of youse?"

My father laughs. "Charlie took a drive. He's the wheelman. Went to fill up the tank."

She knocks loudly on the soggy tabletop, right beside my pale white home fries, and speaks even louder: "Charlie! Dry spaghetti going to waste!" I feel stirring near my ankle; it abates and the waitress departs.

Then I hear it: "I'm not Charlie! And my daddy is mean!"

I optimistically chop up Ben's spaghetti, in case it can be salvaged. But it can't.

"MY DADDY IS MEAN!!"

I knock on the table from above. "That's right!" I spit out. "I *am* mean! I go to diners without batteries. I'm the worst. I suck!"

There's no answer from the dirty floor. But my father responds while digging into the battered chicken: "Kids!"

I wolf down my omelet and vow—once again—this will be the last visit to Brooklyn. Even though it won't be.

*   *   *   *

Because of the leave for graduate school, money is suddenly a problem. I'm having trouble making the rent. When she was in grad school for five years, I worked full-time, so it was never critical. Now I've got NYU tuition, mediators' fees, attorneys' fees. My dues are in arrears to the National Air Traffic Controllers Association. And the muffler is ready to drop clean off Lovey, our nickname for our Taurus station wagon.

Also, we had a joint savings account totaling almost $14,000, which I didn't think about during the first weeks she was back with her parents. Last month I was shocked to find it now contains $23.52, and she defiantly asserted the withdrawal was rightfully hers. I was still hopeful of reconciliation, so I didn't escalate. What I don't know is that was yet one more mistake on my part.

*   *   *   *

And suddenly my life is altered forever.

It's Independence Day and I'm dropping off a sleeping Ben because we watched fireworks from my brother's roof. She answers the door, hands Ben to her father, and then steps out onto the stoop. "We've got to talk," she tells me.

Again?

A university liked her dissertation, which examined Jacques Derrida's repudiation of French age of consent laws. She's been offered a job. Visiting professor, full-time, a one-year gig filling in for someone on sabbatical. In a state fifteen hours away by car.

"Well, Ben will miss you," I say calmly, dumping tea into the harbor.

She spends nearly four minutes explaining why Benjamin needs to live with his mother. I listen politely, then leave.

And so it begins. We see more of the professionals than ever. Lots of visits. I've finally accepted that my wife will never return. But accepting that Ben and I will be separated? That's not an option.

It seems apparent to me, and most of those closest to me, that a child should never be separated from a parent he loves. So now if I have to fight, I'll fight. I believe it's a rather straightforward argument, and I can't imagine a court would disagree with me. Ben should remain where he's happy.

*   *   *   *

I'm out of work early and realize I don't know how to spend the time. It hits me how long it's been since I've visited a bar by myself. Her, Ben, work—it's been years. There's heavy traffic, which may concern a flashing yellow amber alert for an abducted little girl. Funny how I never paid attention before. I pull off and head toward an old haunt, Bunratty's Still in Glendale. The place is like Rockefeller Center: I may not desire to go ice skating, but to hear it had closed would be depressing. As I park the wagon, I notice the third green leaf on the neon shamrock burned out.

The decor is petty larceny. That is, every wall is covered with stolen traffic signs from the Auld Sod. *MOTORWAY 5 KM.* Directional signals in Gaelic. Red yield shapes with *GÉILL SLÍ* in the center. Every barman, waitress, and regular customer who steps off Aer Lingus is required to bring another hot item.

I belly up and order a draft Harp. In Ireland the law says you start drinking Guinness at age six but I've had bad experiences with that black brew. If I want pot roast and gravy and mashed potatoes, I'll eat off a plate, thank you, not slurp out of a mug.

The place is nearly deserted, just two old guys falling off their stools as the Mets and Yankees both grind out wins. Dennis plops down the Harp, parks before me with one leg up, and leans in as though the mirror isn't lying and he's the customer and I'm the one tending bar.

"Marital troubles, eh?"

He's from the other side of the pond so I hesitate; who knows what goes on there? They eat blood for breakfast, for Christ's sake.

I wipe foam with my tongue; drinking's like riding a bike. "Who told you?"

He snorts. "Shit, man. This is my living."

"What?" I hold up my bare knuckles. "The ring?"

"Didn't notice." He rocks on one leg. "It's *you*, boyo. Shit. Haven't...what's it been? Six years? Never see your arse in here." He shakes his head. "Marriage's killed more bars than liquor license people. Every time."

I take a bigger swig, showing I haven't lost a step. "I've been in. Now and again."

"Bullshit. Haven't seen you since...shit."

"My cousin Timmy's bachelor party. Maybe...eighteen months ago."

"Well, la dee dah," he says, in that way the Irish have of saying effeminate things without sounding effeminate. "Used to work with a fella. Long-time barman. *Many* years at the stick." He nods toward the keg handles. "And Eddie used to say funerals are great for business. But weddings...hell, they're death. The death of good bars."

I smile. "Well, I'm back."

"Any chance of..."

"No. *No.*"

"That was that red-headed Jewish girl you'll be divorcing."

"Well, she's Jewish. But that's not why we're divorcing."

"And no chance?"

"Nope."

Dennis finally smiles. "Then you won't mind me saying she had a great arse."

"Not now I don't. Last year I would've..."

The crowd erupts at Citi Field but neither of us look. Then he says it: "Should find yourself a nice Irish girl."

I channel Rita Moreno and sing off-key: "One of your own kind! Stick to your *own* kind!"

The nearest old guy pivots, and Dennis doesn't get the reference. "Huh?"

A real swing-and-a-miss, quoting Sondheim in a joint like this. I'm out of shape. I've left this life. "Look...even my mother stopped lighting candles. Ya know, for me finding some Sheila or Mary Patricia."

"And now you've a kid."

I push my empty mug at him, the most ancient of gestures. "Now I've a kid."

He barely moves as his long arms reach over to refill the mug, yet his feet remain planted while capping off a perfect head. "I've a kid as well. In County Cavan..."

"County Cavan," I repeat, not knowing what to say.

Dennis has been out for about 15 years, so there's no telling the last time he was a real father. At least, my idea of a real father.

"My kid's in County Queens," I say. "She's trying to take him. To Indiana. I don't know why..."

We both watch the game; it's mutual relief.

"You know, Michaleen," Dennis says finally. "Saw something interesting. Right in that toilet."

I smile. "Men's or ladies?"

"Oh, men's! Definitely the men's." He pauses so he can get it right. "Just over the last urinal. Down the end. And I was doin' my business and there it was."

"Joyce? Yeats?"

Dennis seems to speak to himself. "'She may be gorgeous,' says the wall. 'But just remember somewhere some other fella is already sick of her shit.'"

I'd like to think at some point I'll have a comeback for this type of misogyny. For now I just drink up.

*   *   *   *

My attorney is kind. And I'm learning—far too slowly—that kindness is never a quality you want in a lawyer.

I found Hillary through my union's Employee Assistance Program at no cost, which just about summarizes it. At our first "exploratory" meeting she professed to believe more in mediation, arbitration, or even reconciliation than in litigation. Stupidly, I hired her anyway.

Now we're huddling and strategizing for our first court appearance. Hillary smiles too much when discussing the new job in Evansville. After she asks me about the school's reputation, I run out of patience. "Who cares! It's Indiana! She's taking Ben!"

We talk a lot—the debt clock ticking hourly—about motions and legal precedents and filings. I'm viewing all this as mere formality, checklists the court requires before ruling that Ben cannot leave Queens. I tell Hillary about my friend Dan from the Stewart tower; he and his wife divorced and then bought houses next door to each other in Westchester so their daughter is always "home" no matter which parent has custody. That's my goal—that Ben always has two parents nearby. But Hillary doesn't seem optimistic, and finally I ask her if there is something she hasn't revealed.

My lawyer sighs and tells me of a recent ruling in New York State: If a working mother must relocate in order to provide for her child, then so be it.

For several long seconds, I simply stare. And blink. Finally I speak: "A working mother? What about a working father?"

She smiles without humor. "Well...the courts...they tend to favor mothers. Overall. It's...well, it's just the reality. You need to know that going in."

I feel myself continuously blinking, and can't seem to stop. "But...what if the father is the better parent? That's what the court needs to decide, right?"

Hillary sighs again, and quietly explains that the day I "allowed" her to take Ben to her parents' house was the day I de facto ceded custodial rights. Legally, I tacitly granted consent to my son not living with me.

Now my brain itself seems to blink. "But!" I breathe and regroup. "But...I didn't—"

"Look, Mike, I'm just saying what the courts—"

"But I didn't *know*. I didn't know they were leaving for *good*. I hadda get to work! I was on my way out the door. Late for my shift. She said they'd be at her mother's. I figured we'd talk that night. Sort it out. What was I supposed—...I mean, I thought we were just having an *ar*gument. I didn't know Ben was being *taken*—"

Hillary gently smiles and holds up her hand. "One thing at a time. Let's write this all up so I can explain it to the court."

Being given a task is an instant salve. I open my laptop and begin typing.

We're moving forward. Soon I'll have my day in court. For now and forever, I'll be the plaintiff and she'll be the defendant.

*   *   *   *

My best friend is Sam, but we probably only see each other six or so times a year. In the summer, at least, we have a ritual: once a month, we hook up at a batting cage to whack the hell out of some balls. Since he lives in Jersey now, we alternate between cages in Teterboro, near the tower where he works, and the excellent cages in the Five Towns, at the ass end of JFK.

We were both stationed in Dover, working midnights. His real name is Samir, and though he goes by Sam it's ridiculous to assert a Muslim could fully assimilate into the United States Air Force before, during, and after 9/11. He's as secular as I am, but in modern America you don't get to say, "Well, I'm not *really* Muslim..." It's like saying in 1938 Germany: "Well, my *parents* were Jewish..." That he's a third-generation American and his grandparents own a Lebanese restaurant outside Detroit is academic. Everyone knew the M-word was stamped onto his dogtags and he was excused from shifts at the end of Ramadan. Eventually, the same week they sent me to Iceland is when they shipped Sam's ass to Bagram.

Down in Delaware we started hanging out because we both came from New York—he grew up in Jamaica. Until then I hadn't palled around with anyone from the city; in fact, the whole time I was in I avoided being labeled a New Yorker. But looking back, I realize I befriended Sam because he was openly ostracized after September 2001 and I admit I defend underdogs. And I love being contrarian. We were thrown together working those long, lonely shifts when the only air traffic was dead bodies returning from overseas in secret, and eventually we started getting nostalgic for our childhoods back home. One night we'd discuss Roll-n-Roaster sandwiches and the next would be Dr. Frank Field's weather reports. The RR train, Ching Chow in the *Daily News*, the suicide of Donny Manes, commercials for the Nevele resort. We both drove back home once a month, so we alternated cars and pooled gas money. Slowly we discovered each had something besides airplanes; I told him about psychology and he discussed performing comedy. He hasn't done it yet, but twice a year I rate his material for him. Every stand-up needs a hook, and he's the Muslim air traffic controller—can't miss.

One night driving north in my Saturn I told Sam if I ever got married, he'd be my best man. Several years later he was. The irony of a Jewish bride, a Muslim best man, and a WASP justice wasn't lost on this former altar boy; thankfully the FDNY didn't honor us with a float in the Broad Channel parade. As for Sam, he made the same offer in return, but I haven't had to rent a tux yet. He's been engaged for four years now, and the date hasn't gotten closer.

I'm leaning on Lovey. Sam's about 15 minutes late, but that's no surprise. It's a Five Towns month so he's suffering bridges and tunnels. I'll have to E-ZPass it next month. When his Buick pulls into the lot I purchase the tokens; he buys when we're in Jersey. I pull my batting glove out of my right rear pocket and select a piece of aluminum. Sam walks up just as I settle on an unusually heavy stick.

"Trying to kill somebody?" he asks.

"Just the ball."

There are two things we understand yet never discuss. Neither wears batting helmets. And we hit first, talk later. I use up three tokens, he uses four, then I use two more. Finally I step outside the cage.

Sam smiles. "Swinging too quick. Overanxious. Like you wanna murder the ball."

"I *do* wanna murder the ball."

"Any particular face on that ball?"

He steps in and I watch. He, on the other hand, swings late. But then it's always easier to recognize other people's errors.

A half hour later we're overheated and done, and I feed coins into this George Lucas contraption using vacuum cleaner hoses to slide Good Humor bars down a chute. I'm chocolate eclair and he's toasted almond. I sit on the bench with both legs spread wide and he stands against a bat rack.

"How's the bit coming?"

"The TSA?" He nods. "Almost there. Working on a thing about liquids and gels."

I shrug. "Ya know...*all* the bits don't have to deal with airports. You can do other stuff. Growing up. The restaurant. That Ramadan bit?"

We pause. Finally he broaches it: "So you're in some wild shit, huh?"

"Yep."

"But it's just one year, right? I mean, she won't stretch it into more or whatever. They'll be back?"

"Good question. She's saying one year..."

"You know..."

I stop eating. "Yeah?"

Sam stops too. "You just keep talking about Ben. Not losing him. Which I get. Completely. But...not for nothing. Marriage is over too. Haven't said much about that."

Those little chocolate crumbs melt right onto my forearm. "Not much to say."

Sam sits down. "But...this is me. I mean...you loved her. Right?"

For days I've been tracking weather at work; a front has been sitting over the Tri-State area, and the unstable atmosphere and humidity have made it unbearable. I suck on the empty stick.

"Look," I tell him. "I'll lay it out. Just for you. Three years ago. Pregnant with Ben. So...I took her out. What she wanted most of all. Westbury Music Fair." I pause. "Air Supply."

I watch Sam; he stops mid-munch, his face recoiling. "What the fuck! Over!"

"It's worse. Afterwards we stood in the back. So's to sign the program. Finally one guy came but wouldn't sign."

He disgustedly throws his stick into the can. "The small guy?"

I shake my head. "The other one."

Sam slumps back down. "Jesus...*Jesus!* Air Supply..."

"Yep."

He's trying to make sense of it all. "I mean...I knew you loved her. But...Jesus!"

"You'll find out. With Debra. You'll see."

He tilts his head. "I dunno...*Lost in Love. All Out of Love*...Jesus!" Sam quickly stands up. "Let's not mention it again."

That sounds fine. I don't know that we'll talk about it forever.

*   *   *   *

Judge Rhonda Westphal is a small mountain of a woman, well over 300 pounds, and she wields that gavel like a lion tamer cracking a whip—fast and accurate. She has white hair and smooth ebony skin and a large gap between her front teeth. And she has more power to directly affect my life than any other human being alive. Yet she never utters my name. Never speaks to me. Never even looks at me.

Hillary wears a skirt way too short for her 49-year-old legs, and when I see the other attorneys I understand—this seems to be a young woman's game, particularly on family issues. There are dozens of lawyers in the massive hallways, and each one viciously taps out texts and shows more thigh than a Rockette. When I make my way to the empty men's room, my senses are overwhelmed by electronic beeping and pantyhose.

At the defendant's table, her attorney is leggy and quick-tempered and mean-spirited. Everything you could want when suiting up on Sutphin Boulevard. She dismisses our claims and concerns and makes a convincing counterclaim that western Indiana is the only spot in all 48 contiguous states where a PhD in Psychology could ever find work, and she asserts this as if it's common knowledge only an inbred moron would dispute. Hillary flails and sputters, losing on points round after round. Incredibly, no one mentions Ben or his needs.

I nervously look about. Rabbi Cohen is several yards behind his daughter; her mother is minding Ben today. I pivot backwards and make eye contact with Katie and my mother, and both clearly realize this is all going very, very badly. In the car coming here, the three of us were already making plans to turn my bedroom into Ben's room, with me sleeping in the living room for now. With me as the custodial parent, Hillary wants the court to know Ben will not be deprived of anything. That car ride now feels as though it was days ago.

When the talking is over, the judge silently communicates with a young woman—also mini-skirted—who whispers into the ear of justice for a good four minutes. I'm learning these young firebrands are the power behind the thrones, making life-and-death decisions hourly. Finally Judge Westphal nods and speaks briefly but loudly.

The plaintiff, she says, must start developing trust in the mutual relationship both parties share as parents, which will be in the best interest of the child. It actually takes a few seconds to realize she's referring to me. *Me!* Trust? Has Your Honor confused the plaintiff with the defendant? I'm not the one wanting to move Ben to Indiana.

She continues speaking. The best interest of the child is most important. And she, Judge Westphal, will not hamper any woman's ability to support a child in this troubled economy. Women already are severely disadvantaged by unequal pay for equal work, and the historical record only reminds us of the challenges still ahead in establishing true equality. We should all celebrate this awesome opportunity offered the defendant. Her attorney is already snapping shut her briefcase.

I feel as if I'm drowning—as though I'm one of those people who doesn't know how to swim, thrashing about in deep water. Hillary is quietly taking it all in, and I gently touch her arm, silently imploring her to take action, *some* type of action.

But events overtake me and the gavel falls. Evansville it is. For one year anyway.

I have no way of knowing this lightheaded feeling will return time and again.

My mother and Katie hug me and we don't look at the other table. I wouldn't even know what to say. But somehow I do notice the defendant's own skirt is considerably shorter than any during the years we lived together. Is there yet another secret playbook? For decades to come I'll continue to question if the very course of my son's life was dictated by hem lengths.

*   *   *   *

Among the many things I don't know is Evansville is not now, nor will it ever be, about a job opportunity.

*   *   *   *

It's busy in the tower but finally I'm relieved for a meal break. I don't eat, and instead I go downstairs; the elevator runs just to the 14th floor, and from there the tower is accessible only by a narrow staircase. I head to the men's room and enter the last stall. Without unbuckling I sit fully clothed and lean my head on the cold tile wall.

Life without Ben. Yes, we've been hammering out the visitation agreement for Evansville. But it's just that—*visits*. For the next year, I won't be living with Ben and he won't be living with me. Laying out the next day's outfit and discussing the colored stripes in his shirt. Watching his tiny fingers scoop the dough from the inside of a bagel, leaving the crusty covering as though it were an orange peel. Carrying him home after he falls asleep in Lovey. Somehow, Ben and I both have to make it through this year, and then we can exhale.

I sit until my head aches from the cold. Finally I return and again speak to planes.

*   *   *   *

It's taken a week, and we've signed all the paperwork. Now I'm at the deli on Sutphin Boulevard, cattycorner to the courthouse, waiting on line for a roast beef sandwich; I've already grabbed chips and Pepsi. The hydraulic thing above the heavy front door hisses and I look and it triggers a memory.

When we were together, she used to pontificate about the caste system between Ashkenazi and Sephardic Jews, but I never bought into it. I'm an American, so even if the whole "all-of-us-are-created-equal" jazz is pure bullshit, it's bullshit I happily buy into for the sake of democracy, or what's left of it in the United States of Morgan Stanley. Meanwhile, she always asserted that because her last name was Cohen, a member of the blessed tribe, life had designated her first class while the rest of us unwashed masses squeezed into steerage. I learned how Cohens are forbidden to marry prostitutes or come into contact with dead bodies.

One time, on a three-day getaway to Bermuda, we were delayed at JFK while they loaded a casket right below our window. Of course, she didn't want our quickie vacation in Elbow Beach postponed any longer. But she let me know—for the record, mind you—*tech*nically a Cohen wasn't supposed to fly with a stiff in the belly compartment, on the off chance the dead guy was a member of the tribe. So I let her know *tech*nically—for the record—we Mullens had an ironclad Hibernian rule as well: No one in my clan is permitted to ride on Amtrak unless it has a bar car. She didn't find that amusing.

And the reason I'm recalling all this is Alfred Cohen, my soon-to-be-ex-father-in-law, is standing under the door's hydraulic thing and can't pretend he doesn't see me.

"Hello, Michael."

"Morning, Rabbi." For years I used his first name, but although I'm polite, instinctively I've gone back to Rabbi Cohen. Forget Paul Simon: I won't call him Al.

I always felt he was a genuinely nice man, one of those guys who perpetually smiles. Even my father got along with him, trading tales of the Polo Grounds and Horn & Hardart. Now he tries that smile, but he's met with stone. And I know he's contemplating what he's lost as well. In the years ahead he'll truly miss me at the Seders and the barbeques in Westchester.

We always had this one thing, something no one else had, not her, not her mother, not even her stepbrother Adam. Back in the day, during the Kennedy era between Korea and Vietnam, he'd done six months in the Reserves as an Air Force chaplain. He'd been running from Uncle Sam all throughout CCNY and Hebrew Union College in Cincinnati, and his draft board finally got him with a direct commission to captain. He was stationed in McGuire down in Jersey, and they didn't put too much on his plate. Conducting Sabbath services, counseling drunken Jewish airmen in the brig at Fort Dix, consoling Newark or Jersey City families if they lost someone in Weisbaden or Manila or a plane crash. But it gave us a connection, both of us in the same branch, the same blue uniform.

The truth is, he always liked me. And I always liked him. But the gates are clanging shut now. For good.

His smile fades. "This kid Harvey's got some arm, huh?"

I visually check my roast beef. "Couldn't say. Haven't had time to follow 'em."

He nods, but clearly it doesn't concern the Mets.

"You still at LAG?"

"It's L…G…A."

He pauses. "Mike, I—"

"Don't."

He just stares.

I continue, "Really…I just don't wanna hear it. Blood is thicker. Fine. You gotta do what you gotta do. But I don't have to listen. Cause I don't. Not anymore."

The rabbi seems disappointed in me, as though I confessed to something much messier than he'd been prepared to absolve. "It's not that simple, Mike."

I'm watching the guy on the slicer. How hard is it to stack meat on a roll?

I smile grimly. "Know what? It is. It really *is* simple. Taking a little boy and moving him…far away from his daddy. Even though he loves him. It's pretty simple."

There's a pause long enough for the rabbi to jump in, but he's got nothing. So I add, "You can slice it any fucking way you want, but there it is."

The guy behind the counter looks up, but I'm staring at the rabbi. I've never dropped an f-bomb on him before, yet he doesn't even blink. Must have counseled some foul-mouthed Airman Basic Rosenberg or Berkowitz in a court martial hearing back during the Cuban Missile Crisis. Instead he plays it obvious.

"You're a young man. You still look at the world all black-and-white. Life is…more about shading."

I let out an audible sigh. "Shading," I cluck. "All due respect…you're the one in the morality business. But when the chips are down…it's about *shading*."

He shifts so he's standing closer to me. "You're an intelligent guy, Mike. But you've got a temper."

"That what she said?"

The rabbi coughs as though he misspoke. "No! No, I don't mean that type of temper. I mean...you don't hear things at times. And when you get angry it clouds—"

"Please!" I say, forcefully enough so he steps back.

Finally, the counterman reaches across with my sandwich, wrapped mummy-fashion in thin white paper so I can carry it ten feet to a table.

Her father nods sadly. "I'll pray for you, Mike."

"No," I say. "Pray for Benjy." Now I'm done with him, once and forever.

*   *   *   *

As for that Google logo, we find the answer on Wikipedia, presumably accurate. The original concept was for all six letters to be decked out in primary colors, blue-red-yellow. But the graphic designer said the *L* became a secondary color—green—because Google doesn't follow the rules. Ben nods, and I believe he understands.

But I've been spared the difficulty of telling him the court's decision. His mother already debriefed him, and he speaks matter-of-factly about moving to Indiana. So we google the term *Hoosier*. Calculating the distance makes my throat hurt.

*   *   *   *

I've gotten home late. There's a thick manila envelope wedged into the tiny mailbox in the lobby. My attorney's return address. I hustle into the apartment, tear it open, and start reading.

> AGREEMENT made and entered this _____ day of _____, 20__, by and between HER residing at HER PARENTS' ADDRESS (hereinafter the "Mother"), and MICHAEL PATRICK MULLEN, residing at MY ADDRESS (hereinafter the "Father").
>
> WITNESSETH:
>
> WHEREAS, the parties were married on July 30, 2008, in Queens County, New York and subsequently filed for divorce on July 30, 2013; and
>
> WHEREAS, the divorce will be resettled at a date to be determined; and
>
> WHEREAS, there is one (1) fruit of the marriage, to wit: BENJAMIN COHEN MULLEN, born December 1, 2010 (hereinafter referred to as the "Child"); and
>
> WHEREAS, based upon the order of the court—

I stop reading.

There's an odd sound in my ears, getting louder.

The fruit of the marriage.

Ben.

The fruit of the marriage?

Ben!

My ears are pounding. And I wonder—for the first time but not the last time—if all this will kill me.

*   *   *   *

I continue telling Ben about the state where he and Mommy are moving. There are lots of farms there, I point out. Maybe you can ride a pony when I come visit. We use Google to learn about neighboring states. Illinois. Ohio. Kentucky.

Ben is startled. "The grass is *blue*?" he asks incredulously.

    *   *   *   *

I'm a lame duck and hypersensitive about it. So I find myself disappointed when Ben acts up—which has been quite often. Doesn't he realize how precious these days are? At other times, I get bored the way only the primary caretaker of a toddler can get bored. It's the dirty little secret of parenting: the best job in the world, yes. But conversing about Buzz Lightyear and Harold the Helicopter eventually takes its toll. So the cycle renews—engaged, bored, guilty, engaged. And then I'm maudlin, stealing kisses and hugs when he clearly feels they're inappropriate. I steal them anyway.

    *   *   *   *

I'm not sure how this fell into place, but for the first time since 2006 I'm preparing for a date with someone other than her. On some level, I think it's a mistake, because I've been miserable company ever since my day in court. Then again, Katie isn't wrong that I could use a distraction from thinking about Indiana.

I would have guessed I'd eventually get back into the game with a colleague from the tower. There's always a steady stream of

Fucking New Guys coming through LaGarbage—many don't stay long—and some of them aren't guys at all. In fact, some have made my head turn away from the screen at times. After all, the FAA actively promotes diversity. But instead it happened at NYU, in that Understanding Grief seminar.

After class I queried the professor over the methodology for differentiating depression symptoms from grief symptoms. But during his rambling response I mistakenly mentioned I'm an air traffic controller so he started speaking slowly, in the I-hope-you-understand-this-because-you-must-be-a-moron voice pseudo-intellectuals use for anyone not generating W2 forms from universities or media conglomerates. Afterwards, the young woman behind me smiled and blatantly said she was headed to Starbucks off Washington Square, and I just as blatantly told her so was I.

Her name is Velveeta Smith, so on top of my already tall pile of anxieties is the real concern we'll hit it off and develop a relationship and find happiness in each other's company, which of course will mean I'll have to explain to quite a few incredulous friends and blood relatives that, yes, her name really *is* Velveeta Smith. In fact, I've already begun composing responses to the quips I'll hear.

But although I don't know how the moniker was bestowed, or exactly what ethnic brew stirred up those freckles and strawberry blond curls, Velveeta Smith is cute as all hell. And even though she dresses in baggy layers of NYU violet-and-white sweats and hoodies, somehow all that cotton doesn't hide a sexy curvy figure and a nasty scar on her shapely right calf and a red-and-blue Chinese tattoo at the base of her smooth spine and a pared ring inside her shy belly button.

Not drinking coffee has never hampered me at Starbucks so I chose an Italian soda and paid for her latte macchiato venti mocha whatever-the-hell and from the lilt of her left eyebrow I could tell she was impressed I treated, like she was out with a grown-up. Because the thing about Velveeta Smith is she's a hell of a lot younger than me. So young she used the word *bae* while texting.

In fact, in the break room the next day I jotted down the following, a sloppy scalene triangle summing it up:

MPM...................1978

VELVEETA..........1991

BEN......................2010

But what the hell. She blew on her latte and we discussed the axis of psychology and sociology and she talked about conducting research on the career aspirations of kindergarten kids based on gender breakdowns and I told her about the psychological make-up of a control tower during summer thunderstorms and when Velveeta Smith smiled—the point of her left knee parked in the side of my right thigh—I felt a charge that emanated low but soon coursed through my whole body.

I asked her to dinner for Sunday night, calculating it's a good first date night, weekend but without the Friday-Saturday anxiety nexus. In no time, that smile returned.

Now I'm flowing into traffic on the 59ᵗʰ Street Bridge (screw the tunnel and E-ZPass). I'm deciding where I can stash Lovey and its noisy exhaust system for an overnighter if the stars really do decide to align. Presumptuous I know, but the FAA spends a considerable budget providing us with contingency planning so I bought a Trojans twelve-pack when stocking up on blue Huggies at Walgreens. I'm way too early; the plan is to meet Velveeta Smith at her apartment off Broadway at eight. But I roam the East Village until finally finding the holiest of grails—an old-fashioned broken meter, not the shared kind. Now I slowly hike back toward NYU.

On St. Mark's Place, I inhale incense and think about that kindergarten project of hers. I know it sounds crazy after sharing close quarters with a sweet woman, but my strongest reaction at Starbucks was when she mentioned her kindergarten research. So Velveeta likes kids. No wonder the very thought of Italian soda has made me smile.

I walk and wonder and wander through the maze of NYU and non-NYU buildings and read posters touting the upcoming bands at a new club: *Ground Zero Mosque. Tighty Whiteys. Ayn. Barbara's Bush. Sam the Butchers. Flatulence. Roy and Siegfried. The Skid Marks. Grassy Knolls. Bananafish. Grilled Toe Cheese.* Slowly and concentrically I wash up on Velveeta Smith's doorway at two minutes before eight. She buzzes she'll be right down and minutes later my heart leaps when she steps through the foyer.

Seven years. Seven years since I felt the emotional-physical-sensual tug of kissing a woman lightly on the cheek and telling her for the first time how pretty she looks and seeing her smile while her nostril wings flutter for just a moment, silently telling *me* I smell good. And probably *at least* three years since a woman smiled at me the way Velveeta Smith just did. Not since Meghan down in Oklahoma City.

We've been texting for days, and I've been downright giddy every time I turn on my phone and see the text icon. She agreed on Indian, and the joint I selected is perfect in two ways: it's dark and nearly always empty. We're there in no time and settle in. Then the guy with the sitar moves away, the waiter uncorks the bottle of red I remembered to bring, and Velveeta pops in some papadam.

She looks gorgeous. Gone are the layers, the hoodies, the rah-rah athletic gear, and instead the clingy blouse and short skirt reveal treasures I only imagined while seated at the long wooden table in the seminar room. She's even dabbed on a bit of make-up and I can't help feeling honored and grateful...it's for me. *Me*. Thank you, Velveeta Smith. No doubt she debated on the blouse veeing apart from two opened buttons or three, and I want to assure her the winning vote for three isn't lost on this appreciative fan.

But it's so much more than deconstructing body parts, juicy though they may be. I've forgotten what it's like to be with a woman, just one woman for an evening. A woman who isn't faulting me with her eyes or waiting to say something to spoil the night. Disapproving, dismissing, denigrating. In recent weeks my mind has rewound over how she treated me during the last few years of our brief marriage, and it's safe to say I've passed through the denial phase; I now realize I'd been afraid to acknowledge what was virtually contempt. Velveeta reminds me I've missed so much about being with a woman, and didn't even realize it. Her eyes when she tells me something I never knew, her laugh when I lob in some shtick, her upper arms when she tosses back her hair. I love being with a woman and now I realize losing this is yet one more item on a long list of items taken so abruptly and perhaps permanently. This list of discovering what I've lost continues to expand.

"Do you want to get a couple of things and share?" I ask.

She smiles widely. "I was just gonna suggest that. That's lit!"

The sitar strains waft from the rear and I sit up taller. Seven excruciating years.

The waiter has memorized our order—reassuring us he'll bring naan right away—and I can wait no longer. The soft light from the street highlights Velveeta Smith's strawberry blond halo, and I reach back and retrieve my wallet.

"I know we haven't talked very much," I say, aware of my awkwardness and yet not caring. "But I want to show you something."

I flip open the wallet so the fold naturally exposes both my Exxon Mobil card and a Sears portrait of Ben holding a ship's wheel. "That's my son. He's three in December."

She smiles perfunctorily, then says, "Nice."

The light from the street seems to shift momentarily, and her hair darkens.

"His name is Ben."

Velveeta nods.

I'm holding the wallet at an odd angle, with my wrist inverted uncomfortably, so I finally slip it back in.

"This place smells amazing," she says. "I passed by like a million times. But I never crossed over."

I pour more wine, hers first. "So Ben's with me right now. His mother...well, we're still working out...stuff. For now he's with me."

"That's awesome." I find it impossible to process exactly what that overused word means.

The waiter arrives, busily throwing down bowls of mango chutney and raita, extra napkins, a sizzling platter of vegetable samosa and pakora. Velveeta's face lights the way I'd wanted it to light at the Sears two-by-three, and she snaps a photo of the appetizers.

I dab at some tamarind sauce and bluntly dive in: "So do you like kids?"

Her front teeth pull at the crust of an overly puffy samosa and she finally utters a rather weak, "Sure."

I'm watching her eyes now, probably way too intently, and I can feel the happy expression on my face ten minutes ago has evaporated—likely for good. "I mean...with your project and all. What you told me. With the kindergarten kids? I figured...you know. You really liked kids."

She leans in and says, "As long as they're someone else's!" Then she breaks into a giggle I think lasts much too long.

I stop chewing and realize at once the meal is over, the night is over, Velveeta Smith is over. Now it's all about running down the clock in as painless a manner as possible, like during a disastrous shift at LaGarbage when it's nothing but diverted and canceled flights. I openly look at my watch and realize my lamb biryani hasn't even arrived yet. Of course, the waiter has disappeared.

Eventually I pay for everything including the tip and walk Velveeta right to her door. Though we're side-by-side on Broadway, I've already entered my post-Velveeta Smith period. She's talking at length—too much, actually—about how corporate psychology consultants for Fortune 500 companies sold their souls. I actually might have found the topic interesting had events progressed differently.

We're at her foyer; I smile broadly. "This was nice. Thanks."

Velveeta's forehead crinkles. "Are you okay?"

I may step back from her, but I'm not entirely certain. "Sure."

"You seem a little...distant."

My smile remains. "Tired. Got a long shift tomorrow. Mondays are tough."

She sighs. "Take care, Mike."

During the long walk back through the East Village I realize, of course, I'm a flaming asshole. On some level, I know a 22-year-old woman doesn't have to spring into cartwheels over toddlers. I understand I might have spent many fine days and even finer nights in the company of Velveeta Smith and those occasions would have absolutely no bearing on my ability to parent Ben. In fact, I realize she may even have come to enjoy Ben's company in due time. Yet when I reach Lovey I'm back to weighing the benefits of dating and masturbation. And it's a dead heat.

My phone vibrates; a text from my sister Katie:

Hows the big nite w/ Cheddar Cheese?

I decide not to respond as I start the engine and that noisy muffler kicks in.

*   *   *   *

When the muffler finally falls clear off Lovey, it's a relief. Ben comes with me to Midas on Queens Boulevard. I've owned quite a few cars, so I know the drill—sure, they guarantee the muffler itself for 700 years, but they get you on pipes and clamps.

Ben is not feeling well, and I hold him in my arms. We're standing inside the garage, watching them work the hydraulic lift. Looky there, buddy. Lovey is up in the air.

He lifts his head to ask, "The *blue* station wagon?"

Then he pukes, violently and seemingly without end. On my Icelandic flag T-shirt. My jeans. My Reeboks and socks. My shoe*laces*. Others who are also exhaust system-challenged peer out from the waiting room to watch.

It ends finally, and Ben cries softly. I kiss his hair and rub his back. There's no need worrying about a second wave; he's already thrown up more than he weighs.

I tell the Midas manager I think it's best we swing by another day. He's yelling at two Pakistani assistants: one should lower the wagon, the other should get a mop. Then I spread a tattered Air Force blue blanket across the front seat, and violate a cardinal law by strapping Ben in beside me, sans car seat. With all the windows lowered, it doesn't smell as bad as I would've thought.

It's okay, buddy, I repeat over and over. I quote what was inscribed on his first baby bib: *SPIT HAPPENS*. He leans against me, speaking softly about the color of vomit.

*   *   *   *

The New York Mets aren't far behind in the National League East. Sure, I'm a contrarian, but I can't turn my back on the Mutts. When Ben was six months old I dressed him in a blue-and-orange jumpsuit with booties to match and we took him for his first game. She kept repeating he'd never remember it, but I didn't care. So now among the things I'll send to his new home out West are a Mets T-shirt and cap. Thankfully, blue, orange, and white are all favorites of his. He'll be living just down I-64 from the Cardinals, so he needs inoculation before he goes.

*   *   *   *

The landlord and I finally chat and I make plans to move—giving up the apartment is the only way to keep my job, stay in grad school, and pay the lawyers. I've toured NYU dorm rooms the size of prison cells. But I always knew where I'd wind up.

My younger brother Kevin has a two-bedroom joint in Astoria, down near all the 20-something grad students, unpublished writers, and aspiring musicians. Only his loft is in a brand-new building constructed specifically for hipsters and other Gen Xers and Yers with serious bucks and an unobstructed view of the far side of the East River. For those of us born in Queens, it's amusing as hell to see the borough finally gentrified and hear 30-year-old gay magazine editors from Wisconsin talk about Jackson Heights like it was just invented. Of course, one of the dirty little secrets of New York City real estate is that a lot of young struggling kids aren't struggling at all—they're posing at struggling while their parents are paying the $3,000 a month for those lofts you see in romantic comedies and TV sitcoms. They just pretend to struggle—as if life itself is another zip-lining course or summer spent volunteering in Haiti. But they know, and their parents know, and their landlords know, that eventually they'll move out of those lofts and settle in Glen Cove or Montclair or Darien or Hastings-on-Hudson.

I call Kevin and he helps me transport the big dresser to her mother's house; I don't want her moving guys coming into what's now de facto my apartment. We wrestle it into my wagon and then sit on the hood; I pass him my Pepsi but he retrieves a spring water. He eats macrobiotic while I just keep putting on weight. My kid brother is taller than me, a hell of a lot richer than me, and quite a bit more centered than me. The bastard. I'm parked at a hydrant, the flashers flashing.

"So when's she leaving?" he asks.

"A couple weeks."

A few years back, Kevin got married himself, though it was an odd coupling that didn't last. In all, they spent less than a year under the same roof. But the good news is there were no kids. The whole transaction was cleaner than the Dutch turning New Amsterdam over to the British; they both had MBAs so their pre-nups covered everything from light bulbs to coat hangers to shower curtains. It's funny— the night he told me they split up, I felt sorry for him. Now I envy him.

It's doubtful he'll marry again soon. In fact, maybe never. Because he seems happier than ever.

He swigs the water. "So...ah, where are you gonna be?"

"Whattaya mean?"

"I mean...you staying here? Keeping this place?"

"Nah. Can't swing it. The lawyers' bills're killing me."

Kevin wipes his brow. "Uh huh. What about Eileen's?"

I've already considered my mother's place. "Uh uh. Can't. I mean, it works just sleeping over now and then. But I can't move in permanently. You know. With my hours. And my shifts. Getting in at all times. She'd wait up all night on midnight shifts. And get up to make me breakfast. She'd never get any rest."

"Yeah..."

I finish the Pepsi and say nothing.

Kevin's not like the rest of us. I don't think of him any longer as Irish-American, or an ex-altar boy, or a kid from Queens. He probably doesn't either. He didn't consciously reject us or any part of his past; it's just money people have a culture all their own. They're like Amish, or Hasidim in Brooklyn. In a way, the cult that welcomed Kevin is democratic—they don't care where you're from so long as you kneel and offer a novena for nine straight days in front of the Charging Bull statue down in Bowling Green Park. For money people, Wall Street is the Vatican and cash brings transubstantiation. He was shaking off Queens long before he got back from Wharton, so it's pretty ironic his seven-figure pad is in Astoria. Besides the loft, there's the Land Rover and 33.3% of a cigarette boat. Plus, a summer place in Sag Harbor and a new girlfriend every time I change the batteries in my smoke alarms. But he's a good kid. And he's my brother.

We both know that starting next month I'll be sleeping on the couch in Kevin's apartment (the spare bedroom is his office, where he speaks to Chinese traders when most of Astoria sleeps.) Maybe for a few months, maybe the better part of a year. Nearly all my possessions will go into storage at the Stop & Stor in Elmhurst. A couple of floor-to-ceiling cases of books, some softball bats, an Air Force footlocker, an 18-speed bicycle with 15 working speeds, a box of wedding photos. Part of the anxiety of moving is that hoarding our belongings makes us face the stark reality of just how little we truly possess.

Kevin never quite offers and I never quite ask. But he'll rescue me from homelessness. Without ever discussing it. In the end we'll stumble through such decisions in the wordless communication perfected by Irish-American brothers.

*　　　　　*　　　　　*　　　　　*

By early August, the tan line where my wedding ring had been has disappeared.

*　　　　　*　　　　　*　　　　　*

I'm finishing a swing shift, paying back a newbie who covered me so I could swear out a deposition. I'm seated next to this guy Wayne, and during breaks we talk. That is, he talks about sex. I've known guys like this in high school, and in the service. The funny thing is, like a lot of carnally-obsessed men, he's somewhat physically repulsive, with buttocks so abnormally large it looks like he's stuffed the back of his jeans with National Weather Service telexes. At shift's end, he's waiting for me.

"No offense, dude. Really. I know you care about your kid and all. You do you. But...you're divorced. You've gotta get laid, dude. I mean...*ser*iously."

I shrug. "Yeah...well."

"No, seriously. I mean, like, tonight."

Tonight? That's not on the blue Post-it in my pocket:

> - *Lion King tkts--$??*
> - *call Hillary/notary!!*
> - *switch for 28th?*
> - *adult mouthwash & kid shampoo*
> - *wagon—Midas DONE!*
> - *A+D diaper cream/wipes*

"Who?" I ask.

Ten minutes later I'm following his black BMW Z3 out of the employee lot and contemplating that a controller's salary isn't so bad with no kids or attorneys to support. Soon we're in Manhattan, southbound on Broadway and passing Letterman's place at way too fast a clip. In the theater district, he brakes violently and cuts across three lanes to park. I slow down more cautiously.

We meet where I figured we would, in front of a canopy advertising the topless joint upstairs. I follow Wayne's large buttocks, and he acts as though he's home.

I try not to look at the four girls onstage as we work our way toward the back. The DJ is spinning *Maneater*. We find seats at a small round table with three chairs, and Wayne beckons a tall girl in an orange G-string walking offstage.

"Hey there," Wayne says.

Her smile makes it clear she's seen him before, but she isn't happy. "Hey hey..."

"Wanna come have a drink?"

"Maybe later."

I laugh at Wayne. "Quite the ladies' man..." Now I spot another woman walking by, but she's a waitress, not a dancer. She's wearing an overly sexy outfit—high heels, red gym shorts, and a small top exposing her tummy and pushing her considerable cleavage up and out. I nod at her.

"Hi, guys."

I smile while Wayne orders a Heineken; I'm feeling patriotic so I ask for Sam Adams. Then I say, "Would you like a drink?"

She hesitates, but then nods. "Sure. Gimme a minute. I've got a break soon."

After she leaves, Wayne turns to me in disbelief. "Dude! What the fuck!"

"What?"

"You're supposed to drink with *naked* chicks. Off the *hook*. Not waitresses! Nobody goes home with the waitress. It's cray cray."

I shrug. "She seems really nice. Besides…she's the cutest."

As Wayne sulks, I recall joining a dozen enlisted men for a bachelor party at a strip club down in Tampa. This senior master sergeant—a guy old enough to have fathered some of us—lit up a cigar and said, "Boys, the first rule in topless bars is the best chests are the ones you can't see." At the time, I had no idea what he meant.

Our waitress has returned, carrying a tray with our beers and a seltzer for herself. Wayne and I dig out cash and throw way too much of it onto the tray. I smile and stand up and she sits next to me.

"So how're you guys doing?"

"I'm Wayne. This is my buddy Mike. We work together."

"Hi, Mike."

Wayne starts jabbering about the Hamptons, where he's got a timeshare with guys from the JFK tower. Then, without the pretense of explaining why, he gets up and leaves.

Very subtle.

I steal a few looks at this woman. She's short and stacked and probably from a big Italian family in Massapequa Park. Relatives in illegal basement apartments violating the Nassau County fire code. They all get together on Christmas Eve for seven types of fish at her Aunt Rose's and then head to Midnight Mass. She's got long dark hair and she's all curves and cambers, no sharp angles anywhere. I like that she's not emaciated—though of course any heterosexual male over the age of 12 would be insane to utter such a thing to an American female. My eyes remain focused above her clavicle.

I'm not sure what to say. "I guess you know Wayne, huh?"

"Sort of. We've crossed paths."

"Uh huh." A long pause. "So I didn't get your name?"

"Gina."

"Gina..."

Another pause, even longer.

She makes a stab. "So where do you guys work, anyway?"

"I'm with the United States Government."

She doesn't like the sound of it. "Which branch?"

"Federal Aviation Administration."

"That right? Doing what, exactly?"

"I'm an air traffic controller. LaGuardia. We call it LaGarbage."

She seems to perk up. "Really!" Now her brow crinkles. "You putting me on?"

Without giving it any thought, I reach back and remove my wallet and open to my photo ID with the USDOT seal. Immediately there's movement on all sides. She covers the wallet with both hands. The nearest chunky bouncer starts speaking into his earpiece, and a second chunky bouncer crosses the dance floor in about five strides.

Earpiece squats down beside me. "There a problem, officer?"

I'm slow, but I get it. I quickly flip the wallet closed and tuck it away, this time in my front pocket. "Not at all."

The second bouncer hovers. "We're good in here," he tells me. "We're *good*."

"I'm sure you are."

"What precinct you out of?" he demands.

"I'm not a cop."

Both bouncers look at each other, and then at Gina. "He's an air traffic controller," she tells them.

"A *what*?"

"You know. He speaks to the planes."

I smile my best I'm-not-a-cop-even-though-I'm-barrel-chested-and-stocky-and-I've-got-an-Irish-mug-and-I-was-born-in-Queens-and-I-went-to-Archbishop-McCarthy-Memorial-High-School smile.

Earpiece stands up. "You expecting to park a seven-forty-fucking-seven in here, or what?"

Gina waves them away, then laughs. "They don't dig the steenkin' badges."

"My bad." I lean in. "Mind if I ask you something?"

"Ask." She's all business again.

"Your belly...those rings. Doesn't it *hurt*?"

"Everybody asks that. Sure. Sore for days."

"And the tattoo...right next to it. Man. Your stomach's been through a lot."

She smirks. "That's nothing. I almost had a Caesarean. *That* would've sucked. I mean, wearing these tops. Lucky I had a good O-B guy. He waited it out and we did it the old-fashioned way. I probably wouldn't've gotten this job." She shakes her head. "They don't wanna see a scar. Not there."

Finally, I shift and get comfortable. "So you're a mom."

She smiles for real now, one hell of a pretty smile. "You bet."

"Girl?"

"Uh huh. Almost fifteen months."

I smile back. "Cool. My guy's two and a half. He'll be three in December."

"What's his name?"

"Benjy. How about her?"

"Ashley."

"Pretty."

"Teeth?" she asks.

"We haven't lost any yet."

"Right." She hesitates while the DJ increases the volume on *Milkshake*. "How about the potty?"

I shake my head. "We're not ready."

"Gotcha."

I lean sideways so I can dig the offending wallet out of my front pocket. This time I'm discreet and leave it in my lap, while I worm out two recent Sears portraits. I slide them onto the table.

Gina really lights up. "Oh, he's gorgeous!" she says. I can tell it's not just a line. She actually means it. Then again, Ben *is* gorgeous.

She looks into my eyes. "I don't have any photos. I mean...*on* me."

We both have a good laugh at that line.

Gina crosses her sexy legs and everything sways provocatively. But I'm watching her eyes now, her rather stunning brown eyes. "Lemme ask you," she says. "You think there's a difference? 'Tween boys and girls? I mean, right from birth?"

"Oh, definitely."

A different waitress stands over us, but I've still got half a bottle. Then I realize I'm supposed to buy Gina another $10 seltzer. So I do, and add a $5 tip.

Gina gets right back to it: "So to you it's nature, not nurture?"

I lean in. "Well, I think it's both. I mean, do I treat Ben different? Cause he's a boy? Sure. I mean...I doubt if he's my daughter I'd throw him in the air. Least not so high. Or wrestle as much. But bottom line...boys and girls act different. They just do."

She nods emphatically. "See, I hear you. My mom...Ashley stays with my mom. Three of us live together. My mom says they're all the same. But I'm just not sure."

Maybe I was wrong about Massapequa Park. Could be Staten Island, or even south Brooklyn. I want to ask where Ashley's father is, but I can't do that.

Instead I tell her, "Just watch 'em when they're in preschool. You can line up a whole room full of 'em. Half boys, half girls. Then the teacher'll dump a box of toys on the floor. The boys'll run toward anything with wheels. Or wings. Cars, trucks, trains...planes. The girls'll pick up dolls and animals. Then the boys'll start shooting each other with juice box straws."

"I know!" She laughs loudly and I can tell I've made her night. "Meantime the girls'll be cooking!"

"You watch. Ashley'll pack her own overnight bag next year. Telling you what shampoo to buy her. Boys still forget to brush their teeth when they're in high school."

She shakes her head. "I respect what you're saying. I really do. But think about it. All of that—all that behavior. The toys, how they dress, how they groom. That could *still* be due to how they're raised. You know? I mean, if we treat them different from the minute they're out of the womb, and start slapping blue and pink on everything, then...of *course* they'll be acting all that out by preschool. How could they *not*?"

I take a long swig and tell her, "Maybe you're right. I can't argue with that. We carry all this stuff around with us and it affects our kids in so many ways...it seeps in. I've read about how little girls are always told not to be aggressive. I'd like to think if I had a daughter I would always encourage her. No matter what."

Gina stares at me, saying nothing for long seconds. I take a swig, only because it's a socially acceptable way to keep busy. Then she says, "You don't come here."

I shake my head. "Nope. I'm sorta...a project. For the guys at work. I mean, since my divorce. They're all...you know..."

"Sure. I could tell."

"But I'm glad I came," I say quickly.

"Divorce sucks," she mutters.

I nod. "But in my case...well, I've got Benjy. I just wanna be with him."

Gina leans forward. "And Benjy's one lucky kid."

Suddenly, the second bouncer hovers again.

"Sir, if you'd like a private dance...there are ladies available. Gina's gotta get back to work."

A dance? A private dance? Actually, I'd rather chat with Ashley's mom. I shake my head and stand up. "Guess we'll catch up next time, Gina..."

She smiles that pretty smile. "Take care, Mike. And take care of that little guy."

I smile too. "You bet I will."

Before I can finish the Sam Adams, there's Wayne, right at my elbow. He's staring at me, his face contorted into a question mark.

I tilt my bottle upward. "You were right. Just what I needed. Thanks, dude."

*   *   *   *

She's gone to Israel for a seminar. At least, that's what she tells me. Who really knows who she's with or what she's up to these days. I'm starting to question—did I ever know? It's occurring to me far too slowly that she can be devious, and clearly has been for some time. I doubt I'll ever know even a modicum of her deceptions. And those doubts make me feel sick whenever I focus on them.

As painful as it is, I acknowledge old patterns. So much mendacity, but not in a Southern mansion—in a tiny Queens apartment. An early March night a year ago: I'm watching the Mets in spring training, Ben's dozing in his sleeper swing, she's reading. Then the buzz of a text. She reads quickly and blushes like she blushed years earlier when we first swam naked at midnight in the Pacific off Catalina and I kissed salt water off her neck as she wrapped her legs around my waist and suddenly the light from a distant shore flickered across our wet hair and her nipples pebbled and she blushed. I ask about the text, and she looks up, surprised I'm still in the room, or perhaps surprised I'm still alive. Then she says, "School."

But her travels do leave Ben with me for a week, an unexpected pleasure. Unfortunately, though, I have work. So I start calling relatives. I can't run my mother into the ground just yet; Ben's only two, so there'll be plenty of times I'll need to call on her.

My sister Katie is closest in age to me, just one year behind at Saint Rita's for all eight years. More than anything, Katie loves taking Ben for the day—she even bought a car seat for her favorite nephew. So he's hers on Tuesday. She and Chris have no kids, though we all know they're trying, and we all know what a great mom Katie will be. Of course, the universe gives plenty of kids to people who burn them with cigarettes and beat them with closed fists and forget to feed them. So there's that.

I wait for her in the food court in the main terminal at LaGarbage. Katie is a voice-over actress and good enough to actually make a living at it, working freelance out of an Integrated Services Digital Network studio right in her apartment; from my selfish perspective, the best part is her flexible schedule, just what a primary childcare provider needs. She's coming from Manhattan so if she gets stuck on the Triborough, I'll bring Ben to the tower with me. But it would be the fourth time this summer.

I've brought the stroller, and it's a good thing, because Ben is out like a proverbial light. It's funny. A grown man sleeps with his mouth open, and it ranges from disgusting to alert-the-authorities creepy. But a two-year-old boy does it, and you want to take a photo with your phone, which I do. I finish my pizza, then finish his pizza, then finish my Pepsi. Then I wait.

"Hey, Mikey! He likes it!"

I stand up and Katie gives me a violent hug. She's the redhead in the family, and she wears it long. Though last month Ben pointed out Aunt Katie's hair is not, in fact, *red*—and all three of us discussed the hue at length. She squats down and tweaks his chin, and he stirs.

"Careful," I whisper.

She smiles broadly. "My Ben Benny Benson!"

"Let him stay that way for a while."

Finally she stares at me, then steps back. "You don't look too good, Mikey. Putting on weight. And your eyes..."

"Thanks."

We transfer the diaper bag, apple juice boxes, A+D diaper cream, Baggies filled with Cheerios, Thomas the Tank Engine, a spare pair of shorts. And of course Dog.

"So how long's he with you this time?" Katie asks.

"A week."

"And she's where?"

"Israel. Psychology seminar."

Katie shakes her head.

I raise a brow. "Yes?"

"Taking Benny Benson Bennington away! Selfish bitch."

"Whoa!" I glance at Ben. "Easy…"

She sneers. "Puh-lease. Aren't you pissed?"

"I'm still…hopeful."

I see them to the parking lot and jog to the tower: four minutes to shift time. As I wait for the elevator, I think back a few years. After the inaugural barbecue at my brother Tommy's when I introduced her to the mob, Katie raved about her for days, telling me it was a redhead thing and I wouldn't understand. And it was Katie who insisted she enter the Kris Kringle lottery that Christmas, even before we married, an historical break with Yuletide protocol.

But that was then. Things have changed. And I guess that's forever too. I keep learning new meanings of forever.

        *   *   *   *

Nearly all my correspondence from the FAA and NATCA is electronic, so sometimes I forget to check my slot in the row of wooden mailboxes at work. But today I do, and find a typed note that could have come from any printer:

> *Dear Shit Head. Your a REAL pain in the Ass. Your NOT the only Father in the World. So grew a fucking Pair AND spair us all the BullShit with sick Days. Earn you're fucking Pay!!!!*

I crumple it and prepare a jump shot for the wastebasket, then stop. Instead I press out the wrinkles and fold it neatly, so during my break I can copyedit it.

        *   *   *   *

I realize her side has to be told as well.

Of course, I never envisioned us on separate "sides"—I thought we'd always be just one side. Her and Ben and me. *Our* side.

In print, as in life, people become suspicious of black and white. Flat characters—can't have them. The difference between a competent psychologist and a hack lies in the shading, no? And telling all makes it at least understandable, if not forgivable. Yet I can't tell all, because I seem to be missing critical components.

Actually, I *didn't* have a clue. I mean, of course there was arguing. But we were both groping through career adjustments. Respectively finishing and starting grad school. Living in a 1-bdrm/EIK with a two-year-old. Of course there was arguing.

But slamming-your-fist-down-on-the-dining-room-table arguing? I'm-taking-Ben-and-moving-in-with-my-parents arguing? I'm-so-unhappy-I-can't-ever-see-staying-here arguing? I-can't-stand-to-look-at-you-anymore arguing? I've-fallen-out-of-love-with-you arguing? No. Never. Like I said—clueless.

I envisioned dying together when we both had wispy white hair; sometimes in my dreams I still do. I never envisioned the rancor and acrimony of the American judicial system. In fact, despite it all I would broker a truce right now, and reboot this dying marriage.

As a chronicler, I know I need to tell her side. Staying probably wasn't easy. Leaving couldn't have been easy. Conducting this secret job search for teaching positions in other time zones—I doubt even that was easy. And deciding to separate a two-year-old from his parent: how easy is that? I'm sure she has a tale to tell. I'm sure my character comes across better on this page than it did across our queen-sized Sealy.

Can't I step back and see things as she must have?

I can't.

*   *   *   *

I'm supposed to alert a US Airways inbound to a Comair commuter sneaking up too quickly on his port wing.

Instead I'm fighting back tears and for one nanosecond the scope blurs. I breathe deep and will myself, then place my left hand over my helmet.

"Cactus four-two-seven, turn right heading zero seven zero. Ma'am, you have traffic off your nine o'clock."

"LaGuardia, Cactus four-two-seven, traffic sighted."

My nerve endings are more frayed than the 30-year-old equipment we rely on. Only this time it's not Ben. Or Judge Rhonda Westphal. Or the New York State Supreme Court. Or even her.

This time it's Dog.

I'm certain Ben was dragging him this morning when we left for Stop & Shop. Then again, I'm not entirely sure. We were running late—as always. And I rushed getting him in and out of Lovey—as always. Ben was up high in the kid's throne on the shopping cart, staring at cereal boxes, when he turned to me with a strange expression.

"Daddy? Where's Dog?"

A little later, after I bought him a Curious George coloring book and we loaded the groceries through the tailgate, I tore apart the second seat area. We found dirty napkins, blackened pennies, petrified French fries, dried-up baby wipes, parts of Happy Meal toys, a yellowed *Daily News* weekend Kids section from 2012, two missing Matchbox cars, a bowling alley pencil, and a long bolt and washer the Ford Motor Company undoubtedly believed should still be attached to a nut. No Dog.

There are many categories and subcategories of children's tears, including the unexpected kind, like when I accidentally men-

tioned dining on reindeer in Iceland, and Ben sobbed I had eaten Ru-
dolph. I expected the loud type—wailing, ear-piercing, throat-
constricting—when he eventually runs dry and sputters into red-
cheeked sniffling exhaustion. I was wrong. Ben was quite controlled.
Stoic, even. He remained that way even after unloading the groceries
and tearing apart the apartment. He hovered while I dumped the tall
kitchen trashcan onto the tiled floor, all 19 gallons. Still, he was in
control. What happened instead was worse, much worse.

Later, at my mom's, she was preparing grilled cheese for him,
and just the way he likes it, untoasted rather than toasted, so after a
minute or two under the broiler the yellow cheese turns puffy and
brown, yet the underside of the bread is soggy and doughy. I filled his
sippy cup with apple juice and found him at the dining room table,
tears slowly rolling down both cheeks.

"Buddy!" I called out, and he pushed back his chair and awkwardly rushed toward me, burying his head into my belt area. I rubbed
his hair and swore I'd keep searching. My mother said she'd call Katie
and Chris, since Ben had spent most of yesterday with them. I promised to retrace our steps since last night.

By the time I left for work I could barely look at Ben's face. I
hugged him tightly and kissed my mother. On the way to LaGuardia,
listening first to a Pearl Jam CD and then Green Day's *Warning*, I
found myself loudly cursing. Funny how Dog and not the New York
State Supreme Court ignited such anger.

"Jetlink four-two-four-zero, descend to two five and hold."

"Jetlink four-two-four-zero, say again, LaGuardia."

Jetlink, please take the shit out of your ears, sir. I repeat it.

"Jetlink four-two-four-zero descending to three five."

"That's *two* five, sir."

I stare at the box of cold moo shu pork and unused pancakes and hoison sauce next to my weather charts and I shake my head.

During both breaks I spoke to Ben, but his voice was lifeless, and he didn't even want to hear what one wall said to the other wall ("Meet ya at the corner!"). I began thinking of bizarre places to search late tonight. The car's spare tire compartment. The refrigerator's fruit crisper. My Air Force duffle bag. The Christmas decorations closet. My sock drawer. Ben's sock drawer. The bathtub. The microwave.

I stare at the scope and realize I'm filling up with tears. They're not falling, but they're in the sluice. I feel them backed up, the way the automatic return in a bowling alley spits balls down that long chute. What the hell!

It's not just the usual stress—you know, guiding pressurized aluminum tubes safely to Earth, blah blah. No. I'd be just as rattled on an off day. I'm rattled. Rattled over whomever the hell calls himself Mike Mullen these days. I don't even know the reflection flashing back from the scope.

Is it official? Have I morphed into a wuss?

Is that what fatherhood does, turns you into a wuss? Or, rather, is that what it does to those who care and allow it? Lord knows my father never succumbed to wussydom. Centuries of men didn't. But it's a new era and I'm wussifying as we speak. And am I turning Ben into a precious snowflake that won't learn to fend for himself?

I was never a macho asshole, but I was never a wuss either. I've always been a man. A guy. I've talked about the Mets with strangers. I nodded when people spoke of killing terrorists. I like airplanes and cars and gas stations and junkyards and barbequed burgers and baseball and boxing—and breasts. I make no excuses for liking *Family Guy* and CollegeHumor.com and Austin Powers movies and Ed Norton's sewer jokes on *The Honeymooners*. I love The Three Stooges, provided—of course—we're not talking about Shemp or Joe Besser or that godawful Curly Joe. I know how to curse. I like humor wrung from bodily functions. I play *Sweet Child O' Mine* at ear-splitting volume and I love the first beer of the night in a strange bar. I like video games in which I blow up stuff. I like watching shit thrown off roofs. I liked the kick on my shoulder from firing a rifle down in Texas. I know the major players and actions in World War II, prefer a stick to an automatic in the right car, stop on the sidewalk to watch electric trains, and eat dirty dogs off Sabrett carts—with sauerkraut. I can discuss the strengths and weaknesses of each of the Corleone brothers at length, *including* Tom Hagen. Obviously I don't stop and ask for directions when I'm lost, but I also don't *talk* about it, which is even worse. I liked *High Noon* from what I could follow the day Ben was born. After a week or so of showering in the same tub, I clog the drain with body hair.

Now this whole drama with her and Ben is having yet another unseen effect: It's turning me into a wuss. There's no denying I've cried more times in the last year than I have in the last ten. I may begin crying right here—here!—if the first officer onboard Jetlink Flight 4240 doesn't listen more closely.

What the hell is this?

When I was stationed in Dover we had an airman break down in the tower one night, and it wasn't pretty. It was an all-male crew and after they took him away, the awkward jokes started. I didn't join in, primarily because after my lost year on anti-depressants, I figured there but for the grace, etc.

Like I say, I've never been the asshole type, not in the macho sense. Even back in grammar school I usually didn't join in on ostracizing and at Archbishop McCarthy I made friends with Puerto Ricans, when the unwritten rule was only hang with people whose last names started with *Mc* or *O'*. In the Air Force I took shit voting for John Kerry and at LaGarbage I took even more shit voting for Obama. But I didn't care. No one could screw with how I handled a scope, so I never worried.

Now I'm not so sure.

A damn piece of canine-shaped stuffing is about to knock me off the scopes. Wuss is way too tame. There isn't even a word strong enough to describe this state.

"Cactus four-two-seven, cleared for localizer, ma'am. Winds at zero-one-zero from nine-zero."

"Cactus four-two-seven cleared."

I've never said it aloud, but I guess for years I haven't wanted to become one of the New Dads springing up in certain neighborhoods. Okay, I'm cranky. But you know the guys. You see them in Soho or the Upper West Side and of course in Brooklyn and now even Queens. To me, they usually don't have any upper body development and in fact they always look kind of sickly. On city streets they wear shoes that expose their toes. If they're balding by age 28, they shave their skulls; if not, they get their hair cut by girls. They probably wax away body hair and own far too many gels. They've got neat clothes and black glasses and shiny accessories and wear baby Snuglis and tote around $9 coffees. They use phrases like "That feel when..."

They don't drive and they rarely drink alcohol other than wine and they've never clenched a fist with the intention of punching another guy. They can't jump-start a dead battery or light a decent barbeque. They sit cross-legged with tablets on the bench at the park, occasionally telling Brandon or Caitlin or Tyler how really important it is to share, but always calmly. Their wives make more money, have more defined biceps, and speak louder and more frequently at parties. Perhaps parenting itself has become another narcissistic fashion, like eating kale or organic Brussels sprouts from the food co-op. So maybe the pundits are right: Now children don't *earn* trophies—they *are* the trophies for preening parents. Like me.

So are those the only two choices? Join the burgeoning army of Todds and Coopers and Tanners? Or crawl back into the cave with my father?

Can't I live a life devoted primarily to two things: 1) loving Ben and 2) loving talking to airplanes and the often shitheaded pilots who fly them?

I use Tom's of Maine Whole Care Peppermint Natural Fluoride Toothpaste—it fights cavities, whitens, facilitates fresh breath, and helps fight tartar. My father brushes his teeth with baking soda. There's the divide.

"Jetlink four-two-four-zero, cleared for localizer, sir. Winds at zero-one-zero from nine-zero."

"LaGuardia, Jetlink four-two-four-zero." Pause. "Cleared for localizer."

Well. Someone's listening. "Affirmative, sir."

I suck it up once more, in this year of sucking it up and sucking it up. My definition of manhood keeps shifting, but sucking it up always seems to be an intrinsic component.

When my tour finally ends I descend the stairs and speed-dial my mom. I know she's about to watch the 11 o'clock *Eyewitness News*, since she's of a generation that still accesses corporate media at Pavlovian times.

"Hello, Mikey."

"You get caller ID?"

"Who else would it be?"

I lean against the pool table. "How's he doing?"

"He's out. Finally."

"What time?"

"Bout ten."

"Ten! Jeez…"

She says nothing.

"Did he cry again? Dog?"

She clucks by way of an answer.

"What's that mean?"

"Look…these things happen, Mikey. Things get lost. Maybe it'll turn up. Maybe not. Say a prayer to Saint Anthony. Either way…things happen. He'll be alright."

"I do thoughts, not prayers," I mumble, reaching back to slam the purple four ball into the pack. It's one thing to be a bigger wussy than your father; obviously I'm a bigger wussy than my mother to boot. "So he cried?"

"Look…he's a kid. Kids cry, Mike. He'll be alright."

I sigh.

Then my mother says, "She called tonight."

"Who?"

"*Who*. Princess Di. Who else?"

"Oh."

"Benjy got on with her and the next thing...he's in tears. Poor little fella. Telling her all about it."

"Uh huh."

"Then he says she wants to speak to me."

"And?"

"And so she asks me what happened to the dog. I said I didn't know. So she hung up. Very pleasant girl you picked."

"I'm on my way. You need anything?"

She chuckles. "Just that Dog."

I slot out a 16-ounce Pepsi and Doritos, neither of which I should consume, as Mayor Bloomberg would happily point out to all wussies within earshot. I'm thinking even though it's dark, I could drive the wagon over to the civilian parking garage, where there's lots of light, and tear apart that second seat again. I may have missed something, so I munch and drink and strategize.

Replacing Dog, by the way, just isn't an option. Two years ago, I came out of Citi Field for the first time after they razed Shea and walked with Sam to his car, parked in Corona. It was a hot after-noon and street vendors had set up shop right on Roosevelt Avenue. A dreadlocked Rasta type working out of a Chevy van was pushing the saddest-looking collection of stuffed this and sewn that. Ben had just played with Gretchen, a neighbor's yellow Lab, so I grabbed the near-est mutt and gave the Rasta one buck. Right now I'd easily pay a hundred bucks for Dog. More.

Finally I head out. The last departures all pushed back and the airport is nearly empty. That's why it's a shock to see anyone standing at the fence behind the ominous warning: *US GOV'T PROPERTY— NO TRESPASSING.* Especially my sister Katie.

I step through the gate. "What?"

"Hey, Mikey."

"What? You okay? What? Everything?"

She smiles. "Calm down."

"You drive from the city?" Katie nods. "Where's Chris?"

"Home." She comes close and hugs. "How you doing?"

"I'm fine. I mean...what?" I look at my watch: *23:22.* "It's...after eleven."

"I spoke to Eileen before."

"Yeah?"

"I ran into a friend. Needed a lift to Queens. Figured I'd drop him off here."

I just stare.

Katie's smile grows wider and she reaches into what I now realize is too large a bag for a late-night jaunt. Her right hand holds him by both tattered ears.

"Dog!" I exclaim. It frightens me how quickly it occurs. I hadn't felt it coming and I didn't even know it was in me. But tears burst forth, not flowing but gushing. I let out a self-conscious cry that's meant to be a laugh but betrays my relief and gratitude.

Katie seems fascinated, and her eyes light up. "Look at you!"

"Shit." All at once I'm wiping awkwardly at my face, grabbing Dog by his hind legs, and hugging Katie in thanks. "Shit!"

"Mikey! Look at you." She steps back to see me anew. "Now I get it..."

I breathe deep. "Get what?"

"Ben Benny Benson. He drags Dog around pretending he's his. Turns out he's yours! Ben is your beard. Who the hell knew?"

I snort-laugh-cry in response.

"It's okay, Mikey. I won't tell."

I rub my face dry and raw. "I'm a wuss."

Katie's smile fades. "What?"

"I'm a freaking pussy."

"What's that supposed to mean?"

As usual, I flash on my father. "Can you picture Tom? I mean, crying over Dog?"

"No." Suddenly her voice is angry. "But I can picture him beating the hell out of Benjy. With his belt. Strap end...buckle end."

I nod. To change the subject, I hold up Dog. "Where was he?"

"Trunk of my car. Put him in yesterday. Bennington and I were at the mall. We didn't wanna lose him."

"Thanks..."

"Listen. Cut the shit. What's with the pussy stuff?"

I shrug. "I dunno."

"What? You serious?"

My legs are heavy and I lean against the fence. "Look...this whole thing. The whole thing. With her. I dunno. I was just so...blindsided. I still can't believe it. All I want...all I wanna do is be a good father..."

I stop because the door opens, but it's a guard; all the controllers from my shift long ago followed the Grand Central Parkway to where the lampposts turn from metal to wood and it's the Northern State Parkway, guiding them right to their Long Island split-levels. The older ones are in Nassau County, the younger ones in cheaper houses further out in Suffolk County. "I'm...I dunno. I feel like the older Ben gets...the weaker I get."

Katie shakes her head. "Boy, you're a freaking knucklehead." She hugs me, then gently slaps my temple. "Wacko! You've never been so strong in your whole stupid lousy life." Then she adds: "Now stay strong!"

I walk her to her car and pay for the parking. Later that night, I tell my mother to wake me before she leaves for early Mass. I want to watch Ben when he first stirs in the morning. I've got to be there when he sees who's resting on the blue pillow beside him.

*   *   *   *

It's the last week of summer vacation. My last week with Ben. But back at our apartment I find he's become sick, hot to the touch, his forehead singes my hand. The damp washcloths keep sliding down over his eyebrows. I crowd into his toddler bed, my arm across his thin, beating chest.

By morning the fever breaks and he wants mini-bagel pizzas for breakfast.

*   *   *   *

And then finally the summer is just Ben and me.

She's gone ahead to set up their new apartment, some un-known academic supposedly driving her. The rabbi's wife, soon my ex-mother-in-law, is afraid to fly so she'll Amtrak Ben to his new home. Working backwards, and accounting for all the connections, they'll depart Penn Station at five a.m. on Labor Day.

I'm not up for driving them to Penn. I consider dialing 718-441-1111, but several friends and three local siblings volunteer to take us. I let my oldest brother do it.

I sit in the back of Tommy's Chevy Tahoe, the one he uses for work, with my arm wrapped around the car seat. It's chilly; summer is ending fast. The horizon is black, but Ben is awake and humming soft-ly. He wants to know what color the Queens-Midtown Tunnel is.

Over the past few weeks, I've spent hours speaking long-distance to Annabelle, my mentor from Queens College. We've re-mained friends in part because she always thought I was an odd combination, a would-be air traffic controller interested in shrinking the heads of other controllers. Now she's teaching psychology in Rhode Island, and I've abused her hospitality by calling repeatedly.

Because she's black, Ben once rubbed his face with his hand and asked me why some people's cheeks are dark.

Annabelle gives great suggestions. A *Disney Cars* knapsack that serves as an object of transference. The idea is when he carries it, he's carrying around a piece of you-know-who. Inside is a photo al-bum, and every picture is of Ben with paternal relatives. Stamped, self-addressed envelopes to send me his drawings. A framed portrait for his bedside: *Daddy and Me*. A Fisher-Price tape recorder so I can send him recordings of myself. Talking. Laughing. Irish lullabies.

Ben's wearing the knapsack when our echoing footsteps ring out across Penn Station. Tommy does what he's come to do, and takes her mother off for coffee. There's nothing but empty benches at this hour on a holiday. I sit down alone with my son. The object of transference is working all too well: He'd rather devote his attention to it than to the person it represents.

Fathers and sons.

"Buddy," I say softly. "I wanna talk."

He shakes the new tape recorder. "You bought the red one."

"You hafta go. On the train. To see Mommy."

My sentences come in short, staccato bursts. I'm breathing deeply in between the syllables. "And don't forget. I'm coming. To see you. Real soon."

He punches at the recorder's bright yellow buttons.

"I'm coming soon. On the airplane."

"The *blue* airplane?"

"Uh huh. Blue. Real soon. I'll be coming." The pain in my chest feels acute enough to warrant a hospital bracelet.

He looks at me. "I'm gonna *carry* this. It's mine."

I nod. "I love you. More than. Anything."

He hits the *PLAY* and *REWIND* buttons simultaneously, and the machine emits a screeching sound of metal-on-metal.

I wince. "More than. *Anything.* Buddy."

Ben slaps at the Fisher-Price logo.

"I wish...I could go. With you."

"To Indiana? The brown house? With Mommy?"

I nod. "First Washington. Then another train. Then Chicago. Then *another* train. Then Indiana."

I reach out and hug him close, even though he's struggling. I put my mouth close to his ear. To sing. "In Dublin's fair city…"

He shakes his head as if in response to a question. "I *don't* have a doody diaper."

"That's good. Me either. I'm coming soon. To visit."

"You coming *now*?"

"I can't. I have work. And school. This week."

"At the NYU?"

I nod. "At the NYU."

My brother is there, and her mother, and the white-haired porter Tommy tipped excessively. Pushing a metal cart. He lets Ben ride on top of suitcases. And he lets me accompany them to the platform.

My last hug is suffocating, and probably too tight. I kiss Ben's forehead, and both his cheeks. "Bye, Benjy." I brush at his yellow hair, straighten his blue shirt, pat his red tape recorder. "Be good. And be happy. You're my favorite…buddy."

He squirms away, then runs ahead of his grandmother. They board, and I watch him race down the aisle. He picks a window seat in front of me, and I stand on the platform and rap at the glass. He's almost three, so he's on the far side of enjoying a good round of peek-a-boo. But he gives in, maybe for my sake.

I know even now reminders of shared moments will crowd my autumn. A commercial for *The Croods*. Spotting a box of mini-bagel pizzas in frozen foods. A miniature Thomas the Tank Engine popping out as the car wash attendant vacuums.

Then her mother lifts him up, and they move to the far side of the aisle. I can barely see him through the glass. I pantomime a shrugged-shoulders questioning look to her. She yells there will be

New Jersey farms on that side of the train. I shake my head. Ben has thrown his knapsack onto the floor and is carefully ripping an emergency evacuation card into semi-even strips.

Somebody cries out *"ALLL A-BOARD!"* in that laughably anachronistic diction. As if it weren't 2013. As if the country still traveled by rail. Norman Rockwell fathers waving sons off to college. Jobs in the city. Troopships bound for the front. I'm in a time capsule buried under the new Madison Square Garden.

"I love you, buddy," I mouth through the colorless glass.

Ben leans into her mother's shoulder and refuses to sit with his legs in front of him. They're arguing like an old married couple. My last image is of him pulling on the fold-down tray table.

The front end of the train must be approaching Newark before I stop peering down the tracks.

And then all there is to do is turn and go up the escalator. Passing gray walls and ceilings, neither black nor white. All shading. The rest of a life is awaiting. According to the Aetna HealthFund tables I've been sent by my union rep, I still have another 52 to 56 years to live.

BOOK TWO

It's a summer of numbers, and unlocking the ancient secrets of mathematics, especially simple addition. We count and we count and we count, and the world gently slides into much sharper focus, just knowing there are 54 squares on an Eggo waffle and Citi Field is 4.3 miles from our apartment and Earth is the third planet from the sun and it's two more nights of sleep until Wednesday, when there's outside morning playtime at preschool. And the LaGuardia control cab tower where I work is 198 feet above the runway complex.

Unless you count the sections partially cut off on the corners, because then there are 68 squares on an Eggo waffle.

When we fly to visit my sister Kerry's family in Florida, I teach Ben to count the number of rows to the emergency exit. He counts and adds and weighs and measures and slowly, methodically, carefully, surely, patiently, gratefully, graciously he begins to understand just a little bit more about everything than he understood before. And therefore so do I.

Instead of analyzing the color of clouds, he counts clouds. It's five months until Christmas, Ben tells me one day. I tell him he's absolutely correct. But he isn't finished. And it's five floors to the roof on Uncle Kevin's building (where we're *never* allowed without an adult). I also teach Ben that *a dozen* is less than *a billion*.

An NYU friend posted this on Facebook: *DID YOU KNOW? The average four-year-old child asks 437 questions a day.* Of course, it's on the Internet so it must be true.

He counts the Cheerios bobbing in his milk. Walking to the subway, he counts fire hydrants (while I explain such a rusty apparatus helped save Grandpa Tom's life). He counts stars. On a hot night while I'm reading to him in bed he attempts to count my chest hairs but gives up underneath my ribs. When we shop for a new toy box at Ikea, he counts Swedish meatballs at lunch (although he won't eat the ones that touched the lingonberries). And he counts airplanes from the LGA tower when I can't arrange childcare and once again he's forced to "visit" Daddy at work.

When I play my Beatles CDs in the car, Ben wants to know why it takes 4,000 holes to fill the Albert Hall; in fact, so do I.

He first grasps the concept of infinity when my mother sneaks him to Mass one Sunday and Monsignor Lafferty refers to "a world without end." That leads to a lengthy discussion the next day about beginnings and conclusions, which segues into yet another viewing of *The Lion King* and yet another chorus of *The Circle of Life*.

In mid-summer he asks for four mini-bagel pizzas instead of the usual three. I wonder if he's hungry and he shakes his head, explaining the third one was lonely so he wants two pairs. In fact, he counts the entire contents of the box.

I count the days he is with me. I even count the hours.

*   *   *   *

It's a summer of departures and arrivals.

Ben returns to LaGuardia on a hot Friday in May. Within minutes after their 737 taxis to a halt, I'm waiting at the happy end of the jetbridge, my FAA identification strung around my neck. She and

Ben are among the last to exit and when he sees me squatting near the ticket counter his face quickly lights up—but then just as quickly he looks down and clings to her forearm.

He's never reacted to me like this before in his life. In fact, I have to gently pry him from her to finally get a hug. I smile at her, believing Ben's back home for good.

*   *   *   *

In Evansville she enrolled Ben in Temple Tots; somehow she managed to find a conveniently located synagogue in the birthplace of Indiana's Ku Klux Klan. It seems clear he's on track for the Jewish thing. I know it rankles my mother and others on my team, but I won't battle her on this one. I'm an agnostic but I seem to be evolving into a secular humanist, so how can I fight for a church I deliberately left behind? Also, I believe it's nice to be given something as a kid, some sort of ethical structure. A framework, as it were. So hopefully you can grow up, start thinking for yourself, and question it. Then reject it.

Apparently the rabbi's daughter has fervently rediscovered her religion. But I'm not questioning it, even though some are saying she's driving yet another wedge between Ben and me. I think that's paranoid, though a few members of my posse have begun believing the worst of her. I'm not at that point. Now that Indiana is behind us, I'd like to stay positive and work together to figure out the next 14 or so years until Ben graduates high school. We all could use some normalcy. So call me optimistic.

*   *   *   *

It's my first full day alone with Ben since he returned from Evansville. We're on the widest part of the Grand Central Parkway, heading East with the fairgrounds on our left as we cruise toward the Van Wyck and a trip to the Coney Island Aquarium. Ben's in his perch, strapped into the car seat in the center of the wagon, riding high where I can see his face drooping onto his left shoulder. He's out for a nap with Dog in his lap.

I'm not sure how to interpret why Ben's been acting so strange the last few days. That hesitance at the end of the jetbridge last week lingered, albeit sporadically. He has never shied away from hugging me, kissing me, holding my hand. But ever since she walked him off that plane, it's as if Ben knows something about me that I don't. He'll forget it for hours at a stretch, and then revert as if recalling absent instructions.

I pop in one of my favorites—Warren Zevon—and sing along, ignoring the bright orange *CHECK ENGINE* light on the dashboard. Lovey needs new tires, a new battery, new suspension. But the money I don't have to spend on those things has already been promised elsewhere. *Send Lawyers, Guns, and Money.*

We're in the left lane and inching up toward 70 miles per hour. Then, before any sane person can even fathom why, the silver Mini Cooper in front of me slams full on the brakes. My brain instantly calculates this dipshit only just grasped he's four lanes away from the Harry Van Arsdale Jr. Avenue exit and therefore the lives of multiple strangers—men, women, children, pets, Dog—should be endangered, since that's clearly a better option than doubling back on Queens Boulevard an exit later. I can see the undercarriage of that crappy little car as the brake lights tilt upward from the sudden de-acceleration. My brain simultaneously calculates neither the laws of physics nor the God I prayed to at St. Rita's School when I still believed in his existence will be enough to prevent me from rear-ending this oh-so-selfish prick in my 4,300-pound station wagon. But I recall the words of Bob Hoover, the greatest pilot who ever lived: *Fly as far into the crash as possible.* I brake and steer and brake and steer and the wagon jerks and then it squeals, it slides, and it shimmies and now we're juussstttt past the Cooper's left rear quarter panel as we kick up last winter's rock salt and plow through the grassy median, pass the prick, and fishtail back into the fast lane. All this in the time it takes to grimace. In the patch of rearview mirror above Ben's head, I instantly see that—miraculously—for the first time since Robert Moses built the damn parkway, no one is tailgating in the left lane. It all happens so fast I don't even get a look at The Selfish One piloting the Cooper.

The wagon rights itself as though it's on tracks, and we continue. But the adrenaline, as always, has burst onto the scene and now wants to stay. I feel my pulsing vessels and pound the steering wheel with the meat of my palm.

"Cock*suck*er!" I hiss in fury at what a careless, faceless stranger was prepared to take.

And then I hear it.

"Cock*suck*er!" Ben chimes in.

The rearview shows he's more than stirring; he's positively alert.

I make my living finding the right words to express myself on a moment's notice during flashes of terror and distress. But for once, I'm vocally challenged, and I falter. The lecture about saying bad things just won't program itself. Instead I say what I truly feel: "I love you, buddy."

For the first time since his return, his smile is genuine. "I love you, Daddy."

Ben is back.

*   *   *   *

I live with my brother Kevin in his apartment in Astoria now, sleeping on his sofa. So Ben is de facto living here now as well, sleeping on the love seat facing the sofa. No formal discussions were held about any of this. It all just evolved. There are times when I think Kevin's completely wrapped up in his own life. But then I came home exhausted one night over the winter and found he had spent over $200 on *Disney Cars* bedding, towels, pajamas, slippers, toothbrushes, sippy cups, plates, bowls, utensils, etc. I'm forever surprised by family.

*   *   *   *

Through the mediator, she unexpectedly suggests I stop calling Ben every single day he's with her—why not weekly, so it's more "special"? I refuse, politely asking how a psychologist could suggest that. Of course, when Ben's with me, she hardly ever calls.

During those nine months between September and May I took ten trips to Evansville, home of the Purple Aces. I negotiated countless shift swaps to patch together four-day jaunts until my work schedule became hieroglyphics. In April a nightmare woke me; I was expected at work but couldn't confirm the date on broken phones.

On nine occasions I flew, but Evansville's airport only serves the greedy major airlines so I found lower fares elsewhere, hopping Southwest to Louisville or Frontier to Nashville, transiting Baltimore one month, Philadelphia the next. I'd pick up a rented Chevy Geo or Ford Focus—anything for $20 per day—and Interstate it to Evansville. I booked the lowest rates with Indian-born franchisees running Motel 6s and Super 8s.

Once the good people at Thrifty forgot my reservation for a child safety seat, and I dug in until they borrowed one from Budget.

During Christmas I snagged six days off in a row—no small accomplishment but I worked double shifts as payback. Holiday airfares were too high so I was forced to drive Lovey. The old girl wasn't sure she was up to it. On the 23rd—eve of Christmas Eve—I was merging off the George Washington Bridge when the car alongside honked. Thankfully I didn't extend the finger since it was a Garden State trooper; apparently I was so distracted by dashboard lights I'd nearly taken off the Crown Victoria's mirror. He inspected the brown bag of bagels for Rabbi Cohen, realized I wasn't transporting poppy seeds across state lines illegally, and wished me happy holidays. Of course, an Irish surname on a license often invites White Privilege. Like when the cop reads *MICHAEL MULLEN* and smiles: "You drive safely, okay, *Mike*?" As opposed to what Sam once heard in Dover: "*Hands*, motherfucker! Lemme see some fucking *hands*!!" Eventually the left headlight died in Pennsylvania and a radiator hose blew in West Virginia. But I picked up Ben to celebrate at Econo Lodge.

It was a strange and quiet Christmas.

The monthly visits soon fell into a pattern. Someone other than her always minded Ben at the off-campus apartment: her mother,

her father, a graduate student. I arranged pick-ups and drop-offs with them, which was easier. In fact, I didn't see her at all between December and April and only communicated via the weekly mediation conference calls. I phoned every day but Ben picked up himself. My sister Katie wondered if she was even in Indiana, or living elsewhere; I didn't pursue it. Probably I didn't want to think about it. Instead I'd pull up to the apartment and toot the horn—BAH, BAH-BAH-BAH, BAH, BAHHH—and Ben would come running.

We'd spend the next three days at horse farms, kiddie arcades, or petting zoos, or walking along Dress Plaza by the Ohio River. We traveled as far west as St. Louis and as far south as Nashville. But most visits we gravitated toward Louisville, taking Route 64 east-bound and laughing at signs for Santa Claus, Indiana. We visited Churchill Downs and the Louisville Slugger Museum, but Ben got a bigger kick out of Colonel Sanders' statue outside KFC headquarters. We ate many cheap meals at Waffle Houses, but eventually branched out, with Ben even sampling catfish. He and Dog toured Dixieland in rented car seats while discussing life and art and popovers.

Early one Saturday at Red Roof Inn, Ben watched *Curious George* on his bed while I still dozed on mine. Finally I stood up to stretch, exhausted from another long journey. Ben pointed: "Daddy! What's that?"

I looked down. The nine-hour snooze had produced a major urine erection, one threatening to burst through my boxers; my instinct was to turn away but I forced myself to play it calmly and not give in to generational taboos. "That's my penis, buddy."

"But…why? It's so big today…"

"Yeah…well. Cause I have to pee now."

As I stood over the bowl, Ben watched me. "Do all daddies' penises get big?"

"Pretty much, yeah."

"Does my penis get big when I'm a daddy?"

"I think so, yeah." Mercifully, he returned to *Curious George*.

Between visits, the intervals—though they never extended more than four weeks—began feeling much longer after January. Each arrival found Ben taller, leaner, more eloquent. His growth spurts occurred not when I strapped him onto carousels but during the long gaps when I talked for hours on end to airplanes at LaGarbage or napped on Kevin's love seat, my face pressed against the *Disney Cars* spread.

In the fall, I financed these sojourns with MasterCard debit plastic. Those funds dried up after Halloween, so I switched to Visa, and ran into its $10,000 limit by February (and was promptly alerted my credit wouldn't be extended by a friendly Mumbai-based rep named Woody). So by March I used American Express, and by May—the week Ben returned—the folks at Amex froze my account. Meanwhile, the mail continually brings offers of new cards.

It was the longest winter of my life.

In my line of work annual physicals are mandatory, not optional, and my last one didn't go well. During the first year without Ben, I gained 32 pounds, which was no mystery considering I eat such crap and at such crappy hours. The wastebasket at my workstation is a Jackson Pollack of gyros and pork buns, calzones and fajitas, pad Thai drenched in gallons of Pepsi. The extra pounds helped drive up my blood pressure, which was promptly reported to the FAA.

February was the nadir. On a snowy Thursday I visited the 7-day clinic on Northern Boulevard and the physician's assistant confirmed what I'd suspected about my two-week-old cold: bronchitis. Anything involving the vocal cords is life-and-death in my profession; up in the tower bronchitis is discussed in hushed tones, like rotator cuffs in professional baseball clubhouses. So I begged for oral steroids and he finally gave me antibiotics, even though he called it unnecessary. Unnecessary for him, not spending nine hours a day speaking to airplanes. The next morning I borrowed whatever cash my mother had and used it for prescriptions and taxi fare, then Long Island Rail Roaded to MacArthur Airport, to fly Southwest to Chicago and then connect to Louisville.

By 10 p.m. I was at Midway, listening to the gate agent explain the receding snowstorm had forced the cancellation of all southbound departures. And there were no meals, phone cards, taxis, or hotels, since after all this was a force majeure situation—in aviation the golden rule is, always blame God. So where does that leave us agnostics? As an FAA-licensed controller I could have occupied a cockpit jumpseat, but there were no cockpits departing for anywhere that night. I opened my wallet and realized I had exactly $74 to last through four days and several states. My flights, motel, and rental car were booked and vouchered and I retracted a folder of "paperless" confirmation sheets. I sat in a plastic chair, emailing Super 8 and Alamo. I was cold, tired, and hungry. My throat ached as I considered the collection agencies, the NYU probation, a possible FAA suspension, the way Kevin's sofa dug into my kidneys. Over the last few months I not only gained weight, but started taking longer naps and lost interest in dating. I realized I'd be sleeping on this plastic chair in Midway, where chairs aren't nearly as comfortable as at O'Hare.

Then I clicked on my phone and saw I had forgotten to charge it yesterday; the Nokia had morphed into a $250 paperweight.

Ben would be waiting up for me, counting hours out loud. Or tossing in his bed, wondering why Daddy hadn't come. Daddy always came when he said he would. *Always.*

I managed to find the last telephone booth not shipped off to the Smithsonian and croakingly placed a collect call to Evansville. Once again, she wasn't around; instead her mother answered.

"I have a collect call."

"What's that?"

"I have a collect call, ma'am."

"Oh...they still have those?"

"It's collect from...what is your name, sir?"

I opened my mouth and at that very instant, *that exact moment*, the vocal cords making my entire life possible finally decided to shut down, utterly and completely. My brain forwarded signals— *Michael Mullen, Michael Mullen*—but the complete oral network went dark. I grunted, then groaned.

"Sir?"

I grunted and groaned once more.

"*Sir*? Are you on the line?"

"*Mmmm...*"

Her mother chimed in: "Who is it?"

"Sir?"

I closed my eyes and willed my larnyx into action: "*Mii...Mii...MII!*"

"Sir?"

"Who is it?"

"Who's on the line?"

"Al, get off the line."

"Well, who is it?"

"*MII! MII!*"

"Al, it's the operator. She's got a collect call."

"Collect? They still have those? From who?"

"Ma'am...I think he's hung up."

"Well, who was it?"

"Forget it, Al!"

"*MII! MII!*"

"I couldn't tell you, sir. Thank you for using AT&T."

Then all I heard was a dial tone, and I kept it to my ear, long after the screechy message about how if you'd like to make a call…

I rested my forehead—my hot, bloated, burning forehead—against the icy metal support of the phone booth. Everything hurt.

During *High Noon* while we waited for increasing contractions, I envisioned travel. I envisioned many things, but travel was paramount. Of course there'd be travel. I'm an aviation geek. Airplanes, hotels, future memories to fulfill. She and Ben and I would buzz through airports continuously. But not like this.

*   *   *   *

With Ben away, I'm bored and spending too much time online, surfing one meaningless site after another. Yes, I know—the ultimate First World Problem.

Somehow I stumble upon an essay, and start reading. Then I defy Internet algorithms because by the third paragraph I'm *still* reading. The author had me at the title: *WHY ARE DADS ALWAYS PORTRAYED AS JERKS IN MOVIES, TV & COMMERCIALS?* Why indeed? I click on the byline: *J.T. Livingstone is co-founder of Fathers Are Critical Too.* I visit FACT's site and find myself nodding.

I'm hit with two emotions simultaneously—shock that other fathers also are mistreated by the courts, and fear that the Evansville decision was not the anomaly I believed it was, but rather the rule. Dozens of poorly written blog posts sound as though they were transcribed in the back of Judge Rhonda Westphal's courtroom.

My organs constrict over paternal horror stories. The former CEO who resigned to spend more time with his kids—and was promptly hit with child support bills based on his *potential* salary of $1 million annually rather than his *actual* salary of one-tenth that. The dad on Long Island whose ex-wife married a cop, so every time he picks up his kids he's pulled over and strip-searched. The fathers whose children have disappeared to other states, countries, continents.

There's a FACT chapter in Queens. I log on under a phony name—Jimmy—to learn more.

*   *   *   *

It's very early Sunday morning, deader than dead. At 4 a.m. I made a bagel run and brought back a dozen for my co-workers and left them on the cabinet with the bottled water; a small overture. Now the Circadian Rhythm Effect means I'll be napping later on instead of slapping together Legos with Ben. I'm so bored I google *circadian* and absorb factoids. Our biological clocks indicate best coordination at 2:30 p.m. and fastest reaction time at 3:30 p.m.; so why don't the Mets schedule more day games? Then I stumble across this: highest testosterone secretion takes place at 9 a.m.

Now I recall something submerged. On that last Saturday morning—just before she left with Ben and never looked back, in the final hours of the death throes of a marriage—she silently seduced me. I awoke to find her above me, red hair across my face, lips on my chest, breasts ballooning alongside my ribcage, thighs straddling my hips. My eyes widened and we both turned toward the crib, where Ben slept in a blue Onesie. She touched her finger to my lips and I followed her naked form into the living room. The sofa was piled with Ben's toys so we fell onto the carpet. It was our first sex in over three months; it would also be our last. The entire transaction took place in silence. And I ended with a nasty rug burn on my knee.

A week later, after she and Ben vacated the premises, I remember a sickening feeling. Had it been guilt intercourse? Worse, was it precautionary—covering a pregnancy? Was she ending things the same lustful way they began? Or just saying goodbye? I remember hoping this was an overture. But she left me lying on the floor.

"You want any coffee, Mike?"

"No, don't drink it."

It's Maurice, better known as Moe, on my right today. He's one of the most decent people at LGA. Tall, trim, silver-haired, all pleats and tweeds. My mother would say he stepped out of a bandbox, whatever that means. He's buttering a toasted sesame.

"I wanna thank you," he says. "The election. I heard."

"Oh. No biggie—"

"Nope! It was like a heavenly choir."

Two months earlier, Moe had run as a shop union delegate. Compared to the other jamook on the ballot, Moe was hands-down smarter, more articulate, and a better controller to boot. Back in the day, after Clinton's idiotic Don't-Ask-Don't-Tell, Moe was kicked out of the Navy; some homophobic admiral in San Diego—no doubt deeply afraid of being yanked from the closet himself—booted Moe without so much as a hearing. Just a few days before voting, at a closed-door meeting of the rank-and-file, the jamook's loudmouth supporters kept calling Moe "unfit" for office. So I stood up and challenged them to quit speaking in code about Moe's discharge "for the good of the service." If they were homophobes, own it. A few days later, Moe lost in a landslide.

"A heavenly choir! You sound gay, dude!"

He smiles wanly. "It's like what's happening with you now. Your custody stuff."

I swivel my chair and ask for clarification.

Moe stares. "Well...they figure you should forget custody. Move on. Focus on...airplanes. You know. Like a *man*."

I stare out at Trump's gaudy 757. "Is that how *you* feel?"

"Absolutely not. Eliot and I were just saying...it's heroic." Then he adds, "Keep up the fight, Mike."

*   *   *   *

Ben and I run into my long-time neighbor Jackie, who lives two doors down from my mom. He's a little over five feet tall, with horribly crooked teeth and rheumy eyes. We all grew up playing with him in St. Rita's schoolyard—dodge ball, box ball, stickball. Early on, we didn't quite grasp he was 30 years older than us yet still had the mind—and spirit—of a child. He has gray hair now and still lives with his mom, though we all worry what will happen when she exits.

We each serve humanity in our own way, and I drive Jackie and our mothers to the cemetery on Long Island annually to visit the graves of Jackie's dad and my sister. I've been doing it since my discharge. The women sit in the back and Jackie straps in up front with me, talking baseball. He's both more insightful and more civil than the loudmouths on talk radio.

Now Jackie does what he always does: He hugs both of us and offers his standard greeting. "I love you, Mike! I love you, Benjy!"

He also tells me the Mets are going to the World Series next year. What I don't know is that Jackie's right.

*   *   *   *

I never finished the final paper for that Understanding Grief seminar because I was in Evansville, so NYU officially notified me of academic probation. Because I'd been granted a break from full-time status, the FAA also was notified and my grant eliminated. Days later, my union rep told me a missed shift due to a delayed flight from Indiana generated an official warning letter, the first in my career.

Then in January, I was assigned—against my will—to working ground control. Even invoking the oldest joke in the business ("They're called *air*planes, not *ground*planes") didn't help. One day I was contemplating a legal invoice and somehow didn't notice two 737s, United and American, almost bump wingtips on Taxiway Foxtrot. The new tower allows us a view of every inch of the runways and taxiways, so no excuses. Photos of would-be airport fender-benders usually make *USA Today*, but thankfully social media and dying old school media were asleep. Even so, I finally received that inevitable work suspension, one week without pay. Also a first in my career. I used the time to fly to Evansville.

Meanwhile, various credit agencies are threatening me with collection methods just short of violence. Despite my NYU probation, I continually apply for student loans, and use these payments to fund my ravenous attorneys. I don't know this is an incredibly stupid way to pay bills. Because student loans, unlike gambling debts, can't be discharged through bankruptcy and—like murder and treason—have no statute of limitations. Which I'll soon learn.

*   *   *   *

Ben developed a cold, either in Evansville or Queens, or perhaps in the filthy rarified air of that 737. I'm killing 14 minutes waiting for his prescription at a pharmacy near LaGuardia, gazing through magazines. I gravitate toward *TRANSPORTATION*, but the aviation mags are old.

I find myself in front of *FAMILY*. Well, I've got family, no?

Parents is in front, and the largest headline screams: *What Moms Need to Know Now!* I thumb through: *The Moms' Guide to Fall Fun*. Another: *Moms Share Toddler Secrets*. I backtrack to the contents. *Essay: Nothing Beats a Mother's Love. Mommy 101: Class is in Session*. Involuntarily, Judge Westphal comes to mind. I hide *Parents* behind *Hockey News*.

Then I pick up *Parenting* and sigh. *Moms Dish on Best &
Worst Pediatricians. The Mom Channel: What Should Kids Watch?
Mothers and Other—*

This one I hide behind *Monster Truck Review.*

*   *   *   *

It's Thursday afternoon, so I'm taking a long break in Lovey,
my battered old Taurus wagon. The *CHECK ENGINE* light continues
glowing. I've driven to the far end of LaGuardia and parked near the
Marine Air Terminal, an Art Deco structure overlooking my old Little
League field, home of countless childhood traumas.

For months now, once a week she and I have dialed an 888
number and spoken for 45 minutes each time with Jessica Goldstein, a
mediator certified through a state Community Dispute Resolution
Center. Jessica methodically talks with us, then her partner the attorney converts the notes into legalese; the goal is to develop a legally
binding divorce and custody agreement without incurring the expense
and rancor of lawyers. We've discussed health benefits, Jewish and
Christian faiths, visits to grandparents, summer vacation, preschool,
Christmas/Hanukkah, vaccinations, Easter/Passover, haircuts, potty
training. Recently we discussed Halloween for 20 minutes; I'd take
Ben trick-or-treating early, and she'd take him later—she insisted on
separate costumes. I cautiously started believing relations are improving. Even Jessica suggested a full-fledged joint custody agreement
seemed imminent. Normalcy!

Of course, the premise is she and Ben will live with her parents in Queens. So sharing dinners and holidays and vacations won't pose logistical challenges.

But several weeks back she casually told Jessica—and me—the job market had dried up here and she's looking elsewhere. It hit me hard, and I questioned how someone with a PhD couldn't land a job in New York.

Now Jessica questions the same thing. "I think we've made real strides here, guys. But...some basic presumptions. All our work—visitation, school, holidays. All of it. It's...based on living in the same city. Presumably New York, yes?"

"The Federal Government assigned me to Flushing," I put in.

"Right. Michael's locked in. So...we're agreed on New York then, right?"

Already I can tell this conversation will change my life—not in a good way. I stare at the Little League field, then Rikers Island. Finally she speaks, and she seems annoyed at Jessica. "I told you. I have to go where I can secure a decent job. And Benjamin needs to be with his mother. If I found a job here...I'd take it. But we've looked and there are none. So we have started looking elsewhere..."

We?

Jessica coughs. "Like where?"

"Other locations."

"New Jersey?"

"Well, I've been...given an offer. In Israel."

It's one of those moments in life when you realize the bad thing is happening, and you've been waiting—and yet you're still not prepared. *Israel!* Among the many, many thoughts crowding my brain is that *no* court in New York State would ever allow this.

My capacity to be shocked never ends. I'm speechless.

Jessica sounds even more flustered. "But...I mean...*wait.* We've been speaking for months now. You, me...Michael. In good faith. About mediating. You both said you wanted to avoid a trial. For your son's sake. We've come so far. Kim's already—she's drawing up final papers. Just a few minor things—Halloween, Thanksgiving. It's entirely based on living *here.*"

She's not backing down. "I have to go where there's work..."

"I'm a bit confused," I interject. "Are you saying...you're looking to go overseas but Benjy stays with me?"

"Absolutely not," she responds. "A child needs his mother. I have a bond with Benjamin you'll never have. It's the natural order."

I'm speechless again.

Jessica cuts her off and says we'll continue next week.

*   *   *   *

I finish my shift and email my attorney; in the subject line I use all caps: *ISRAEL!*

Hillary tells me to come in first thing tomorrow.

All those months of mediation. Was she deliberately misleading us? Again and again, I attempt to decipher her thinking, and each time I fail. I simply don't know her.

That first afternoon home from Lenox Hill, with me stretched out on top of the comforter in bed for hours, Ben puckering his lips like a fish as he surveyed his new home. Suddenly it hits me—why was she in the other room that wondrous day?

And so mediation is over. Now it's back to litigation, and joint custody is dead as well. Now I'll seek being the custodial parent. In other words, my fate—and my son's fate—will once again be in the hands of strangers. But I remain optimistic, believing that the parent who puts Ben's needs first will be heard. It's only right.

*   *   *   *

It's Monday evening and I've finally located the address for Fathers Are Critical Too. Only it's a dimly lit bar hiding under the elevated 7 train in Jackson Heights. I parallel park the wagon, stick the meter receipt on the dashboard, and behold the dingy front door: *F.A.C.T. MEETING TONITE—1930 HOURS—MEN ONLY!!*

The bartender points toward the restrooms and I work my way back. Hammered into the wall is a small plaque:

> *Any Man can be a father, but it takes someone special*
> *to be a Daddy*

I involuntarily smile; Katie gave me the same plaque last year.

It's early, but as I step into the brightly lit room I see most of the wooden folding chairs are occupied; about fifteen men are present in the semi-circle. Up front someone hung a sheet emblazoned with the words: *SAVE THE MEN!* The Alpha Dog sits beneath it, in a discolored pleated armchair. His slicked hair is parted in the center and he sports a moustache that faded from popularity soon after the Rough Riders returned from Cuba. He wears a sleeveless sweatshirt, exposing an impressive set of guns, as well as letters on the front I can't quite read.

I don't belong here. I just know it.

This is pure instinct on my part, like at work when I instantly seek out a specific flight because something tells me it's deviating off course. This doesn't feel right, and I'm wary. I select the chair furthest away from the crowd. The pre-meeting chatter ceases; we're all waiting on Alpha Dog, who presses fingers to temples. Finally our leader retrieves oversized eyeglasses Elton John would have rejected as too ostentatious during the Philadelphia Freedom tour. Now he stands.

"Gentlemen, welcome!"

There are a dozen muted greetings.

"I see we've a new member this evening." Oddly his head has swiveled away from me, so I glance to his left as well. But then those Dr. T.J. Eckleburg glasses quickly pivot to me.

I nod. "Evening."

Our leader speaks: "My name is Owen. Only Owen. In this room we dispense with last names. Please introduce yourself."

"Sure," I respond. "I'm...Jim. Well, call me Jimmy."

Again, it's instinct. I remain on guard: If this man is capable of time traveling to a 1978 Pearle Vision store, who knows what other dark powers he possesses?

Greetings are thrown my way, and I smile tightly.

"Welcome, Jimmy. Is that Jimmi? With an I?"

I stare. "Jimmy *has* an I."

"No. 'Stead of a Y. Jim-*mi*...Anyway, you're a man among men tonight. Two things bind us. We're all men. And all fathers."

Everyone nods.

Owen isn't done: "And I should warn you—you're free to act as a man in here. Not like...out *there*. In here...you can scratch your balls. If they itch—scratch away. If you wanna burp, burp. If you wanna fart—" He lifts his foot clear off the ground and lets one rip, right in the contralto to countertenor range. "Fart! Is that clear?"

"Yeah," I say. "But I'm good."

"Fair enough. First things first. I'm a father. Three kids I haven't seen in five years. Thanks to a judge. Whose name won't pass my lips. All these men, they have similar testimonies. Briefly. If you will, Jimmy. What's *your* testimony?"

I shift in the chair and cough, two of the world's oldest delay tactics. "Well, I'm getting divorced—"

This draws a snort from my left. "Ain't we all, brother!"

"Yeah. I have one son. He's three. And...well, I've spent some time in court. And like it said. On the FACT site. About how the deck seems stacked. That's how it feels. I feel like the deck is stacked. I mean...my wife—my *ex*-wife. She keeps trying to cut me out. Take him away. And the courts—it just seems stacked against me. I'm trying to remain optimistic. I mean, this is America. It just...at times it doesn't seem *fair*."

There's a low buzz; apparently I struck a nerve. I see nodding.

Owen seems pleased as well. "Welcome, brother! I can tell you're one of us. You're a dying breed, my friend..."

I'm forced to play it straight. "What's that?"

"You're a *man*. An endangered species now. Yep! The world is killing us off. Forget the polar bears. Men will be extinct before ice caps melt. *Real* men. Not pussies!"

"Fuck the pussies!" someone yells.

"Fuck 'em!" shouts a grandfatherly guy.

Owen purrs. "The courts! Congress! God knows the White House!" There are more shouts, some of them quite guttural and not at all human. "They want our balls, gentlemen! What say ye? Forget your guns. Shall you surrender your *balls*?"

"No!"

"*Fuck no!!*"

"Gentlemen," Owen continues. "Need I remind you! The NYPD wants to change regulations. In place for over a century! So now there'll be *two* physicals. One for men. And...one for cunts."

There's a loud rebuttal, but no negative response to that vile word. *Shit.* My instincts were right.

"They wanna let 'em all on the job," a white-haired guy yells. "Even if they're five-foot-nothing and ninety-two pounds. But they still get sick pay that special time of the month." Laughter erupts.

"Firemen too!"

"Same at the post office!"

Owen's just warming up. "They don't want kids to have dads in their lives! Especially boys. Don't want 'em learning how to throw a ball. They should throw like girls. Or learn how to fight. Boys shouldn't fight—they should *reas*on. You know, reason with bullies. Like we did with Hitler and Tojo! The *Enola Gay*, it dropped a whole lot of reasoning on the Emperor, eh? They don't want boys growing up around *men*."

I'm looking at his Stephen Crane moustache, which oddly remains in place. Then Owen moves and I finally see what's emblazoned on his chest: *I Haven't Had A Bitch—Until I've Had Her Three Ways!*

"Jimmy! Come up here. Share. You're with brothers. Tell us about the women destroying you. Tearing you down. We'll listen."

I find myself standing. But I don't walk up front. Instead I ask, "What's the deal? On Roosevelt? Do they ticket at the meters?"

The white-haired guy nods vigorously. "Yep. Denver boot!"

"Uh huh." I move. "I just gotta feed the meter. I'll be back."

The bartender doesn't even look up as I rush past, keys in hand. I'm at the wagon in seconds, and I turn the ignition before the door closes. The tires squeal as I pull away.

On the sofa at Kevin's place I'm watching Louis C.K.; what I don't know is that within a few years I won't be able to watch him without contemplating sexual allegations. My phone rings and I see it's Katie and I smile. Last week I spent 90 minutes telling a social worker why Katie and Chris would make the best parents in all five boroughs. I also submitted an online essay in their defense.

"Whattaya doing?" she asks.

I laugh. "I'm painting my toenails with little cotton balls between them. My hair's in curlers. And I'm watching *Sex and the City*. With my two boyfriends, Ben and Jerry."

Katie sighs. "Jesus. Never a dull moment with you. Now what?"

"Nothing. Just screwing around. What's happening?"

She breathes deep. "Well…you ready to be an uncle again?"

*   *   *   *

Some friends just don't get it.

I meet my old buddy Kenny from Archbishop McCarthy High at White Castle. Like millions of other novice drinkers, we always wound up there for belly bombers at 4 a.m. For years, we shot baskets near Bell Boulevard, then went for sliders. As we both put on weight, we skipped the basketball and started meeting directly at the Castle.

We both order a #1, mine without cheese, and he asks if I'm kosher. He's Irish-Catholic but an accountant, so he knows from mixing meat and dairy. We sit in a back booth as I politely ask about his job, girlfriend, even the monster SUV parked diagonally. Finally I give him all five acts of my tragedy. He nods, seemingly sympathetic.

Then he says, "I don't get it."

I ask what, and he says, your kid going to Israel. I explain, he's my *son*. And he says, but you can visit him. I explain it's across the globe. And he repeats, but you can still visit.

Finally I stop responding. I know—here, now—there'll be no more basketball. No more belly bombers. No more Kenny. Some friends just don't get it.

*   *   *   *

I loved *Close Encounters of the Third Kind* as a kid; for months I made mountains out of mashed potatoes. Now I'm up late with Kevin, watching it again. Only this time, I think—what the hell? Richard Dreyfuss just gets on that ship and leaves behind three kids? Leaving a spouse, sure. Shit happens. But leaving your kids? Talk about science fiction.

*   *   *   *

I'm roaming Stop & Shop, searching for an end-of-the-aisle pyramid of peanut butter. Ben will be with me for the weekend.

Choosy moms choose Jif

My phone buzzes and I check it: *Restricted*. Curiosity wins.

"Mister Mullen?"

"That's right."

There's a pause. "This is Jessica Goldstein."

"Hey there." I assume she's rescheduling a mediation session. Yet her tone sounds downright funereal.

"Mister Mullen...I shouldn't call you. I mean, I can lose my certification. I want you to understand what this means. Me contacting you directly."

It does strike me as extraordinary. For months now she's re-stated her policy of never speaking to either party unless we're both present. She always makes a show of hanging up first on our calls, and every email ccs us both. If shopping carts had emergency flashers, I'd switch them on beside the cereals. "I do understand."

Kid-Tested, Mother-Approved!

She sighs. "My partner and I've had a strong disagreement. She doesn't know I'm calling you. Kim knows the legalities. But...*I* know the people here."

"Yes you do."

"We've handled one hundred four cases now. And...well, one hundred and three were settled without litigation. Our track record is perfect. *Was* perfect. Everyone settled through mediation."

"I know."

Jessica pauses. "This business about your ex-wife. Only finding work in Israel."

"Yes?" I move toward dairy.

"If I were you I'd hire a lawyer. Quickly."

Hey Moms! Don't forget the power of cheese!

"I already have a lawyer..."

"Good. I wouldn't waste time. It sounds...like she's planning to flee the country."

Flee. The word hits me. Leave. Depart. But *flee*? *With Ben?*

I'm stunned near the pharmacy.

Recommended by Dr. Mom

"Did she tell you something? I mean...did she say she was—"

"I've already said way too much. I'm...seriously jeopardizing my certification here. I like practicing in New York State. I really don't want to move."

"Okay."

"You can't ever tell anyone I contacted you. Do you understand? It's important you understand."

"I do understand."

Seconds pass in silence near movie rentals.

Join Reel Moms!

"Michael...I think you're a decent man. What always struck me is your attitude. For ten months now you've always stressed what's good for your son. And your ex-wife...well, she only talks about her career. Or maybe...it's her libido."

"Hmmm..."

"I hope you have a good lawyer. Good luck."

"Thanks." I'm about to ask what's next but the line goes dead.

My question is answered on Monday, when I receive a certified letter signed by Jessica and her partner notifying me mediation is terminated. The cc indicates an identical copy was sent to her.

*   *   *   *

It's late afternoon; Ben didn't have his nap. As soon as I said we're leaving the park, he melted down and cried. But I'm not concerned, because once he is strapped into his car seat, he'll be out. Sometimes I even drive around at night just to lull him to sleep.

I'm holding him in one arm and pushing his Little Tikes car with the other when an older woman suddenly jumps in our path. She circles me and stares into Ben's face. "Honey! You okay?"

I decide to let this play out.

"Do you know this man?" she asks. "Where's your mommy?"

Ben stops crying and clings tighter to me, actions I'm guessing don't indicate I'm a marauder. But she continues. "Is this man hurting you, honey? Do you know him?"

Ben gives a WTF expression. I pat his back, and he mutters, "Daddy, I'm tired…"

Now I pivot to see her clearly as Ben clings harder. "Are we just about done?"

She shrugs. "Predators stalk children in parks!"

"*Parents* take children to parks!" Now I regroup, breathing deeply. "So you also accost *women* carrying crying children?"

The sneer reappears. "Statistically, most predators are over-*whelm*ingly male—"

I turn away as she babbles.

*   *   *   *

I'm convinced my brother—and roommate—is tired of experiencing my never-ending woes. But I'm wrong. This afternoon, Kevin calls me to his desk, where he's bathed in late sunlight. I need to see something, he says, opening a file on his large screen desktop. It's a stranger's face—a middle-aged man, bald, glasses.

"Who's this?"

Kevin shrugs. "Kasper."

He clicks to another photo of this guy, this time with her, taken at that psychology seminar in Israel; his arm's around her waist. A photo of them on a Caribbean beach, where he looks like her father. More photos—seminars, lectures, academic cocktail parties. The most common locale is Evansville. And then, to my horror, both of them at the off-campus apartment with Ben, who doesn't seem happy.

I look up. Kevin nods, as if acknowledging words fail.

He quickly briefs me, summarizing downloads, including Kasper's employment history, CV, court records. He's a psychologist, but an academic who never practiced. He taught in Haifa for years, and recently moved to Tel Aviv, although he's Catholic. And he just spent a year's sabbatical in Evansville. Kevin says he's originally from Bulgaria.

"Well, the brown socks and shoes on the beach gave that away," I mutter.

Until last year, he lived with his wife and four kids in Haifa.

"What?" I ask. "You mean…he left a family for *her*?"

Kevin shrugs. "He left them for someone…"

I breathe deeply and realize it's a good thing I didn't know about this. There might have been violence. I mean, way back when I cared. Like last month. And I can't help asking again. Just who *is* she?

        *   *   *   *

About monogamy.

The fact is, shortly after we were married, before she became pregnant with Ben, I fell in love with someone else. It happened during annual recurrent training in Oklahoma City. Now, any day that doesn't reach triple digits there is considered chilly. We'd finish class by three, and the sun was still broiling at four when I'd take a swim at the Days Inn. It was so hot you didn't need a towel; you stepped off the ladder and nature blow-dried you. One afternoon I climbed out of the pool and found myself on a plastic lounge chair next to a classmate, a fellow controller I'd smiled at during the morning donut scrum. (The most dangerous location in North America? Standing between air traffic controllers and free Krispy Kremes.) She had long blonde hair and a blue-and-red swimsuit. Talk about your primary colors. I quickly wished I did have a towel.

Meghan worked up in Providence, which I straightaway concluded was good—not too far, but definitely not too close. We started talking poolside, goofing on the meteorology consultant who became tumescent when lecturing us on the airborne hazards of radiation fog versus advection fog. Pretty soon it was dinnertime so we took my rented Dodge Caliber to Applebee's. Oak City—like most places in these United States—is all about restaurants advertising on national television, so it's the same menus with the same mozzarella sticks and same bottomless Cokes and same Death by Chocolate. While we waited, they handed us one of those flying saucer shaped things that lit up and buzzed and flashed red when it was time to be seated, and we tossed it back and forth like it was radioactive. After we ordered, we imagined a maniacal employee recklessly combining dishes in the kitchen—coleslaw soup, Buffalo sushi, deep fried Jell-O, zucchini pudding, roasted garlic mashed brownies, bacon and ketchup juice, salsa ice cream.

She was a hell of an attractive woman, but what I remember most was her laugh. Jesus, what a sexy laugh. And laughing was about all we did in the following days, sitting in the back and giggling at the guest instructors from Lockheed Martin and MIT as they yapped about upgrading to Next Generation Air Transportation System. Texting each other from four feet away: *NextGen? We didn't even get LastGen!* It's lucky we didn't earn detention, or get sent home with demerits. On the penultimate night, we took her rented Pontiac Vibe to Outback and stayed until the waitresses were counting their tips at the table next to us. When we got back to the Days Inn, I walked Meghan to her room, one floor above mine. She smiled and asked if I wanted to come in.

And there I was. Literally on the threshold. My father had stood in a thousand portals during his career, smelling the smoke and feeling the heat through the door on the palms of his hands and wondering whether to swing an ax or retreat. Fight or flight.

I smiled and went back to my room, where I got damn little sleep that night.

But let me clarify. I'm not looking for extra points because I was the only one in my marriage who didn't color outside the lines. In fact, I still look back at that Oak City trip as the time I cheated. I didn't so much as hold Meghan's hand that week, and when we caught our respective connecting flights in Dallas, we lightly hugged and rubbed noses like Eskimos, each afraid to deploy lips. But the way I laughed at what she said, the way I watched her peripherally in class, the way we shared the same apple-caramel-dessert thingie at Bennigan's with the very same spoon—all that felt like cheating. Meghan made me feel alive in a way I'd never felt in my marriage, even on its very best days. She made me feel interesting and engaging and funny and attractive, which I didn't even realize I wasn't feeling. And I loved making *her* feel interesting and engaging and funny and attractive, because she allowed me that, and even encouraged it. But when I walked that extra flight to her motel door, I felt like I cheated.

Even so, I'm not proposing fidelity is the finest of virtues. In fact, I'm not even sure human beings are meant to be monogamous—what we don't know about our own species dwarfs what we think we know. But when I wake in the morning and my frontal lobe slowly drums its daily reminder—*MARRIAGE OVER! MARRIAGE OVER!*—my first thought isn't about her possible infidelities. It's my slow realization about how miserably unhappy *I* was in that marriage. Even though I never would have left.

*   *   *   *

Another quiet Sunday morning. Once again I'm with Moe, who's reading a thick book by David Foster Wallace that isn't *Infinite Jest*. He looks up. "Anything I can do?"

My response is immediate: "Yes."

I hear words tumbling forth, as if someone else is speaking. "I think my wife—...*ex*-wife. She's having an affair. Maybe long-term. Maybe multiple affairs. I dunno. She's got a boyfriend in Israel."

"Hmm..."

"She says she's got a job offer there. It's bullshit. It's a boy-friend. And she wants to bring Ben there. She keeps saying, over and over. Short-term. Just a visit. Just for a while. I think she wants to take Ben there. I mean like...one-way."

Moe leans in. "What can I do?"

"Eliot. Still with El Al?"

He nods. "Every Landing, Always Late..."

I pause, certain he knows. "I need a PNR, Moe."

He expels air. It's quite illegal these days for airline employ-ees to share information electronically stored in Passenger Name Records. Even before the 9/11 insanity turned airlines into the Gesta-po, it already violated privacy laws. At an absolute minimum, his partner Eliot could lose his job in reservations at El Al.

"Okay."

I lower my voice. "You sure?"

"Yep."

I've contemplated this for days, even while denying it. "July or August," I say quickly, as if Moe might reconsider. "Most likely Tel Aviv. Probably nonstop. Kennedy. Newark? Forget her...don't bother with Cohen. Just check Mullen. That's Ben's passport."

"Okay."

He scoots back to his workspace and pecks at his laptop.

As an excuse to expend nervous energy, I take a break and slot out Hostess pies and Nestle Quik; I ingest all this sugar and dub it breakfast. When I return, there's a slip of paper facedown on my chair.

I read, as Moe nods grimly. It's a printout of Eliot's email.

"Jesus H. Christ!"

My eyes zip past airline jargon—fare codes, billing data, extraneous crap—focusing on the simple, chilling facts:

> *Pax: Cohen-Mullen, B. (minor)*
>
> *LY 8/29 Jul 14*
>
> *JFK-TLV; 0 stop(s); 10 hours, 30 minutes*

Nonstop to Tel Aviv, departing in July! What's more, Cohen is Ben's middle name; there's no hyphen before Mullen. Sirens wail in my head. But I hear Moe's voice.

"What?" I somehow hope the letters and numbers realign.

"You were right about the other thing."

I look up. "What other thing?"

"It's a one-way ticket."

*   *   *   *

It's a summer filled with bile.

Up in the tower, old-timers like to quote an ancient air traffic control maxim—that sometimes when we're dealing with an ignorant or difficult or English-challenged crewmember, we engage in "wishful hearing." We tell ourselves they comprehend us, even though they've provided no verification that our message was 1) sent, 2) received, 3) understood, and 4) remembered. But we pretend that we have communicated despite no evidence to support all four suppositions.

This summer I'm forever filled with bile that won't recede, and a sickness that won't abate. I can say it now. Now I can say that I've known for years that she is duplicitous, untruthful, deceitful. Unfaithful. Known it. Known? Not really. Not known it. But yes, known it. The way we know the deepest truths in life, truths that don't require evidence or photographs or affidavits, the truths we feel through our skin. I engaged in wishful hearing, wishful seeing, wishful wishing. Her lies were so thin that on some level she was challenging me to challenge her. Yet I'd see Ben smearing his forehead with applesauce in his highchair and I'd know that addressing this would mean the three of us would never again share an eat-in kitchen. So I bore down into wishfulness.

Of course, we're not in that eat-in kitchen anyway. Which only increases the bile.

At the time, I refused to input such damning evidence. After all our promises? Plans. Dreams. She couldn't. She could not.

She could.

So I wishfully heard and wishfully saw and wishfully imagined Ben in his highchair stained with Motts. And pretended not to hear and see and think and feel. That's why it's a sickening summer, bilious and dizzying at once.

Finally I got tech savvy and found the password for her email account. What I found wasn't pretty, and I stopped reading early on. Then I clicked the "About" sections on some of her LinkedIn connections, and began making my own connections.

What I don't know and would be shocked to learn is that the bile will go away but it will leave a mark, despite what the professionals and the books all repeat as a mantra. The bile is a poison that I'll have to live with for the rest of my years. Betrayal has an infinite shelf life. And—like a cockroach—it can survive an apocalypse.

       *   *   *   *

Hillary has called about 15 times in two days. She's apoplectic a subpoena must be served—immediately. Even she realizes that mediation has run its course. Judge Westphal is on vacation and apparently half the judicial branch of Queens County is in the Hamptons or some such place; Hillary's worried if the window passes and Ben gets on that flight to Israel, it will all be over. My attorneys argue over logistics—they won't employ a process server, apparently because too many are numbnuts and could screw this up, and we'll never get a second chance if it goes sour. Hillary insists I use someone who knows her well, preferably one of my blood relatives. I've learned there are dozens of rules to this serving game: It can't be done by me, or by a lawyer, or on a Sunday, etc.

I've roped Tommy into this mission. I'm not happy about it, but it's got to be done.

Last night I told her she could pick up Ben at the Georgia Diner in Elmhurst at 10. Then I rehearsed Tommy multiple times, just as Hillary rehearsed me. We got here at 9:15 and parked my car up front and tucked his Chevy Tahoe way in the back, the better to downplay its Multark Construction signage. I'm springing for breakfast, but he's no hungrier than I am. My wrist will fall off if I keep angling it to look at my watch; I don't know how millennials live without them. Watches, not wrists.

We're sitting in a window booth, perpendicular to Queens Boulevard, with a clear view of the steps leading to the vestibule. I've parted the tall vertical blinds so I've got a clear sniper's view of the entrance. There's no way she'll get past me.

Tommy theatrically sighs. "Jesus, Mikey. Clemenza. In the Georgia Diner. 'Leave the subpoena. Take the Linzer Tortes.'"

I nod nervously. "Either that or learn Hebrew. I can't read backwards at my age."

My brother chomps on wheat toast and stirs his coffee. He's silently letting me know he's aware of the stakes.

It strikes me I haven't been alone with my oldest brother in quite some time. In fact, a very long time. He is not a guy to fuck with, not after years of carrying pipe and swinging sledgehammers. High on his impressive left bicep is the Semper Fi tattoo he got near Lejeune, but even in a tight work shirt you can't see it. He wears a goatee and a small earring and heavy work boots seven days a week. He's a man, but he's never been a dick. Somehow he carved out a piece of the world for himself and quietly jettisoned any ugliness he breathed on 116th Street in Rockaway and in Catholic schools and on Parris Island. He simply rejected much of life's bullshit.

He met his business partner Terry Tarkington at a union meeting when they were laid off after the first Bush recession. Together— Irish-American and African-American—they've built Multark Construction and nice lives for about 45 employees and their many dependents. Once a year, Tommy and Rosemary join Terry and his wife Jo to take all four of their kids on a Disney Cruise, or they drive to the Outer Banks, or they fly to Bermuda. Tommy even asked my father to stop referring to Terry as colored, and the old man did. But then Tommy was always his favorite. Not because he's the oldest, or because of the Marines, or even because of the name. Tommy is the one who least seeks my father's approval, so naturally he gets it.

Tommy and Terry don't use off-the-books labor and they provide decent health benefits their accountant warned them dips into their own executive compensation fund. Both have *OBAMA* stickers on their matching company-owned Chevy Tahoes, and Tommy's got a nice home in Douglaston he built himself. They charge customers more, but they market themselves as artisans—quality costs, as Katie's voice-over narration on the company homepage conveys. Last year Rosemary told us Tommy donated a four-figure personal check to AIDS Walk New York after his favorite admin died.

And Tommy and Rosemary have twin daughters. Ever since Liz and Kelly were born, I've watched him rock them to sleep and help them decide what color shoes to wear and listen along to their Miley Cyrus and Taylor Swift tapes. He and Rosemary have instilled in them that they are strong and smart and beautiful and capable.

In short, he's been an outstanding role model. But somehow I didn't realize it until this summer. What I don't know is of all the relationships that will see me through the next two years, my bond with Tommy will strengthen the most.

I launch a discussion I've back-burnered. "Lemme ask you..."

He says nothing.

"The last few years. I mean...up until she left. You've been...a little...I don't know. Distant."

He snorts out a laugh. "Wow."

"Wow?"

"Yeah. Wow. You're a piece of work."

I shake my head. "I don't get it."

"I'm freaking distant? *I* am?"

"Well, not now. But...before. During my marriage."

Tommy stirs. "You need a new history book there, pal."

"Meaning what?"

"You! You're the one, my friend. You practically told us all to go fuck ourselves after you met her. You worked yourself up everybody wasn't gonna like her. Nobody *didn't* like her. But you worked yourself up anyway."

"Well, I dunno. She was...different."

"You were a little hard on Eileen there for a while. No?"

"Whattaya mean?"

"Look, Mikey. So you wanna marry a Jewish girl. I mean...all due respect, big whoop. For Christ's sake. It's two thousand and something. You make such a big stand about it. Sure, maybe Tom would be an asshole. What else is new? You could marry Maureen O'Hara and he'd say something stupid. But not the rest of us. Telling Eileen to shove the church. All of that. Nobody said anything! *You* were the one brought it up. Nobody really gave that much of a shit, to be honest. Not even Eileen. I mean, what's it to us if you marry a freaking Hindu? For Christ's sake. You act like it was *Fiddler on the Fucking Roof*, like Eileen was gonna disown you. 'I have no son named Michael...'"

He shakes his head. "You never even gave Eileen a chance. What the hell? Eileen treated that girl golden. From day one. She was trying to learn how to cook kosher freaking meatloaf! But you had your panties all up in a twist."

I have nothing to say. He's right. Absolutely right.

"Okay," I say finally.

Tommy nods. "Okay. So don't be a douchebag. Everybody's on your side. Always have been."

He sips more coffee—it's nervousness, not caffeine—and then leans in. "I'm gonna give you some free advice, Mike. You take shit way too personally. All kinds of shit. *Way* too personally. You gotta learn to focus on people you wanna be with. Screw the jerks. *Screw* them."

I make eye contact, then drop my gaze. "Wow. I didn't know ex-Marines could be so insightful. Or count to ten. Or grip a spoon."

"Whoa! Funny guy." Tommy smiles, holding up the thick envelope with Hillary's seal. "You gonna ask the waitress to do this?"

"I meant *thank* you…"

"You bet your sweet ass."

I check my watch: 9:50. "Let's do it. What you're gonna say."

My brother shakes his head. "I'm gonna say…'Hey, you look great! New hair? Lose weight? I love those shoes!'"

"Cut the shit."

"Fine. I'm gonna say, 'I have—'"

"No!" I can't hide my impatience. "You've gotta say her name first! You've *got* to."

"Fine." Tommy slurps at his cup. "I'll say her name. Then I'll say, 'I have some papers for you. You've been served.'"

I nod. "And what if she wants to argue? Call you names?"

Tommy shrugs. "She'll be talking to dead space. Once this is in her hands, I'm outta there. 'Less she's gonna lay down on my hood. I'll be pulling away on two wheels."

I expel my breath; my eyes are on Queens Boulevard, the subway side. "Here she comes," I say quietly.

All in one move, Tommy chugs down a last swig, grabs his thick ring of keys and the envelope, nods grimly at me, and scoots out. I slump down as if waiting for Sonny to enter the toll plaza; goddamn Tommy for bringing up the Corleones. My line of vision is perfect: I wait. And wait. Then...her right foot is on the top step when I see the glass door open and now Tommy is facing her. I'm not close enough to read lips, but then I don't have to since pantomime tells the tale. I see her hands reflexively come up for the envelope, I see him nod grimly and trot off, I see her tear open the seal.

Tommy's Tahoe quickly shoots out of the parking lot—not quite on two wheels, but the suspension creaks when he takes the hard right toward Queens Boulevard and blows through the yellow light across four islands of traffic. In the distance a horn blares.

My phone rings; I knock a juice tumbler as Tommy speaks.

"She says there's a lot I don't know about my baby bro. Everybody thinks she's not nice. But you're not so nice either."

"What'd you say?"

"'Try the veal. It's the best in the city.'"

My chest constricts. "I love you, man."

"Yeah, yeah. Forget it. We'll talk later." And he's gone.

Hillary advised I didn't even need to come. In fact, she argued against it. But I'm here. Not because I doubted Tommy's competency; the guy has 45 people working for him. I came for the woman who's leaning against the handicapped ramp and rifling through papers. Believe it or not, despite all that's happened, I think it's the right thing. I may very well be unhinged, but I'm concerned that she understands.

Now I throw down the tip, quickly hand cash to the Greek-speaking woman up front, and within two minutes push open the same door. She's still reading and doesn't even see me.

I'm close enough to be struck. "You have any questions?"

She looks up, staring at me with venom I never saw before. Those same eyes that looked at me so differently? How is it possible? Who knew this pendulum had such reach? Was it always like this?

"You're a real son of a bitch! You know that?"

I nod and instantly it's as if I'm guiding an aircraft with engine failure; Hillary's voice echoes and it's all instinct. And adrenaline. "I'll see you." All instinct and adrenaline.

She's cursing at my back now, and I walk toward my car as she hurls foul words we both know have less potential to sear since our eyes no longer meet. I can see the station wagon. She recedes. Further than ever, she recedes.

*   *   *   *

We're snuggled in for the night, nowhere to go and nothing to do. I need several waking hours of not thinking about subpoenas.

Kevin is in Sag Harbor and I've got the best of both worlds. First, time with Ben until he conks out. Then, time with myself. Specifically, a phone on airplane mode and a fresh bag of Pepperidge Farms as I stream *The Right Stuff*. It won't be the same without a big screen, but it will do.

Jesus. Curled up with cookies. I'm more effeminate hourly.

It's a Berenstain Bears evening, and tonight we're reading a favorite: *Trouble at School*. After Grizzly Gramps uses cookies to

teach Brother Bear about division, I think about my stash of Nantuck-
ets up in the Cabinet-Ben-Doesn't-Know-About-Yet. Then he asks
what division is, a fair question. He rests against my chest and it takes
a while, but I decently explain how numbers are divided, and why.

His response probably seems both linear and logical to him.

"Do you love Mommy?"

I don't even blink. For once, I'm prepared. I've been waiting
for this over a year, and I can see the pitch lobbed in, fat and juicy.

"Yes, I do," I lie.

At first he doesn't respond, yet I know he's skeptical. I wait.

"But you're doing divorce."

"Yes."

"Why?"

"Well, divorce doesn't mean people don't love each other anymore. It means they...shouldn't be married. Or shouldn't live
together. Because they disagree on...stuff. So they decide not to live
together. But we both love you."

"Stuff?"

Another fair question, but I bullshit: "Grown-up stuff."

Ben sighs. "But you love Mommy *now*?"

"Yes. I do."

"So we'll live together?"

"No. Like I said...we figured it's better not to live together.
This way everybody can be happy."

"But you said you love her."

"I do. I mean...of course. She's your mommy. So of course.
I'll always love her cause she's your mommy. And she'll always love
me cause I'm your daddy."

"But..." He falters, regroups. "She said she doesn't love you."

I grin tightly, but don't respond.

"You only love her cause she's Mommy. You don't *love* her?"

"Well...I used to love her a different way."

"What way?"

I shift under his weight. "The way daddies love mommies. I mean...the way husbands love wives."

"Not anymore?"

"Well, like I said. I love her cause she's your—"

"*No.* Like before."

"Well, no. I don't love her that way anymore."

I don't want to break the silence, so I wait, staring over his blond hair at the digital face of the alarm clock near my sofa. *7:54.*

"Where did it go to?"

"Where did what go?"

"The other love."

"Huh?"

"The *oth*er love. Not the Mommy love. The other love. Where did it go?"

And once again he's done it. I think I'm prepared, I won't be stumped, I'll be ready with one swing to knock this ball clear out.

Instead I'm silent for way too long.

Finally I answer: "I don't know where it went, buddy."

*   *   *   *

It's a summer of diners again. Only not for food.

Ben is with her so I've shifted into non-Ben mode, when my only concern is guiding thousands of people safely through the stratosphere on through the troposphere and back to Earth. My shift is over and I hear an urgent voicemail from Sam. In a twisted and selfish way, I'm almost glad he sounds anxious; someone else is having a crisis. We agree to meet on the Upper West Side at Tom's, the coffee shop on Broadway used for exteriors on *Seinfeld*.

When I arrive, Sam's already secured a corner booth. I scoot in opposite; whatever it is, we're in silent agreement we'll order first.

He hasn't had dinner, so he goes all out, a bowl of minestrone and a hot turkey sandwich. I get one of my late-night standards, cheese blintzes; I always ate more Semitically than my ex-wife.

We discuss Ben and Tel Aviv. Finally I ask what's happening.

Sam nods. He's off his game, rambling about new material. Last weekend I received a postcard from a club called FunnyBonez, listing him alongside 15 others.

"I wanna talk about area codes. Back when the city was just 212. All five boroughs. The pre-718 days. Before all the stupid cell phone shit. The 646—"

I grimace as if at a foul odor. "*Lame*. What's next? 'Member when KeySpan was still Brooklyn Union Gas? Gee whiz! And, hey, remember Checker cabs? They sure had some big back seats…" I shake my head. "You're gonna be a *remember* comic?"

Sam pretends I've hurt him. "Think it's easy? Get your ass up there. Just a mic. It's goddamn *hard*."

I lean back. It's time to explain the urgent voicemail.

He makes eye contact. "'Member bout a year ago? Maybe two years. We were talking bout…Ben and all. You said something like, 'You'll see when you have a kid.'"

"Yeah…"

"Debra's pregnant."

I lean way across the table. "Wow."

"Yeah."

"Wow…"

"Um hmm."

"Holy shit."

"Yeah."

"Wow. So…are you *hap*py?"

He leans forward too. "Yeah…ya know…I think so. I mean, I think I am. Really."

Finally I smile. "Don't have to apologize."

He sighs, as though he's shedding skin. He looks calmer, older, happier. He looks…better. "Yeah."

I raise my glass and we toast. Then we fist-bump and finally his smile spreads.

"What's Debra's take?"

"She wasn't feeling well. Had this doctor's appointment in Jersey City. Told her I'd go with her and she said, nah, it's probably nothing. So…she's real happy. But only if *I'm* happy. You know."

"Sure."

I stare at Sam's dark arms. Debra is paler than Lady Gaga locked in a closet all winter, so I'm imagining how the kid will look.

Sam smiles; he could always read my mind. "A swirl. Chocolate and vanilla on the same cone."

The waitress puts down coleslaw and pickles. I notice she's very sweet and I smile at her, reminding myself I'm technically single again. In fact, it's not technical—I *am* single.

Sam shifts so he's almost supine. "So. We're getting married. I need you for the best man thing."

I drop the pickle. "Holy shit! Big night! What else? You're getting braces?"

"Baby. Marriage. FunnyBonez. Yeah, that's it. For now."

The waitress drops off Cokes and I wrestle with the straw.

"So?" he asks. "Best man?"

"Maybe. Depends what's on Netflix that night." I blow the paper covering off my straw and it catches Sam in the left ear. "What the hell? Have to ask?"

"Thanks." We both drink. "So...any advice?"

I lean in again and he leans in too.

"Parenting. It's the best thing ever gonna happen to you. *Ever.* Better than falling in love. Better than sex. Better than anything. Absolute best thing. And you'll be terrific."

"I'm not so sure…"

"I *know* you'll be terrific."

"How come?"

"'Cause you just said you're not so sure."

*   *   *   *

After work, I stop at my mother's, where Ben spent the afternoon. She's flipped a shoebox onto its side, zig-zagged string across

HALF THE CHILD · 140

the opening, cut out a back door, and turned it into a cage for a plastic Simba. Ben is thrilled. It's nice to know she's still got it.

To be honest, my mother and I always had an okay relationship but we were never particularly close. It was nothing personal—just the usual thousands of years of mothers and sons pulling each other's reins. That is, we weren't close right up until the time my marriage imploded. Lately we've been charting some new waters.

While Ben naps, she turns off *Jeopardy* and asks me how I'm holding up. Fine, I say. No, she means really. Fine, I repeat. Then I make eye contact. Oh, I say.

I see she's really asking about one of her greatest fears. Without forming the words. She's asking about 1998.

Just before my twentieth birthday I spoke seriously about taking my own life. There's obviously little need to add I didn't follow through. But I lost most of 1998 because of it, when I had that gap year from college and worked construction and drank in Sunnyside and slept with a divorced mom. Later, when I took the physical at Fort Hamilton, the old petty officer that had me turn my head and cough gave me a seven-page form and knowingly and under penalty I checked *NEVER* next to anti-depressants. So much for Don't-Ask-Don't-Tell. The Air Force never did learn about Prozac. Since then so much changed I feel I've lived several additional lives. But I don't think I could ever really be back in 1998 again. Of course, I don't know. It's a frightening thought.

"Don't worry, Ma."

"It's what I do."

I look at her. "You know...I never doubted you. You know. Loving any of us." I indicate Ben curled up on her sofa. "That's what I wanna do with this guy."

She nods.

"I just don't want him to ever...you know, question if I love him. Not for one minute." My voice lowers. "I know what it's like not to feel loved by your father."

"So make sure he doesn't," she says quietly. Then my mother does this thing she often does—she just starts singing. Her scratchy voice starts in on *Love Me Do*.

Now it occurs to me that my sister's anniversary is next week. "You having a Mass said for Lizzie?"

She stares at me. "Don't I always?"

I pause. "That night. Me and Katie. On the stairs..."

"Yes."

"I can still see Lizzie."

My mother shakes her head. "You...the others. You remember differently. When you think of your sister, you see her at that age. When she died. But I'm her mother. For me...it's different."

I pause. "What do you mean?"

She stares again. "When I think of her...I think of her in my arms. As my baby."

I don't speak for a long time. Then I tell her, "I'll take you to the Mass."

*   *   *   *

I'm starting a swing shift, and our supervisor's briefing makes it clear this humidity will combine with an unstable atmosphere and provide a lifting source for a whole lot of moisture. In other words, thunderstorms. Motherific thunderstorms, from what the System Command Center is predicting.

Technically, JFK is in the serious shit, not LGA. We're 11 nautical miles away, great-circle distance as the crow flies, not that very many crows soar over the Van Wyck Expressway. But both LGA and JFK—along with Newark and a whole bunch of smaller fields within 100 miles—are all bound together like hostages trussed at the wrists and ankles, because bad weather in and around New York City means all the runways in use will be closed and reopened and over-lapping arrival and departure patterns will be continually remade and we'll all suffer as one until the moon rises high after midnight.

Then again, who knows? The worst of it could skirt past Co-ney Island and bounce out to sea, but not before killing a few shitfaced drunken summer speedboaters en route.

When I was in the service I took an advanced meteorology course at Keesler Air Force Base in Mississippi with an absolute weather legend, an old-school forecaster they still talk about for his prognostication skills and sheer brilliance. He was so good the senior officers never scolded him for wearing white athletic socks with his service dress uniform. And he used to repeat the same mantra all the time: The best climate expert in the world, using the most advanced technology science can provide, is capable of one thing and one thing only—predicting weather for no more than the next ten minutes.

I stare at the online forecasts and a realization washes over me. Predicting weather is no different than predicting relationships. In fact, ten minutes seems optimistic.

*   *   *   *

We're on a hard wooden bench in the courthouse on Sutphin Boulevard and Hillary is speaking too fast. It occurs to me: As much as I regret all that's happened, she may regret it even more. Starting with answering the phone the first day I called. This is one case that won't be settled through reconciliation. But we're all in now.

"First I'm going to request they revoke Ben's passport."

I nod. "So tell me…Westphal's on vacation. Do we get another judge?"

"Yes. Judge…Bullard."

"Is it a woman?"

"Yes."

I pause. "Are they all women? I mean, the ones dealing with divorce and kids?"

Hillary laughs. "Not always. It seems that way." Then she leans in. "Mike, I…"

"Yes?"

"Well, I just…I want you to be prepared. I mean…you're a great dad. You love your son. But…be prepared. I've seen this many times. Family Court is the one place you don't want to be a man."

Before I can respond, I look up to see the defendant arrive. Along with her new attorney. This one isn't mini-skirted; in fact, she's wearing pants. But when she glances at me I almost shiver. Since Ben came along, I've spent many, many hours watching juvenile enter-tainment. There's no denying it; the resemblance is beyond dispute.

Her new attorney is Elphaba. The Wicked Witch of the West.

Soon we're standing before Judge Bullard in a small anteroom serving as a temporary office. She's seated at a rather modest desk found in any cubicle in what's left of Corporate America. I study the face of justice but can't conclude much; she is old, tired, perhaps even bored. Her assistant whispers constantly in her ear as Judge Bullard scans scores of pages pertaining to the life of my three-year-old son. In so little time he's generated more than his weight in dead trees.

The Fruit of the Marriage.

Suddenly the judge recoils; she beckons her assistant and whispers harshly. Then she addresses Elphaba and Hillary.

"Counselors…clarify something."

"Absolutely, your honor," says Elphaba.

"Sure, judge," says Hillary.

Judge Bullard holds up a weathered hand. "Counselors! You're telling me it's been…a *year*? And these parties still aren't di-vorced? Can someone explain?"

Hillary shifts nervously. "The parties chose mediation, judge. They hoped—"

Elphaba rudely cuts Hillary off; clearly there's no penalty for such behavior. "Your honor…my understanding is there were…temperament issues. Mediation became impossible. There were too many…anger issues..."

I turn imploringly to Hillary. But Judge Bullard speaks: "I want all the parties up here. *Now*."

We all shuffle to the desk. Then, shockingly, the judge grabs Hillary by the shoulders and positions her facing front on the right. "What is the plaintiff's name?"

I nod. "Michael Mullen, your honor."

She moves me next to Hillary. Next she positions the defendant on my left, and then Elphaba. Once again, I'm rubbing arms with the woman I exchanged vows with before a justice six years ago.

"Are we ready?" Judge Bullard asks.

I look about nervously. Is there no end to the theatrics of the judicial system?

The judge stares. "Are you both of sound mind and body?"

We nod, and we're sharply instructed to speak up.

"Are you both here of your own volition? With no coercion?"

I respond quickly, like in basic training, and she follows suit.

"Are you prepared to end the marriage you willfully entered into in…" She peers down. "2008?"

We respond.

"You both realize this is permanent? This marriage will be dissolved for now and all time?"

We respond.

"And you are fully committed to taking this step?"

Oh God, yes! Please!!

We respond.

Finally, Judge Bullard nods. "Then New York State officially grants your petition for divorce. You are no longer married."

I look to my best man Hillary for guidance. What now? Toss her garter? Then I make accidental eye contact—*just* a second—with my former bride. Her face reveals nothing.

Judge Bullard has the last word: "I want all of you in Conference Room C. You have unsettled issues with this...move. Alright? Let's get things worked out. I want you to settle these issues yourselves. *Not* through court. Alright? Take as much time as you like." The judge stares. "Good luck to you. Alright? And to your daughter."

"Our son," I say instinctively.

But justice's back is already turned.

Now we're settled into Conference Room C. But we won't be discussing Israel, or Ben's passport, or the El Al flight I'm not supposed to know is already booked. Instead it's Elphaba's show. She's Michael Jordan in here, and the rest of us are nameless teammates and opponents who'll grow even fuzzier on the highlight reels.

"Mister Mullen, how many hours a week do you work?"

I cough and shift. "That's in the paperwork we filed."

Elphaba shuffles folders; it's all method acting in court and some still seek motivation. "Ah, right. Plus overtime, yes? And mandatory training in Oklahoma—"

"Only once a year."

"*And* graduate school. That doesn't seem to leave—"

"I'm not in graduate school. For now."

"For *now*...okay. Well, you're a busy man. So clearly when Benjamin is *with you*"—she inserts air quotes—"he isn't always *with you*. He doesn't spend all those hours with you yourself, correct?"

"My family helps. Just like her family helps."

She laughs, but with absolutely no mirth. It's theatrical and hollow, like justice itself seems to be. "Yes, indeed! *Helps*..." She shuffles folders she doesn't need to see again, because she's actually reading from a Post-it. "Obviously Benjamin spends much time with…Eileen Mullen. Exactly how much time, would you guess?"

"It varies."

"It varies. Okay. How about…Katherine Mullen? Does that vary too? And Kevin Mullen? Thomas Mullen, Junior? Rosemary Mullen? All that time varies? Does Benjamin ever manage to spend some time with *you*, or is it always your mother, your siblings, your siblings' spouses, your siblings' unmarried same-sex partners—"

"I have to work. To earn money. To pay rent."

"Ah! That's funny. Because my understanding is you're currently living with your brother. Do you have canceled checks from what you've paid him?"

I've almost forgotten Hillary, but finally she speaks. "I'm not sure…where exactly are we going with this?"

Elphaba doesn't even respond, and remains focused on me. "So you spend quite a bit of time at work, yes?"

Throughout this long, hellish journey, I've fought an internal war to keep my temper in check. Time and again, I've felt bile rising in my throat—and I've suppressed it. But this woman seems intent on nurturing my worst impulses. "Well…some of us work for a living. Not all of us spend five years in grad school living off someone—"

Hillary touches my arm.

Elphaba turns to her Post-it. "Mister Mullen, do you work with Benjamin on improving his vocabulary?"

For seconds I say nothing. "Yes."

She locks eyes. "Do these lessons include the word…*cocksucker*? In your estimation, is that appropriate vocabulary for a three-year-old? The word *cocksucker*?"

"Ben repeats things he hears…"

"Things he hears from *you*! Yes? It was *you* who said cocksucker to him."

"I didn't say it *to* him! I said it in front of him."

"Ah. You think that's appropriate? A three-year-old should hear such language?"

"He was asleep when I said it!"

"He was asleep? Well, you just admitted you said it in front of him. And if he was asleep, how then did he hear it? And why did he repeat it to his mother?"

I turn to Ben's mother but she's not even facing us; her gaze is out the window.

Hillary speaks quietly. "I don't think this is productive," she puts in timidly. "Are there other issues?"

"Mister Mullen, how long have you been licensed to drive in New York State?"

I shrug. "I haven't always lived here. I served in the mili—"

"When were you *first* licensed in New York?"

"At sixteen."

"Right. So then you have a fair command of New York State driving regulations."

I'm more than tired of all this. "Sure. A fair command."

"So then you're aware of New York State Section 1229-C?"

"You might as well be speaking Mandarin Chinese now. And you know it."

Elphaba clucks dramatically. "No, it's not Mandarin Chinese, Mister Mullen. It's New York State law. Designed to protect the lives of children. This law's been in effect since…April first, 1982. It requires all children under the age of four riding in an automobile to be properly restrained in an approved car seat. Have you heard this?"

"Of course. Ben always—"

"And yet last year when Benjamin was only two years old—two! You allowed him to sit in the *front* seat. And with*out* a car seat. At *two*! Isn't that correct?"

"He was sick! He had just thrown up—"

"Did you notify Benjamin's mother he was sick?"

I sigh, and stare at the table.

Elphaba nods, jotting meaningless notes on a legal pad. "I'll take that as a *no...*"

Hillary dares to speak up: "Is there anything else?"

Elphaba smiles. "Well...yes. Mister Mullen?"

I look at her.

"Mister Mullen...do you feel three years of age is the appropriate time for children to be instructed in sexual education?"

I sit up straighter. "Why not say what you mean? Just once? Just...come out and say something without all the bullshit prelimin—"

Hillary touches my arm again.

"Certainly." Elphaba smiles her mirthless smile. "I won't use foul language like you. I hope that's alright. But I'll put it another way. Mister Mullen...do you believe a father should show his three-year-old child his erect penis as a means of instructing—"

"That's complete bullshit!"

Elphaba turns to her client, still gazing out the window. "I'd been warned about your temper, Mister Mullen, but—"

I turn to Hillary. "Jump in any fucking time!"

Hillary opens her mouth but—once again—Elphaba beats her to the punch. "Mister Mullen, we can leave the room if you'd like to yell at your attorney…"

"I'm not yelling at her!"

"I see. You're yelling at *me*. Well…then I think we're done. For now."

She makes a big show of stacking folders and slowly scraping back her chair. Her client follows her toward the door. But not before Elphaba adds one more sotto voce aside directed, of course, not at her but at me: "I thought controllers were so calm and cool. Good Lord! Remind me to book flights out of Kennedy now…"

*   *   *   *

My sister Kerry calls from Florida, asking about Ben and court. I answer by rote.

Just last year, Kerry was at the center of the family's crisis command center. She found something strange while soaping her left breast; she's a nurse so she knew a specialist in Fort Lauderdale. I flew down with my mother and since the flight was oversold with spring breakers I used my license to bum a cockpit jumpseat. At the hospital the exchanges with my older sister were awkward and filled with pauses. Then we all spent the next few months doing what American families do when there's a medical calamity in the 21st Century: We sent cards and stuffed bears and cartoon emails and six kinds of gourmet brownies.

Thankfully, the chemo worked and she got better. But she couldn't bask for long, because my own shit show occurred during her convalescence.

She says she wishes she were closer to New York, and I believe her. Now she asks how I'm holding up. What can I say? I know, Mikey. Hang in there.

It's pretty much the same conversation each time.

Then she says her stepson outgrew his *Toy Story* bedspread and pillowcase set, and maybe Ben would like it. Should she send it so I'll have it for when Ben sleeps over? Don't bother, I tell her. Ben may be sleeping in Israel soon. My optimism is dying fast.

*   *   *   *

There are 18 families listed on the docket for Judge Rhonda Westphal today. This is Queens County, New York, USA, so that means I'm standing on the most ethnically diverse patch of land in the known universe. That's not hyperbole, it's a statistical reality confirmed online as quickly as blue-red-yellow-blue-green-red Google. Even so, outside the door there's a complete listing of all 18 couples—posted right where a mezuzah would be nailed—and it's almost silly. If this were fiction, names would have to be amended to sound less stereotypical.

> *Abbruzzi v. Colletti*
>
> *Chung v. Chung*
>
> *R. Patel v. L. Patel*
>
> *Fernandez v. White-Fernandez*
>
> *Mullen v. Cohen*

I take a seat. Within minutes I complete a statistical analysis and I'm shocked to realize it's quite damning to any vessel transporting XY chromosomes. All 18 mothers are here. Some are poorly dressed, some are loud and rude, some are sneaking texts when the bailiff turns away. And some strike their children without caring who witnesses a backhanded cuff. But all 18 are present.

Conversely, there are only six fathers here today.

Through the course of the day, when those names are called and then called again, explanations will be offered for the absentees.

The father returned to his home country, your honor.

The father's serving a two-month sentence on Rikers Island on unrelated charges.

The father's respecting the mother's restraining order.

The father's being held at the 115th Precinct due to these abuse charges.

The father has a separate court appearance in Brooklyn.

The father didn't respond to the subpoena.

The father's whereabouts remain unknown.

It's not particularly hot, yet four of the five other fathers are in shorts, and two are in tank tops, one a bona fide BVD wife-beater. Among all 18 families, I'm the only father wearing a suit and tie.

Based on appearances, none of them seem to feel how I do: that Judge Rhonda Westphal holds their very lives in her hands.

*   *   *   *

I'm meeting my sister Katie and her partner Chris for the annual foray to the Bryant Park film series. Only this year Ben is along and the feature is *Bye Bye Birdie*. He and I get there early, spread a blanket, and unload dinner from Cosi. I desperately need a night not thinking about Israel.

While we munch, Ben says Katie told him she wants to get a baby. I say I know. He says he and Grandma Eileen prayed in church and asked God to help Katie. This shocks me, but I only nod. He nods too, under his Lightning McQueen cap.

Now I see Katie's red hair making its way through the crowd, and she skips over and swings her hysterical nephew through the air. "Master Benjamin Ben Benny Benjy Benson Bennington Ben-Noodle-Head the First!"

Chris mockingly offers a handshake: "Good day, Michael."

I answer sternly, "And a fine day to you, Christine." Then we laugh and I hug my common-law sister-in-law.

While Chris and Ben discuss *Disney Cars*, I smile at Katie. "This just in…guess who's lighting candles for a bambino?"

Katie's eyebrows rise. "So miracles do *hap*-pen…" She says this in "Deep South." Her standard bread-and-butter is a patois marketed as "US General American," but she's also adept at New England, Mid-Atlantic, and all varieties of greater New York.

The title song starts. Katie and Chris and dozens of other women—as well as quite a few men, and my only son—jump up and dance along with Ann-Margret's skirt twitching.

$$*\qquad *\qquad *\qquad *$$

Bob M., the tower manager, is in an unusually decent mood and visits the break room on the 14th floor to shoot the shit with us. I look up from a 2009 *Aviation Week* and nod, and he nods back. Why is he hanging with the rank-and-file? Finally I conclude he's probably acting on tips learned at a management seminar.

I've never had a run-in with the guy, but he's screwed enough colleagues for me to know he would screw me—high, hard, quick—without him having to consider it first. He falls in with loudmouths jawing about the Yankees and what a bust A-Rod's been postseason; nothing you couldn't parrot from a thousand calls to WFAN.

"I was gonna take the kids to the stadium," says Rusty, an older guy. "It runs like two hundred bucks now. Parking, hot dogs. Freaking ridiculous."

Bob M. dramatically shakes his head. "Don't mention kids! I had a tee time on Saturday. Rockville Centre. Course I never played. But I gotta babysit!"

There's a chorus of groaning and *Oh shit!*.

"That sucks," chimes in Wayne, always eager to suck management teat. "Whose kids?"

"Mine!" says Bob M., and there's raucous laughter. "My wife's got me by the short ones. I got out of it, like, three times. She's doing something with her sister and I'm nailed. I gotta babysit from Friday till Sunday. Nailed!"

More groans, curses, sympathetic chuckles. And now I've walked around the pool table and stopped a little closer to Bob M., someone who could obliterate my career and transfer me from Flushing to Fairbanks.

"Hey, Bob," I say, and everyone quiets as I glimpse Wayne's furrowed forehead. "I've gotta ask you something."

"What is it?" Bob M. says calmly, slipping from Guy-Who-Wants-To-Hit-18-Holes-In-Rockville-Centre and back to Guy-Who-Holds-Both-My-Balls-In-His-Surprisingly-Small-Hands-Now-That-I-Notice-Them.

"How can you babysit your own kids?" I may have spit it out too quickly, in an effort not to sound too confrontational. But Rusty literally steps further away.

"How's that?"

"I mean...how can you *babysit* your own kids? They're your kids too. Right? How can you babysit them? Only *other* people can babysit them, right?"

Bob M. nods the same nod he offers when sitting on a review board, preparing to vote on the length of the suspension. "Interesting point, Mike." He makes a show of looking at his watch and then, just like that, he's gone.

Things are silent for a few beats until finally Rusty speaks up. "Hey, Mullen...what the fuck, over?"

I say nothing. Some things are hard to articulate.

*   *   *   *

My mother and I learn Ben's obsession with colors is passing.

We're at an indoor medieval dinner somewhere near the ass end of The Meadowlands and we're explicitly instructed to root only for the green knight. I wait, breathless, when the wench in the lime bodice hands us our emerald pennant. I fully expect Ben to insist we move to the red or even blue section, which we can't because the house is packed. My insides tighten as we prepare for a joust of our own in Row 11.

Instead, Ben shrugs and turns to munching a roasted turkey leg as big as his calf. I let my breath out slowly, smile at my mother, and pick up a spare rib.

That sweetest, most elusive entity of all: progress. *Huzzah!*

*　　　　*　　　　*　　　　*

I'm laying out Mrs. Paul's fish sticks on a cookie sheet and it's no simple task; Ben insists on the same number in each row. Now he yells that my phone is ringing. You ignore caller ID at your peril; I look down and see it's not good: *AMEX CUST SVC*.

"Mister Mule-an?"

"No."

"Sir, I'm trying to reach Mister Michael Mule-an."

I'm guessing Bangalore or Delhi. I quit prolonging the inevitable. "This is Michael *Mullen*…"

"Ah! Mister…*Mul-len.*"

"Yes. Who is this?"

"American Express Personal Credit Card Center."

"I see." Ben looks up from an episode of *Arthur*.

There's a pause. "Sir, I am calling about your account. Ending five-five-six-one."

"Yes."

"Sir, as a security precaution can you tell me your mother's maiden name?"

"No, I can't. For security reasons. This is an unsecure line."

He pauses again. "Sir, you have an outstanding balance on—"

"I know." I peer at Ben, completely focused on *Arthur*. "Look, you sent me notices. Voicemails. You're calling. But...*look*. We can talk all day. I just don't have it."

Static from the developing world buzzes my eardrum.

"Excuse me?"

"Sir...why do you not have the payment?"

"*Why?*" I breathe deeply. "Well, my ex-wife wants to kidnap my son to Israel. I mean...that's the *main* reason. There are others..."

"Sir, you agreed to make a payment on April—"

"Did you hear me? My son is being kidnapped."

"I understand, sir. But the payment was—"

"*No.* Don't say...don't say you understand. What's...do you have children?"

"No, sir."

I utter words I once swore I'd never utter: "Well, if you did then you'd understand." *Damn!* Before Ben was born I hated it when people played that card. Who the hell have I become now?

"Sir, I—"

"Look. It's really simple. I can pay my lawyers. And keep my son from being kidnapped. Or pay Amex. It's...I mean...it's not really a contest." Then I add, "I'm sorry."

"Sir, if we don't receive a payment by the fifth—"

"My credit rating'll be screwed. You'll break my arms...."

"So can I indicate you'll make a payment by the fifth, sir?"

I shrug. "I dunno. All depends on how the kidnapping goes."

I've stopped listening. Fish sticks don't take very long.

    *   *   *   *

We've got a court date but Hillary can't make it, voicemailing me she'll be presenting final arguments in another custody battle, this one in the Bronx. Replacing her is the youngest attorney at her firm, a sort of Midwestern-looking guy with blond hair and Scandinavian features named Cal. Like a lot of people who moved here at 22, he speaks about New York City as if the rest of us don't understand its charms.

Hillary indicated today is just formality, a reading of the summaries of both cases so Judge Westphal can consider all points before blocking the move to Israel. To me, it's such an absurd proposal, dragging a child across the world and away from his home and most of his loved ones. I can't even conceive of a wise adjudicator who would allow it. I stand with Cal at the plaintiff's table and she stands with Elphaba at the defendant's table.

The judge's assistant drones on about Benjamin Cohen Mullen so the court reporter can record the pertinent names and dates. Then she nods toward Cal, and my attorney du jour stands and explains why Michael Patrick Mullen is requesting he become the custodial parent of the Fruit of the Marriage.

All throughout, however, I'm watching Judge Westphal, and it's quite clear she's off somewhere far away. We all listen to Cal's flat Nebraska monotone, yet the judge has reading glasses on, low on her nose, and she's immersed in a document I'm certain is about some other fruit of some other marriage. Even when Cal pauses for effect, she neither looks up nor stops tapping a pencil. Finally Cal moves into homestretch mode, and lets loose the phrase "best interests of the child and the child's father." Now the judge looks up. She drops the pencil, removes the glasses, and stares.

"Counselor," she says, so softly Cal doesn't hear it. I flinch.

"—incumbent upon this—"

"*Coun*selor," she says again.

It's clear Cal's stride has been altered. "Yes, your honor?"

"Would you approach, please?" Then, for the first time ever, she stares directly at me. "You too, Mister..." She lets my absent name trail off, not pretending to search for it.

My chair scrapes loudly since I push it back so quickly, but I'm following Cal's long strides toward the bench. Suddenly it's a hot Texas afternoon during basic training and I'm still learning how to stand stiffly at attention. The open windows let in so much traffic din that only Cal and I can hear the judge.

"Counselor." Now there's the unmistakable edge of incredulity, even annoyance. I'm sweating as if it really is Texas, and cursing whatever parent in the Bronx took Hillary away. Somehow Cal has screwed up, that much is clear, yet I don't know how.

"Your honor?" he says meekly.

She leans forward, and involuntarily we both lean inward.

"Are you saying your client is requesting...to be *cus*todial?"

Cal nods furiously. "Yes, your honor. It's all documented—"

She glances briefly in my direction, as if an open window had gatewayed a bothersome insect. "And your client is the father?"

"Yes, your hon—"

"And the child's mother? The woman in the blue suit?"

"Yes."

The judge sits back. There's a loud sigh, and I truly can't tell if it's genuine or for effect; from what I've seen of the judicial system, on most days it's all a high school play in search of a drama coach.

That feeling comes over me once more. That feeling our lives are about to be altered yet again. And not in a good way.

"Counselor…let me explain how it works in my courtroom. In *my* courtroom, unless the mother is a prostitute or on crack, she is always awarded custody." She pauses. "*Always.* Do you understand?"

I say nothing, I do nothing, I feel nothing.

"But, your honor," Cal sputters. I can sense him desperately regrouping. "The Nineteenth Amendm—"

Judge Rhonda Westphal raises her hand. "You have your Constitution. I have mine. Go sit down please."

Almost immediately, she announces she very much supports the defendant's efforts to further her career by working in Israel for one year. It's an excellent opportunity for a working mother, and after all, the child isn't yet in kindergarten. Therefore both parents will share joint custody, with the mother as custodial parent.

Just like that. The ruling I thought would take days.

Joint custody. The most grievous oxymoron in all of law; how exactly are we jointly raising a child while living on separate continents? The judge adds that the father, of course, will be allowed visitation in Israel on dates agreed upon by both parties.

I may regret it for the rest of my life, but I act through instinct, not premeditation.

Committing the most grievous of sins, I speak up in court, and address the judge without being acknowledged. I'm on my feet and my voice cracks, but I plead. *Your honor, please…Don't allow my son to leave the country...I'll never see him again...She booked a one-way trip...On El Al...Please...They won't be back...She wants to take him away for good!*

Elphaba, of course, is *shocked* by such charges, and now she's on her feet. Her client dramatically shakes her head. The judge actually pounds her gavel and we all sink back into our chairs. Then she commands me to stand again.

I need to learn trust, I'm lectured by Judge Westphal. I need to address my temper issues and my anger issues and most of all my trust issues. My child's welfare is dependent upon *both* parents trusting each other. And communicating with each other. I need to put my child's needs first, not my own. I need to learn to *trust* the defendant.

The defendant nods at this.

I sink back down again. And my only thought is, I'm too old to learn Hebrew.

*   *   *   *

Back at Kevin's I find myself googling *constitution u.s.* and I quickly discover the relevant nugget:

> *Article. [XIX.]*
> *[Proposed 1919; Ratified 1920]*
> *The right of citizens of the United States to vote shall not be denied or abridged by the United States or by any State on account of sex. Congress shall have power to enforce this article by appropriate legislation.*

Quite straightforward and surprisingly simple. The language specifically refers to voting, yet after more googling I learn most legal scholars view it in much broader terms, as equal opportunity among genders. That said, like far too many laws of the land, this one has been ignored fairly often since 1920, on everything from women earning equal pay to women serving in combat.

I've always believed it's disgraceful how women have been treated in this country—by Congress, courts, cops answering domestic disturbance calls. I recall how Katie had to sue to obtain her first apartment, and how my mother was fired from her part-time teaching job when she became pregnant with Kevin. And how Airman Rebecca Truman—yes, the Air Force refers to women enlistees as *airmen*—was denied a rightful spot in the Dover tower. But apparently violating the 19th Amendment cuts both ways.

Hillary doesn't answer my voicemails. I wake up when Kevin notes it's 3 a.m. and I'm stretched out on the couch still fully dressed.

*   *   *   *

I'm on a break, but I'm still in the tower's management pod, just past the small set of stairs leading to the Grand Central Parkway side rather than airside. I'm staring out at the endless conga line of arrivals snaking over Westchester and into the Bronx and then right onto Runway 22. For someone who spends his life speaking, I have little left to say. I've told it to my mother, my siblings, Sam, Annabelle. What else is there to enunciate?

The government I'm working for at this very moment. That I served in uniform. That I salute with my hand over my heart at Citi

Field. All its guarantees and promises have seismically shifted under me, as surely as the Earth is shifting under that Airbus, its dangling landing gear blindly clawing at air as it fights to return to terra firma.

I think of the quiet night when Moe told me he's appealing his discriminatory discharge to the Pentagon. And then he muttered, "Yeah, the Pentagon. That was no 757..." My head snapped and I rolled my chair closer. And we talked about the experts we respect who question official narratives.

I'm learning to question. The worst part is that, for the first time, I'm questioning my relationship with Ben. Has our bond—the surest bond we both have—somehow become vulnerable?

*   *   *   *

As always, a hard copy of the monthly schedule is posted on the union bulletin board. I have an electronic version so I rarely glance at it, but someone added comments in red Sharpie, so I move in. At the bottom of the alphabetical roster, right under Wes Yardley, is this:

MIKE MULINS KID

Ben is slated to work three shifts a day, all 31 days.

*   *   *   *

I'm back at the VA Hospital in Fort Hamilton, only this time instead of bringing Ben to visit his grandfather I'm bringing my mother to visit her husband. As we enter the lobby I tell my mom to go ahead and I'll come fetch her later. She gets on the elevator and I head to the information desk.

Ten minutes later I'm at the opposite end of the building, filling out a lengthy form on a wooden clipboard. I wish I had my DD-214, with all my discharge information, but this wasn't planned so I guess at some dates. Finally I hear a nurse call out, "Mullen!"

I stand before her huge desk. There are about 20 people in the room, all men, representing a cross-section not only of races and ethnicities but the wars that brought them here: Afghanistan, Bush Junior's Iraq, Bush Senior's Iraq, 'Nam, Korea, even some hanging on from WWII. *H.W.* and *W.*—so many wounds inflicted.

Fathers and sons.

"What's the nature of your problem?"

Can my parents hear her booming voice five floors above us? "Excuse me?"

"Your *prob*-lem," she says slowly. "What is it?"

I lower my own voice. "Well...I'd like to speak to...um, a counselor. You know. To discuss some...issues."

"Right. What issues?"

"I'm not sure..."

"Well, if you're not sure...then how can we *help* you?" She's staring at me. "You wanna take a guess?"

"Well...I...I've been having problems. Um...marriage problems. Financial problems. You know."

"Substance abuse?"

"What?"

She speaks slowly again, obviously convinced I'm a moron. "Are you engaged in substance abuse?" Unfortunately, when she speaks slowly, she also speaks loudly. Two 'Nam-era guys with stereotypical gray ponytails look up.

"No."

"Suicidal thoughts?"

"Well..."

She leans forward. "Have you had suicidal thoughts?"

I lift the spring-like device on the clipboard and slip out the paperwork, then stuff it into my back pocket. "You know what...I'm fine. Really. I'm good."

For the first time, she smiles. "Great. Morales!"

I decide to wait in the lobby.

*　　　　*　　　　*　　　　*

It's a summer of waiting for the wheels of justice. Specifically, for the parameters of a very detailed legal agreement.

Hillary finally calls. Ben is allowed to live in Israel, but only for the next ten months, and with ample visitation from me; he must return to Queens County next summer before starting kindergarten. Justice is done with us—for now.

*　　　　*　　　　*　　　　*

My phone buzzes and I check the time. Friday, almost 7 a.m.

"Yeah?"

She says her name but I already know it's her. Ever since the Israel ruling, my feelings have hardened. I've tried, and tried, and tried to give her the benefit of the doubt, but now I too am starting to believe the worst about her. It's a dark mindset. I'd give anything for a time machine and a do-over.

"Is Ben alright?"

"Yes, he's fine."

"Where is he?"

The connection is crystal clear and my head sinks into my shoulders as I involuntarily grimace: *Don't say Israel, Israel, Israel...*

"He's with my parents. I told you...he's fine."

"Okay. Where are you?"

"In the city."

"In the city. And Ben's in Queens. Okay."

"I'm calling to tell you something."

"Okay."

"I got married last night."

"Hmmm..."

She seems unsure of what to say, as if she calculated I'd be talking. I'm not.

Finally she breaks the silence: "Do you have any questions?"

I cough. "Well...I haven't received any divorce papers. You're not...I mean, this isn't bigamy, is it?"

She clucks in disappointment, or perhaps it's substantiation. "No," she replies impatiently. "The divorce is final."

"Well...like I said, I didn't...get anything. When was it final?"

"What?"

"I said...when was it final?"

She clucks again. "I'm not...*why?*"

"I'd like to know."

"Tuesday."

"Tuesday." I cough again. "And last night was Thursday."

Now she is silent.

"Who did you marry?"

"*Kasper*," she says, as if this is obvious. To her it probably is.

"Well...I haven't gotten any papers."

"Your attorney can pick them up at the courthouse. On Sut-phin Boulevard."

"Uh huh. Is that what you did?"

"What?"

"Is that what you did? Picked them up at the courthouse?"

Her voice sounds far away, further even than Israel. "Yes."

"I guess we'll have to do that."

It's as if she had something else to say, but now won't say it. Instead that far-away voice breaks in: "Well...goodbye."

"Goodbye," I tell her.

*　　　　*　　　　*　　　　*

And now it's a summer of crying.

Over and over—unprovoked, unpredictable, unexplainable crying jags. They come on unexpectedly and are hard to shake.

Not Ben. Me.

*　　　　*　　　　*　　　　*

And once again, it's a summer ending in farewell. Once again, I'm saying goodbye to Ben.

But I can't say once again my heart is breaking. In fact, since last week I don't even feel I still have a heart. I feel somewhat discon-nected from all that. I just need to safely see Ben off to his new home in Israel, as per the written decree of New York State. During the last few days I've been rather calm about it. That's all I need to do.

I still have hours to go. I'm in the old brick row house in Queens, where I was born and raised. There are people everywhere. I'm in the center and yet I don't feel like I'm there at all. And suddenly I recall something. When I was young, there was a TV repair shop called CULLIGANS a few blocks away, and of course it's long gone now because who the hell repairs televisions in 2014? But the place sported a large neon sign out front, with those nine letters—C-U-L-L-I-G-A-N-S—lighting up the boulevard in bright red lights. Except the funny thing was, for years the *G* was in disrepair; it neither lit up completely, nor darkened entirely. Every night, year after year, you could see the other eight letters shining brightly well into the night, but the *G* would sputter and blink and gasp. The gases inside even gave off an odd, constant hornet-like buzzing. Now I'm that faulty *G*. I'm here, amidst other bright lights, but I'm sputtering into dimness.

And I want time to move into reverse. To when I, not Ben, was the child. A time with no cell phone stores or tanning salons, no bottled water or sea salt or red velvet cake. No online unfriending. When tattoos were primarily found in carnivals. When there were typewriters and phone booths and flip tops on cans. Telephones with cords to unravel, cars with vent windows bent back, TVs with rabbit-ear antennas pointed toward the Empire State Building.

I breathe deep—and try to be strong.

The people who love me the most are in full celebratory mode. My mother even skipped Mass at St. Rita's this morning to help Katie and Chris decorate the entire first floor. The theme is blue and white, punctuated by plastic Israeli flags and Stars of David throughout the living room. It's a new and hybrid holiday, with blue and white noisemakers, blue and white streamers, blue and white confetti. A banner is strung over the fireplace: *MAZEL TOV BEN!*

There are platters and bowls and dishes from Ben's Best, the kosher deli up on Queens Boulevard. Of course, this pleases my son no end—*Ben's Best!* And the airport he'll be flying to is Ben Gurion! Earlier this afternoon I helped him count the toothpicks holding up the colored cellophane wrapping on the meats. Katie continually refills baskets with blue corn chips and blue potato chips.

Chris has set up a karaoke machine and Tommy's daughters Liz and Kelly are singing with her but although I'm staring from about 15 feet away, I can't understand the song. Sam and Debra are here, as are Moe and Eliot. I hear Sam and Moe comparing and contrasting Teeterboro and LaGuardia, which should interest me, but I walk away. Eliot rubs Debra's tummy, which seems odd but maybe isn't.

The door opens and my brother Kevin arrives straight from his summer pad in Sag Harbor. He's accompanied by a beautiful young woman and I smile and shake her hand. Everyone says she looks amazingly like Jennifer Lawrence, a point made so often they start calling her J-Law and now I'm even further confused.

The twins and Rosemary came here with Terry, the co-owner of Multark Construction, along with Terry's wife Jo and their two kids, T.J. and Ellie. That's because Tommy drove to Brooklyn to pick up the man sitting in the far corner. My mother said Tommy laid out the ground rules before they even left the VA. No nastiness, no cracks, no bullshit of any kind—or this will be the last day pass he'll ever get and the only sunshine he'll see will be the benches outside Fort Hamilton. And so my father mingles with gays, lesbians, African-

Americans, single parents, and a Muslim comedian, all to celebrate a three-year-old Jewish guest of honor. But clearly he took Tommy's warning seriously; he smiles and chats with anyone walking by, nurses his Solo cup of juice, and even claps along to *Hava Nagila*.

My mother's in the kitchen, frying up dozens of homemade latkes as appetizers. And heating knishes and kosher pigs in blankets. She offers me a latke in a napkin, but I shake my head; I haven't eaten since yesterday. Rosemary arranges blue and white serving trays, and now I see Ben helping his aunt count as well: "Grandma said twenty!" Jo dishes applesauce; sour cream isn't an option in this house. Terry and Tommy take turns behind the bar, serving up everything from booze to wine to Juicy Juice.

The phone rings and it's my last surviving sibling, Kerry down in Florida, calling to wish Ben safe travels.

Sam borrows the karaoke microphone from Chris and then announces he's written fresh material just for tonight's occasion. The women leave the kitchen and crowd in to watch. Katie hands me a Pepsi, but I don't drink.

"Thank you, folks. Thanks very much!" Sam points at Ben, eagerly sitting puppy fashion on his knees up front. "You, sir! We've never met before, have we?"

Ben giggles into the microphone and it echoes inside my head. Sam holds up the plastic shofar Chris found at Party City. "Can you tell me, sir? What is this object?"

Ben pipes up without the microphone: "It's a shofar!"

T.J. and Ellie and the twins repeat: "Shofar! Shofar!"

Sam nods dramatically and inspects the plastic horn. "I see!" he says finally. "Well, that explains it. A man came up to me before and said, 'Shofar? Sho good!'"

There's lots of laughter, but to me it doesn't sound like laughter. I pull out a dining room chair, even though the table is being used as the buffet. I rest my head in my hands. Although I'm staring at carpet, I can feel others in the room glancing my way.

I breathe deep and look up. I hear Kevin warn Sam not to tell the one about celebrating in the back of the limousine by blowing not the shofar, but the chauffeur.

Someone yells out, "There're kids here!" But Kevin laughs and J-Law playfully slaps his thigh. Then Katie slaps his other thigh.

Sam's back in control. "Hey, Kevin! I do a solo. Seriously. No, no, seriously. I kid the Jewish people. But…it's out of *love*. Love! After all, they have the best tailors in the world. They're the only ones we use for washing and ironing the dishtowels on our heads. We tore up the contract with five Chinese brothers way back in 1400 A.D."

I can hear my father guffawing at that one.

Sam has gotten serious. Or maybe not. It isn't that the room is spinning. It feels more like *I* am spinning. My senses send false signals, like in a poorly made 1960s avant-garde film, fisheye camera lenses substituting for an acid trip. But I can hear Sam.

"Ben, we want to wish you lots and lots of luck in your new home. We can't wait to see you when you return. And I hope when you get back you're still not writing 5774 on your checks!"

There are giggles and groans. "Saw that coming," says Terry.

Sam wraps it up. "Thank you, folks! I love you, Queens! I love you, Ben!" I see him hug my son.

My mother says something about the soup being on, though of course there's no soup. There's shuffling and stretching; I can hear Terry dropping ice into Solo cups.

It's a scene entirely manufactured by love, and I know—the brain has more layers than that blue and white cake on the dining room table—I *know* I'm lucky to have a son, family, friends. The popular term now is *privileged*. I know all this. And yet none of it matters. It truly doesn't. Not in this moment. Not anymore. I can't evaluate, or calculate, or weigh and consider and adjudicate with the coldness of a Judge Rhonda Westphal. I've crossed over to where reason can't stand its ground and love can't save. Right now I feel anything but lucky. Because knowing I'm loved does nothing at all to prevent me from considering what I contemplated last night at LaGarbage, as I stared up the Hudson River toward the Tappan Zee Bridge and imagined outstretched arms as I plunged.

There's a general movement toward the Ben's Best trays and the salads and the rolls piled high on the table and I move in the opposite direction, away from them all, away from the guest of honor, away from all that love. I stumble toward the narrow front hallway, where we always forgot to take off our snow boots after making igloos and forts. Where my mother hung her Céad Míle Fáilte plaque. Where my father yelled at us to close the goddamn door because he wasn't paying Con Ed to heat all of goddamn Queens. And once again I forget to close that goddamn door.

I make it to the stoop and lean over and heave, but I haven't consumed anything in 20 hours and whatever's in my stomach remains there. My legs finally give and I slump onto the bottom step. I lean forward, and it begins. I'm sobbing and banging my fist on brick. I punch and I sob and I punch and I sob.

The safe arrival of Flight LY 8 in Tel Aviv tomorrow morning seems far away.

Someone has opened the screen door and is standing behind me. My guess is Katie. Maybe my mom. Maybe even Sam. Instead I feel strong arms on my shoulders and realize it's my older brother.

For long moments we don't speak.

"I can't do it. I can't do it…"

"Sure you can, Mike."

"I can't say goodbye."

"You will. He knows you're the rock. He worries about her. Worries she's never coming back. He can't count on her. He never worries about you. *You're* the rock."

More long moments pass.

"I'm gonna die, Tommy."

"No."

"I am. He'll be with her. He'll be okay. But I'm gonna die from all this."

"No, you're not. If you didn't have him…maybe. Maybe you would die. But you *do* have him. So dying's not an option."

"I can't do it."

"You'll do it, Mikey…"

And now our neighbor Jackie is standing on the sidewalk in front of us. "I love you, Tommy! I love you, Mike!"

Tommy waves and responds softly, "I love you, Jackie…"

Now those strong arms help lift me to my feet. And my brother walks me back in.

My mother pretends to be slicing sour pickles but she's really looking at her middle son in the hallway. Then she crosses to me, holds up my bloody knuckles, and bends to gently kiss them. She is humming. *Love Me Do.*

I move back into the living room. Katie makes eye contact and smiles at me, and I see she's been crying as well. Ben has his ear pressed against Debra's tummy but he can't hear the baby. Then she gives him a copy of *Oh, The Places You'll Go!* and asks Ben if she and Sam can come visit him. He nods enthusiastically and tells her, "You can come with my daddy. He always visits me. Everyplace. He always comes."

Someone tells me grab the roast beef before it's gone, but I still can't eat. I move with a tight and false smile on my face. And then I feel a tender pat on my shoulder and I turn. It's my father. I look at him but neither of us speaks.

Time passes. The cake is cut and we're all singing to Ben, and though I don't know what we're singing, we're calling him a *fellow*. Rosemary and Jo are passing out blue and white cups of coffee. Gifts are unwrapped. There's a line for the downstairs bathroom. The twins cuddle up on the sofa. Ben yawns. He's going to be on a red-eye out of JFK in just a few hours.

And now the doorbell rings, even though the front door is open. Tommy says, "I've got it." I see the pantomime of him shaking hands with Rabbi Cohen, and the sweep of my brother's arm as he invites him in. The broad smile and quick wave in return indicates the car is double-parked, or they're running late.

Everyone is standing now, and Ben is being hugged and hugged and hugged. His loved ones fall in line, even J-Law. Grandpa

Tom kisses his forehead and Katie openly cries. Grandma Eileen is last, and after she straps on his knapsack he throws both arms tightly around her. He looks neither happy nor sad. I've seen that look before.

I'm in the hallway, with my hand outstretched. Ben grabs it and we take the stoop slowly and walk toward where the Chrysler is in fact double-parked with flashers on. I stop in front of old Mrs. Bloom's house and squat down.

My face is buried in his shoulder and tears are flowing down both my cheeks. I know I'm speaking, wishing him safe travels, telling him I'll see him soon, expressing love that can't ever be expressed. I know this, but I don't know what I'm actually saying.

Now Jackie is standing near us in the dark. "I love you, Mike. I love you, Benjy."

We both tell him we love him, and he hugs Ben goodbye. Just as I stand we hear someone yell: "Bennington!" Katie runs barefoot down the sidewalk and when she reaches us she pulls something from behind her back. Ben smiles—finally—and grabs Dog.

Jackie speaks up: "I love you, Katie. Your red hair is pretty."

She hugs him. "I love *you*, Jackie. I wish every person in this whole wide world was just like you!" Jackie blushes.

At the car, I nod at Rabbi Cohen, who's behind the wheel and babbling about the Mets pitching. She's seated in the back, next to the car seat, and then steps onto the sidewalk. Ben hugs her. Stops. Turns. Then hugs me.

I help him off with the knapsack and buckle him in. Ben is tired but he smiles at me. "How many days till I see you, Daddy?"

"Twenty-two, buddy."

I know now I won't make it. I'm saying goodbye for good.

After I straighten up, she moves awkwardly around me. Then she sees I'm crying, and seems genuinely surprised by it. But ultimately she says nothing.

As she buckles up, I lean through the window and whisper, "His last name doesn't have a hyphen…"

And now something occurs that has never occurred. This brave little man, with more than three years of farewells under his belt, gives in to his massive grief. He yells, "Daddy!" And now he's sobbing as well.

Out in the street, I pull and pull on the rear door handle until finally the rabbi hits the power locks. Once inside, I awkwardly hug Ben in his car seat and whisper over and over again: "Shhh…it'll be fine…I'm coming soon…I'll see you soon…everything's gonna be *fine*, buddy." She stares out her side and doesn't speak.

I don't know how long it takes until Ben stops crying, but I convince him—and possibly myself—that I will see him in three weeks. Now I'm back on the sidewalk, waving cheerfully, and watching the huge Chrysler push away. They leave and I retreat to the home of my childhood.

Inside, there are tears and harsh words away from the ears of the kids. But I'm immune to it all. I barely say goodbye to my friends and family and accept hugs woodenly. Finally I stretch out on the sofa where we spent idle days as kids when we were sick. It's not sleep, but something like sleep overtakes me, my mother rocking nearby. I hope rest brings strength.

Grandpa Al has one thing to do, and it's early afternoon when he finally does it. My phone beeps and I retrieve an email from rabbi-al1937@aol.com: They have indeed arrived safely in Tel Aviv. We researched it recently, and found *Aviv* is Hebrew for spring and symbolizes renewal.

Ben has started his new life at his new home in Israel. Now, as always, I have to remain strong.

BOOK THREE

It's a summer of language, of reading and writing and speaking. Letters form words, words form sentences, sentences form all sorts of magical things. Life is the greatest of locks, and language the finest of keys. Especially for a four-year-old.

Ben and I discuss the old trope about how Eskimos possess 100 words for snow, and soon we're researching it. First we learn the real terms for Eskimo: Inuit and Yupik. Neither Ben nor I are surprised by those many indigenous names for snow—only someone who's never seen or felt the stuff would think one word could cover it.

I've taken up boxing again, so I give Ben lessons in our hotel room in Tel Aviv. Facing him on my knees, I demonstrate four basic punches—straight jab, cross, uppercut, hook. I mention how this last is driven by kinetic energy, and Ben asks, "Connecticut energy?" Later, I hum *The Air Force Song*—drilled so deeply into my brain in Texas it'll never be dislodged—and Ben wants to know why the blue is *wild*. And *yonder*.

Some language, of course, I never share with Ben. Like when a guy in the tower gripes about an NFL quarterback he perceives as cowardly: "That dude's always bleeding from his mangina."

And some language is complex. I'm unsure how to explain to a four-year-old the only guaranteed certainty in life is anyone who employs the phrase "I'm not racist" will immediately follow that phrase with a racist statement.

My phone vibrates and Ben asks if the call is *moot*. I laugh, and explain many of my calls are both *mute* and *moot*.

Nighttime always culminates the same way for us—first we read together and then as Ben snuggles in for sleep, I sing to him. Of course, the reading introduces new words, phrases, concepts. His library of books is ever expanding, and I never throw out those he's outgrown; *Pat the Bunny* sits proudly alongside a child's first encyclopedia. But singing also spurs interest in language and imagery and lyricism. Songs he's heard 1,000 times contain unwrapped bounty. Even *Molly Malone*, our favorite tune of all time. He wants to know why Dublin is a *fair* city. And we use Google Images to retrieve photos of both cockles *and* mussels. Which are not the same as *muscles*.

After I buy Ben new shoes, we go online and learn that metal thing to measure your foot is called a Brannock Device. When we visit Citibank in the Platinum Building in Tel Aviv and the ATM asks which language we'll be using today, Ben pleads with me to log on in Korean. So I do. And after withdrawing the equivalent of $60, the screen tells me: 고맙습니다. We both laugh hysterically.

His new favorite joke is, "I called the zoo but the *lion* was busy." Of course, the first time Ben heard it I had to explain to a child who is primarily familiar with wireless telephones why *lion* is a play on *line*, as well as what *line* means in this context.

While watching the Mets—the suddenly dominant Mets—we play with new sounds heard on the recaps and highlights: *Yoenis Céspedes, Jacob deGrom, Noah Syndergaard, Jeurys Familia*. I tell Ben that, hands down, Kirk Nieuwenhuis seems to be his favorite. So naturally he asks about the term "hands down," and soon we're googling, and surprised to learn it originated with horse racing.

Another day I say: "You're right as rain." And Ben responds: "Rain? Why?"

When I play my Beatles CDs in the hotel, Ben wants to know why the show is for the *benefit* of Mr. Kite.

Thanks to my attorneys, I learn that my son is not in fact my son; he is "the infant issue of the marriage."

It's a summer of language, both English and Hebrew. His four-year-old brain is a tabula rasa and soon he's jabbering in a hybrid Engrew. Or Heblish. It's a phenomenon I later learn is called code-switching by linguists.

It's a summer without Ben. And yet my son's love of language continues to touch me, even from thousands of miles away.

Last summer Ben wrote his initials—a rather shaky *BM*—in the rear side window of Lovey during an August thunderstorm. Then he wrote *DM*—for Daddy Mullen. Months later, when it was cold enough that frost covered the car prior to an early morning shift, I spotted those four letters re-emerging from the past, quite apparent again due to the perfect combination of light, temperature, and moisture. And I ached in lonely misery because I so missed my boy.

It's a summer of language, even when language is woefully inadequate.

*   *   *   *

The crying thing was scaring me. Driving on the Jackie Robinson Parkway, watching a Mets game, at night in bed, even at work. It was entering a critical phase.

I kept willing myself to make it stop. Eventually, after my first trip to Tel Aviv, I was successful. What I don't know is that the respite was temporary.

*　　　　*　　　　*　　　　*

Spending time with Ben has changed how I view just about everything. Trees, birds, music, orange juice, sink stoppers, the Presidency, sidewalk cracks, pencils, war, twigs, death, words.

I call it my Squirrel Theory. Until I was about five I was fascinated by squirrels. I'd sit at our living room window, watching these odd, furry creatures running, climbing, chasing, eating. And just where were all those nuts coming from, anyway? Yet after age five, squirrels disappeared, not just from Queens but entirely. Until Ben started toddling and they reappeared. We brought peanuts to the park, and I observed squirrels again.

I think of this while supposedly watching airplanes.

*　　　　*　　　　*　　　　*

Once more, I call Annabelle, my former Psychology professor. Once more, she listens patiently while I rant. I fear I'm sounding paranoid, describing how Judge Westphal ignores my lawyer but makes small talk and chitchat with the opposing attorney. But this time something's different; I'm sensing she's had enough of me.

I stop. "Listen…I'm really sorry."

"About what, Mike?"

"Going on and on. I mean…it's been tough. Ya know? I feel like sometimes…"

Annabelle's voice seems at once clearer, as though the connection has improved. "I have to be honest with you, Mike. I wouldn't be truthful if I said otherwise."

"Yes?"

"I'm quite worried."

I bite my lip. "Worried? About Ben?"

"No. About you."

*   *   *   *

So we've spent nearly a year in the Israeli Phase. When Judge Westphal lectured me on this excellent opportunity, she failed to mention how I would afford ten round-trip airfares and hotel stays during the ten-month period. My El Al fund soon ran dry, even when I supplemented it with additional student loan money for courses I'm not taking. So I play with fire, by bumming cockpit jumpseat rides with U.S. airlines operating to Tel Aviv, which now is just American, Delta, and United. Technically we're only supposed to flash our ID when traveling on government business, but most airlines won't turn away FAA employees. The usual routine is I sit in the cockpit for takeoff, answering any crew questions about air traffic control; when we're at altitude they usually suggest I move to an empty seat in the cabin. It's don't-ask-don't-tell, and I fear the day Bob M. summons me to discuss how I'm using my government ID as a de facto credit card.

As for Israel, I want to like it more but I can't. Of course, it's a beautiful locale, and nicer than many other places. But I feel toward Israel the way I feel toward Indiana and the courthouse and her parents' home—they all remind me of the sheer misery of separation.

For a while, we tried. Without discussing it, somehow we all agreed to reboot on my first visit; instead of picking up Ben in a public place, I was invited to their small house in a suburb called Bat Yam. I took the rail line and found the address and was asked in. After Ben jumped into my arms at the front door, she and I smiled at each other and Kasper formally introduced himself. Ben excitedly showed me his room—complete with *Disney Cars* poster—and then his mother took him to get changed. Kasper and I were alone in the kitchen and he offered me Limonana, a local lemonade, and nervously showed me photos of his four children and even his parents in Bulgaria. I was shocked to learn Ben was sleeping in his sons' room.

While she was still upstairs, I spoke very evenly, just as I rehearsed to myself, without a trace of anger or machismo. "Kasper...you seem like a nice guy. Hopefully we'll all get along. But I just want to say...my son'll be living with you now. And if you ever hurt him in any way...well, I'll kill you."

He stared at me, perhaps wondering if this was American humor. Then he nodded. "Ah. You see, I am a father as well. So I appreciate your...thoughts."

"Good."

Ben came down and I thanked them for the lemonade and he and I set out by rail for Hotel Shalom near the beach. After that night, we met at the train station.

And so it's Indiana again, only without rental cars and waitresses who draw crucifixes on the checks. In fact, considering it's probably the world's most famous state built on a religion, Israel seems quite secular; I've seen far more Hasidim in Brooklyn than in Bat Yam (which we learn means Daughter of the Sea).

I visit Ben's day school and his empathic teacher tells me Ben is frustrated not knowing Hebrew; I point out he seems to learn quickly, but she frowns and says not to the other children. She explains Ben misses his father very much. I swallow hard and softly ask how she knows this. She replies, "Because he told me when he was crying."

We go to parks, walk the streets, ride the trains. Ben's palate expands a bit—he tries schnitzel and even couscous. The falafel vendors are ubiquitous, but he won't sample, though he soon loves the pastries known as bourekas, especially with spinach. When I order shawarma, he picks the meat out of my pita. By evening we're back at Hotel Shalom. Which, of course, means both hello and goodbye.

Eventually I meet Ben's friends, Amit and Omer, and we take them to the beach.

On the micro level, there's nothing wrong with the visits. But it's not parenting. Ben has a life here—and I drop in monthly with gifts and Krembo marshmallow treats.

Despite my seniority, I can't take off every holiday I'd like, so I wound up working Christmas Day. On Boxing Day I flew to Tel Aviv to spend a belated holiday with Ben at Hotel Shalom. My checked bag was filled with gifts from my family and me. Of course, I still embrace secular humanism, but my reasoning for celebrating—backed by the courts, for once—is that Ben spends Jewish holidays with his mother's family and Christian holidays with his father's family. Ben, of course, is eager to celebrate as many holidays as possible, particularly when they're celebrated with gifts.

By winter these trips completely tire me—physically and emotionally—and I can't wait until Ben returns home. Or what I certainly consider home. I worry that I'm sinking further into...what exactly? An existence I fear and refuse to acknowledge—a solitary life as a single man intersecting with Ben's world but not shaping it.

She still doesn't pack a knapsack for him, so I travel overseas with clothes, books, toys, and toiletries for my son. On the second pick-up at the station, she "forgot" to pack Dog. On the third visit, she simply shrugged when I asked. On the fourth visit, she said Dog went missing, and by the fifth the search had been called off. Ben stared at the tiled floor as I calmly peppered her with questions.

The next day I texted Katie about Dog and she responded: *What fresh hell is this?* Still, I absolutely refuse to believe she would do something like this intentionally. Since we first separated, she developed a phobia about "her" clothes and toys for Ben not leaving "her" house; Ben and I even joke about him wearing "daddy's underwear" and "mommy's underwear." But it couldn't possibly manifest like this. I refuse to believe she eliminated Dog to keep him from me.

By March even Ben is tiring of my visits; not of me, thankfully, but the hotels and restaurants. He asks when I'm moving to Israel.

And now I face a horrible scenario. It's the Saturday night before I depart, and Ben's behavior is absolutely wicked. He throws a kebab at me during dinner and pulls his hand away from mine while boarding the train. Back in the room, he calls me stupid. I dislike being a disciplinarian even under the best of circumstances, and I hate having to use our precious hours for punishment; even so, the alternative of doing nothing is much worse. And above all else, I'm his father. So Ben discovers even hotels have time-out corners, and I scroll online while he stews near the curtains. By bedtime, he's sweeter than ever, and hugs me tightly.

*　　　　*　　　　*　　　　*

Sam emails us the new baby is named Henry, and Ben asks why. I falter a bit—sometimes people have reasons to pick names, and sometimes they just like certain names. I email back, using the shoddy hotel WiFi, and Sam explains Henry was Debra's dad, who recently died. Ben considers this. Then he says, "So Debra has a new daddy."

*　　　　*　　　　*　　　　*

For me, finding the right words becomes increasingly harder. Like when I hitched a U-Haul trailer from College Point onto the back of the wagon and cleared out all my belongings from the Stop & Stor in Elmhurst and packed up all our stuff from Kevin's apartment. The timing was good. J-Law has become the longest relationship of Kevin's life, even longer than his marriage. In fact, we've all stopped calling her J-Law; her name is Nicole. And although Kevin proved to be the finest of brothers' keepers, by last fall we both knew it was time to move on. Particularly after I stumbled to the bathroom in my boxers and encountered Nicole stumbling out in bra and panties.

A few weeks before, without any notice, my mother suddenly told me Mr. Hannity—just five doors down from our family's row-house—was fleeing to Florida and would rent his narrow three-bedroom place to me for $1,500 a month, scads less than market price. A small backyard for Ben's Little Tikes car, and best of all a room of his own. Hillary was ecstatic, instantly filing papers with the court: Mr. Mullen's new living arrangements not only offer space and security, but proximity to Ben's extended paternal family. It also means I grocery shop for my mother now when shopping for myself, so we don't worry about her schlepping milk and juice.

After Kevin and I loaded Ben's toddler bed onto the wagon's luggage rack, words failed me yet again. I turned to Kevin and said nothing. He smiled and—unusual for him—gave me a hug.

"Thanks for taking pity on your loser brother," I blurted out.

But Kevin wouldn't play along. "You're anything but a loser, man. I've been watching you all this time. With Ben. He's the luckiest kid in the world."

*   *   *   *

Hillary mails me a motion Ben's mother filed suggesting a visitation schedule. But something's wrong here. The cover page is stamped in red ink: *INVALID*. And now I see why. The Fruit of the Marriage has been repeatedly—and erroneously—referred to as *Benjamin Cohen-Mullen*, not once, but in 17 separate references. Hillary stapled a copy of Ben's birth certificate, highlighting my son's correct, hyphen-less name in yellow ink.

To be clear—I would have been willing to discuss hyphenating Ben's name, but upon his birth it never came up. Her lawyer is framing my opposition as some sort of patriarchy, but my lawyer counters this is an attempt to legally marginalize the Father.

What I don't know is this ridiculous and illegal effort to change Ben's name will continue for years. I'll constantly need to correct teachers, principals, and coaches, and whenever I protest I'll be laughed at as an obsessive-compulsive oddball. He's even angry over punctuation! Eventually, she'll assert that a mother's maiden name as a middle name is *always* assumed to have a hyphen. And I'll respond, "You mean, like that dark day when President Fitzgerald-Kennedy was killed?"

For now, the effort has failed, and the entire motion will have to be re-filed.

*   *   *   *

Back in February I told Annabelle how confused Ben was on many of our phone calls, because he'd be in bed in the dark in Israel and I'd be eating lunch in New York. Or he'd be having breakfast and I'd be sitting up after midnight. Annabelle devised a brilliant solution to help Ben understand. On my next trip, I unwrapped two special packages. One was a large flashlight and the other a deflated beach ball we took turns blowing up, Daddy providing much more hot air than Benjy. When the ball was fully inflated, Ben was delighted to discover a globe. I turned off the lamp and together we pointed the flashlight directly at Tel Aviv, and then found New York City on the dark side. Then I slowly rotated the ball while Ben held the flashlight steady, and Israel faded into darkness as the sun rose over Montauk. After I returned home, I called Ben and he asked me if I could see the giant flashlight from my airplane.

*   *   *   *

She's here in New York, but my son remains in Israel. It's a world upside down.

We're in a conference room in the courthouse in Jamaica so Hillary and I can respond to an Order to Show Cause filed by her new attorney. Three summers, three attorneys for her, and I can only imagine the backstories. The latest is a sickly looking guy with a bandage on his forehead, and he's running down a list of reasons Michael Patrick Mullen has issues with anger and, therefore, *potentially* with violence. Meanwhile, he's the one looking like a victim of violence.

This is a theme that has returned with increasing frequency over the past year, and I admit it confuses me. I've never been accused of excessive anger and I've certainly never been accused of unjustified violence, during my marriage or at any other time in my life. Why these false accusations? And why now?

Hillary says nothing, and I shake my head repeatedly. Of course, if I don't object I'll be acquiescing, but if I do object I'm putting that infamous temper on display. The charges are read. Isn't it true I've fired assault weapons? Yes, while serving in the military, though there's a difference between assault weapons and assault rifles so—. And engaged in pugilism? Yes, again while serving in the military; does New York State not support our troops? And I've used foul language in front of the defendant, the defendant's attorney, even the child himself? And I once yelled at the child? And I once yelled at a television when the New York Mets lost a playoff game? I decide to defuse this insanity with levity by asking for a jury of my peers, comprised entirely of National League fans from Flushing. But her attorney taps his bandaged forehead, frowning rather than grinning. Finally he drops the big one: Isn't it also true I threatened the life of the child's stepfather in Israel last year?

I let out a groan and tell Hillary this is absurd. But the paperwork is filed with Judge Westphal. Who promptly agrees Mr. Mullen would benefit from Anger Management counseling, and so orders. The truth is dawning on me rather slowly.

*   *   *   *

I'm on the subway, returning from my accountant's office, where her assistant itemized expenses for a possible bankruptcy filing, which seems inevitable now. At 59th Street, I'm again contemplating life without Ben. But other forms of loneliness are crowding these long spells as well. After the Velveeta Smith debacle I'll admit I became apprehensive about dating. Then recently a brilliant idea hit— why not follow up with someone I already know? Of course, human beings can't be freeze-dried and thawed out upon demand. But still…

The other night I looked up FAA contact info for Meghan, that controller from Providence I'd spent several happy days with in Oklahoma City. I won't deny that while sending off an email, I recalled that invitation upstairs at the Days Inn.

Happily, she responded. And to my sheer delight, she wrote:

Great to hear from you, Mike!!

We lob messages back and forth, until finally I broach getting together. I could drive there. Or any chance of you visiting NYC?

By Queens Plaza, she responds. As luck would have it, Meghan will be in Manhattan next month. She plans to visit old friends with her husband. It will be a fun road trip for their baby daughter. I sigh, and wish her well.

*   *   *   *

I'd almost forgotten publicly ostracizing Bob M. for griping about babysitting his own kids. Now my boss has asked me for a ride—rampside, out among the airplanes—in his government-issued Jeep Patriot. All those familiar voices from the tower tumble forth from the low-hanging radio as we cross two active taxiways and angle into a sweet location for plane spotting. He stares out the windshield as he speaks.

"I don't like you," he says.

I nod and don't respond.

"And you sure don't like me."

Again, I say nothing.

"But I'm having one honest conversation with you. Then...you're on your own."

I wait. It's his theater, so why should I fumble for lines? I'm going to play this existentially, and not show emotion.

"You remember in the service. No ranks, no bullshit. Completely off the record."

"Sure," I tell the dashboard. "You *say* it's off the record. Only you can't un-remember anything."

I'm looking away, but I sense Bob M. smiling. We both watch a US Airways 737 rumble by. Soon that livery will be retired, thanks to the latest merger, as that long list of dead airlines grows longer. And then American capitalists will secure their ultimate victory and all airlines will merge into one—like in the old USSR.

"Some guys were born to do this job," he says. "Um, gals too. I mean...they're just born with perfect skill sets. But those guys, they're usually just brilliant at talking to aircraft. Nothing else in life. When they're not working they watch Cartoon Network marathons."

Despite my attitude, he actually has my interest; I've long believed the same.

"Then there's guys like you—smart about the job. But also smart in other ways. And you go in different directions."

I look at the huge U.S. Naval Academy ring. When I was on hiatus from college and taking anti-depressants, Bob M. was throwing his white hat into the Maryland sky in front of the President.

He looks at me. "I've been over your record three times. Talk about a golden boy. I read every military fitness report—Christ, that guy in Keflavik sounded like he was wet when he wrote it. 'Finest Senior Airman ever...' Which also raises something else. Namely, why you had a four-year degree and you were enlisted. How come you never applied for Officer Training School?"

Now I stare at his ring. "I have trouble respecting authority."

Bob M. sighs. "Look, I've even asked some older guys. Everybody says the same thing. *No one* ever fucked up his career so quickly. It's incredible. If your file was just the last two years, you'd be out on your ass by now. It's the early stuff—commendations, perfect reviews. You're still running off those fumes. And, mister...the clock is ticking."

I consider remarking about mixing fumes metaphors with clock metaphors, but for once I restrain myself.

"Lately it's all reprimands and write-ups. You pissed away all that good will. Forget busting *my* balls—that's your mulligan. You had people up the chain looking at you. For years! You think every knucklehead up there gets government grants? To go study psychology? Of all damn things. Jesus. Then you can't even pass a three-credit class at NYU. All the rabbis you have! *Had.* Fucking *had.* People in the Region making plans for you. Brand-new job carved out of nothing. With this budget! Twice a year Congress shuts us down, but Mullen's getting a brand-new job. Hell, a guy on New Jersey Avenue knew you by name! This guy's at DOT headquarters and he knows Michael at little old LaGarbage. I'm there for a meeting and he mentions you. Incredible. And you pissed on him. You piss on everybody. I'll be damned if I can figure out—"

His phone beeps and he quickly reads a text message.

Now I speak: "You identified the timeline. Two years ago. You know why."

Bob M.'s voice softens. "Sure. And in case we forget...you always remind us."

My head snaps. "Meaning what?"

"Meaning...well, maybe you like this stuff. I don't mean what's happening. I mean...talking about it. You talk way too much. Reminds me of a professor I had. This admiral. Guy was shot down, spent time in the Hanoi Hilton."

I set my jaw and say nothing; let him fill the void.

"Look... you're not the first divorced guy. I'm not unsympathetic. If you didn't have such a hard-on for me...we could've talked. Worked stuff out. But...you don't like officers. Mister Friend of the Working Man. That's clear. Even though I ignore a lot of shit. Like whenever you decide it's Bring Mike Mullen's Kid to Work Day."

The idling engine revs. "Your annual physical, used to be a cakewalk. Now you've been flagged. Right? Big red flag, *hyperten-*

sion. Fifty milligrams of something...Losartan? Thirty-six and now you're flagged for a stroke risk."

"That's just for high—"

"Doesn't matter. That's how the agency looks at it. It's all about *risk.*" He taps the dashboard. "I'm giving free advice. Knowing you...you'll tell yourself I'm an asshole. But you, my friend...don't suffer fools well. You're a bright guy. But you don't deal well with people who aren't bright. And, mister, you act like you spend your entire day at a fools' convention. Not a good trait. Especially for an enlisted man. It's a little snobbish."

I stare out the passenger window. Because on some level...I fear he's right.

He talks into my left ear, the way I spoke into Father Dinnigan's in the confessional as a child. "You can play this whole management sucks thing. But...*I'm* responsible for what happens out here." His hand sweeps the runway complex, and the many planes creeping on taxiways. "So far...it's been chickenshit stuff with you. The worst would've been dented horizontal stabilizers. Fuck the airlines—they've got insurance, right? Well, I'm not gonna let you do real damage."

Now my emotion comes out: "I *hate* people don't take this job seriously. You think that's me? I took an oath!"

Bob M. points to a Delta 737 easing onto Runway 22. "Right there—a hundred and fifty strangers. Times how many a shift? Parents, kids...babies. They're cattle in the back of a truck. Strangers control them. Like you. When you're up there...I'm gonna say something you won't like. But I'm gonna say it. You gotta pretend *your* kid's on every plane. That's the only way I know to get through to you. Pretend it's *your* kid in the air."

I breathe heavily through my nose, like when I boxed in Dover. And suddenly I see my arm move, as if on its own. It moves toward him.

My hand is moving because I find I can't argue with his logic.

He shakes my hand. "We'd better get back."

Once parked in his *TOWER MANAGER* spot, I notice not one but two new sets of colorful kiddie golf clubs in the back seat.

*   *   *   *

It's a Wednesday afternoon and I'm standing on line at Five Guys in Terminal B so I can purchase a Styrofoam container of fats, oils, sugars, and carbohydrates to bring up to the tower with me. I know I should be dieting and exercising, and I vow things will change next week. Of course, this burger and those fries cannot do what a visit from Ben would do. Now I notice a few customers ahead is a guy from the day shift—a nice kid named Devin. He's the chapter representative for the National Black Coalition of Federal Aviation Employees and we always bust each other's shoes; I recently texted him *#BlackControllersLivesDontMatter*.

Devin picks up his order, then turns and stops. He's with a young woman.

"Mike! What's good?"

I shrug. *Utter despair. Nihilism.* "Same shit, different day..."

"He's a friend from upstairs," Devin says to the woman. "Mike, my girlfriend...Anna Wilkins."

She smiles as I shake her hand, and a distant, far distant, bell slightly rings. I shouldn't, but I stare at her. Anna is a beautiful woman in her early 30s—bright-eyed, long-limbed, full of energy. I say hello and she says it's nice to meet me.

And I want to tell her…we've met.

Your full name is Shi'anna Wilkins, and I've known you most of my existence. In the oddest of ways, it's as if we were sprung from the same loins. Thomas Mullen Sr. helped give life to six children, and one little girl died. But then at great personal risk he marched into a hellish inferno and gave new life to yet another child, Shi'anna. And here you are. Here we are.

Instead, of course, I just tell Anna I hope to see her again, and Devin says he'll catch up with me in the hellhole. As they walk away, I watch them. And before they reach the exit doors, I see her turn and look back at me.

*   *   *   *

I'm in Manhattan, at a comedy club called FunnyBonez. Last year Sam crapped out and canceled his gig here, citing the upcoming marriage and baby. I was concerned he was walking away from stand-up without giving it a chance, but happily I was wrong. Because he's just taken the stage.

His life has been busy too, only with positive developments. I served as best man at the wedding in Hoboken, and it was a fantastic night—the wine, the food, the band, that undulating belly dancer. During my toast, I pretended I'd just discovered Sam was Muslim, or I never would've hung out with him; and does the government know this guy talks to *airplanes flying past Manhattan*? "Too soon!" Sam yelled. Meanwhile, Debra intentionally sat me beside her college roommate, a nice woman from Chicago, a chef at a Hilton. Her name was Lizzie, just like my dead sister, and she was bright, engaging, attractive. We danced one dance and then I found excuses to avoid her.

Later, at the bar, she cornered me. I looked at this intelligent, personable, absolutely lovely woman, whom most men would be thrilled to court. "You know we've been thrown together, right? We're supposed to hook up tonight."

I could only manage: "Oh..."

"Good toast, by the way. You're a funny guy. Anyway...let's get our story straight. How about this? New York...Chicago. Too much work doing the long-distance thing. Okay?"

I nodded. Yes, my fear of dating kicked in. But it wasn't just Lizzie. My heart stung all night, because there was no way I could arrange for Ben to attend; this was the first major event he had missed. My fear was he'd miss dozens more.

The baby arrived in April and dramatically changed Sam's life. Not just in the usual ways. But an infant did what years of talking to airplanes hadn't: Henry provided Sam with his best comedy fodder.

I'm genuinely laughing now, not because he's a friend I love. His material was always language-based, but now he's an excellent mime, standing before us changing an imaginary baby. A clean diaper in his mouth, an ankle in one hand, a dirty diaper in the other hand, his foot vainly searching (*Tap! Tap!*) for the pail and not finding it. He's actually hysterical, and Debra and I hug as the audience roars. But we really react once the baby starts pissing in Sam's face, recalling the old boardwalk game where you shoot water at the clowns' mouths. Simply put, he kills.

So I was right. I had told Sam he'd be terrific at fathering.

*   *   *   *

At my mother's birthday dinner, I mention when Ben will return from Israel. My siblings start jabbering and a family reunion is planned. Katie calls Kerry in Florida, and soon everyone's onboard. A contractor Tommy works with has a waterfront McMansion for rent on Long Beach Island in New Jersey, so that's that.

My mother seems especially happy, particularly after it's pointed out all her grandchildren will be together. Once Ben arrives from Israel, that is.

*   *   *   *

Delaware is an odd place with an odd Napoleonic complex, like a small man always itching for a fight. What else explains *THE FIRST STATE* license plates? Back when I first arrived in Dover I explored up and down Dupont Highway, which the locals call Route 13, and for a small state it offered surprisingly large vistas. I was yearning for something, but didn't know what, and instead found places to drink. For some reason not geographically apparent, Dover loves BBQ and I tried them all before settling on Little Richard's, right outside the base. Sam and I thought it hysterical that if military intelligence types spied on him, their reports and clandestine photos would confirm their only active-duty Muslim spent an inordinate amount of time eating spare ribs.

Little Richard's is where I met Loretta, a divorced woman ten years older, who'd been stranded with two young kids and a rusty Plymouth by a chief master sergeant eager to be transferred anywhere she didn't live, like Baghdad. She was an assistant admin at Bayhealth headquarters and often banged in sick so we could spend the entire day in bed. I don't like that term MILF. But it's hard denying my track record with divorced moms.

I abruptly broke it off when Loretta kept mentioning marriage—cowardly of me, I know, but I was only 24. So I spent more time on base, seeking new avenues to expend energy. I finally found it on the 436th Airlift Wing Boxing Team. A former coach from the Air Force Academy rode us hard. It was great exercise, and I loved channeling all that youthful frustration and anger by slugging it out legally and safely. Though looking back I have no idea why I was so frustrated or angry. *Then.*

All this comes forth while I'm browsing online for an inexpensive gym. But instead of choosing a unisex spa with computerized equipment, a juice bar, pink dumbbells, and Zumba instructors, I descend into a hellish basement in Woodhaven to visit the Ring of Fire boxing club.

The place is as old school as a *Bowery Boys* flick, and at first there isn't a woman in sight. I immediately realize I like this, and then I immediately question if I'm misogynistic, and then I immediately question why wanting to train among my peers is misogynistic, and then I immediately cite many institutions where both men *and* women prefer to be among themselves. While I internally debate, I'm interrupted by the manager appearing before me. The manager is a she.

Her name is Archie and she seems to be easing into her 60s. She has dark skin and an odd—Caribbean?—accent and though she's graying and battered, the shoulders and biceps in her ripped sweatshirt speak of a body that once dispensed violence.

We take a tour, and I realize, with an icy combination of excitement and concern, this place is truly hardcore. Down in Dover we fought in baggy cotton shorts and T-shirts, with heavily padded gloves and headgear; true knockouts were rare. But the boys at Ring of Fire are stripped to the waist, and pounding away with hard gloves at nothing but exposed flesh from the beltlines to the hairlines.

I agree to a month's membership, but since the place is deserted, I offer Archie $50 for a private tutorial, and she points toward the ring. I hesitate, then quietly say I've never hit a girl before, so I don't know if training with her is a good idea. She laughs in response, but there's no mirth in that laugh. Within an hour she has me sweating through drills, then hitting the catch pads. We start on the heavy bag, and even I realize how pathetically rusty I've become. I climb into the ring with her, and she dares me to throw punches. Of course, her aging reflexes continually deflect my fists time and again, and I stumble as she continually taps me upside the cheek. Finally she speaks.

"Most dese guys—they headhunters. You a body puncher. Dat's rare. Most knockouts are to da head."

I nod; what she says rings true. It's all due to Eddie Conway in the fourth grade. For a month he made my life at St. Rita's miserable, shoving me on line in the schoolyard, pushing me in the cloakroom, slapping me in the head in gym class. I sat at home and seethed, and when Tommy arrived on leave from the Marines and said I seemed too quiet, I blurted out I'd like to slug Eddie right in the nose. Tommy shook his head, explaining not only was Eddie taller, but too much could happen when a punch traveled so far to impact a small target; instead, I should aim for a much closer and bigger target, his body. So the following morning in the schoolyard, before the snide remark could leave Eddie's lips, I punched him as hard as I could in the stomach and he sank to the concrete, right next to the nuns' old Rambler station wagon. Three other kids who'd been similarly tormented by him all cheered. And fourth grade became tolerable again.

This drama repeated itself, as dramas tend to, when Ben quietly told me in January about a bully named Yosef, who trips boys when they're running. I listened carefully and we discussed it at length; I stressed the importance of using words rather than violence. After I returned home Ben seemed reluctant to discuss it by phone. On my next visit, in February, he confirmed words hadn't helped, as they so often don't. So I told Ben since words had failed, he had every right to defend himself. Then I demonstrated technique. We didn't have long to wait; the very next day, Yosef tripped him. So Ben punched him in the stomach, and once again it worked. Now he and Yosef are buddies. But I anticipate this will soon be raised in court by Ben's mother.

I start telling the Ballad of Eddie Conway to Archie, but she doesn't care. In fact, she doesn't want to know anything about my life, or work, or family. And I realize I like that. It's actually a relief. No talk of lawyers and judges in this one oasis; it's almost a new identity, one not consumed by the custody soap opera. Ring of Fire is a silo, closed off from the rest of my histrionic life. I hand Archie a check and tell her I'll be back.

And God help me, but I have only one thought as I drag my aching body into the shower; I'm so tired I forget to feel guilty for thinking it: I just can't wait to hit someone.

What I don't know is, each member at Ring of Fire must step up once a year during the monthly Friday night bouts. I will soon meet the opponent I'll fight this summer, a man considerably larger than me. Hugo Concepcion. But I will tell myself, what have the last few years been if not a lesson in digging deep and meeting challenges?

*   *   *   *

My email volume increases tenfold as we prepare for the reunion at the beach—excited missives on bedding, groceries, sunscreen. Tommy suggests I pick up Ben when he arrives at JFK so we can travel directly and save time. So I email my ex-wife, because we seem somewhat more civil when communicating electronically:

> *Hi. It'll make things much easier if we meet at baggage at JFK next Thurs. To avoid traffic to NJ. All Ben needs is any favorite toys/books/etc. And Dog, if you've found him. Please let me know. Thank you. M.*

A few hours later, she responds:

> *That will be fine. We leave for a short vacation tomorrow and will not be near a phone until we get to NYC.*

I follow up:

> *Okay. Where are you going for vaca?*

She answers:

> *Somewhere warm.*

I don't know that these are the most important emails I'll ever receive in my life.

*   *   *   *

I'm not sure I have the right address, because I'm standing in front of what looks like an abandoned building in Hollis, an area of Queens I rarely visit. There's no need to add it's a "run-down" section of Hollis, because for blocks and blocks that's all I've seen. I hear loud voices so I enter, assuming this is the location for my first court-ordered Anger Management group session. I take one last look at poor battered Lovey, hoping she'll still be sitting next to this cracked sidewalk and rolled-up carpeting in an hour.

The front foyer is empty, but it opens onto a large conference room that once must have been a restaurant or nightclub. Signs indicate a storage area for broken furniture, and a halfway house for recovering addicts. There's a large circle of men in the center of the room, and I work my way toward them. An older Filipino guy spins his wheelchair in my direction and calls out.

"Welcome! I'm Doctor Navarro! Come join us…"

Despite his cheer, the atmosphere hardly seems collegial, unlike the Fathers Are Critical Too gathering. There are about ten men in all—Latino, Asian, African-American, white. They may not represent an accurate demographic slice of America, but they do seem to fairly represent the face of the men's exercise yard at Rikers Island any given morning. I slide into an empty metal chair, between a black man who even while seated looks close to seven feet tall and well over 300 pounds, and a grizzled pale teenager with a red do-rag and a Confederate flag tattoo on his forearm.

Dr. Danilo Navarro nods at me. "Please introduce yourself."

"I'm Mike." Obviously I spoke far too timidly, because there are snickers and even a loud kissing sound. Is it my demeanor? My hair? My dress? I carefully selected an ensemble of a navy blue golf shirt, tan chinos, and brown lace-up Dockers, hoping to fit in with my new angry friends. But clearly I've already committed a faux pas.

Dr. Navarro holds up a hand. "People, please! Thanks for coming, Mike. But first...you don't have any weapons on your person right now, do you?"

I shake my head.

"Good. Because we have a zero tolerance policy. Not just on firearms, but also knives, switchblades, clubs, blackjacks, nunchuks, brass knuckles, box cutters, mace..."

"I understand," I say, hoping there are no loopholes and fearing a ninja star will sizzle through the air at any moment.

"Good, Mike. Well, we're running through someone's story. Your story will be next. We've all got stories..." He pats his wheelchair. "I've a story too. I obtained this vehicle at twenty. The owner of a bodega objected to me robbing him again."

I nod as a tall, thin man named Rocco continues his saga. His black hair is piled high on his head and there are multiple gold chains under his wife-beater, but even though those smooth arms and sunken chest are quite undefined, he still exudes a rather menacing persona.

Rocco's tale is as old as dirt. He blew through a red light on Cross Bay Boulevard and was pulled over, but the officer with an attitude who rapped on his window was female! The bitch rapped on the driver's side glass of a brand-new Cadillac Escalade with a flashlight or some shit. So he did what any man would do, and opened the door quickly and knocked her on her ass. But then the bitch's partner yanked open the passenger door and reached in with a club, so Rocco had to respond—here there is much head-nodding and affirmative grunting of the "What-can-you-do?" variety—so he cracked that asshole's wrist with the pipe he keeps under his seat for just such occasions. Needless to say, mayhem ensued. Fast forward the story and now Rocco is here.

A buffed-up Asian man provides the coda: "Mah boy did what he hadda. *Done.*"

Dr. Navarro, however, weighs in. "Are we sure about that, Ray-Ray? The law takes assaulting a police officer very, very seriously. So I'm wondering...if there might've been another way for Rocco to have dealt with this. An al*ter*native. Why don't we think about that? And come back to it?"

Ray-Ray pulls on a gaudy purple bracelet dangling from his left wrist and rocks gently as he murmurs: "This too shall past! This too shall past! This too shall past!"

I'm considering if it's *past* or *pass*, but now another voice yells: "Bitch deserved it! Throwing shade!" There is nodding, as if to say...we've all been there, brother.

"I respect your input," replies Dr. Navarro. "And I certainly would fight for your right to express it. But let's hold that thought for now. Right now I want to bring our newest member into this." He turns his chair toward me. "Mike, what's your story?"

One member of our group lodges a formal protest: "Ain't this some fucking shit! White boy just come in the damn door!"

I'm prepared to wait, but Dr. Navarro remains unflappable: "Junior, you'll get your chance. Right now the floor belongs to Mike."

As I often do when I'm stalling, I cough. But the funny thing is, this time it's more than a delay tactic. Suddenly I really do have a frog in my throat, and somehow it doesn't seem appropriate to ask any of the fellas for an unopened bottle of Dasani water or a Halls cherry flavored cough drop.

Finally, I spit out, "Well, I'm Mike—"

"We heard that!" comes from my right.

I force a smile. "Yeah. So I was sent here by court. Jamaica."

"Criminal court?" asks Dr. Navarro.

"No. Family Court."

There's some murmuring, but I can't decode it yet. The doctor nods. "Ah. I see. Are we talking...domestic abuse here, Mike?"

I shake my head emphatically. "No. God, no! It's...my ex-wife. Her husband. My son lives with him now."

For the first time, I receive a positive response, and it's from the seven-foot giant to my left. "You kick this motherfucker's ass?"

Again, I shake my head. "No. I...well, I sort of *warned* him. I told him...if he ever hurt my son...well, I'd kill him."

The murmuring increases in volume, and Dr. Navarro leans in, his feet riding those metal footplates like a downhill skier. "Mike...let's be clear. Your son's stepfather...did you threaten him with a weapon of any kind? Menace him? Did you hit him or lay hands on him?"

"No. I just warned him. Verbally."

The room erupts.

"Fuck this fucking boy! Hotep gotta wait for this!"

207 · WILLIAM J. McGEE

"Man, this some lame-ass bullshit! Get this motherfucka's ass outta here!"

"Fucking *verbally*!"

Even as he quiets the crowd, Dr. Navarro wheels toward me. "Mike, walk with me please." I get up and follow him, taking a last look at my would-be comrades without arms. At the door, the doctor hits the brakes.

"I appreciate you coming, Mike. But I don't think...this is the right venue. I don't believe you pose a threat to anyone at this time. Do you agree?"

I nod. "I don't believe so either."

"Good. You know...I see this a lot. Guys like you. Custody cases. The legal system...for some reason judges like casting dads as violent predators. I don't know...I guess men have a larger physical presence. Louder voices. But in my work...I deal with violent people every day. I *know* violent people. And you're not violent."

"No, I'm not."

"Well, I have your paperwork. And I'm going to contact the court. In about two weeks. I'll tell them we've spoken. You've completed all the requirements. And I recommend you don't need to return. Will that work for you?"

"Absolutely." I can't shake his hand fast enough.

As I pull away from the curb, however, an uneasy thought does occur. I can't even carve out a place in Anger Management. One more venue in which I don't quite fit. I've never felt so alone. It's as though I'm a demographic of one.

*　　　　*　　　　*　　　　*

It's hard being optimistic because I miss Ben so terribly, but knowing he'll arrive later this week has me relaxing a bit. First Ben. Then the family vacation in New Jersey. A chance to breathe deeply.

I arrive home late Tuesday and pick up the mail. There's an odd-shaped, oversized envelope, and I see foreign stamps and a taped note from the post office indicating it was sent from Israel. I tear it open and see it's signed by an Israeli attorney.

> *29.6.15*
>
> *Dear Mr. M., Mullen:*
>
> *This advises you Benjamin Cohen-Mullen will not re-turning to the United States on 2.7.15. He remain in Israel with his mother. They are on holiday present but will return shortly and you will be contact. Thank you.*

My senses are supercharged; I'm blinking and shaking my head. My ears ring.

Some blows hit you hard immediately. Yet this is the oddest of blows—it will usher in the worst experience of my life, and will resonate with me forever. But it strikes me first in a confusing and haphazard way. What exactly is this about? What is she doing? What does it mean, Ben will not return?

It's midnight as I type the email I know Hillary won't read for hours. Eventually I get into bed. But of course I don't sleep at all. Which the FAA advises isn't good.

*   *   *   *

Her parents maintain they know nothing of the whereabouts of their daughter and grandson. The phone number of the house in Israel is already in my contacts list, of course, and I hit it and let it ring until the tone indicates the voice mailbox is full. I repeatedly dial this number. Over and over again, all day, every day.

*   *   *   *

Abduction.

Some things have a name, and in defiance of the court order signed by Judge Rhonda Westphal, she has officially abducted our child now. Her smoking emails confirming our meeting at JFK seal it.

Those amber alerts lighting up parkways and expressways? Now I wonder if Ben's description will be flashing at motorists.

Of course, now and for years to come, some people will give me a fish-eyed look when I discuss these events. *Well, it wasn't like he was...*really *abducted.* They're quite wrong: Ben *really* was abducted. I'm up all night googling a topic I never dreamed I would need to research. It turns out in the United States only about 3% of abducted children are taken by strangers. The creep in the back of the Dodge van is an anomaly, since nearly all abductions are committed by family members. Usually parents. And in thousands of such cases these dramas end in violence, forced separation, even death. This is textbook abduction.

All morning my phone rings until the battery gives out, and I repeat the same odd details to family, friends, co-workers. My heart beats too fast and I feel lightheaded.

By early afternoon, I realize I'll be at Hillary's office for several more hours, so I bang in sick. With my track record lately, it's the last thing I should do, especially three days before starting vacation, but leaving this office isn't an option. Hillary's partners have gathered us in a conference room, and despite the obvious need for the all-hands-on-deck strategy, part of me calculates that the legal bills for four attorneys working simultaneously are going to be whopping.

Hillary shakes her head. "I never thought she would do it..."

The oldest partner sneers. "Why not? We've seen worse."

Earlier a junior partner reached the newest attorney in Tel Aviv, but her Israeli lawyer proved less than helpful. She had no idea where they were holidaying, but they should be back within two months. My heart froze: *two months*! My worst fear is Ben's mother continually citing how Jewish law dictates a child is Jewish if the mother is; will I be translating Hebrew before an Israeli court?

I'm having trouble keeping up, but our agenda slowly takes shape. We're petitioning an emergency session with Judge Westphal, and requesting the current joint custody agreement be overturned and I be awarded sole custody. She should be cited for abduction, contempt of court, and possibly perjury. There's further talk. Israeli courts. Interpol. The International Court of Justice in The Hague.

Someone calls her New York attorney, the bandaged guy, and his admin claims he's vacationing. An hour later, a fax arrives stating he no longer represents her.

She's down one lawyer. But I'm up several. My New York team advises me I'll require an attorney in The Hague, where I'll need to plead my case that Ben should be returned to me under authority of an international treaty. And possibly I'll need another attorney in Israel, if things there get rough.

I don't dare ask what rough means. And I don't dare ask the cost of all this.

       *   *   *   *

And what of her? The legalities and finances and sheer horror of Ben's disappearance occupy me so thoroughly I've delayed pondering the motives of the…whatever she is. Defendant? Suspect? Culprit? Perpetrator?

Who is she?

It's 6 a.m. and I'm fully awake in bed; so much shift swapping has left me unaware of day and night. I think of Ben, and of her. I focus on the first Thanksgiving after we married, when I worked an afternoon shift. And I looked up and saw her ascending to the tower carrying a moveable feast—even stuffing and cranberries. *Her.*

I can remember waiting for her to walk through a door, then feeling my heart twang. Holding her. Confiding in her. Dreaming with her. This child, now the focal point of strangers worldwide—*we* created that child. *Together.* I didn't understand ripping a relationship in half, yet I accepted it. But ripping a child in half?

How could I have loved what I now realize was a stranger?

       *   *   *   *

I'm back to work, and other than continually dialing that number in Israel, there's little to do except talk to airplanes. My attorneys have taken charge.

Today's the day I was supposed to pick up Ben at JFK, and this morning it finally hit me with the force I knew it would. I passed his room and saw the bags I packed for him last week. New clothes, new books, new beach toys for the rented house. I sat on his bed so long I was almost late for my shift. Everything hurts.

Now I'm on break and Tommy texts me to say I'll be riding to Jersey in his Tahoe. I've wavered for days—why even go to the shore? It's a family reunion, I'm told repeatedly. Yeah, only it'll be a reunion without my son.

Hours later, I'm in the back seat with the twins Liz and Kelly, who jabber like kids setting out on vacation. Which is what they are. By the Outerbridge Crossing I'm asleep, and I don't wake until we're on Long Beach Island.

The house is gorgeous, even though we turned right off the bridge and not left toward more expensive real estate (as the locals say). We're the last to arrive, and as I'm given the tour my siblings address me as if we're celebrating either a wedding or a funeral. My sister Kerry hugs me, saying, "Well, Mikey…about all we can do now is eat and drink for you."

I sleep fitfully on the back porch, counting the many activities Ben will miss in the coming days. After dawn I overhear Tommy on the phone and confront him. He tries to evade me, but I persist; he was canceling a photographer he had booked. His wife Rosemary bought matching white-and-red shirts and blue shorts for all the grandkids, and the photographer was going to secretly take a sunset photo, a present for Eileen next Christmas. But since Ben won't be here…

We road trip it to lunch down in Barnegat Light, but my throat is constricted and I swallow only two spoonfuls of bisque. I can feel my mother looking at me. Back at the house, I quietly ask Kevin to give me a lift to the mainland so I can head home and return to work early. A full-scale family meeting erupts, and I thank everyone profusely for insisting I stay. But my reasoning is sound—I'll be miserable company. And furthermore, my vacation days will be much better saved for trips to court. Or Israel. Or The Hague.

Katie hugs me and says, "The world never runs out of pain…"

On the bus, I realize that the fall I've been dreading has already begun. And I can't even guess when I'll hit bottom.

*   *   *   *

Over this long winter I became convinced I would die soon.

I've felt this before. The last was in San Antonio on my second full day in the military. My prickly scalp was shaved and my freshly-issued boxers felt as stiff as cardboard. I was lying on my rack that felt like a coffin. I remember thinking the trick was not to move, that maybe I could somehow become invisible. Then in the morning I could slip away and sneak home.

Now that feeling is back. And I realize it didn't ever leave. Somehow I've carried it around, through all these years. But it feels very familiar, like it may stay forever.

After the reunion ended, those who love me most gathered round and lifted me up. Katie took charge and called Sam, who in turn called Moe, who notified my union reps. They obtained a list of psychiatrists who could prescribe anti-depressants; after just one visit, I walked out with Prozac. But the harder part of this one-two strategy was finding a psychotherapist, and the list Katie obtained was alphabetical, with no preferences indicated. So I began.

Last week I trekked to Chelsea for a 10 p.m. appointment. I found the late hour rather odd; schlepping 90 minutes by subway each direction? I was met by a Woody Allen lookalike, down to the black glasses and bulky sweater. We transited the waiting room into his office and I parked on the sofa. Woody, who was in socks, crossed to a file cabinet and turned his back. "What do you go by?"

"Michael. Um...you can call me Mike."

"Okay. I don't know much about you. Why did you come?"

I watched his back as he sorted manila folders. "Well...I started Prozac. I've been depressed. And...I guess suicidal. I've been thinking about suicide. You know. *Suicidal thoughts.* I went through this before. So..."

The back of Woody's head nodded. "And...what's been blazzity-blah?"

"Excuse me?"

He still didn't turn. "I said...what's been happening lately?"

I sighed loudly. "Yeah. Well...my son's been living in Israel."

"Israel's nice. I was there recently."

My tone hardened: "He's *four.* Anyway, his mother abducted him."

"Ah ha..."

I coughed, then spoke louder. "Excuse me? Excuse me!"

Woody finally turned. "Yeah?"

"Could you...I mean, would you mind you sitting over here? So I can see you? When we speak, I mean."

Woody padded over and slipped into his armchair with one leg tucked under him. "Tell me...why does it bother you I wasn't sitting down?"

I simply lost patience. "No, no," I responded. "I mean...I've been learning the law lately. There's this legal term—*res ipsa loquitur*. It means...thing itself speaks. That's the case here. The burden's on *you*. Not me."

"Ah. Why is that?"

"Because you can't file and give me your full attention."

"Hmm...what's your dosage of Prozac?"

Before I could answer, a young man entered the waiting room. Without so much as a perfunctory knock, he strolled into the office, head craning. "Hey, guys. You didn't see a red—" Woody pointed, and the hipster grabbed his umbrella and waved at us. "Later, guys."

I watched as he exited, then turned to Woody. "Um...I don't suppose we could close the office door?"

He nodded. "We could. But...mind telling me why?"

I smiled. "Sure. I'm just kind of funny. You know...strangers walking through while I discuss...killing myself. Call me wacky..."

He leaned in. "I'm worried about you. What you're going through. I fear...you view yourself as...*damaged goods*. We should lock in appointments..."

I followed my instincts and stood up. "No need. I'd like to be a big man and throw a check down on the table, like they do in the movies. But to be honest...I'm broke. So I guess that's that..."

"Mitch," he said, "Can I give you a hug?"

I stared at him. "Well, I'm not Mitch. Not that you were distracted or anything. And...*no*. You can't give me a hug. Maybe you can give Mitch a hug when he barges in." I walked toward the door.

Now *he* got to see the back of *my* head. "You should stay!"

I held up my hand. "See, you're not getting it. It's not that I'm not doing therapy. I'm just not doing it with *you*."

He looked hurt. "I care about—"

And then I was out the door. One down.

A few days later, I met the second candidate on Katie's list. There was no first name, just an initial: *R. Miller, LCSW*. I'll never know what the *R* stood for. She curtly indicated the specific spot where I should sit; when I did, she directed my ass exactly one sofa cushion to the right. Then she told me not to wear cologne in the future. I detected an accent and asked where she was from; she replied Bulgaria. Kasper's home country. So I asked to use the bathroom, and walked straight out onto Madison Avenue. Two down.

But today Number Three has proven to be the charm. In fact, after just one session, I tell him that my nickname for him is Goldilocks. He smiles and says he's flattered.

*   *   *   *

We've returned to Jamaica, same courthouse, same courtroom, same Judge Westphal. But this time there are differences.

One difference is we've been bumped to the very front of the calendar, and *Mullen v. Cohen* is the first case called. Another difference is the defendant's table is empty; that lawyer with the bandaged forehead had no desire to be disbarred for aiding a criminal act, so he sent an identical fax to the court stressing he no longer represents her.

But the most extraordinary difference is Judge Westphal. For the first and only time, she refers to me by name, and asks that I stand. Then she says, "I'm sorry for how this turned out, Mr. Mullen." I nod and say nothing.

The court asks if the Father has had any contact with the Child, and Hillary says none; I see the judge grimace. Now things move quickly. The joint custody agreement is abolished, and I'm awarded sole custody of Benjamin Cohen Mullen. Just like that.

I'm also given a statement by the judge I can bring to the Court of The Hague so it can issue a worldwide decree forcing her to return Ben to me. If not, Interpol may prepare an arrest warrant.

Here in Queens, the missing defendant is found in contempt of court, and possibly faces perjury charges as well. The gavel falls.

*   *   *   *

As she so often does, Katie sums it up: "You found a shrink named Paco! And he talks like Tony Soprano. Incredible…"

He's a handsome man, an aging Latin lover type, the sort of guy who could get away with wearing an ascot. Back in the 1950s, he was an adolescent punk in a Cuban street gang, The Nacionales. Then he got jumped and stabbed, and a nurse at St. Vincent's suggested with his good looks he should try out for the chorus in *West Side Story*. He did, and within months he was the understudy for Baby John, ironically enough a Jet, not a Shark. He continued acting in Broadway musicals even while earning his graduate degrees and conducting therapy for Catholic Charities. Eventually he opened his own practice. But he's still capable of breaking into song. Or doing a Fosse-like slide across his office floor. His real name is Alejándro, but he's been Paco since gang-banging days. He also uses the F-word excessively.

His primary job now is to keep me alive until Ben gets back.

By the second session, I busted his shoes by imitating the Dos Equis guy in the commercials: "I don't always employ neo-Freudian therapy, but when I do…"

We've been recapping the custody saga—focusing only on what unfolded after she walked out and took Ben to her mother's. Paco's been frantically taking notes, like a wire service reporter witnessing the Hindenburg docking. He continually interrupts to ask about her: Wait, she really allowed you to support her through five years of marriage while she earned two graduate degrees, then left you the night before you started at NYU? She once didn't speak to you for seven consecutive days? She told you if she developed cancer she would absolve you of your vows? When Paco pried out of me that she kept her parents' address on her driver's license all during our marriage, he smiled in recognition. He even correctly surmised intimate details about our sex life.

Then he asked if I would object to him seeing my sister Katie. It surprised me, but I agreed. The next day, she visited Paco, and first they made small talk about her dream gig— the interior cabin voice inside every Lexus vehicle. But within ten minutes they were done. Months later, he will explain. He cheated a bit, because he felt the drama of my situation wouldn't allow for a more leisurely form of therapy. And quite frankly, he couldn't determine if I was a reliable narrator, or a patient who enjoyed spinning myths. My matter-of-fact descriptions of her outrageous behavior could be masking my own cries for attention. Once Katie settled in, he inquired about her ex-sister-in-law and—I was later shocked to learn—Katie replied that abducting Ben was the most evil act she had ever witnessed personally. So I became instantly reliable.

I only want to focus on discussing the abduction. But he's slowly expanding the discourse. My mother. My father. Nuns. Bob M. at LaGuardia. Katie and I huddling together the night our sister Lizzie died. We've got our work cut out for us.

*   *   *   *

I'm en route to Manhattan again, only with my mother beside me. She does so much and asks so little, I happily grant her two frequent requests: drive her to visit my father at the VA and drive her to a church near Madison Square Garden for confession.

When I was a kid I often tagged along with both my parents, though I never understood why they would seek penance in another borough. Now that I'm tall enough to see the spire of St. Rita's from my mother's stoop, I completely get it. In fact, I wonder if Manhattan is far enough.

"Forgive me, Father, for I have sinned. It's been one week since my last confession. I argued with my husband over our six children and I—"

"Eileen! You're a dear! All those cupcakes. And remind Tommy, he's serving the eleven tomorrow."

What surprised me is why my mother felt the need for a midweek confession, and couldn't hold off until Saturday. She said she's feeling something she swore she wouldn't—hate in her heart. In my post-abduction stupor I was so clueless I had to ask why. She paused and said, "My ex-daughter-in-law…"

I drop her right at the front steps, and tell her I'll be cruising. A cell phone isn't an option for my mother, so we're rolling old school, where I'll keep circling the block until she appears. But now a funny thing happens—no more than 30 seconds after I pull away, I come upon an empty, legal parking spot. In Manhattan. On a weekday afternoon. And my mother missed it—I feel like those Bigfoot trackers whose cameras jam at the critical moment. After sticking the meter slip on the hot dashboard, I impulsively walk back up to the church.

I've always detested that smug line about no atheists in foxholes—it's the ultimate insult to those of us who've rejected whatever big tent we were assigned at birth. It questions our intelligence, our courage, even our honesty and integrity. The reasons I first left Catholicism, then Christianity, then all organized religion, then all faith, are myriad and complex and not apt for a bumper sticker, fortune cookie, Tweet, or meme. But my foxholes haven't sent me back here; it's the air conditioning.

Authors often invoke the flickering of candles, the scent of incense, the dirge of organists. But for me, the first sensation is the overpowering sight and smell and even creak of wood. Entire forests have been chopped to bits for each of these enclaves. I spot my mother on a confessional line up front, and duck into a back pew.

Pushing aside the kneeler and sitting down, I remember my favorite poem by my favorite poet, Walt Whitman, and his meditation on animals:

Not one kneels to another, nor to his kind that lived thousands of years ago

I look up, and there he is, dripping in blood and gore; what odd energies ran through the veins of artists who undoubtedly wept as they lovingly detailed the nails and thorns and spears. Once again, my mind returns to its most frequent theme.

Fathers and sons.

I shake my head, just as I see it's my mother's turn and an usher assists as if he's strapping her in for Space Mountain at Disney. The ultimate father and son story. Even if the entire drama played out just as they say, I can't abide demonstrating love by putting your own boy through such misery and suffering. And why ask an Abraham to do the same? Why not truly demonstrate love for us all and stop the clock—sparing all the sons and daughters to follow. Now *there* would be a story to tell.

As for the legend of the son, they say he suffered just as the rest of us do, but even within the confines of the drama that isn't true either. Yes, he felt those bloody nails—absolutely. But he saw hunger and he fed, he saw pain and he alleviated, he saw death and he breathed life. Good role modeling, undoubtedly, but ultimately we come up short. The rest of us may bear our own pains, but we can't lay hands on those we love and assume their aching. And I've discovered that's the greatest pain of all—the impotency to ease the burdens of those we love. If I could, I'd sign and notarize right now to assume all of Ben's tears. But I can't. Nothing done to me pains me in the way Ben's travails do.

And so I sit. And sit. It's the same old story. The nails and the thorns and the spears play out as they always do. So many people I love find comfort here, and I'll always wish them well. Meanwhile, I wonder once again where my son is right now, and the tsunami of shock, pain, fear, and fury assaults me anew. I miss Ben so much, but unlike the father worshipped here, I have no preview of how our drama will unfold.

Now my mother makes her way down the aisle, and when she sees me she registers surprise, though clearly not because I scored the Moby Dick of parking spaces. As I help her down the front steps, she finally speaks: "I *thought* I heard a bolt of lightning hit the roof..."

I can't help laughing. "Nah, I got bored in the car."

Like Whitman, I'll continue singing a Song of Myself. Just as we all do.

When we get home, we're greeted near the stoop by our neighbor. "I love you, Mrs. Mullen," says Jackie. "I love you, Mike."

As I watch him hug my mother, I decide he's the only saint I still believe in.

*   *   *   *

Paco is quite serious today. He didn't open by discussing Mets pitching or Jerry Orbach (whom he worked with on *The Fantasticks*). Not that he cheats me on time; it's as if baseball or Broadway warms him up. I ask what's happening.

He nods. "Well, this isn't easy, pal. I've been thinking about this ex-wife. And something called...Parental Alienation Syndrome."

Amateurs have been diagnosing her for two years. Bipolar. Borderline Personality Disorder. But Paco always maintains you can't truly diagnose patients you haven't met, though he once referenced "Narcissistic Personality Disorder."

He leans forward. "You need to hear this. All her efforts—the moving, the lawyers, ending mediation. Claiming the only fucking jobs are in Indiana. Or Tel Aviv. Even that stupid hyphen. It's all designed with one goal—to marginalize you to the point of eliminating you entirely. She's intent on destroying your bond with Ben. *Intent.* I know that sounds highly dramatic. But that's what the abduction's about. Her actions speak to it. At this point...I worry she's fucking capable of anything."

I listen respectfully. But despite it all, I question Paco's reasoning. She has to know by now she can't erase me from Ben's life. We have an unbreakable bond.

*   *   *   *

So now I'm on KLM, my ticket paid in part by my mother; it's always uplifting to mooch off a septuagenarian on a fixed income for a "loan." My schedule is a ridiculous patchwork due to all the shift swapping I've been forced into; after working a full eight hours, I taxied it from LGA to JFK. Then we sat through a three-hour delay the airlines blamed on weather, but I called the JFK tower and it was due to pure summer congestion. Once we were airborne, I slept fitfully for less than an hour, yet even then I dreamed of Ben. I stared out at complete blackness and my soul ached.

We've landed in Amsterdam, and I try not to be rude as I hustle toward the jetbridge. In the airport restroom I change into my Court Suit, then run downstairs to the rail lines. This is Europe, where the free market isn't a religion Jesus invented in the stable in Bethlehem; the ground transportation systems are efficient, quick, clean, inexpensive, safe, and environmentally friendly. In America, of course, we believe the Lord wants us to fight continual Middle East wars for oil, so we can all park our fat asses in eight-cylinder SUVs and spew carbons during day-long traffic jams. I hustle onto the train and ride smoothly from Schiphol Airport directly to The Hague, or *Den Haag* as I soon learn it's called. Amsterdam—where my hotel awaits—is in the opposite direction so I drag my carry-ons since I'm due to meet my Dutch attorney within the hour.

There's not much in Den Haag besides the world-famous Court of International Justice, and after stowing the bags in my lawyer's Saab, we proceed to the Peace Palace and enter the room where *Mullen v. Cohen* will be deliberated. But it's a quick deliberation. This case is all mine; in fact, it's as if we're arguing "Resolved: Smoking Isn't Harmful" before the Tobacco Growers Association of North Carolina. I don't know a word of Dutch—it's a series of guttural, Germanic-sounding barks—but I watch the panel as they read translations of Judge Westphal's ruling and glance at the empty defendant's table. They seem to say, *"Wait! Hold up. This American dude is invoking the Hague Convention on the Civil Aspects of International Child Abduction? Seriously? We wrote that shit! Damn. Next case!"*

And so I win one. For once. But it's a considerable victory, and not bad for a guy who hasn't showered in more than a day. The clock has begun ticking, so Benjamin Cohen Mullen must be returned within 30 days to his father in Queens, New York, USA. Or Interpol will issue an arrest warrant. One of my deepest concerns is somewhat allayed when I'm assured both the United States and Israel are signatories to the treaty.

I awkwardly thank the court and follow my lawyer into the hallway. I lie through my teeth when the newest member of the Mullen Worldwide Legal Team politely inquires about that wire transfer; it is coming soon, yes? *Yes*, I tell her. *Very soon.* She asks me to a late lunch but I check my dual-time zone watch and calculate I've been up for 38 hours, so instead I let her drive me to the train station. In no time, I've passed the airport again and arrived in Amsterdam, and I'm so bone tired I decide to splurge on cab fare with some of the $200 Kevin slipped me yesterday, who correctly assumed I'd be short funds. After converting to euros, I hail a taxi to my hotel, and finally shower. It's about 5 p.m. I'm hungry, and knowing I'll need a good night's sleep I resist "napping." Instead I head downstairs and out into the busiest street, the Damrak.

The Indonesian food smells delicious, so I select a small place and have bakwan and beef rendang and two Anker Beers. Now I'm back out on the streets, and I wander the busy section near the rail station. I buy Ben souvenirs—an orange baseball cap and a plastic tramcar—and chocolates for my mom, a small payback for my plane ticket. On every corner, cafes proudly display marijuana leaf symbols in their windows. American fellow travelers can legally imbibe, of course, provided they don't bring any of these plants or baked goods back onto KLM. But I have no such luxury, tempting as it is to bake my brain now. The FAA maintains a zero tolerance policy, regardless of the country where the products are bought. I can just imagine explaining a failed urine test to Bob M.

So I keep walking in the direction of Anne Frank's house. Now I'm in De Wallen, the infamous "windows district," where prostitutes of varying ages, races, genders, and persuasions beckon to pedestrians behind plate glass. I'm a man, clearly a foreigner in my Reeboks, and I'm alone, so I generate more than the usual amount of knocks and waves. Somehow, I knew I'd wind up down here, and the extra euros in my pocket sealed it.

I stop before a narrow window and smile at a short, curvy, dark-haired woman in a red teddy. She smiles back, then quickly opens the door and I'm inside. We briefly discuss the transaction and I hand her euros. Now she yanks that street-front curtain closed, locks the door, and shows me to a rather small bed. I pull out a sheaf of three foil-wrapped condoms but she shakes her head and extracts one of her own from a tiny box. I've forgotten what it's like to be in a civilized country.

Her English is halting but perfectly clear: "What do you call yourself?"

"Jim. *James*. And you?"

"I am Aya. A-y-a."

"Aya..." Last winter Ben and I discussed palindromes.

I undress to my boxers and sit beside her. It's been a long time since I've engaged. I'm worried about the same thing men have worried about for centuries, but as soon as she slips off that little red teddy and firmly places my hand on her thigh, all concerns fade. I begin caressing her, higher, lower, and after a moment—if we choose—we can both close our eyes and pretend we're with others. The hot lights apparently must stay on. I smile at Aya and gently move my face toward hers. She abruptly puts the palm of her hand on my chest.

"No," she says quietly. "No kissing."

Huh? I can fondle, squeeze, stroke, even more—but I can't kiss? My anatomy responds, and it's not good. I'm thinking this is like hitting a solid double to the opposite field and then running due north from the batter's box and straight across the pitcher's mound before sliding into second and avoiding first base. No kissing?

My euros would have been better spent on the many homeless crowding the Damrak near the sex museum. Aya tries. I try. But it's no use. I gather my clothes, collect my souvenirs, and shrug sheepishly. I assume she, of course, has seen this. Maybe not.

As she slips back into the teddy, she tells me, "Not all men need to kiss, James. You must be...romantical."

Within 24 hours, I'm back at JFK, hoping to forget this trip.

*   *   *   *

I call and call and call the house in Israel. No response.

*   *   *   *

I find a pink "While You Were Out" message in my mailbox. Who would call me at LaGuardia? I read it and my mind seems to flip, like a person falling down stairs. It's dated yesterday, at 5 a.m., with no number given:

Your wife & son called; pls call back ASAP

I lean against the soda machine. I'm not sure I can move.

Is all this cruelty a simple test of wills? An effort to fracture me—physically, mentally, spiritually? At 5 a.m.! My OCD—which has served me so well in this tower—haunts me every time I touch my phone. I can't *not* try once more, and then the failed call reinforces my desire to try again. And the misery grows. But to call me at work...

I'm still not sure I can move, yet it's time. Once again, I have to separate my current abduction reality from the reality of talking to airplanes.

The shift starts and I'm seated next to Stephanie; I work departures off Runway 13, she works arrivals onto Runway 22. It's a typical busy summer afternoon at LaGarbage and growing busier hourly. I see traffic already stacked up over Westchester.

I will myself to forget the pink message for now, and focus on Runway 13.

Once, at a Cohen family barbeque, her cousin asked why LaGuardia even has a Runway 13. Isn't that bad luck? Why don't they just repaint it *Runway 14*? I popped open a beer—where to begin? First, I explained, over at JFK there are actually *two* Runway 13s, 13-Left and 13-Right. Second, in aviation numbers are simplified and zeros often dropped, in large measure to make communications easier to transmit, particularly during a crisis. Therefore, Runway 13 is actually shortened from Runway 130. Third, Runway 13 is actually 130 because it's 130 degrees on a magnetic compass heading; in the opposite direction, the same patch of concrete is a separate runway heading numbered Runway 31, short for 310. Because 310 minus 130 equals 180 degrees. See? Fourth, numbered runway headings are dictated by many factors, but primarily it's often the prevailing winds, which facilitate takeoffs and landings. In North America, westerly winds actually make Runways 13-31 and their perpendicular corollaries,

Runways 4-22, quite common. I swigged my beer and thought, I translated Aviation Geek-speak into American English rather well.

"I still say it's bad luck," the cousin spit out.

Bad luck or not, today I'm launching departures from all measly 7,000 feet of Runway 13, out over Flushing Bay and Citi Field and into the Wild Blue Yonder. My job now is to eject metal tubes hurtling down Runway 13 toward the Mets dugout, while Stephanie alternately accepts metal tubes onto Runway 22 inbound from the Bronx. Of course, 220 minus 130 equals a perfectly perpendicular 90 degrees, the configuration of nearly every traffic corner. In other words, Stephanie waves hers through on the green while I hold mine up, and once one of hers clears the intersection, I quickly wave another through while she ensures nothing comes in too quickly. Decades ago my grandfather was on the job as a traffic cop, and his primary post was directing vehicles from a pedestal in Columbus Circle. In theory, his grandson's career is not wildly different.

Stephanie smiles as I settle in and attempt to focus. About a month ago she ran into me in the employee lot as I was finishing my shift and asked if I was headed to court. I was somewhat startled—has my life devolved into a punchline?—and I said no, not always. Then last week in the elevator she mentioned growing up in a large Greek family, just blocks from LaGuardia. So naturally, I asked, "Astoria?" And she said, nope, Corona. It was her idea of a joke, albeit one only enjoyed by natives who know Astoria is the Athens of New York City. "Opa!" I told her.

"United Express four-four-five-seven, clear to land Runway Twenty-two," I hear her say.

"United four-four-five-seven clear to land."

I speak. "Frontier three-eight, hold short Runway Thirteen."

"Frontier thirty-eight, holding short Thirteen."

Smoke quickly dissipates as United's wheels touch runway, and I watch...watch...until *now*, clearing the intersection. "Frontier three-eight, clear for departure Runway Thirteen, sir."

"Frontier thirty-eight, departing Thirteen. Thanks."

And on it goes. I swig a Pepsi, even though Archie at Ring of Fire wouldn't be happy; she would have me drink water and hack at a truck tire with a sledgehammer in preparation for meeting Hugo Concepcion, mano a mano and fisto a fisto.

"American seven-eight-five, hold short, sir."

I can't *not* think about Israel. My phone is off; there's no way I'm going to screw around up here. Actually, I've found my sharpness has been compromised lately, though it's hard to identify why. The FAA has even cleared Prozac—officially Fluoxetine—for pilots, so it's not the meds clouding my brain. It's that empty house in Israel.

"Southwest four-two-two, clear for departure Runway Thirteen, ma'am."

"Thanks. We'll see ya."

It's a beautiful day, what aviation types refer to as "clear, blue, and 22," although New York City smog doesn't allow visibility of 22 miles, even from this height. And Stephanie's arrivals are handed to her from approach control only about ten miles out. But we've got a great view of all those toy metal tubes. I watch and watch.

"American Eagle seven-seven-four-two, hold short Runway Thirteen."

And here it comes. That punch in the chest hits me in bed, in the shower, behind the wheel, up here. Ben. I miss him so much. That feeling just slams into me at times. But the worst of it, worst of all—I wonder does he miss me? When does he cross over so the obsession of wanting to speak to his daddy lessens rather than intensifies? Four weeks? Five? Ten? When do I fade the way Southwest 422 is fading over the World's Fair grounds? Goddamn! At 5 a.m.! I breathe deep.

Now Wayne, working Ground Control, calls out from across the tower: "Mike! Ground traffic!"

"I got it," I say calmly. Voices are seldom raised here.

A construction vehicle attempted to quickly cross Runway 13 at Taxiway Sierra but obviously wasn't quick enough. For some reason the truck has stopped on the active runway, perhaps searching for loose debris.

I update my metal tube, a Bombardier CRJ700: "United Express four-four-three-niner, gonna need you to hold there, sir. Ground traffic ahead of you. I'll readvise."

"United four-four-three-nine…okay, LaGuardia."

One player has stepped on a teammate's foot, so now our rhythm is completely thrown off. Stephanie and I exchange glances and nods; we're middle infielders silently assessing runners on base and a dangerous hitter at the plate. Her last arrival is on the deck, but mine can't proceed. So we'll skip a rotation for me and she'll clear two arrivals in a row, since my United Express 4439 still can't depart yet. We communicate all this without saying a word.

Stephanie talks to her guy: "Delta five-five-niner, clear to land Runway Twenty-two."

"Delta five-five-niner, roger that, LaGuardia."

I'm watching the construction truck that hasn't moved, and I know Wayne is asking the Port Authority about it. I can only hurry up and wait, as we used to say in the military. And waiting isn't good for me these days. Waiting means my mind returns, repeatedly and repeatedly, to that four-year-old boy I haven't spoken to in so long. And that call—not to my cell phone, but to the LGA tower. At *5 a.m.* What's the expiration date on a parent? What week should I circle on my calendar when I'll be forgotten?

"Port says they found metal scrap," Wayne says. "They're moving!"

And, sure enough, I can see the truck completely clear Runway 13, and safely edge past the perimeter. My runway is free from debris. And so I will myself to forget the 5 a.m. call and the little boy, and return to matters at hand.

"United Express four-four-three-niner, clear for departure Runway Thirteen, sir."

"United four-four-three-nine, departing Thirteen, thanks."

A second or two pass. Now there are muted voices, and for one bizarre nanosecond I think it's Ben's voice—at long last!—finally calling me. In fact, my name *is* being called. But it's not Ben. It's a feminine voice.

"Mike!" Stephanie barks. "Christ!" For the first time in my career, I'm slow to respond—which in our line of work means another fraction of a second passes. And United 4439 is into its takeoff roll. She correctly ignores me and speaks to her aircraft: "Delta five-five-niner, need you to go around, sir! Traffic ahead of you!"

There's no response from Delta 559, which I can see is a Boeing 737 almost returned to Earth.

Stephanie won't relent: "Delta five-five-niner, go around. Ground traffic at your twelve o'clock!"

I somehow see now what I didn't see before, which is the entire panorama. I've cleared United Express 4439 and it's on full takeoff roll on this short runway, applying power and rumbling right toward the intersection of Runway 22, the same runway where Delta 559 is about to touch down, just to the port side of my airplane.

What we all know up here is the lack of a response from Delta 559 doesn't mean they didn't hear Stephanie; it actually could be a good sign—they're too busy enacting established procedures to chatter with ATC. In this instant, we just don't know yet...

Now she's imploring: "Delta five-five-niner, go around, sir!"

"Fuck!" someone says.

"Oh, God..."

Even through the thick glass of the tower we can hear the high-pitched whine of the 737's engines as the Delta crew guns it. They've certainly heard Stephanie. *"Christai mou!"* I hear her murmur; others are speaking but I don't know what they're saying. I've never felt so sickened in my entire life. And even now—at the apex of this drama—part of my brain registers that this sickening feeling even surpasses the sickening feeling I had opening that letter from Israel weeks ago.

United Express 4439, the Bombardier I gave the green light, is plunging down Runway 13 and crossing Runway 22 now, with no hope of braking even if the crew was aware enough to attempt it. Meanwhile, the 737's engines whine and we watch and watch Delta 559, and finally the nose lifts and *just* before it settles onto Runway 22 it surges upward in the classic "go-around" maneuver. *Up!*

Delta 559 clears Runway 13 just as the United Express tail clears the intersection. Smoke billows from both 737 engines as the plane rises abruptly, appropriately enough shaking the very windows we're looking through, and I can see gear retracting and flaps extending. Now both aircraft ascend from LaGuardia simultaneously, and for a moment they resemble a fireworks formation as they take to the skies in sync on either side of us—one veering left over Flushing and the other veering right over East Elmhurst. A few lucky drivers on the Grand Central Parkway are viewing an unscheduled air show; as it so often does, terror unintentionally generates beauty.

There are voices too loud for a control tower now, and more people here than necessary. In all my years as a controller, I've never heard panic at this volume. I quickly turn and see Bob M. approaching. One of the managers, an older guy named Andy, already has parked himself at my elbow.

"Mike, let me slide in," Andy says.

I remain seated, composing my thoughts. "I just need—"

"I'm holding departures!" Wayne calls out.

Now Bob M. stands beside me, speaking evenly and coolly: "Mullen, get up. Let Andy in. Go wait in my office."

"I'll—"

"Let Andy *in*," Bob M. repeats.

The ultimate time-out. For the first time in my life, I relinquish my post upon the direct order of a supervisor, and I stand awkwardly and move toward Stephanie to let Andy take command. Now she looks directly at me and although it's no more than a second, it's a look I've never received from a peer. It's not disgust and it's not even anger; it's a mix of pity and shame. She turns away quickly and continues speaking to Delta 559, which is on an emergency loop right over my alma mater, Archbishop McCarthy Memorial High School.

And now we all hear the captain of Delta 559: "What the hell, LaGuardia! Somebody's got his head up his ass down there!"

Stephanie's soothing voice talks him through a deviated route, while another controller assumes command of her conga line of arrivals. A supervisor hovers. Everything slides into place, smoothly and automatically, just as it's supposed to, just as we've all been trained.

"My office," Bob M. says.

I turn, but in the wrong direction and I'm moving away from the stairs, not toward them. To an untrained eye, I probably appear drunk. I've seen it with others before, so I'm aware on some level I'm suffering from very mild shock. But I know it's nothing like the shock felt in that Delta cockpit. As for United Express, chances are that most onboard have no idea how closely fate just breathed so hotly on them.

I'm suddenly conscious of that which I ignore every day: the latch on the small gate at the top of the stairs; the security camera broadcasting who is ascending from below; the frayed floor tiles as I stumble. From across the tower a union rep calls out: "Mike, don't say a word! Wait for counsel!"

Counsel, I think. Lawyers, attorneys, barristers. Could there possibly be room for more counsel in my life? I exhale deeply, grab the empty Pepsi, and leave the tower.

As I wait for Bob M., I recall that cousin of hers. Maybe Runway 13 *is* bad luck.

*　　　　*　　　　*　　　　*

I'm meeting Hillary, though there's little to discuss since we have no idea which continent or high sea my son is on right now. We strategize, but until the 30-day window expires and the arrest warrant is issued, there isn't much to say or do. On another note, I mention I may soon be fired by the FAA for gross misconduct endangering scores of lives. Hillary gasps. Then she suggests we do everything not to allow the "other side" to learn of this development.

As we talk, I re-dial the number in Israel. No answer.

*   *   *   *

It's been a week since The Day of The Near-Miss. Still no news from Israel or any other country harboring my son. Meantime, I'm the highest paid admin in the FAA's Eastern Region, changing printer toner. Of course, soon I may not be paid at all.

I deserve whatever I get. When Bob M. closed the door, I assumed I'd be in his office for at least an hour; instead, I was on my feet and gone within three minutes. It was as if he'd already prepared his speech, and perhaps he had. Effective immediately, I'm on modified assignment, pending further investigation. Undoubtedly there'll be a hearing, and I should seek advice and counsel from the National Air Traffic Controllers Association. I am not to ascend to the tower under any circumstances, under penalty of immediate dismissal. A supervisor is waiting to administer a breathalyzer and urinalysis. Finally, I should leave immediately after that and take the rest of the day. Before long I was pressing the down button on the elevator.

Within minutes of reaching the employee lot, my phone rang; Moe remains active in NATCA and the LaGuardia union team was alerted. Our conversation was awkward; what could I possibly say? Moe urged me to get some rest, and I mumbled something. Through the windshield, I craned to see the top of the tower. I knew by now Delta 559 had completed its go-around maneuver and landed safely, and so the captain was calling Delta's dispatch office in Atlanta, his Air Line Pilots Association rep, and maybe even Bob M. Free from Federal Communications Commission prohibitions, the captain would rip up the wireless lines the way he wanted to but didn't from the cockpit. Just who was the fucking numbnuts who almost had us T-boned? Is he gonna wipe the shit stains off the cockpit seats? Is he fucking fired yet? In the old days, pilots sometimes waited outside the tower elevators, hoping to settle such situations with fisticuffs. I also know some airline Crew Scheduling offices post this:

> *What's the similarity between air traffic controllers and pilots?*
>
> *If a pilot screws up, the pilot dies.*
>
> *If ATC screws up, the pilot dies.*

Then my phone rang again. It was Sam, who had befriended Moe at Ben's party. Bad news spreads fast in NATCA.

"Dude…"

"Yep."

"Anything I can do?"

I stared at the base of the tower. "You mean like Superman? Screw around with the axis of the Earth? Turn back time?"

"Well…I was thinking more like coming to Queens. Buying you a brewski."

I sighed. "You're the best, man. Really. But I'm going home. Assuming I remember to stop at the red lights."

Sam's voice lowered. "Go easy on yourself. So…you shit the bed. It happens."

"Not like this. Clear, blue, and twenty-two. No excuses."

No excuses—including that pink message from 5 a.m.

Instead of going home, I found myself at my mother's place. Where I immediately did two things. Called Israel—no answer. And googled *LAGUARDIA NEAR-MISS* using the "Past 24 hours" function—no hits. I explained to my mother exactly what happened, and used terms her father the traffic cop would clearly understand. My partner allowed an airplane to land on a runway that formed a cross with another runway. And I—oh so wrongly—allowed a second plane to take off on the other runway just as the first plane was landing to cross that intersection. When I mentioned it could lead to termination her face turned ashen and she said she'd light a candle.

Subsequently I told and retold this story to others, mostly civilians. Those outside aviation were quite forgiving and granted me absolution—you were momentarily confused by that construction truck, who wouldn't be? Air traffic controllers, that's who. Professionals. My job is to handle dozens of distractions, night or day, in all weather and visibility, without ever endangering lives or property. So now I'm the SWAT team leader who shot the hostage, the surgeon who left the clamp near the aorta, the judge who freed the serial killer. I keep googling and so far, no news.

Masochistically, I logged on and looked up the particulars of Delta 559 and United Express 4439. I wanted not passenger manifests but FAA records, detailing what the industry terms SOBs—Souls On Board. Meaning *everyone* strapped into those tubes: crewmembers, revenue passengers, infants, airline employees, FAA jumpseat riders...everyone. There were 121 SOBs on Delta 559 and 37 SOBs on United 4439, including an infant traveling—quite dangerously, as I always warn others and never did with Ben—as a lap child. There also was a dog in the 737 belly. So 158 souls, or 159 if dogs go to heaven.

After I got home, I sat in Ben's room, staring at his Buzz Lightyear poster and gently rocking. Among the side effects I was warned about when starting Prozac were prolonged erections—no joke—and something termed "abnormal dreams." At first I questioned what these might be. But now I know.

Ever since the letter from Israel, my sleep has been haunted. By Ben's cries. *Where are you, Daddy?*

Now, Ben's been joined by others. Offhand, I can't say exactly how many voices cry out with him. But I'd estimate about 159.

*　　　　　*　　　　　*　　　　　*

"Jesus Fucking Christ!" Paco blurts out when I describe the near-miss. He lamely jokes about a new merger between Delta and United, but even he knows we've somehow moved past postmodernist irony. We're poking at the embers of pure pain, and sharp tongues have little sway now.

What's worse is my googling finally generated a hit. Yesterday some aviation geek posted a blog item. Maybe he heard the audio of Stephanie's pleas on LiveATC.net. Or maybe he got a tip from a pissed-off Delta pilot or back-stabbing LGA controller. All I know is today the *Daily News* and the *Post* both carried items about the recent near-miss, though thankfully not on the front pages. There used to be an unofficial "Tabloid Rule"—if a screw-up made the cover, the controller was transferred.

I'm not mentioned by name, but it's all about me. So now the same two newspapers that praised my father's heroics have dubbed his son The Tower Sleeper.

*   *   *   *

I find I have two great fears now.

One fear is soon I'll forget a voice, the voice of my own son. That thought fills me with terror.

The second fear? That I'll never forget another voice.

What the hell, LaGuardia! Somebody's got his head up his ass down there!

*   *   *   *

And all of a sudden the entire drama screeches to a halt, as if the projectionist dozed off and the film ran right off the reel as the screen darkened. Hillary emails me this time it's not a bluff—the attached letter verifies her firm will cease working on behalf of Michael Patrick Mullen if payments in arrears are not satisfied *immediately.*

The unspoken part of this is, what if I'm fired and unemployed as well? How can I continue paying lawyers? How will the courts view an out-of-work father? Somehow, in hopping from crisis to crisis, I will myself to stay focused on the most immediate crisis.

It's a particularly dark 72 hours, in a summer that's all about darkness. My family huddles, Katie and my mother supervising the discussions. Kevin has expensive possessions but very little cash flow at the moment, due to a pending and complex deal in Malaysia. Finally, Tommy says he has an idea. A few hours later, my phone rings and it's Tommy's partner Terry; as he identifies himself I realize we've never spoken by phone. Terry speaks softly and bluntly, telling me of the father he hasn't seen since sixth grade. Apparently the old man departed for the Left Coast and forgot to send for his wife and kids. I'm not sure what to say, so I just murmur. Then Terry quietly tells me that Multark Construction is co-signing my personal loan at Citibank.

At first the woman on the phone hesitates when I reference the abduction; you mean, this isn't to buy a deck or a swimming pool? No, it's to buy a *child*. After it's approved, I ask her to expedite payment, and she does. As soon as the FedEx arrives, I rush into Manhattan to the Citibank branch near Hillary's office.

I present a Citibank teller with a Citibank check for $50,000 and she taps away. I ask it be deposited as cash, so I can draw a certified check for $40,000. She shakes her head; it will take five business days to clear. But it's from Citibank, I point out. Yes, but it takes five days. But look at that address—Citibank Personal Loans, Clayton, Missouri. See? Another head shake. But it's the left arm and the right! It's one office of Citibank speaking to another! I understand that, sir. But it requires—

There truly isn't enough Prozac in the world.

A man looking far too young to be management interrupts. Sir, would you join me? I follow him and recap the scenario. Look, I plead, I need this. *Right now!* It's to pay lawyers. In a custody case. My son's been abducted. If my lawyers stop working—

I go silent. The manager nods sympathetically. But the five-day rule is inviolable.

Finally, my begging brokers a compromise. I ask him to pick up his phone—right now, while I'm here—and please call Hillary and explain the check truly has been deposited. He agrees, and after a moment hands me the phone.

The movie resumes.

*   *   *   *

Sleep won't come, so first I call Israel and then I boot up my laptop. Within minutes I'm googling images of plane crash victims.

*   *   *   *

I wake up starved and make my way to the kitchen. Slim Fast. And Prozac. Breakfast of Champions. Look out, Hugo Concepcion. You'll be stepping into a squared circle filled with rage. Soon I'll be at work, where my modified assignment consists of filing old "incident reports," though none of these incidents are as dramatic as my own.

*   *   *   *

I'm sitting on the second floor of the courthouse, and it occurs to me I'm the only man in sight. Downstairs, there's more than enough testosterone—along with lots of weaponry backing up bull-necked guys in cheap uniforms manning metal detectors. But up here, it's the usual battalion of women attorneys. Dozens of mothers who far too often aren't joined by deadbeat fathers. Even the cleaning staff on the second floor is all female—and all African-American or Latino.

They move invisibly alongside Ivy League lawyers, here in America, where professors preach we're all equal under the law's blindfold.

Hillary is delivering to Judge Westphal a stack of documents punctuated by the necessary Dutch signatures, fresh from The Hague. She's also updating the court about the 5 a.m. call to the Father's workplace being the only communication. Technically, I don't even need to be here for such dull administrative duties, but once again I've donned my Court Suit, which is not only becoming tighter around the middle, but also becoming more stained in spots. This morning I received a date for my *other* hearing, the one to determine if I'll continue working as a controller for the U.S. Government.

My phone indicates I've dialed Israel 27 times today.

For some reason I look across the hallway and watch an older attorney speak to a young client. The client looks familiar, though I'm having trouble placing her. She's dark-haired and rather petite, but the short frame in that suit seems surprisingly shapely. Then she turns and I notice large brown eyes and, in response to the older woman gently patting her shoulder, a broad smile.

I get up and cross over to them.

"Hello, Gina."

She turns and her smile grows wider. "Mike! Hi there!"

We stand awkwardly, like dancing bears during the organist's key change. Handshaking seems absurd, but we really don't know each other well enough to hug or kiss. After all, the only time we ever conversed was in the topless bar that night two years ago. Her lawyer helps by politely excusing herself.

"Good to see you," I put in finally.

"You too. How's your boy?"

I shake my head. "He's why I'm here. His mother...she abducted him."

"Oh, my God. Mike!" She reaches out, touching my forearm.

I shrug in a universal what-can-you-do gesture. Maybe Israel and Holland have sharpened my international communication skills. "How's Ashley?"

Gina seems touched. "You remembered her name..."

"Sure. She must be three?"

"Yep. And your guy...is Benny. Right?"

"Close enough."

A door opens from what clearly was an angry mediation session, and both teams burst forth. I confirm Gina is done for the day, then tell Hillary I'll meet her back here in a half hour. We take the elevator downstairs and within minutes we're seated at the coffee shop across Sutphin Boulevard. She orders iced tea and I order lemonade.

"First things first. You owe me a photo of your daughter..."

Gina couldn't be happier to pull out her phone and thumb through several—an adorable little brown-haired version of her mom riding a pony; wearing tights in the park; sitting on Gina's lap on a tram ride. I spend nearly a minute telling her how lucky she is.

Now I'm unsure what to say, but she fills the void. "Ya know...I wanna continue our conversation. About nature and nurture. The differences 'tween boys and girls. We won't have time today..."

"Yeah. I'd like that. I've been thinking a lot about it lately. I mean, gender. The differences, similarities."

She opens a sugar packet and I'm even fascinated by her fingers. "I'm taking a course in gender politics," she says.

"Where?"

"Queens College."

"I'm an alum. So's Jerry Seinfeld."

She nods. "Paul Simon."

"Ron Jeremy, the porn star known as The Hedgehog."

Gina mock-pretends to sneer. "Anyway…I've only got a few more credits for my MS. I'll be done by December."

"Congrats. That's great. What's your major?"

"Adolescent Education. And English."

"Wow! Good for you. You'll be doing God's work." I sip my lemonade, and the moon-shaped slice of lemon bumps my teeth. "Listen…I don't mean anything by this. But…you must meet a lot of guys. At work. I'm kinda shocked you remember my name."

She smiles. "Actually, I'm not there anymore. I was only there for two months that summer. But…that's beside the point. I'd still remember you."

"Why?"

She shrugs. "Well, we talked about our kids. I never did that before or since. And…the whole time we talked? You looked into my eyes."

"They're beautiful eyes," I blurt out. I'm convinced she can see me blush like a geeky seventh grader, like those she'll soon be teaching.

But she's smiling. "Thanks. Those blue ones of yours ain't bad either."

"So you're not there anymore…"

"Did you go back asking for me?"

"No. I was only there the once."

"I can tell. You're what we used to call a *looker*. Just there for a quickie..."

"Unlike my buddy Wayne. The guy I came with."

Gina laughs. "Oh, we had a name for him too."

"Yeah. So do we."

She leans forward. "I should tell you something. That place. All I did was serve drinks. And sat and had club soda and talked with guys—like you. Well, actually...*not* like you. But the other girls. Well, they danced up front. And then they did lap dances. And worked in the back. You know. I passed on that. Some of us were just waitresses. In those stupid Hooters outfits."

I'm shaking my head. "You don't have to tell me. It's cool."

"Well, you've been nice. I wanna tell you."

"Okay."

"Anyway, I was broke then. I mean...broke. Ya know?"

"Yes. I do know. Believe me."

"Yeah. Well, I worked for a company contracted to a cruise line. In reservations. And they outsourced to Mumbai. And then unemployment ran out. And my mother and I trying to make the rent on the apartment. Trying to finish school. And I can't do it all working at Target. Places with real salaries wouldn't hire me then 'till I got the degree. And my ex-husband...well, he started making noise about custody. It was one of those times. You know how it is."

I chug lemonade as I nod. "Yep. I know. I *know*..."

"So one night my friend Sheri comes over. I met her at QC. She's like twice my height—legs up to her chin. She was a dancer in that place for a while. So we sit down in Ashley's room and we start making lists. Like, where I can make money quick. Because the ex-husband, he's being a dick. 'Scuse my language. He doesn't care about Ashley. But hitting me with all these Orders to Show Cause."

I sigh out loud and nod again.

"And he's running up my legal bills. Just out of spite. And texting me. Saying I should cut my hair. Lose ten, fifteen pounds."

I grunt in disgust.

"So…Sheri and I start listing my skills. My assets. And then finally she starts laughing. And I'm like, what? What is it?"

Gina stops, smiling at me. "I'm gonna speak bluntly, okay? You're a nice guy. So anyway. Sheri says, 'Sweetie, you're five feet tall and you've got all-natural double-Ds. If those aren't assets, I don't know what is.' So I go there and try on the waitress outfit, and that was that."

"No wonder," I say, grinning.

Gina playfully slaps my wrist. "Behave," she warns. "*So…*I was there a few months. Know how much I cleared? Almost twelve grand." She's still shocked, even two years later. "*Cash.* Paid off tuition. Lawyers. Rent. Got straightened out. In two months."

I lean in close, my face drawn tight. She leans toward me, her concern apparent. I look both ways, then whisper: "I need cash fast…can I rock that outfit of yours?"

There's that great smile again, and she flicks her wet straw at me, as iced tea hits the already stained Court Suit jacket. I lean back and threaten her with my dried-out lemon wedge. Finally I ask what I've wanted to ask.

"What's the deal with your ex-husband? Was he across the street this morning?"

Gina shakes her head. "No. Actually…he's dead. Killed himself on the Long Island Expressway few months ago. Drunk driving—ran into a pole. He drank too much. Drove cars too fast. He was one of those guys. Everybody said he'd die young. Well…he did. The only good thing is Ashley won't miss him. She barely ever saw him."

"Wow. That's…something."

She seems to search my face. "Does that make me sound cold? I mean, that I'm not that upset?"

"No. Not at all. Marriages end."

"Yeah. Love ends sometimes too."

I swirl my lemonade and watch the ripples overtake each other, first in one direction, then the other. "So what's with court? Why are you here?"

"We're finalizing paperwork. His parents're out in Arizona. They filed this stupid petition. To see Ashley. I mean…what's with people? All they hadda do was call and ask. I'd fly her out there. They're like ninety years old, they're not gonna abduct her. But they have to use the damn lawyers."

I nod, but I'm thinking how lucky Gina is. Just her and her daughter. *Free at last.*

"So, speaking of abduction…" She reaches out and touches my hand, and I feel a shiver. The good kind. "What's next?"

I sit up straighter. "Well…first a talk with Interpol. Then I'll go back to The Hague if I have to. If it escalates. If not…I may go to Israel. That's where they were last seen. I mean, Ben. And his mother. Bottom line…she's got to return him to me within the next nine days. Or she's going to jail."

"My God." Gina shakes her head. "She must be crazy."

I nod. "Literally. Everybody misuses *literally* these days. Especially online. But I mean it—*literally* crazy. Up until a month ago I didn't think that. But now I do."

"And...I mean, how have you held up? You must...I would want to crawl into bed. And just cry. Not talking to your kid..."

"Sure. But I can't. It's not an option, like they say. I've gotta get Ben back. Whatever it takes. I'll do it."

We're both silent for about twenty long seconds, and Gina looks at my face the entire time. Finally she speaks: "God, you must be beating women off with a stick..."

I pull back at this, as if a flame shot up and scorched me. Why the cruel joke? But Gina is smiling and seems sincere, and isn't teasing. Still, I frown as I respond.

Damaged goods.

"Yeah," I say slowly. "I mean...I'm on anti-depressants. I'm gaining weight. I'm suspended. May lose my job. Got a quarter million dollars in legal debts. I flunked out of grad school. My car failed inspection. And if it weren't for my brother's sofa, I would've been homeless for two years. So yeah...of course. Women are falling all over me."

Gina's smile fades as she shakes her head. "You're wrong. Hey. All of that...it's just temporary. You'll come through this."

"Maybe. But still...it's not the stuff you list on Match.com."

She's still shaking her head. "Well...it depends. What you're looking for. Maybe not for some young chick. I mean...sure, you're right. But *women*. Well...women look at it differently. Lemme tell you. There's nothing hotter in this world than a man who really loves his kids. *Nothing*. It's the ultimate turn-on. For a mom, anyway."

I say something in response. She says something. I say something back. But I don't know what we're saying. When you've been locked in a dank basement and suddenly feel the strong rays of daylight's warmth beaming down, your senses don't function properly.

Finally I tell her, "I'd better get back to Hillary." She reaches for her bag but I've got the bill and the tip. As we move toward the door, I decide to satisfy my curiosity.

"I didn't know you were from Queens."

She nods. "Forest Hills."

"Hmm. I was guessing Brooklyn. Maybe Staten Island."

Gina smiles. "Really? Why?"

"I dunno. More Italian families down that way."

"Sorry to disappoint ya. I'm Jewish."

As I hold open the glass door for her, I see my reflection and I'm shocked to realize I'm smiling. Genuinely smiling. I instantly wonder if the reflection is lying. And I also instantly wonder how long it's been since I've smiled like this; a month, at the very least. And I just as instantly chastise myself for smiling at all. Meds or no meds, there are times I wonder if my head will just spontaneously combust on its own.

Outside, I steer Gina to an empty section of sidewalk near the subway entrance.

She looks at me. I cough. I stare. Finally I speak.

"Look...here's the thing. I mean...the last few weeks. They've been hell. I thought...before. I *thought* I knew hell. But this...it's really been hell. Just pure hell."

Gina puts her hand on my forearm. "I know. I mean...I can't imagine. But I believe you. If I couldn't see Ash..." She shudders. "But...you're gonna get him back, Mike. There's no doubt."

I nod. "Yeah. But...here's the thing. I mean...I just spent six weeks in hell. And just now. I mean, in the coffee place. For twenty minutes. That was the first time since—in six weeks. First time I wasn't thinking about Ben. Or airplanes on final approach."

She smiles the smile that makes me wonder if I can continue standing upright. There must be as many English words for that smile as Inuit words for snow. "That's a good thing," she says. "I'm glad."

"Right now...I mean, my life is insane. Absolutely insane. I've got an appointment next week with Interpol. I mean, who says that? Except in movies. *'Sorry, I've got an eleven o'clock with Interpol on Tuesday.'* So...things are just beyond intense right now. All I can do is focus on Ben. Getting him home. Getting him back. Safe and sound. It's all I can do."

"Of course. It's all you *should* do."

I know I'm staring into her eyes, and I wonder is it possible to stare too long into a beautiful woman's beautiful eyes? Should I look away? What do I know from following my instincts?

"But later...I mean, when I get back. With Ben. Hopefully. Then..."

"Yes?"

"Then I would really, really like to see you, Gina."

She laughs. "Really, *really*?"

"Yep."

She kisses my cheek. "Me, too. Really, really! Now go get that kid of yours. I'll be here."

My heart—that vessel I could have sworn was worn out, dried up, unfit for service, blinking *CHECK ENGINE* in orange—suddenly it's soaring. I can feel it taking flight, just as surely as the metal tubes I follow for eight hours at a time. "Yeah?"

"I'm not going anywhere," Gina tells me. And then she's gone, into the subway.

I jog back across the street, grief and joy fighting for headline space in my frontal lobe. Funny thing, how the bliss sears as much as the pain. I'm alive, that much is for damn sure. I am definitely alive. At the courthouse, I turn back to the subway where Gina descended.

I'm not going anywhere!

And now a new thought crosses that lobe as well. I've heard that line before.

*   *   *   *

Another carefully typed note is slipped into my work mailbox.

> *Hay Mulins!! Way to go, asshoal!! Wear taking Bets on how many Plains you bring Down. 100 buckes says you Kill at least 2 hundred. Keep it up, Shit Head!!!!!*

*   *   *   *

Paco is annoying me.

"I'm up to speed on Israel. There's nothing new. And I know all about the hearing at work. Whatever will fucking be, will be..." He places his hands together as though praying. "Tell me more about that woman you met in court…"

"No. Nothing more to tell."

"Well, I think maybe—"

"No!"

*   *   *   *

It's a rainy, nasty day on Long Island, and I'm at the FAA's Flight Standards District Office in Garden City. I've had my hearing—though I wasn't really heard. My union rep and the attorney paid for by the National Air Traffic Controllers Association did all the talking; they cited my commendations, read letters of support, and desperately waved the flag, noting I served in the military during wartime. They advised me it would be best if I didn't speak at all, and I reluctantly agreed. I'm becoming used to not being heard on vital matters affecting my life, liberty, and happiness.

I was touched when Moe showed up and submitted written testimony on my behalf, praising not only my skills and dedication, but my character as well. He even cited my efforts to combat homophobia in the tower during his unsuccessful union campaign; I hugged him in front of the FAA attorneys when he stepped down.

But then the other side stated its case. And what can anyone say? Even as they spoke, all I could focus on were those 158 Souls On Board. Plus the dog.

I finally receive the sobering news: a 30-day suspension without pay; a year's probation, when any serious infraction will mean immediate dismissal; and a demotion to working under supervised conditions until further notice. UFN—my new motto.

I don't mind the time off, of course, though it would be better to have time off if my son was on the same continent. But to lose one-twelfth of my annual paycheck? That's a tough blow to absorb. Filing personal bankruptcy is inevitable now.

Lenny, my union rep, pulls me aside when it's over. "Hey, you should know something, guy."

"What's that?"

"Well...the decision was already made. In fact, paperwork was typed. You were *gone*. If you wanted work in North America? You'd be moving to Canada or Mexico."

I let this sink in. "So what happened?"

"Bob M." He nods across the room at my boss. "He went to bat for you behind closed doors. Argued with the others. Told them you were having personal problems, but you'd pull out of it. Said it would be a mistake to lose a good man like you."

I'm stunned, and I say nothing.

"He must really like you, guy."

Me? The Tower Sleeper?

*   *   *   *

I'm shocked beyond shock. My actions have been so rote for so long, continually redialing that number in Israel at all hours—from home, the LaGuardia tower, my car, Ring of Fire, the courthouse itself. After four rings the metallic sound always indicates the voice mailbox is full, and I hang up.

So I can barely speak when, standing in Stop & Shop, some-one picks up on the third ring. "Erev tov?"

I fight to control the muscles working my tongue. "Hello? Can you hear me?"

"Halo?" It's a young man, perhaps a teenager.

I breathe deep, and fight to remember everything Hillary and her colleagues drummed into me. "Can I speak to Kasper, please?"

"Ah...he is not at this place..."

Breathe, breathe! "Do you know where he is?"

"Who is this?"

"My name is Michael Mullen. I am Benjamin's father. Do you know who I am?"

"Yes, I think so..."

"Are you Kasper's son?"

"Yes, I think so."

I ignore the odd syntax. "Do you know where your father is? Or Ben's mother?"

"No. I do not know."

Breathing... "You need to contact your father. Do you under-stand?"

"I do not know where—"

"Listen. You need to contact him. And Ben's mother. You need to tell them—they are going to be arrested. *Arrested.* The police are looking for them. Do you understand? You have to tell them."

There's a pause; I wonder if he's alone. "I am not involved. I came for today. I—"

"Just tell them. Ben needs to come home."

After we hang up, I breathe even deeper. Fathers and sons.

*   *   *   *

I'm convinced the medication and psychotherapy are a complete waste. Because I truly am out of my mind. And I'm about to take a beating to prove it to the world.

It's a Friday evening and once again I've descended into Ring of Fire, and I'm standing in my corner wearing green boxing trunks, staring at the man I'm about to battle. We're the last of the four three-rounders tonight, probably because we're the heaviest and oldest (not to mention slowest) guys in a club filled with millennial welterweights. I size up Hugo Concepcion, seeking weak spots, and knowing I've got my own. He's a nice enough guy, though he barely speaks English, but he's got about three inches and twenty pounds on me. His arms and legs are longer than mine, so he'll have not only height advantage but reach advantage as well. Still, he's no hardbody; when he bounces up and down I see arms shake and belly jiggle.

Meanwhile, I had planned to use this date—etched in stone—to force myself into shape. It's one thing to diet and exercise so you'll look good for a cruise or a wedding, but it's another when it's necessary to prevent getting pounded into a dirty canvas in Woodhaven, Queens. Of course, I haven't been lazy. In addition to work, my life is and will be a continual series of appointments with marriage counselors, mediators, American lawyers, Israeli lawyers, Dutch lawyers, union lawyers, bankruptcy lawyers, law guardians, shrinks, forensic shrinks, anger management counselors, accountants, and soothsayers. Still, I've hardly trained at all, and it's hard to be optimistic about tonight. I'd like to at least go the distance; three rounds may not sound like much, but boxers know better. I haven't told friends or family about this fight, because I don't want witnesses in case I go down. Archie's strong hands rub my shoulders as the ref jabbers.

Now the announcer introduces Hugo and the crowd goes crazy; I have no idea if it's because he appeals to the heavily Latino audience or if the bloodthirsty mob senses I'm about to get my ass kicked. As the announcer introduces me, I'm surprised I receive a decent ovation, and chalk it up to being a hometown hero, Michael Mullen from Queens.

I have no idea what Archie just whispered, but the bell has rung and we're both circling, coming ever closer in clockwise fashion, as if we're in Australia rather than north of the equator. I throw a jab that misses, then he throws a jab that I slip. I'm thinking going three rounds without touching each other wouldn't be so bad.

That thought ends soon enough. Hugo sends three quick jabs—left, right, left—and the second and third bounce off my chin and forehead. I respond on instinct with a right cross that happily catches more of his nose than I had hoped. We both circle some more, the wolves on wooden folding chairs baying for us to engage. Everyone's been raised on so much movie and TV crap that most people have no idea what a punch in the face really feels like; it overwhelms all your senses, the brain reacting as if barbarians are storming the gates. And before you can fully register what that punch has done, the next one is already en route.

The round continues, as we punch each other's upper arms. I notice, however, Hugo keeps those arms somewhat high, so I wait and I'm promptly rewarded with an opening. I step inside and bury a hard right uppercut into his pancreas; that loud gasp is sweet music, but it's drowned out by the bell.

Amidst the rubbing and chugging of water, Archie whispers fiercely into my ear—*Stay on da inside!* She's right; with his advantage in reach I just can't compete firing away at a distance. We're back at it, and for a moment here in Round Two I think life may be turning—ever so slowly—in my favor. As we gradually meet in the center, I move inside quickly and throw two hard body shots: a straight right to his solar plexus followed by a left hook down lower in his belly. Hugo groans and drops his guard, and I immediately throw another right cross to that sore nose. As the outnumbered pro-Irish contingent cheers, I hear Archie yell, "Yaas! Dat's it!" And I'm rewarded with the sight of red trickling out of Hugo's left nostril.

This combination is my finest hour. Because before I can continue my rather modest rampage, I realize Hugo is the proverbial bear and I'm the stick. He lets out a yell as he throws a sloppy but more than effective hook I should dodge, but it catches me on the forehead and almost puts me down. For a nanosecond it jogs my vision the way images jarringly shift on a buffering video; I try to slip but he's on me, and two more hard punches catch me, one on my left cheek and one on my mouthpiece. I swing underneath and manage to connect with his gut, but I'm in full desperation mode now. And I do what many wise warriors have done before me: retreat. I backpedal, I evade, I cut cattycorner across the ring. A few spectators catch on and I hear booing, but the small part of my rattled brain that cares reasons they haven't earned the right to protest until *their* faces have been smacked by a large, angry man. Eventually we catch up with each other, and both of us throw more jabs, though his still sting. Hugo and I are tied up, pounding each other's backs, when the round ends.

"You winded, boy," Archie tells me, unnecessarily, as I guzzle water. "Tole you—do dat roadwork. And gotta keep going in. *In! In!* And keep dat chin in!"

I stand for the third round and now I feel scared. All this statistical analysis Ben and I routinely conduct has me examining situations now in new—sometimes frightening—ways. It hits me I'm only 67% through this fight, and I wish it were already over. My chin, mouth, cheek, and forehead wish as much too. Those who have never boxed don't realize these gloves feel like lead weights after two rounds. Now Hugo is the aggressor, and he moves toward me quicker than I've seen him move before. I decide the best strategy is to meet him head-on, stay low, work inside. Theoretically, it might work. Just as I throw yet another hook at his belly, he lets loose with his best punch of the night. It's a hook as well, but he's got much better leverage now, and his fist crashes into the left side of my head, even though conventional boxing wisdom frowns on targeting craniums, the hardest human bone. Simultaneously, there's something of an electrical outage at Ring of Fire, because the strong lights above us shift and seem to move from their stanchions. That battered brain of mine quickly concludes, of course, *I* am the object moving rapidly, not the building, and the direction is downward, so those lights briefly blind me as I twist to the canvas. I somehow land sideways, but roll face down. And now I'm breathing in years of dingy Queens boxing ring; I understand my nose is mainlining sweat and blood and even piss—but shit too? I want to move, and consider how to go about this, but then

Archie is helping me, which of course I eventually realize is what a trainer does when her fighter has been counted out.

For three years now I feel I've had my face pressed into muck. Now, finally, it's literal. And as Hugo's arm is raised, I also realize it's truly official: I'm a loser.

$$* \qquad * \qquad * \qquad *$$

It's the day after the fight, and I've got one nasty bruise on my left cheek. Last night the shot to the side of my head hurt more, but this morning that faded and instead the cheek flared up. It would seem I should spend Day One of my 30-day suspension in bed, but I'm out early to meet with my union rep Lenny so we can file an appeal. Pro forma, as they say. Since it most certainly will be rejected.

While showering, I realize I just want to stay under this stream of hot water. Everything hurts again, but not due to Hugo Concepcion. He gets credit for the shiner, but my brain and my spirit and my heart all hurt. Missing Ben hurts so much even an Inuit couldn't devise enough words to catalogue the pain. The drain swallows it all.

I step outside and it's scorching hot, even for August. Though I'm sure the Executive Vice President of Corporate Communications at Exxon Mobil could cite many paid-off scientists to deny anything is amiss, clearly the world is heating up. I'm already aware *my* world is heating up. But here's evidence it's the entire world.

Lovey is parked near St. Rita's, and as I walk my phone rings: Annabelle, my old mentor. I stop under a tree and for once, I steer the conversation toward her, out of guilt for all the hours detailing my messy life lately. But we both know it's a matter of time before we exhaust her vacation on the Cape and her daughter's pregnancy.

"How are things going with the courts, Mike?"

I explain the days are ticking, and soon either Ben will be back with me or else his mother will be subject to arrest. In 92 countries worldwide, from Albania to Zimbabwe, all signatories to the Hague Convention.

"That poor child..." She sighs. "How are things otherwise?"

I laugh sarcastically. "Well, I was just suspended without pay for almost causing a mid-air collision."

"My God!"

"And last night I got my ass kicked in a boxing ring."

"Good Lord...I'm so sorry." And then she says what I wish no one would ever say: "What else could go wrong for you, sweetie?"

I turn the corner near the church and Annabelle's answer is right before my eyes. My station wagon is still parked at the curb. But the tailgate window is missing. I once read that Queens boasts the highest auto theft rates of any American county; the sight of broken glass on these streets is as common as dog shit. But even as I tell Annabelle I'll have to call her back and I step over the shards to inspect, I see there's *no* glass at all in the carpeted rear of the wagon. In other words, this window was knocked *out*, not in.

Later, when I try using any of three dead credit cards to pay at Safelite, the manager explains it. This wasn't the work of a typical Queens thief or punk; the heat became so intense *inside* my car, slowly building to such proportions, that Lovey simply burst. And here I've been thinking my life is imploding; apparently it's the opposite.

*　　　　*　　　　*　　　　*

One thing I truly wish people would stop saying is—*anything that doesn't kill you makes you stronger and wiser*. I'd much rather be weaker and dumber.

*　　　　*　　　　*　　　　*

I'm in a foul disposition and I point to my bruised face, telling Paco I'm a loser. For weeks, that anger Judge Westphal accused me of harboring has flared up in here.

He leans back. "So these two monks set out on this journey of about 500 miles to another monastery."

I'm in no mood today, so I stare at him. "Why?"

"Um...*why*? Well, they had to deliver these important fucking parchments they just transcribed."

"Why not scan them and send them as PDFs?"

Paco's face hardens. "You know...I used to get into rumbles with smartass Irish guys like you. In Hell's Kitchen."

I steal from George Carlin: "I thought you grew up in Hell's Breakfast Nook?"

Now he ignores me. "So *any*way. They're from a very strict order. They're not allowed near women. Can't speak to them, touch them—nothing. And they come to this stream with two nuns sitting there crying. So the nuns explain one can't get across on her own 'cause she's crippled. Excuse me—*hand*icapped. So the younger monk, he straps her on his back and he swims across. Then they thank them and they go their own ways. But the older monk—he's in shock.

And for the rest of the day, it's all he talks about. How could you do it? *Touch* a woman? *Carry* her on your back? You know the rules. On and on. And finally…the young monk stops. And he says, 'Brother, I only carried that woman for two minutes. But you've been carrying her for seven hours.'"

I continue staring. Then I say, "Hate to tell you your business. But these allegories…they're supposed to relate to the patient."

He chuckles. "Keep at it. Keep punching. Should've had this attitude the other night. Hugo would've had little fucking birdies tweeting over his head 'stead of you."

"Fuck you."

Now Paco smiles. "I love you too, my man. Listen up…you're at a critical fucking juncture. I'm not talking about us getting the kid back. We'll get him back. I'm not worried about that. But this ex-wife…you're gonna have to make decisions. You can be like that old monk. And you can carry this psycho around with you the rest of your life. Every barroom in America has some guy pounding back shots and griping about that bitch that fucked him over. You can be that guy. Or you can engage with her when you have to—like to get the kid back. And then *dis*engage. And brush her aside. You really wanna carry her around?"

The anger's left me, and we both know it. I say nothing.

"And another thing. There's a big fucking difference 'tween losing and being a loser. We all lose. But becoming a loser—that's a choice. You're gonna have to decide how all this will shape you."

Then he segues, and asks how come I didn't work Hugo inside like we agreed.

*   *   *   *

And just as it all began so quickly, maybe now it will conclude quickly as well.

Ever since the young man in Israel answered the telephone recently, I've focused just a little more intently each time I've dialed. It's early morning and I'm at home, and I punch by rote. When it's picked up on the second ring, somehow I'm not surprised.

"Halo?"

I know it's Kasper, and I know I have a lot to remember. My attorneys have drilled me on what I shouldn't say, but mostly they've insisted I remain calm and do not—under any circumstances—lose my temper. Death threats clearly are off the table.

"This is Michael Mullen."

"Ah. Yes?"

"Where is my son?"

He clears his throat. "Yes? He is with his mother."

"And where is she?"

"She is with you, yes?"

With me? Is there no end in sight, ever, to all this insanity? I count three very long seconds. "What are you talking about?"

"She is with you? They left for New York. One week ago."

New York! A week ago! Again—three seconds. "Last *week*?" I count to one. "I have no idea. She hasn't contacted me."

"Yes? I am sure you should call her father or mother."

"I'll do that." As I prepare to hit *End call*, I hear him.

His voice retains its usual flatness, but rises slightly. "I would like to ask you…"

265 · WILLIAM J. McGEE

I pause. "What?"

"I would like to ask why you want to put Benjy's mother…in *ja-il*." He pronounces this last word as if it has two syllables. I start to count again, but he's not done. "I think that is rather…*unfair*. Not only to her. But to Benjy. Yes?"

"Yeah, well, abduction is rather *unfair* too," I shoot back, but then realize there's no advantage in engaging. I'm determined—for once—to remain in control of my vocal cords.

"There was no abduc—"

I hit that red button and he's gone.

*   *   *   *

Seven weeks. I can't let myself think it might soon be over, that two months of agony may come to a close. Within hours I could be hugging Ben—who may be only blocks away! I run the distance of five houses and burst in on my mother. Her dining room will serve as Command Central until this crisis is successfully resolved.

Hillary takes the unprecedented step of coming out to Queens when there's no court date scheduled in Jamaica. Eventually, of course, I'll be billed for these hours and her round-trip Lincoln Town Car. My mother is just thankful Katie arrives first, so they can present the pastries Katie brought alongside the coffee that's brewing.

"Ma!" Katie cries out. "You worried about getting Benjy back? Or the damn cheese buns?"

My mother stares at her. "You act like it's one or the other."

I won't lie. They're incredible buns, from the kosher bakery.

Katie turns. "To think he might've been in Queens! That bitch…"

"Watch the language!" my mother says as Hillary knocks on the screen door.

The four of us talk, but my head is buzzing and I'm having trouble concentrating. They munch and drink, but I'm too nervous. It's taken all my remaining restraint not to bolt over to her parents' house, but I'm determined to execute this properly. Finally, the plan is hammered out. I'm to visit the local precinct, which is just a few blocks from their house, and request an officer accompany me to the stoop. Hillary presents me with the necessary documents—from Jamaica and The Hague—that will answer all legal questions. Katie should accompany me; Hillary thinks a female presence will help defuse any potential confrontation. My lawyer shouldn't be there because her lawyer won't be there, and courts frown on situations where only one side is represented by counsel. We are not to discuss the case *at all* with her or her family; all questions should be referred to Hillary by whoever represents her now. We're to ask Ben to come with us, and then we're to leave with him; if not, the police will intervene. And Ben should not return to her *at all* until a court date can be scheduled to address abduction, contempt, and perjury.

We all nod. Hillary says, "These are delicious, Mrs. Mullen."

"Please, take these last two with you," my mother implores.

"Too bad you don't have a rabbi on your side of the family…"

My mother looks up. "Michael's cousin is a Catholic priest."

Hillary smiles. "Yes! A priest is excellent. No offense, Kate."

Katie smirks. "So much for my female presence…"

Now I'm en route to an old school rectory in Little Neck. There's an odd whistling sound as I exceed the speed limit on Northern Boulevard; apparently that new tailgate window doesn't sit right. I've called ahead and my cousin Desmond promised to wait out front. I pull up and there he is. Wearing a Mets cap and a Darryl Strawberry #18 jersey. I stick my head out the window and politely ask him to run back inside and change into the black suit and Roman collar—which is what this is all about.

A few minutes later, he slides in beside me and I awkwardly attempt a hug while the shoulder strap strains. "Hey, Des. Thanks."

Desmond smiles. "Sorry to hear you're in such shit, Mikey."

I pull away and execute a dangerous and illegal U-turn. I always liked Desmond.

My cousin speaks up. "Know what I was thinking before? Remember that time—we were probably about six. At your father's engine company? Down in Rockaway."

"The Nut House."

"Right! Well, they had this like…open house. Remember? All the trucks parked outside. The ladders and the hoses. And we were playing on this big fire truck. Wearing red hats. And you were behind the wheel. I said, 'Look, Mikey! The keys!' And you looked at me like, what the heck. You hit the ignition button and all hell broke loose. Two dozen kids all jumping off at once. Your father running up. He was *not* amused…"

I smile as we speed west. "I'd forgotten that…"

"Your mom's worried about you," he says, as if it's a natural segue. "She says these days you're a…*lost soul*. Her words."

"Yep, that's me. You talk to her much?"

"Well, let's put it this way. We're talking more since your marital problems…"

I'm driving too fast, and make a conscious effort to slow down. "Listen…Des. I wanna be up front. I really appreciate this. You're doing a mitzvah."

Desmond chuckles.

"But I can't be…hypocritical. I mean…I'm using you. Your collar. Your *presence*. Just to get through this nightmare. I'm still an agnostic—that's not gonna change. But I'll do anything I can. If it helps me get Ben back."

"I get it." I think he's done, but he's not: "You know…people have used collars to do terrible things. But getting Ben back is a good thing. So it's cool."

Then he lightens the mood by noting the Mets finally added some hitting to go along with all that pitching.

Now we're outside the precinct. Every New Yorker knows cars are brazenly double-parked and even triple-parked in front of only two institutions—firehouses and police stations. I pull up alongside a junked Oldsmobile with no license plates and dust inches thick on all windows, a long-forgotten impound. How could they ticket me right out front? Desmond follows me inside.

I'm shamelessly willing to play any cards available, even pitching blarney about the Auld Sod with a Sergeant Corrigan. Or Dunphy. O'Mannion. Callaghan. Instead we walk to the desk and meet Sergeant Hui Ng.

He listens intently, reads the court order, and then strokes his face. "Here's the deal," he says finally. "We're all about a*void*ing situations. Not defusing them. We'd rather not *have* a situation. Period.

And sometimes—I mean, I know it's ironic. But even though we're peace officers…well, our very presence escalates things."

"I can understand that," says Desmond.

"Thank you, Father. So…here's the deal. I'm suggesting you two go over to the house by yourselves. To be honest…I really don't think you'll have a problem. But I'm going to have a unit parked one block away. By the bagel store?" He slides me a card. "That's my direct number. *If* there's a problem…then call and we'll be there." He nods at us. "Good luck."

Outside, Desmond observes Sergeant Ng really knows his stuff. Of course, my Uncle Tim—his father—spent 25 years on the job, so this is no small compliment.

As I start the engine, I realize my hands are shaking. I breathe deeply and consciously exhale, like I should have done in the ring with Hugo. Desmond reaches over and grasps my arm. "We're going to get your boy back, Mikey. It's almost over…"

Rabbi Cohen answers the door and can't hide his disappointment at seeing me on his stoop. Then he spots Desmond and a smile creeps onto that lined face, even though they haven't spoken since our wedding. "Hello, Father! Hello, Mike…"

My cousin speaks first. "It's been a while, Rabbi. I hope you're well."

"I'll make you a deal. I'll pray for you…you pray for me. How's that?"

Desmond bows. "Done and done."

As always, I cough. Then I nod at my ex-father-in-law. "Rabbi, is she here?"

"No. She's taking a yoga class."

"Is Ben here?"

He nods.

"Could you please get him? I have a court order."

"Can't we wait till she gets—"

"No. There are officers just down the street. Please get him."

The rabbi sighs, opening the door wider. And there he is. For the first time in months, I'm staring at my son. Later, Desmond will tell me I involuntarily moan.

Ben is half-hidden behind a coat rack, peering out at me with large blue eyes, but he doesn't look at all happy. In fact, he looks downright terrified. And he makes no effort to come closer. Somehow I notice his hair is twice as long as usual, and falls disheveled.

To his credit, Rabbi Cohen intervenes. "Benjy...your dad's here. And your Uncle Desmond. Are you all set for a visit?"

My brain registers the word *visit*, but there are more pressing issues now. "Hey, Ben!" I call out. "How ya doing, buddy?"

He doesn't answer, and looks up at his grandfather for guidance. The rabbi produces a child's backpack I've never seen, with a French flag on the front. Ben kisses him, then tentatively steps onto the stoop.

I've been waiting forever, and I throw my arms around him. But it's like hugging a child mannequin. I turn to my cousin. "Remember Uncle Des, buddy?"

He holds up a priestly hand. "High five, Ben!"

Ben slaps his palm and for a moment I think he'll smile. I thank the rabbi, then guide Ben down the stoop. We're at the car within seconds, and I strap him in. We settle in up front and for a moment I rest my head on the steering wheel. "Oh, God..."

Desmond smiles. "Oh, *who?*"

I finally laugh, though we both know it's pure relief. After we pull away from the curb, I look into the mirror, and see Ben has turned away, staring sideways. "Hey, buddy? You wanna hear the Beatles?"

"Oh!" Desmond says. "I love the Beatles."

"Us too. Right, buddy?"

Ben doesn't answer, and my cousin slips in *Rubber Soul*. The music starts and I say to my son, "Someday you can drive my car. Drive Lovey. Okay, baby?"

Finally, Ben turns. "I'm not a baby," he says softly.

He's been back for four minutes and already I've screwed up. "No! I know. I mean…the song. Baby, you can drive my—"

"That song is stupid," he says to the side window. "Lovey is stupid…"

I stop speaking. After long minutes, I pull onto our street but then remember Katie was taking my mother to the beauty parlor. So I drive four more blocks and park behind Katie's car. "Come on," I say to the boy.

From the sidewalk, we can see my mother under a dryer and Katie texting in the waiting area. The three of us walk in, and Ben lights up when he sees his grandmother. He pulls away from me and runs to my mother, who welcomes him with both arms. She is shedding tears, a rarity for her.

"Bennington!" Katie is on her feet and across the room and squeezing any available part of him. The old Italian woman working the dryer has both hands on her cheeks and smiles at Desmond; she's been privy to this drama for the entire seven weeks.

And Ben is smiling. Laughing. Loving.

Desmond puts his arm on my shoulder and when I turn I can feel myself ready to burst. I'm oh so grateful the real Ben is breaking through, but it certainly isn't because of my presence. Are the women providing something the men can't? Are the antiquated courts actually just in their centuries-old wisdom, because fathers are no more than appendages—nice but hardly necessary? Or is it not about gender? Is it simply about me? Is Ben ready to jettison his father?

Then my mother whispers something, and I see Ben turn. He's still smiling. Only he's looking at me. Suddenly he tears across the beauty parlor. *To me.* He jumps and I time it perfectly and he's in my arms, as I kiss that unruly hair and hold him close.

"Welcome home, buddy! I missed you *so* much. And I *love* you so much!"

His words are muffled, and I gently lift his head from my neck. "What, buddy?"

He looks into my eyes. "Why didn't you *call* me?"

I refuse to add a beauty parlor to the list of public establishments I've cried in over the last four years, during my incessant march into wussydom. But I can't say that aloud, or Katie will kick my ass.

"I called you every single day. Every day. A quillion times a day. More than a quillion—a *dozen* times a day! I didn't know where you were..."

He hugs me tighter.

I owe Desmond much more than dinner, but he accepts the invitation to my mother's place so we can order in Chinese. Family continues to drop by in the hours to come, first Chris, then Kevin and Nicole. By the time Tommy and Rosemary and the twins show up, we place a second call to Hunan Gardens. Ben is ravenous—I've never

273 · WILLIAM J. McGEE

seen him so hungry and he wants more beef-on-a-stick. And to my
mother's delight, he's willing to try broccoli in garlic sauce; I notice
he no longer calls it *green trees*.

My phone rings, and I speak out loud, though not directly to
anyone: "It's her." Then I move to the kitchen.

She comes to the point. "When are you returning Benjamin?"

The threat of imprisonment clearly hasn't dampened her
brassiness. I breathe—*again*. "You should talk to your lawyer…"

"That isn't what I asked. When will you return him?"

"Well…actually we will *not* be returning him. Not until the
court determines visitation. As I *said*…you need to speak to your lawyer. To determine a court date. So you can work out visitation."

"Under the joint custody—"

"There is no more joint custody. You broke that agreement. I
have *sole* custody now. You really need to talk to a lawyer. Judge
Westphal wants to talk to you…"

She pauses a moment. "Let me speak to Benjamin, please."

"He's already in bed," I lie. "All this has worn him out."
There's no way I'm going to allow her brainwashing to continue before I can even have a decent conversation with Ben.

"Have him call me in the morning." Then she hangs up.

Back in the dining room, Katie reads aloud her fortune cookie: *A visitor will stay with you soon.* My mother crosses herself, and
Chris blows Katie a kiss as we silently wish for another overdue child.

It's early, but everyone's exhausted, and since Tommy lives
in Douglaston, it only makes sense he drops Desmond in Little Neck. I
give my cousin a hug and tell him what I've never told him before,
that I love him. He responds, "God love you, Mikey."

We say our good nights and then my son and I walk home. On the sidewalk, Ben asks me to carry him. He's heavier than ever, of course, but I don't mind. Just as I lift him, I see our neighbor Jackie standing in the dark.

"I love you, Mike. I love you, Benjy."

As I carefully ascend our stoop it hits me I've lived in Mr. Hannity's house for a year now but Ben's never seen it. Not even his own room, which has sat empty since the twins and I finished painting it last September. He's too tired for a tour tonight, but tomorrow awaits us. Finally. A tomorrow. Our first since forever.

I'd already laid out new pajamas and a Minions toothbrush and a stuffed candidate to replace Dog. We run through Ben's ablutions in the bathroom and then I lead him into bed. Finally: I sit down beside him.

"Daddy?"

"Yeah, buddy?"

"I'm sorry. Lovey's not stupid. The Beatles aren't stupid."

I smile and brush that crazy hair off his forehead. We'll hit Vic the barber tomorrow. "Shhh...don't worry. No worries, buddy."

Now Ben seems to choke up. "Can you sing to me, Daddy?"

"You betcha! Anything you want..."

"The one from the car. The one you shut off."

"*Baby, You Can Drive—*"

"No. It comes later. The one about...the people."

"Ah." I nod. "*In My Life.*"

Ben nods too, and sniffles. "Yeah. And the other one. Our favorite. The cockles..."

I hug him as hard as the law allows. "You know, I think you're a little nutty…"

He smiles through his tears. "Me? *You're* nutty!"

"No. *You're* the nutty one. Mister Sir Topham Hatt. Did you really think this? Did you think you'd come home and I'd tuck you in? And then I *wouldn't* sing about Molly Malone? You really thought that? You must be really nutty!"

Ben closes his eyes. "I love you, Daddy…"

I close my eyes as well. And I sing.

*   *   *   *

I'm worried about Ben, and I speak to Paco about my son entering therapy. Ben may have been vacationing on the Riviera, but this whole event certainly took its toll on him. Paco says the good news is the way Ben forgave me so quickly for not calling him—as ludicrous as *that* sounds—indicates our bond is quite strong, even unbreakable.

The details emerge in spurts, though some pieces will always be missing and other pieces will never quite fit. Seven weeks earlier she, Kasper, and Ben left for the south of France—or *le Midi*, as it's spelled in a deposition—and they spent a carefree summer. Later they were in Dijon, where I would have staged a rescue of my son even though I hate mustard. Whenever Ben asked to speak to his father, apparently he was told there was no answer. Eventually I felt forced to show Ben my endless record of calls to Israel, and he grew silent.

They hired the new Israeli attorney three days before leaving Israel for France. Her New York attorney faxed his termination upon learning Ben wouldn't return to JFK on schedule. Over the coming years, more details emerge, but nothing of significance is learned.

The most pertinent question of all will remain unanswered, now and forever. *Why?* What was she thinking? What did she hope to gain? How could she not have anticipated I would respond? And—most important—what of Ben?

In the hallway outside the courtroom one afternoon I violate my lawyers' advice and impulsively turn to her and formulate one word: "Why?"

"I'm trying to build a life for Benjamin. And my family."

What I don't know is the most cogent explanation will be offered next year, filtered from her to her lawyer to Hillary to me. The two attorneys will confer in Jamaica, and Hillary will ask, *barrister a barrister*, what her client was thinking. And her lawyer will shrug and say: "She just never believed the father would fight it."

Later, Hillary will say, "I guess she really didn't know you."

*   *   *   *

These late summer weeks are busy. Hillary keeps me apprised of court dates and filings, but there's little required now.

The court orders supervised visitations, awkward encounters wherein one of my siblings and I stand nearby while she spends time with Ben in the Queens Center Mall or the playground or the Central Park Zoo. They're miserable affairs—for her, for me, and undoubtedly for Ben. But in its wisdom the State of New York has decreed this for abduction cases. So be it. She barely speaks to me.

After each visitation I gently encourage Ben to express his feelings, but all the drama has led him to hold those feelings in rather close, which greatly worries me. Thankfully, he makes a new friend, Charlie, when a family from Korea moves in right next door to Mr. Hannity's. We remain busy—not just with haircuts but with new clothes, a new pediatrician, a new dentist. There's also registration for kindergarten. As for NYU, I determine being a full-time working dad won't allow me to continue graduate school. At least not this year. So I'll defer that dream yet again.

Eventually, I'll return to the LGA tower, albeit under strict supervision. In the meantime, I pass my suspension working for my brother's construction company, in a futile effort to stave off bankruptcy. I retrieve my old steel-toed boots and hardhat and Tommy assigns me to a project in Queens Village, tearing down a grocery store. Ben joins me some days, and plays in Tommy's trailer while I collect scrap metal.

Among the many injustices of this brutal summer is the vacation my son and I were cheated out of in New Jersey. So just before kindergarten starts, I take Ben for a weekend down the shore. After he tells his mother we're going away, she asks where.

I quote her own email: "Somewhere warm."

* * * *

I'd be lying if I didn't acknowledge that I'm looking forward to this court appearance. It's not about anger, or vengeance, or cruelty. It's about being human. The urge to see justice done—at long last—

flows through my veins. Only those who can't imagine suffering through the pain of July and August can't conceive of such an urge.

She's hired yet another attorney, and it's time to step up and feel the wrath of Judge Westphal, the same Judge Westphal who granted me sole custody and found her in contempt of court. Now we'll hear exactly what punishment awaits on those contempt and perjury charges; according to Hillary, judges get quite pissed when their edicts are ignored. Katie sits a few rows behind me, ready to text my family about the verdict.

And just like that—it's moot. Or mute. The judge's nasal assistant reads a short statement: All pending charges are dismissed since the child was returned to Queens County. The sole custody agreement will remain in place and Ben will remain with me, but the judge strongly urges both parties to work together in the best interest of the child. Supervised visitation will continue for now. We're all to return in six weeks. Six weeks—less time than Ben was missing.

I turn toward Hillary, and then toward Katie. My lawyer closes her briefcase.

"That's *it*?" I ask.

Hillary shrugs. "That's justice..."

I'm stunned. Forget about *me*—what of the pain she caused Ben? Is there no justice to be doled out, here on Earth, right in Queens? But Hillary's expression makes it clear it is not to be. And I will soon wonder, is her greatest punishment living with her own actions? So I breathe deep and swallow any vindictiveness. *Again.*

In the hall beside Katie I ask Hillary what's next. My lawyer smiles. "Mike, what's next is you should sit back. Relax. Enjoy your son. Enjoy life..."

*   *   *   *

Ben and I are painting the second bedroom in the apartment Katie and Chris just bought in Murray Hill. Since it's near a stretch featuring a dozen Indian restaurants, the locals refer to it as Curry Hill. Overall, square-footage-wise, this place is smaller than their one-bedroom in Chelsea, and her Integrated Services Digital Network studio is smaller. But the critical component is the room we're standing in, the bedroom social workers will evaluate on behalf of someone not yet born. However, work slows after Ben spots the Sherwin-Williams can and we discuss primer versus paint.

We selected a limeade green, and Ben's job is to put masking tape on doorknobs (but not electrical outlets, which he's not allowed to touch). Katie silently elbows me: The closet door has sprung a goiter under Ben's nine layers of tape. I ease the roller into the pan of green goo and remember Gina's comments on gender and the use of blue and pink to subtly guide babies onto male and female tracks.

I never did call Gina, even though more than a month has passed. At one point she called me, and we spoke for two pleasant hours, but I didn't follow up after.

Of course, I've thought of her every single day since, in that painful way of poking at a fresh wound. I thought and thought about her, and I concluded that to me she is simply perfect. Which is the worst imperfection of all. Naturally, perfection means long-term she'll want nothing to do with me.

I just consider myself lucky I dodged yet another train wreck so early. It stings when I think of Gina. But I'm still in one piece.

*　　　*　　　*　　　*

Back at work, I'm in my new role as a supervised basketcase. I stare at the NATCA bulletin board—the usual health warnings and labor union propaganda. Then I spot a notice and freeze: the FAA's annual recruitment of controllers to compete for AirVenture Oshkosh, the coolest of cool air shows, held every summer in Wisconsin.

For controllers, this is the Oscar, the Pulitzer, the Nobel. Many compete but only a handful are chosen. Over several days they work the busiest control tower on the planet, as more than 8,000 air-craft—from World War II fighters to experimental spacecraft—continually land and depart. The 78 privileged few selected are given fluorescent pink polo shirts, worn with the reverence of the Medal of Honor. For years, my supervisors suggested I was capable not only of competing, but of serving in Oshkosh. With marriage and fatherhood, I deferred but didn't abandon applying. Now it hits me. Due to my dismal performance this year, I'll never be tapped for a pink shirt.

In the land where every child is indoctrinated that becoming President is within reach, big dreams don't die easy. Then again, this isn't the first time I've had to face the reality something I deeply wished for will never happen.

So I focus elsewhere. Like the New York Mets—in the World Series for the first time in 15 years! With a starting rotation for the ages. For once, Hillary couldn't be more prescient in her legal analy-sis. She's absolutely right. I should just sit back. Relax. Enjoy my son. Enjoy life itself.

But like any true Mets fan, of course I can't fully relax and I have trouble enjoying. Even before Kansas City clinches in five games, I'm already worried about an unhappy outcome. And I realize enjoying life doesn't come easily to me now.

So I will myself to plunge in. I have my son. All the rest flows from this. Ben is more than enough for me to enjoy a full life. He's everything.

BOOK FOUR

It's a summer of concepts. Together we consider ideas and employ cognitive reasoning and collect all that raw material in hope of shaping something. Certainly I'm biased, but I can see Ben has a fine mind for a five-year-old. It's sharp and inquisitive and—best of all—works in tandem with his even finer heart. Whether this is all primarily due to nature or nurture, I couldn't say. But I'm grateful.

We find we have more questions than ever. Like why a heart is a thing pumping blood but also a thing we give to someone on February 14th. Why don't we give cards shaped like kidneys? Or spleens?

It turns out that whole water-flushes-clockwise-and-not-counterclockwise-below-the-equator thing is a myth. Which I find disappointing. Because for some reason I wanted it to be true.

Ben asks me why Aunt Katie's baby isn't here yet, and I certainly fumble. I just can't explain how Katie and Chris traveled 500 miles to a military town and lived in a Motel 6 for nine days, all the while surrounded by boxes of formula, bottles, diapers, creams, lotions, clothes, toys, blankets, stuffed animals—while Katie recorded a Caribbean resort commercial for a new client from the bed. I can't explain how they waited outside a hospital, a hospital they paid thousands of dollars to on behalf of a young Navy couple, Christians who already had three children and decided 48 hours later they would, in fact, keep their new infant after all. Because they reconsidered having their daughter raised by lesbians. And I can't explain how—despite all the paperwork and fees, lawyers and notaries—all this was perfectly legal (not to mention nonrefundable) under state law. And I certainly can't explain that long 500-mile drive back, with Katie and Chris silently holding hands on those dreary interstates. Instead I say, "I have a feeling we're gonna see that baby soon."

During spring training I read Ben the story of the White Sox first baseman that quit the game (and forfeited $13 million) because the team banned his 14-year-old son from the clubhouse. We discuss kids in the workplace, and how—believe it or not!—even some controllers at LaGuardia are opposed to it. Ben's as shocked as me.

Many things don't make sense. Like in April, when Ben hears an airman shot his squadron commander at Lackland Air Force Base, where I once served. Or when Ben's best friend and next-door neighbor Charlie is called a *slope* by an older kid. We also find that the things we apologize for most often, we usually don't need to apologize for. While the things we truly need to apologize for, we don't.

We contemplate this bizarre election year, and the dramatis personae at the center: Bernie, Hillary, Donald. Ben comes with me behind the curtain when I vote in the primary and we discuss each candidate at length before feeling the Bern.

Other concepts play out. Ben has been with me for all the milestones—first swim, first haircut, first lost tooth, first use of the potty. So we prepare for the next big step: removing training wheels.

I pick him up at Grandpa Al's temple, where he quizzically studies a painting in the hallway. 1 Kings 3:16. Dark oils depict two mothers fighting over a baby, as King Solomon orders a sword drawn, the child wriggling in agony as they prepare to cut it in two. I'm convinced it's beyond Ben's comprehension, so I change the subject.

When I play my Beatles CDs in the car, Ben wants to know how she can keep her face in a jar by the door.

Death, life. War, peace. Crime, punishment. Rich, poor. Hate, love. We contemplate it all. And I've learned that there's the big picture, and there's the small picture. And the small picture may in fact be bigger than the big picture.

      *   *   *   *

These days I keep my head down. I'm working arrivals and this older guy Chauncey ambles up. I doubt we've ever exchanged 100 words total. He's one of these totally clueless baby boomers, constantly trying to put down younger guys by saying clever shit like, "You know...Paul McCartney was in a band before Wings." Very timely. As if millennials walk around humming *Maybe I'm Amazed*.

"Did you know I have two kids?" he asks me.

"No."

He hesitates. "See...their mother. She dumped me. For her dentist. True story. Said, we're moving to Seattle. That was that. Kids were five and six. I talked to a lawyer but...back then...well. I was wrong. I guess. I just let them go..."

"Hmmm..."

"Us older guys...we were wrong. Lots of us. We let our kids walk away." He says nothing for long seconds. "But not you. Your kid will never forget that."

I look up. "Thanks." It's back to work. I keep my head down.

      *   *   *   *

I'm not good at relaxing and enjoying life. I remain on edge, as if something lurks around the next corner. Another salvo. Even though these days Hillary and I only speak to discuss my outstanding bills. But I do enjoy Ben. We spent our first Christmas together with the Mullens and slept at my mother's place. I stayed up until 5 a.m. hot-gluing wooden tracks to a Thomas the Tank Engine train board, and nearly hot-glued my hands together. I felt sick because I forgot to buy the holiday truck from Hess, but Kevin smiled and held up a package; he bought it back in November and told Ben it was from me.

Ben and I fall into a routine, which I always read is what children crave. Kindergarten is a success, and although Ben is in the afterschool program, on many days I'm not working, so he skips. On the weekends, he's in karate and I attempt to enroll him in peewee soccer, but the coach insists Ben—and all five-year-olds—attend *every* practice. I explain his parents live apart; you know, like 50% of American parents. But apparently Coach has managed to lumber 16 years into the 21st Century without hearing about divorce. As always, my mother and siblings come to my childcare rescue when I'm stuck in the tower; sleeping at my mother's has become normative for Ben.

As for his mother, Ben sees her often because she and Kasper moved in with her parents. For how long, I don't know. I keep wondering what will come next.

Even without graduate school, my schedule is full. Once a week I visit Paco in Manhattan, and when Ben's in class I steal time to visit Ring of Fire. Over the cold winter months I find myself getting stronger. Harder. But I still don't fully relax.

*　　　　*　　　　*　　　　*

Ben and I visit Sam and Debra and Henry in New Jersey and we stop for breakfast at Denny's. The hostess asks, "Table for three?"

I look around quizzically. "No, just two…"

"Oh. I thought Mom was parking the car."

*   *   *   *

Last fall we had another supervised visitation scheduled, and we met in the park. As usual, she brought Kasper along. Hillary insisted I always have a trusted adult with me, for two reasons: 1) to instantly alert the authorities over any potential criminal behavior, and 2) to witness and corroborate anything said or done in my presence. We rotated a regular cast of Sam, Moe, Katie, and my brothers; I provided the snacks.

That day was Tommy's turn. We watched from some distance on a bench as she played with Ben on the swings, and then I saw Ben hug her. Meanwhile, she seemed to argue with Kasper, who then crossed the long expanse toward us.

"This poor schmuck looks like he's headed to Gitmo," muttered Tommy.

"Michael?" He pronounces it *Micheel*, so it rhymes with *veal*. I didn't stand.

"Uh huh?"

But Tommy was on his feet at once. I sometimes forget my brother can schmooze clients just like any small business owner. "Hey there. I'm Tom Mullen, Ben's uncle."

287 · WILLIAM J. McGEE

Kasper smiled tightly, offering a limp shake. "Michael? Do you think this should end? This...*watching*?"

I shrugged. "It's what the court ordered."

"I am speaking to *you*. Not courts. Do you think it should end? It is very...*sad*."

I stood too. "You should've thought of that before you helped abduct my son."

"We do not look at it that way...this was all a..." His sentence trailed off, not that I cared. He turned to Tommy. "What do *you* think? Do you support this...*watching*?"

Tommy smiled his client smile. "I support whatever the state suggests. You could say I'm a big law-and-order guy." And that grin grew larger.

Kasper turned, but I called out: "Hey!" He stopped. "You're big with the lectures. Yet she doesn't even talk to me. She's cold as ice. Personally, I don't give a shit. But in front of Ben? Well...you're a shrink, no? Doesn't she know how harmful it is? Having one parent acting so nasty to the other?"

He closed his eyes. "I spoke to her about this. She...will never forgive you."

I looked as Tommy shook his head. "Forgive *me*? For what?"

"For trying to have her arrested."

"Ah! Well then...back to square one. She shouldn't have abducted Ben, no?"

"We do not view it in that way. We do not use that word."

I stepped closer, and Tommy coughed, loudly. I said, "You can use any fucking word you want. That's the word the Court of The Hague used. That's what it *was*."

The following Monday she petitioned the court to end our supervision during her visitations. Judge Westphal immediately agreed.

*   *   *   *

My brother Kevin unexpectedly tells us he's asking Nicole—formerly J-Law—to marry him. They've been together almost two years now, and the man who was so happy to secure a pain-free divorce is now eager to jump back in. As always, I'm stunned by life and the changes it brings about.

Before Thanksgiving I heard again from Gina. She had friended me on Facebook but I was still a little surprised she called. And I was even more surprised when after a lengthy back and forth, she invited me to join her in Brooklyn for a college production of *Charlie Victor Romeo*, the play that recreates cockpit voice recordings of fatal airplane accidents. Of course, I'd seen it before (how could I not?). And I was touched, because she clearly suggested something close to my heart. But I explained how work was jammed up. Plus two weeks annual training in Oklahoma. Then here come the holidays…

She politely said she understood. I said thanks and congratulated her on finishing grad school. Once again, I dodged a wreck.

Paco continually brings her up, but I always change subjects.

On Christmas Eve, Katie asked if I'm ready to resume dating, and I said no but I told her all about Gina as we sprinkled red and green sugar on cookies. Katie listened; we continued discussing Gina while playing a drinking game during *Love Actually*—a shot for every bizarre, inappropriate fat joke. Finally Katie said, "A nice Jewish girl from Forest Hills—slinging drinks at a topless place! As Eileen would

289 · WILLIAM J. McGEE

say…Jesus, Mary, and Saint Joseph. I think when they held you up by your ankles at Elmhurst General and slapped your ass, they said, 'May this one live in interesting times…'"

Early in the new year Gina posted a photo of herself with some handsome jerk up front at a Billy Joel gig at Madison Square Garden. Unfriending her would have been a dick move, but thankfully Facebook offers that option to block new postings and therefore pretend someone doesn't exist. Life, of course, offers no such option.

*   *   *   *

I'm late catching an elevator, because we couldn't find Ben's *Disney Planes* lunchbox. And the LaGuardia construction makeover is making traffic insane.

"Hold it!" I jump onboard and face the other rider; I'm alone with Stephanie for the first time since The Near-Miss. We exchange awkward looks and ascend.

"Hi, Mike."

"Hey. How's it going?"

"Pretty good…"

We've seen each other in crowded settings—the tower, break room, even a holiday party. We've nodded, murmured greetings. But we've never discussed *It*. Even though ten months have elapsed.

I force myself to speak. "I'm glad I ran into you."

"Hmm? Why's that?"

"Well…I know time's passed. But I owe you an apology. I…I should've earlier."

Stephanie looks uncomfortable. "You don't owe—"

"Yeah, I do." As usual, I cough as I falter. "I've been looking at it wrong. All this time—I mean, I keep thinking I just owed apologies to those 158 souls onboard."

She smiles as the elevator stops. "There was a lap child too."

"Yeah, I know. The 158 includes the lap kid. But not the dog. Anyway...I realize I owe you too. So...I'm sorry."

The doors close; Stephanie looks at me for the first time since 2015. "You don't have to say that. I wasn't on either plane."

"I know. But if things had...you know. Well, you would've been a victim too. Not that you did one thing wrong—it was all on me. *All* of it. But...it would've been your nightmare too. Your trauma. You'd always be wrapped up in it."

I hold the doors as she exits. Then she gives me a quick hug, her head averted. "I appreciate it, Mike. Really. I hope...it works out."

Damaged goods. I should print up a nametag.

*   *   *   *

Sometimes Paco annoys the piss out of me, and Katie says that's when he's really earning his money. She knows more about psychotherapy than I do. But still.

We've had lots of fires to put out, what with that little international abduction fiasco and whatnot. I once mentioned we could go years without discussing anything but her and Ben, and his eyes flashed in response. Then he immediately asked about my father. I said we had more pressing issues, like court. But he wouldn't relent.

Once we get past the preliminaries, Paco really digs into the marrow—How did I feel during his beatings? Where specifically did the belt strike me? What was I thinking when curled up in a corner of the bed? Which was the worst beating of all? Why?

"Fuck you!" I bark when he inquires about the belt's buckle end. "I write the checks. I decide what we talk about!"

When I blow up, he gets zen: "I never tell you how to land airplanes."

And so into the muck we dive, head first, wallowing and wallowing. I don't see the point. But ever so methodically he draws me further along. And somehow we're back full circle to Ben. I rail how I've never struck a woman or child in my life, never even considered it. Paco pushes and pushes. And one evening I blurt out my greatest fear. That underneath it all—diaper changings, late feedings, bedtime lullabies—peel it all away and I'm just Thomas Mullen Senior. Ready to pounce.

Eventually we move on to my mother, and different muck emerges.

A few months after these discussions I dragged myself home feeling the full effects of the winter flu. Scraping ice off the windshield in the employee lot, I alerted the afterschool program I was running late—again. Ben was cranky the entire time at Walgreens. After parking, I walked past our door and up to my mother's. Where she served homemade beef vegetable soup and fresh biscuits for us while I told her my woes.

"I'm bone tired. Chills and fever. I've gotta drag him home. Make his lunch. Lay out his clothes. Get him in the bath, then into bed. And start all over tomorrow. Then drag my ass back to the airport." I looked up—she was smiling as she stirred. Smiling!

"Is that right?" she said. "Now…imagine having four. Or five. Or six…"

I sighed. "You win…"

She poured milk and winked. "You'll never be half the man your mother is, kid."

I grinned in agreement, as she started singing *Love Me Do.* Then she suggested Ben stay with her while I slept it off.

The next night was déjà vu, and after I finally got Ben into bed, I brought a hot cup of tea with honey into my room. It was Katie's advice—neither of us can afford throat issues in our jobs. I sipped, then heard a crash. At his doorway, I saw him scampering back into bed. "Get under those covers!" I yelled.

Two minutes later there was more noise, this time a tap-tap-tapping on my wall. I spilled hot tea into my lap because I rose so fast. I cursed and stomped back to Ben's room. He was under the covers, only it was his two little bare feet resting on the pillow, toes wiggling. "Cut the crap!" I shouted, my sore throat aching. "Get to sleep!"

There wasn't a sound while I finished the tea. I actually thought he was out. Until a louder crash indicated he had knocked a dozen books off his shelf in the dark. When I swung open that door and hallway light flooded the room, he was on his knees, hurriedly stacking Dr. Seuss. The fever and chills and body aches were in full bore as blood pounded in my ears; my head hurt and I dreaded another severe throat issue. And clearly Ben wasn't taking me seriously.

I crossed to him in three quick strides and loomed over him, not sure what would happen next. Ben turned and for the first time ever looked at me in fear. All I could see were the blues of those eyes.

The calendar flipped, and it wasn't 2016—it was 1984. And I was in a bedroom five doors down, and a large angry man held a belt in his hand. I'd finally arrived at the moment I feared. On some level, I heard a soft whimper. Whose?

Then I acted...

I plopped down onto his bed. Ben blinked. And I croaked, "Hey, Mister Nutty. If you want to read...just ask me. Now pick *one* book." Ben impulsively hugged my shoulders from behind, and handed over *Just Me and My Dad*. I woke up after 1 a.m., lying beside him still fully clothed.

But two days later, facing a silent Paco, I was more terrified than ever. I came *this* close, I explained. I was ready to draw back my hand. I'm just like my father. The same dreaded disease runs through my blood—

"Enough!" Paco yelled. "You are too fucking much, Mullen!"

I stared at him the way Ben stared at me in the dark.

"We don't get slammed for what we con*sider* doing. We're not confessing impure thoughts to Father McGillicuddy, right? There's a song in *The Most Happy Fella*—Brother, you can't go to jail for what you're thinking!"

I kept staring.

"I'll say it one more time. For the *last* time. Then that's it..." He leaned forward. "You are not—repeat *not*—your father. You have never struck your child. And if you maintain your equilibrium, you never will. It's not fucking hereditary. Like baldness."

For once, the tears I felt welling up were tears of joy. And relief. Had I broken the cycle of abuse?

Paco's voice rose: "You will *not* fuck up at parenting like your father did!"

I found myself nodding; I finally believed him. My greatest triumph!

Then he leaned back. And he said, "You're going to fuck up at parenting in your *own* way."

*   *   *   *

Sooner or later I'll face a rematch with Hugo Concepcion and I'll be damned if I'll suck that smelly canvas twice. The next time it's his turn. Tough talk, I know. But I'm backing it up by stopping at Ring of Fire every opportunity I'm free from Ben or work, and Archie spends time honing my limited skills. Earlier tonight she tied my shoelaces together before sparring, forcing me to concentrate on footwork like never before; at one point I looked like young Jerry Lewis without the crew cut. I've punished myself on the StairMaster, ridden my bike along potholed streets, sweated with the weights. I've also given up Pepsi, and now drink seltzer. My blood pressure is no longer problematic. I'm losing pounds and gaining muscle with a bit of a religious fervor; the question, of course, is how long this enthusiasm will last. For now, I have a specific goal. Archie notes it's a good sign that I've worn out the balls of my socks, as all good boxers do, and that I'm no longer backhanding to ward off punches.

I'm military pressing dumbbells and I look up at the silent TV and groan: *Everybody Loves Raymond*. As always, Ray is acting like either a nine-year-old boy or a mentally challenged adult, begging his wife for either forgiveness or sex. I look in time to see her elbow him

right in the balls, and even muted I know the studio audience is howl-
ing. After all, what's funnier than striking a spouse in the genitals?

Then it's followed by a commercial for whipped topping, in
which it's another father who is a complete asshole, as he's repri-
manded at the refrigerator for sneaking an extra dessert by the smarter
wife and smarter son and smarter daughter, all three shaking their
heads in disgust. Two commercials later, a different asshole father is
hiding from mowing the lawn, but the garage door opens, and the dis-
gusted wife, son, and daughter are holding gardening implements.

I hope Judge Rhonda Westphal isn't watching TV.

*　　　　*　　　　*　　　　*

It's a beautiful morning, and I'm actually feeling pretty good.
I walk Ben to school, and we discuss Charlie's birthday party invitation and what he'll say to his friend Rosie because her grandpa died.
Now, late for work again, I double back to my car. At some point, I
realize I'm smiling.

I'm still smiling as I approach Lovey. Smiling even as the
young Asian woman steps from behind the fender, approaching me
quickly. Am I smiling as she reaches into an oversized purse? I can't
know. But I watch curiously to see what she retrieves.

It's not a gun. It's something worse. Much worse.

She hands me a subpoena.

*　　　　*　　　　*　　　　*

I know when my life winds down I'll assess my regrets, despite the wise individuals who tell us we shouldn't have any. And I know even now most of my major regrets will stem from these past four summers, even if I die at 100. Like a Robert Frost fork in the woods, or a 90-degree deviation for a palm reader, these four years are setting the course for all that follows. Yet of all my regrets, what I don't know is my greatest will always be not firing Hillary.

Later, I'll learn all her partners were on vacation this week, and so Hillary responded to this subpoena in the worst possible way: She legitimized it by answering. Once this Order to Show Cause was put into effect, and argued against by Hillary, and entered on the calendar of—who else?—Judge Rhonda Westphal, it was too late to undo. This request to reopen the case and have New York State take a fresh look at the long-term fate of Benjamin Cohen Mullen? It's completely bogus and legally indefensible. But as lawyers like to say, once the toothpaste is out of the tube, you can't shove it back in.

This toothpaste is bullshit, as all three senior partners will angrily tell Hillary when they return from Nantucket and Westhampton and Ocean City. In this state, there must be grounds to reopen a settled custody decision, and Michael Patrick Mullen doesn't fit any of the required criteria, i.e., physically or sexually violent toward the child and/or other parent; mentally unstable; addicted to alcohol, drugs, gambling, or prostitution; guilty of a felony; financially destitute and/or homeless; etc. So Hillary simply should have filed a brief statement noting the request itself was invalid, with the proper legal precedents attached. Instead, she made the worst mistake of her career by legitimizing it.

*　　　*　　　*　　　*

Late last summer Ben and I built an elaborate sand castle near the Rockaway shore. We labored for hours, the sun burning the back of my neck so fiercely that the collar of my shirt stung for days. And then—just as we neared completion—we dug a wee bit too deep and the shovel hit water, water that first trickled but then gushed before eroding all our work. The castle collapsed in upon itself as Ben and I watched helplessly.

It's quiet on my break so I tear into the thick envelope with the subpoena. And as I do, a piece of paper falls to the floor. I bend to retrieve it, frowning at yet another distorted communication. *THIS PAGE INTENTIONALLY LEFT BLANK.*

*　　　*　　　*　　　*

Scott Fitzgerald supposedly said, "The very rich are different from you and me." And Ernest Hemingway supposedly quipped, "Yes, they have more money." Though Scott was right, of course. They *are* different. How could they not be?

Many of my fellow Americans know that not having money—or not having *enough* money—affects everything, as that *CHECK ENGINE* light continually reminds.

One day in the terminal Wayne walked me to an ATM and watched as I withdrew $60. Then he asked why I didn't extract $100 or even $200—why make extra trips? I couldn't explain withdrawing $60 meant my balance was now $3.13 until payday. It was the same look at the post office when I asked for 14 stamps. Or when I told the attendant in Teterboro—where they don't allow self-service—to insert $17 regular into Lovey's tank. It's why I found my mom ironing my shirt, after she learned I stopped using the cleaners because $1.75 per item was too steep.

When I have a few extra bucks at Stop & Shop, I buy additional cans of soup, knowing that'll be dinner in a few weeks. And whenever I have change, I dump it into Lovey's ashtray, since I'll eventually need to convert it to paper money. One day last February, I had no groceries and every single one of my credit cards was maxed out—except my Macy's card. So I drove to the iconic round store on Queens Boulevard and in the gourmet shop I bought Harry & David pretzels and a Danish ham, and ate ham sandwiches for a week. The oddity of being poor in the digital age.

Now *Mullen v. Cohen* is officially reopened, and somehow I'll have to find tens or even hundreds of thousands of dollars more. Perhaps that's the true end game here—a simple war of financial attrition, not wits or stamina. And one thing is obvious: The lawyers and courts are happy to bleed both sides dry until someone quits from sheer debt. Abusing children is a big, big business.

*　　　　*　　　　*　　　　*

My mother seems tired so Ben and I cook pasta shells and bolognese sauce over at her place; he grates the cheese. We can calculate the number of candles she's lit at St. Rita's over the last four years, but in other ways it's hard to calculate the toll all my travails have had on her. She suffers when her children suffer. And now I know why.

*   *   *   *

All my supporters—family, friends, Paco—are taking my emotional temperature. No one will say it, but I know they're concerned if I'm up for yet another round of legal warfare. Despite all the scars, and the lack of funds, I am certainly ready. If I have any doubts, they're dispelled when Ben slips his hand into mine while walking to school. Or pretends to pull a napkin from my ear. Or smiles at me in the morning.

Somehow she managed to inject a bogus claim into the wheels of justice, but I haven't abandoned all faith in the system. This filing is wrong, and any impartial witness would say the same. Ben is happy living with me, and happy seeing his mother when she is not traveling to Israel or Bulgaria. And so I gird my loins. I have no other choice.

*   *   *   *

"My lawyer works there," Ben suddenly says from his child seat as we're driving on Queens Boulevard. Thankfully I do *not* steer the car into a lamppost, though it takes effort. We're in Kew Gardens, which like Jamaica contains a complex of Queens County courthouses and bail bond agents.

"How's that, buddy?"

He points to a mirrored building. "She works there. She's nice. Mommy told me."

Within minutes I'm calling Hillary. Yes, my attorney explains, Judge Westphal will appoint a law guardian to represent Ben's interests, as well as a forensic psychologist to interview all parties.

But Hillary wasn't notified yet of selections. I advise her she's too late; the other team already met Ben's lawyer.

On Friday morning, while Ben is with Katie, we all meet inside that mirrored building—plaintiff, defendant, attorneys. Her newest lawyer, Joy, seems like her dimmest, but underestimating is a fatal mistake. Joy's office is two floors below, and unlike Hillary she's immersed in the Queens legal universe. My heart thumps when I overhear her refer to Judge Westphal not as Rhonda but as *Ronnie*.

The guardian's door opens and a woman escorts us inside. I shake hands with Ben's counsel. Then she and Joy spend three minutes reminiscing about the wedding of a judicial assistant last weekend, and the drunken fountain dancing taking place in the wee hours. Hillary smiles awkwardly. Finally the meeting begins and Ben's law guardian explains to Helen—no, sorry, it's *Hillary*—to Hillary and Mr. *McMullen* she wants only what's best for Benjamin, and has no personal stake. Her role is to be an impartial and unbiased advocate for the child.

An hour later Hillary and I enter a small coffee shop and already I feel sick. As she eats, I impulsively ask about her twin boys, since I know very little; Hillary explains her husband, working from home, is the primary caretaker. Then I bluntly ask how her marriage is, and she says she knows far too much to ever contemplate divorce.

By 3 p.m., I've walked two blocks further into Kew Gardens to a building saturated with names suffixed with *Esq*. I find the office of the forensic psychologist, the man appointed by the court to evaluate us all. He welcomes me in, then asks if I mind Leon the parrot chirping in a cage atop the very sofa I'm to occupy. Actually I do mind, but what can I say? As we settle in, he reports Joy said this morning's meeting went well.

"Joy? You refer to the defendant's attorney by first name?"

Although he has a droopy face, he flares up. "Is there a reason I shouldn't?"

I shrug. He's a jackass, with a droopy face, so from now on he is Eeyore.

He smiles, but isn't happy. "So? Mister Mullen? How's that temper of yours?"

And there it is. Last year concluded a battle, not a war. It's full-on combat, and once again I'm on defense—clueless, sputtering, unsure. The official apparatchiks all seem to know what I don't. The final abduction ruling was far from final; this bogus filing is far from bogus. And the whole nasty custody business is far from over.

*   *   *   *

I have learned something. There's showing support, and then there's showing support. Just about everyone except the depraved rise to the occasion after a death—that first week there are no limits to the kindnesses shown during the wake, the shiva, the enshrouding, the funeral, the cremation, the burial. Who needs a ride? Ironically, though, real support usually is needed later, after the ceremonies and food are finished.

Long-haul battles are indeed wars of attrition, and quitting is more than an option: I've found quitting actually is the expectation. And don't believe Hollywood sagas. We're a bored and restless race, humans, and we want quick and uncomplicated resolutions. Unfortunately, some struggles take years, or even lifetimes.

The cancer returning, and returning again. The trial when the accused keeps appealing. The addiction spiraling in endless circles and repetitions. The minor leaguer hanging in year after year. The missing in action never coming home from battle. And, now I've learned, the custody fight continuing and continuing.

It would be impossible for me to persist without support, and my support has been my greatest beacon. My mother, my siblings, Paco, friends such as Sam and Moe and Annabelle—if not for them, Ben would have forgotten my face by now, pondering it in the dark of a kibbutz. Few things in life are clear, yet I find critical support is an exception. I've allowed old friends to fall off me like scales. Because true support is either given fully, or not given at all.

And many simply grow bored of such trials.

Those of us at the center of these heartaches, we feel the impatience from you. We see it in the fraction of a second before eye contact is broken. We hear it in your "I see..." comment. We read it when your mind makes itself clear without employing words. Words formed but not spoken. You're *still* obsessed with this? You haven't given up yet? Why not let it go? Don't you want it all to be *over*?

Long ago I stopped caring about those who can't or won't understand.

*   *   *   *

And then there's the hardest concept of all to understand. Death.

303 · WILLIAM J. McGEE

I've worked a day shift and I turn onto our street and see it's completely blocked by emergency vehicles with flashing lights— NYPD, FDNY, EMS. My stomach constricts and I back out and park a block away, then walk to where a crowd has gathered near the corner. Kids on bicycles are laughing. I scan the throng and—*relief!*— spot my mother speaking to several neighbors.

She shakes her head. "Terrible, Mikey..." I look to where a rubber yellow sheet covers the front of a Kia, then turn back. She nods. "Jackie. That sweet, sweet man..."

"No!" I shout, nonsensically. "He always crossed at the green!"

Mrs. Ahearn clucks. "I guess God needed another angel up in heaven..."

"He's already got plenty!" I snap. "What about us?"

Within hours, it's online: *ARREST IN QUEENS TEXT DEATH.* A distracted 19-year-old didn't realize the light was solid red until Jackie splattered onto his windshield. It's a world in which both the crimes and the punishments never seem anywhere near proportional to each other. I feel anguish and anger. Then shame. My mother says to keep Jackie's mom in my thoughts and prayers. I tell her, "I do thoughts, not prayers."

Later I pick up Ben, and wait until he's in bed.

"Buddy...we need to talk about something. Something sad."

He picks at his blanket. "Divorce?"

"No. Someone died."

"Grandpa Tom?"

"No." I'm stroking his blond hair. "It was Jackie, buddy. He did everything right. He crossed at the corner. Waited for the green.

But this person—he drove through the red light. And he hit him. And Jackie died."

"So he's a bad person?"

I sigh. "Well…that's the thing. He did a bad thing. A really bad thing. But I dunno…maybe he's a good person. Good people can do bad things, buddy."

What the hell, LaGuardia! Somebody's got his head up his ass down there!

Ben keeps picking. "So God put Jackie in heaven?"

I nod. He's already had two years of Temple Tots, and he's on course for the Jewish path. Then there's Grandma Eileen, sneaking him to St. Rita's and talk of heaven when she thinks I don't know. But I won't assail any beliefs. Not at this tender age.

"My Grandpa Al should pray for him."

"Good idea. I'll tell him Jackie's name. Uncle Desmond, too."

"But we won't see Jackie anymore..."

"No, we won't, buddy. I'm gonna miss him too. I knew him since I was a baby."

We're quiet for a long time. "Daddy?"

"Yeah?"

"Who's gonna tell us they love us now?"

I pull him up for a hug. "I guess we will. That's gonna be our job now."

       *   *   *   *

Paco says Ben displays remarkable resiliency for a child his age, and I should be grateful. I am. Even if I wish he didn't have to display such remarkable resiliency.

*   *   *   *

I'm back in Kew Gardens, aimlessly lost on a Thursday evening, acting not like a native of Queens but rather like the many flight attendants from Texas and California who double and triple up in crash pads and call it Crew Gardens. Ben is at her mother's for a few days, and I'm consciously trying to use time without him to address long-standing issues. Squeezing in more sparring at Ring of Fire. Inquiring about re-entering graduate school. And putting to rest a would-be relationship that doesn't want to rest.

Once again, Gina contacted me. Only this time she was somewhat business-like in her tone. She fully understood I was focused on other things, but she would like to meet once—just once, please—to clarify a few things. What could I say? So now I'm looking for the agreed upon wine-and-cheese place near the school where she just landed a job teaching seventh grade English. Finally I spot the joint, but of course there are no open spaces. I spend another ten or 12 minutes circling aimlessly. There comes a time in every New Yorker's life when you deliberately park where you know you'll get a ticket—though hopefully not get towed—because cumulatively the fine is less than the aggravation. I squeeze the wagon in behind a minivan, but every inch of Lovey from Ben's car seat to the trailer hitch is squarely in a bus stop.

Gina's already there, of course, since I'm 15 minutes late. She's dressed in her teacher's yellow blouse and light summer skirt and looks more beautiful than ever; so beautiful I actually stumble saying hello and repeat that I'm sorry for being late. We shake hands like it's a business deal, and I settle in and ask about the new gig. She's cautiously happy, but it's only summer school and she hopes they ask her back in the fall.

"English. My favorite subject."

She seems surprised. "Really? A guy involved with airplanes?"

"Sure. What novels you gonna have them read?"

Gina swirls her glass of wine. "Good question...*Huckleberry Finn* has the N-word. *Catcher in the Rye* has the F-word. I proposed Alice Walker and they laughed at me. All these insane book burners and Board of Ed freaks out there. And that's in decadent New York." She moves her shoulders, as if literally shaking them off. "Screw 'em. Next week my kids'll meet Atticus Finch!"

I raise a clenched fist. "Preach." Then I ask, "How's Ashley?"

Gina smirks. "The one crying her little head off? At four a.m.? When Mommy has a new job?"

"Cutting a tooth?"

"Bingo. You're good, Mister Mullen. I'll give you that."

"I'd love to meet her," I blurt out; I mean it, though I had no idea I would say it.

Gina's reaction is a bit scary. She stares at me. And stares. But says nothing. Long seconds pass, and then it's as if she returns. And she quietly asks how Ben is.

"He's hanging in there. I don't know how. But he is."

She nods. "And...how're you doing?"

I sigh and tap the thick wine menu against my palm. That's my response.

"Oh, no. Lemme guess. Your house burned down. Right to the ground. Or...your horse died? Your big toe was amputated! Locusts! Frogs? All *ten* plagues? Am I close?"

I shrug. "Pretty much. I've been demoted at work. And I'm back in court. She's fighting for custody. *Again*."

Those gorgeous brown eyes grow even wider. "You've gotta be kidding me! After kidnapping a kid! Shouldn't she be in jail?"

"Um...not according to Judge Westphal. All charges were dismissed. We're starting from scratch. Rebooting. She could wind up with custody."

Gina's face falls, and she can't hide her concern. "Oh, Mike..." I may be wrong, but it's as though her guard lowers a bit. "I'm sorry."

"Thanks. So...I'm still pretty much a mess."

"You don't look a mess. How are you coping?"

"By punching a big heavy bag. I've taken up boxing."

The waitress asks what I'll have, and notes the lady's drinking pinot noir from the Willamette Valley. I order a tawny port.

After she leaves, Gina smiles. "Tawny port, huh?" She seems to be teasing me—though maybe not. Like I know anything about how women think. I stop myself; why separate human minds by gender? *How women think*. What absurd, divisive crap—more pop bullshit to sell books and blogs and radio shows. Women think like men think: with their brains. And I'm being rude by not responding.

"I started drinking it when I lived in Iceland."

"You lived in Iceland. See? I didn't know that."

"When I was in the Air Force."

She nods. "Ah. Well, thank you for your service."

I groan. "Oh, God. I hate that."

"Okay. Then screw you. I'm not thanking you for your freaking service. I didn't ask you to join the Air Force."

We laugh simultaneously, and it feels good. For a few seconds we just look at each other and don't speak. But I have to plunge right in, right where the nexus of + and - is sweetest. It's the same ancient story, the oldest of all stories. Some hairy guy went off to slay a beast and came back and another hairy guy was walking along with the hairy girl he liked, and they were giggling and pretending to give each other flats on the backs of their hairy heels as they wandered down to the watering hole, occasionally stopping so one could bump a hip into the other one. And the universe sent a sharp blade into the beast slayer's chest. It's the pain that unites us all, even though each of us carries his or her own flavor. In my case, it's a story extending from Tricia Conlin at St. Rita's to a cashier at Carvel in high school to three different classmates at Queens College to Airman First Class Rebecca "Becky" Truman down in Dover to right here at this table. That first time you see them holding hands in the cafeteria. Getting into his car. Slow dancing with him. It's the muscle reflex that never leaves you. And once again, I plunge.

"Was your boyfriend in the service?"

"My boyfriend?"

"The guy. I saw your picture…at Billy Joel."

"Oh!" Gina says. "I see."

She takes a nice swig of pinot noir as the waitress delivers my port. I wonder how many she's had. School ended hours ago.

"No," she says finally. "He's not the service type. He's more the type who uses every waking minute to make money. That type."

I nod along. "Well, he's pretty good-looking. From what I could see."

She laughs, and I'm thinking maybe the fermented dark grapes are having an effect. "You know, you guys are all too much. Always comparing dick sizes."

"Yeah. Pretty much."

Gina leans in. "Okay. I'll just lay it out. He *is* pretty good-looking. Although…well, it's not like he has blue eyes…" She smiles oddly at that and looks at mine. I scrunch my brow, but she's not done. "And he seems pretty rich. I don't know *how* rich. But he's got one of those new apartments in Long Island City. Facing the river. And he drives this…Model Seven or something."

I nod. "Seven Series. BMW. I think base price starts around eighty K."

"Yeah. That's it."

I keep nodding. "Well…you must be pretty happy."

Gina leans even closer and smiles at me. "I really am. I'm quite happy." I fight to keep as blank a face as I can; I asked for it. Then she adds, "Especially since we broke up about two months ago."

Something's happening now, though I can't really identify it. It's not external; it's *inside* me. And I don't think it's a nuts-and-bolts issue—nothing related to cardiac or pulmonary or digestive, nothing having to do with the many, many intricate moving parts that keep the show on the road. But it's happening, somewhere deep inside me. Something is opening. And I know it's real.

"Well, I'm very sorry to hear that," I tell her. And I break into a huge grin.

She holds up her glass. "To our kids…"

I clink. "And their lucky parents…"

We both drink in silence and I decide for once not to fill the void. In an odd way, it feels nice. But eventually Gina shifts nervously, crosses one exquisite leg over the other, and nods at me.

"So here's the deal. I mean…why I called you. It's actually about this guy. I wanna tell you the story."

I've got a half glass of port and a car that might very well be on the business end of an NYPD tow truck; where am I going?

"So last summer you said you were gonna call me. And then you didn't. And then last fall you said you were gonna call me—and you didn't. And then around the holidays I asked *you* out. Since…you know, it's not 1952 and all. But anyway, you blew me off. So far I'm right?"

Now it's my turn to shift nervously. "Well, I—"

"It's okay! Really! It *is*, Mike. I'm not busting chops. Just…setting it up. Okay?"

I don't respond, and she continues. "So, anyway…it's not like I have to go out with someone. I've gone years not dating. It's not like…a *need*. But then…this guy came along. I met him at my friend's wedding. On New Year's Eve. He asked me out and I went. And, yeah, he was good-looking. And, yeah, he had bucks. Like I give a crap. And…well, he was nice enough. In some ways. But…"

I simultaneously signal the waitress and lean in as I observe, "There's always a *but*..." Then I order another round and sit back.

Gina nervously jiggles that exquisite limb. "So...anyway. I was bugged about something. Not at first. I mean...eventually."

"What?"

"Well, after like the second date I asked him if he wanted to meet Ashley. And he was...kind of weird. The first time, he said it was too early. The next time—it was some bullshit about making it more *special* by waiting. Like...huh?"

"Sounds like Ben's mother. When she's not with him she only calls him once a week. To make it more *special*."

Gina looks horrified. "That's terrible!" Then she drains the rest of her pinot noir because the waitress is delivering the fresh round. We both thank her.

"Anyway...so I keep going out with him. And he's always making these big plans. Let's take a cruise, let's go to Mardi Gras. After one date he wants me to go to Guadeloupe. I'm like, why Guadeloupe? And he's like, there's a place with a topless beach, you'd love it. I mean...who asks someone to fly to a topless beach on the second date? Not that I have a problem being around topless people, but he doesn't know that."

"Not cool," I concur.

"And he's got all this money and yet he's a shitty tipper. Which is also not cool. I mean...I don't mean to dump on him. But that's something I hate. I worked as a waitress. And...I remember when we had iced tea. At the courthouse. And I saw you gave the waitress like a thirty percent tip. And I'm thinking, this guy is filing bankruptcy, but he's tipping waitresses."

"Actually," I clarify, "I had lemonade."

Gina laughs. "See, that's the type of geeky thing you do. Normally that would drive me crazy. Somebody saying something like that. But you say it, and it's cute." She shakes her head. "So, anyway. After two months of this he invites me out to dinner. At this place in Harlem. The Cecil. Hard to get a table. Big, big deal. And I just wanna settle this thing. Get to the bottom of it. Ya know? So I get dressed up and he picks me up on Queens Boulevard. He had this thing about not coming by the apartment. We drive into the city, and I'm thinking about that Frank Sinatra song. About taking shiny cars to Harlem? So we get there and I order half a lobster—what the hell, right?"

I nod. "Right."

"And so we're having a drink and I say to him, I don't want to pressure you. I really don't. But I'm a little hurt you don't want to meet Ashley. I mean…she and I are a team. You know? And we can do whatever you want. Very caj—just swing by the apartment. Or meet in the park. Or have lunch. Just so…the ice is broken."

Gina takes another healthy quaff. "So you know what he says? Huh? He says, you know that song *Jersey Girl*, by Springsteen? And so of course I tell him. It was written by Tom Waits, not Bruce."

"Although," I put in, "Bruce did add a verse."

She grins, and for the first time since we shook hands she makes physical contact, by reaching out and patting my bare forearm. "Ex*act*ly. So anyway, he says, well, it's like in that song. And I say, what're you talking about? And he says, well, that line about taking that little brat of yours and dropping her off at your mom's. That's kind of how I'd like it to stay with us. And he just smiles at me."

I get it, and I'm a bit stunned. And I mutter, "What a dick…"

"Exactly," agrees Gina. "What a *dick*. I felt like...somebody punched me in the *heart*. So I'm really just done. You know? I never gave a crap about BMWs. And all that. I'm just done. And I call the waiter over, and I say, can you give us separate checks? So I paid for half a freaking lobster I never ate. And I didn't have the teaching job then so basically I ate Ramen noodles for a week. And of course he's yapping about how he'll pay for it, and don't do this, and don't over-react, and he'll drive me home. And I'm like—*no*. I'm leaving. You're not dropping me on Queens Boulevard. Goodbye."

"Wow." I shake my head. "I don't know what to say..."

Gina sips, then shrugs. "What can you say? So now it's ten o'clock at night in Harlem and I'm looking for the 2 train but instead I wind up on the B train. Whatever. And finally I get on the subway and I sit down in my black dress and my best heels from Zappos and I just start crying. I mean...really crying. And I don't cry that much. But I'm *bawling*. Have you ever cried on the subway?"

I think of the Claritin ad the day Ben was born. "Yep." And finally, I act first, and reach across and squeeze her hand.

"And so I'm crying away and all of a sudden there's a Kleen-ex in my lap. And I—I mean, I didn't even see her. This old lady next to me. Looked like a Jewish bubbe from Rego Park. Or Forest Hills. Up in Harlem! At night! She says to me, 'He ain't worth it, honey.' And that's when it hits me, ya know? And I say to her, 'No! He *is* worth it, he really is!'"

Gina looks at me, and I'm not afraid to say I'm confused.

"I'm not talking about the dick. I forgot him about a block from the restaurant. I suddenly realize. I'm crying over this *other* guy. This dorky guy. You won't believe this guy! You know what he did?"

All I can do is shake my head. And drink.

"This guy is such a dork. He walks into a topless bar and he sits down with a half-naked woman who's spilling out of her clothes. And then he pulls out pictures of his *toddler*." Those eyes are dancing. "Can you believe it!"

That thing that opened inside me earlier? Now I know what it calls itself.

I manage a small grin. "I bet she was hot..."

Gina waves me off. "She was okay. But this dork...I mean, he's been driving me crazy. He was married to someone out of a fucking Stephen King novel. Excuse my fucking language. I'd like to smash her, the number she did to this guy. I mean...he's wrapped up tighter'n a damn mummy. And..."

"Yeah?"

"And...after two years—...*two*! He remembered my daughter's name. Ya know?" Her voice breaks and Gina gulps hard, swallowing air. But she continues, "And he even said he wants to meet her. And I've been dying to meet his kid. I mean, so he's the guy I was crying about on the subway. You know? Crying over some dorky, clueless guy."

I'm floating around above the table now; I don't really feel I'm *at* the table any longer. "I see..." I nod and squeeze that hand. "So what did the bubbe say?"

Gina barks out a laugh. "She said, 'Honey, some things we have to do for ourselves.'" Then this beautiful woman leans in and looks right into me. "So...now you know, Michael Mullen. Why I asked you here."

I sit up straight. "I get it."

She looks at me, then at the candle flickering off our faces; it's as if she sees it for the first time. Quickly, she runs her left hand over the flame, as if to test its potential to burn. She turns back to me.

"Here's the part where you tell me how you just remembered you've got that thing. And then you race out of here. See ya..."

For some reason, I run my hand over the candle as well, only I'm much more aggressive, and the flame actually does singe me a bit. Not that I care.

"Listen to me," I say. She looks and we lock eyes. "*Listen...*"

"I'm listening."

"You've gotta understand. What you're doing. I mean...you can say a lot of things about me, but you can't say I'm not being honest. I'm being brutally honest. The thing is, no woman wants to hear this. Some of 'em would throw their wine in my face. But Ben—he has to come first. For now. Until all this insanity stops. I'm sorry. But it has to be like that. Adults fuck up their own damn lives. But kids...we don't have the right to fuck up their lives. I mean, anymore than we will anyway. But we can't in*ten*tionally...I believe that if you have a kid, then the kid comes first."

She nods. "Duh! That's what makes you Mike Mullen. Why do you think I'm here?"

"But his mother—you've gotta understand. I have no idea what these courts are gonna do. I thought everything was good...and it's *not*. It just goes on and on. And she could take him anywhere. Indiana, Israel...the Moon. And I'd have to go right after them. That's just the way it is. Not forever. But for now."

A small grin starts at the corners of Gina's mouth. "I love travel."

"It could be for a while…"

"They have elementary schools everywhere."

I shake my head; she's just not getting it. "Jesus, Gina! It could be freaking Australia!" Where the water flushes counterclockwise, just like here.

She pretends she's singing a non-existent song. "We eat shrimp on the barbie. Ashley and I aren't kosher…"

"*No!*" I look up in embarrassment at the next table. "You're just *say*ing stuff like that. I mean…don't get me wrong. I appreciate it! I really do. More than…you'll know. I think about you constantly…*all* the time. I'll be sitting there…and I'll be wondering what you're doing." I breathe deeply. "You have *no* idea how much I want to be with you!"

A soft sigh escapes. And she whispers, "Finally…"

"But this is *real*. I mean…you should know. This is my fucked-up life."

Those brown eyes have never looked bigger. And she leans in so they grow even larger. "You know something? I don't think your life is half as fucked up as you think it is." She lets that sink in, then adds, "I bet Ben doesn't think so either."

Now all I can do is sigh, and slowly—as slowly as that dangerous molecular solid known as *ice* eventually breaks down to a less ordered state, and therefore fails to pose a deadly threat to aviators the world over—as slowly as that, I melt. "Don't say you weren't warned…"

"Do I look scared?" she asks.

"We'll see…"

And then, not like a woman who spends time with seventh graders, but rather like a woman who spends time with preschoolers, Gina sticks out her tongue at me, and laughs a silly yet sexy laugh. "You know, there's a psychological term for you, Mister Mullen. It's called...being a double cocky doody head. *No. A triple* cocky doody head!"

"Triple!" I cry. The ice breaks, and I soar. "I know you are. But what am I?"

"Your face and my butt!"

"Well, I happen to be made of an elastic substance," I inform her. "And *you* happen to be made of an adhesive substance. So therefore—"

With one hand, she reaches out and strokes my cheek, while with the other she knocks back the very last of her pinot noir; then she slams the empty glass down. "Okay, that's settled. Now...I've gotta get home. Ashley's asleep. But I've gotta correct papers. I'm paying for your tawny port. Then you can point me toward the E train."

I frown. "Negative. Number one, I'm paying. And number two...I'm taking you home. My car is a little less than eighty K. I mean, Blue Book. But at least it's made in the USA."

She runs her tongue over her teeth, in contemplation. "You can pay. But only if I pay next time. And you don't have to drive me..."

"Actually, I do. You're not taking the subway. Not on my watch. And you're not getting dropped on fucking Queens Boulevard."

She pauses for a moment. Then her answer is that full-blown Gina smile, the one I haven't seen all night. "Okay, sir..."

After the waitress thanks us effusively, we walk to my car; on one side of the street I'm on her left, closer to the curb, and on the other side I'm on her right, again closer to the curb. Just as my mother advised me. Miraculously, Lovey hasn't been towed nor ticketed nor molested in any way. I open Gina's door for her and as I round the rear of the wagon, I see her lean over to open my door, also something my mother advised me about. And this tiny gesture—incredible as it may sound—brings me more peace and joy than I've known in a very long time.

While I'm double-parked outside her building, we agree to re-boot this whole hot mess, and start with a tabula that is rasa. We're going to meet in two weeks, on a Saturday, which happens to be the day after I'm scheduled for a rematch in the ring with Hugo Concepcion, but I don't tell her that. I'm hoping I don't show up for this date with two black eyes. Yet I have a feeling it won't matter.

I walk Gina to the glass doors, and we wait while her mother buzzes. I consider kissing her, but I decide not yet. Instead, we hug.

"Say hi to Boo Radley," I tell her.

"*Arthur* Radley," she corrects.

*   *   *   *

"My *man!*" shouts Paco. Then he jumps up and channels his old mentor Jerome Robbins as he glides past the file cabinets; for a moment I think he'll dance on the coffee table, even though he's 72.

"Chill!" I say, but I'm smiling.

He slides back into his seat and leans toward me. "So? Where are we taking her for this date of ours? How should I dress?"

*   *   *   *

I'm at Donovan's Pub in Woodside, which some claim is home to the best burger in the city. But I didn't come for food or drink. It's a retirement party at the FAA's mandatory age of 56 for Andy, the guy who took over my shift when I was removed from my post. Hanging with drunk controllers from LaGarbage is the last thing I feel like doing, but it would be poor form not to appear.

I find the private party in the back room. It's free wings and potato skins but a cash bar, and I order myself a seltzer. Andy spots me pronto, which means I'm free to leave any time now, even though I just arrived. We chat about his new beach house in the Outer Banks. Of course, two aviation geeks can't discuss the Outer Banks without mentioning Kitty Hawk, and soon we're considering how Wilbur and Orville lived such very different lives, with one dying in 1912 and the other in 1948; the kid brother lived to see Chuck Yeager break the sound barrier. I wish Andy well.

Moe invites me to join the union reps at a small table, but before I can even plan an exit strategy, Bob M. quietly asks if I've got a moment. The union reps exchange meaningful glances as I follow him out. We wind our way through the party, back past the bar, and onto Roosevelt Avenue. Finally he turns to me, beer bottle in hand.

"You're looking squared away these days, Mike."

"Well, I've taken up boxing."

He winces. "I got my ass kicked doing that at Annapolis."

I smile politely, eager to move on.

"So...I've been back and forth. But after a few Amstels...I figured what the hell. I hope you'll listen to what I'm gonna say."

The 7 train screeches overhead en route to Citi Field. "I'm listening."

"You've really manned up. Since last summer. Your record is spotless."

"Thanks. I mean...considering I was never formally trained in changing printer cartridges."

He laughs. "See, still got the wiseass edge. But you've toned it down. You do whatever you're asked. You never complain. Your work's been excellent. Nobody can say a bad word about you."

I decide to laugh too. "I hope all the fools realize I suffer them much better now."

Bob M. sucks his Amstel bottle. "So...hear what I'm saying. But don't respond. Just think about it. Go home. Mull it over. Just *think*..."

"Okay." I ponder the agenda. The new movie about Sully Sullenberger's Runway 4 departure going into the Hudson River? (For the record, I was off that day.) The Congressional hearings on privatizing air traffic control? The governor's plans for the LGA makeover?

He draws a deep breath. "You ought to consider a transfer. Someplace...well, *any*place. Someplace where you'd be a bigger frog in a smaller pond."

I lean back, resting my foot against the outside wall of Donovan's and staring at the theater that became a church. "Why would I wanna leave one of the busiest facilities in the United States? And go somewhere smaller?"

"Because your career is dead here," Bob M. blurts out. "I mean...not officially. But I'm talking no ranks again. Just laying it out. You've got too much baggage here. Everybody you work with looks at you and thinks about one lousy fucking afternoon. Forget all the thousands of perfect shifts. And here's the thing—even if you're up for promotion? You'll never get it. Cause everybody'll scream, 'How can you promote *that* guy? After what *he* did?'"

I find I have no response. I'm not angry, and I'm not ungrateful. But he's hit me with a lot to digest. And for years now it seems like I've been continually hit with a lot to digest. Paco has this theory—he calls it his Stool Philosophy. Life is a stool, and most people have legs for Relationship, Career, Family, Pursuits, Pets, whatever you care about. You can have one wobbly leg, or maybe two, but you can't survive on three or more wobbly legs. And LaGuardia's been my most stable leg for a year now. Until this custody drama plays out, I can't handle more instability.

"Thanks. I'll think it over."

Bob M. shakes my hand. "I'm not bullshitting you. I'm trying to help."

Now I remember something. "So I have a question..."

"What's that?" He drains the bottle.

"Last year. The hearing. I heard you went to the mat for me. I was on my way out, and you saved my whole freaking career. What's left of it." I stare for a moment; he's a bit flushed and his eyes have narrowed from afternoon drinking. "Why'd you do it?"

Bob M. smiles. "I owed you one."

"Me? You owed *me*?"

He teeters for a moment, more shitfaced than I realized. "Yeah. That time two years ago. When you made me look like an ass-hole. In front of the whole shift. About babysitting my kids. Shit...I was *pissed* at you. Really pissed. For a long time. And then it finally hit me. Why I was so pissed. Because you were right, for God's sake! You *can't* babysit your own kids. You were absolutely right."

I laugh at this, and Bob M. joins me.

"Hell...my wife wants you over for dinner. These days I play golf one Saturday a month. The other days I'm with...them. Donna finally asked me...what happened? She thought I ended an affair or something. Finally I told her. Mike Fucking Mullen happened. Your name is a punchline in my marriage now."

Another 7 train screeches by, cars rattling as if they'll fall right off the elevated tracks and splatter on our heads. "Well, I'm glad I helped."

He asks if he can buy me a beer, but I pass.

*   *   *   *

Ben has news, even if he buries it behind updates about his friend Charlie's new bicycle and the blimp sailing over the park today when he was with Mommy. I'm serving him spinach pie and fruit cup and what we call Corn-on-Ty-Cobb, and pouring 2% milk into a sippy cup. After I get everything onto the table and Ben slides in, he chatters something about the baby and also about how Charlie's bike can—

I lean in. "What? Baby? What baby?"

He looks at me. "Mommy's baby."

"You mean...*you*?"

"No!" He gives me his Daddy-is-nutty look. "A *new* baby. Her *tum*my. I felt it."

"Her *new* baby..."

"The baby's coming soon. I have to *help* with it."

I sigh. Katie's right. Never a dull moment.

*   *   *   *

At the batting cages near Teterboro, I confide in Sam that Bob M. advised I transfer out of LaGuardia. He takes a few practice swings, then nods.

"I know it sucks to hear, dude. But...maybe he's doing you a big solid. It could be best. Trying a new venue. Hell, at least you live *here*. Towers all over the damn place. MacArthur, Farmingdale, Westchester, my dump...plenty more." He smirks. "And there's always John Fitzgerald Kennedy..."

Sam knows the world looks at LaGarbage as JFK's little brother, the old-school domestic dump that can't handle the big wide-bodies, the long-hauls, the internationals, while JFK is celebrated as the Ellis Island of the 21st Century. But the dirty little secret is we LGA controllers look down at Kennedy crews; our longest runway is 7,003 feet and theirs is 14,511 feet. Working LGA is like working an aircraft carrier in a hurricane. If I'm to take a demotion, I'd like to go further away than nine miles down the Van Wyck Expressway. But as always, my movements are tied to Ben; wherever the court says he will live is exactly where I will live.

I've just used my newly pumped up muscles to knock the crap out of about 50 balls, and my T-shirt is stuck to my back.

"There's only one LaGarbage," I reply.

Sam swings. "There's an old joke about this French guy, Pierre LaFitte…"

"I know. I think I told it to you."

"Well, then you remember the punchline. 'You suck just *one* cock and guess what people call you…'" He puts down the bat. "That's you, man. All those LaGuardia people remember that one fuck-up. So maybe it's time for new faces."

I change the subject to his impending stand-up gig. Once I had such pride in being among the very best at the most demanding airport on the planet. Now I've stopped calculating losses.

*　　　　　*　　　　　*　　　　　*

We're back at the VA Hospital in Fort Hamilton, Brooklyn. I drove here with Ben because things, as they say, have turned for the worse. Of course, betting against Tom Mullen Sr. has never been a lucrative undertaking.

We talk in a lounge with a sweeping view of New York Harbor. My father is frailer and less angry—*finally*—now that he's 75. Clearly the last months have taken a toll. Could he actually be frightened in a way he never was in DaNang or a thousand smoking tenements? The powerful and once-violent physique is now hunched, and nubs of bones protrude where they never protruded before— shoulders, chest, wrists. Undoubtedly he still believes he could climb an FDNY ladder while carrying a fully-grown adult, let alone Shi'anna Wilkins.

What I don't know is even he is recognizing limitations.

325 · WILLIAM J. McGEE

He plays with Ben on the cheap government-issued sofa. Amazingly, he's good with the boy, who giggles uncontrollably. Who knew my father had a way with kids?

He asks me fact-based questions about my situation—the judge's name. What's my lawyer saying? That's the court on Sutphin, am I right? Then he recalls a courthouse fire he once fought.

He points at my eye. "How'd you get that mouse?"

"Sparring. I've taken up boxing."

"Good. Toughens you up."

I don't bother explaining how Judge Westphal has toughened me far beyond Hugo Concepcion's abilities. He downplays his own condition—he's been in tough spots before. I supply the word "quadruple" when he falters.

I've had decades to hold him up to the light from every possible angle. By now I've let go of most of it. I'm sick of wondering if he's a product of nature or nurture. We all know how in March 1965 he landed with the first major American combat units in Vietnam. And none of us living in that tiny row house can really imagine what it felt like running into burning buildings, let alone running back in again, and again. But in thousands of ways, we've all stormed ashore as well. I've dissected all there is to dissect.

"It'll be a real tough thing if they take away your son," he says unexpectedly. I see there's no bitter irony behind his remark. In fact, he uses the word *son* as if it comes naturally to him.

Fathers and sons.

Ben's on his knees near the windowsill, staring at the Verrazano Narrows Bridge. He points to a sailboat off Coney Island.

Colors, numbers, letters—they all come together. He observes and recites at once: one red sail, two yellow, one says USA...

My father scratches at the hospital bracelet. "You the one fell in that time? Off the, um...catamaran."

I shrug. "Could've been anyone."

I know to him kids can be separated if you try hard enough, though they're easier to maneuver as a clump. Herd them close so they stick. Counting crewcutted and pig-tailed heads on the beach at Rockaway. Standing on the boardwalk on a Saturday in an FDNY shirt. His dark eyes taking inventory while slamming the wood-paneled tailgate shut on the station wagon. Saddle up, troops, we're moving out. Flicking ashes out the vent window, treating traffic on Cross Bay Boulevard as if it formed just to thwart him.

Mercury embossed in chromium script on top of the wood paneling. Mercury. A glob breaks off, and you corral it back into the mass.

Fathers and sons, I keep thinking.

And I recall the time he told Katie she was his favorite son. Such moments were the true mile markers, as he lived a separate and clearly happier life in The Nut House. Which is where he was when Lizzie died. In her one and only searing outburst my mother shouted at him that he was there to save Shi'anna Wilkins but he was nowhere to be found when Elizabeth Mullen died. I was lying flat on my belly in the upstairs hallway and heard it all—including his silence.

Now I watch him patty-cake with Ben. The lounge smells of iodine and spinach. I look at them and wonder just how many lives are really issued within the one life?

"We bought Grampa's black robe," Ben says.

Now the iodine's passed, and it's all spinach. "I think that was more your battleship gray, buddy."

"No, it was *black*," he says, stiffening.

My father stands. "Black, schmack." Ben breaks into giggles.

The old man puts out a liver-spotted hand for the boy, and the tattered robe flaps open, very nearly exposing him. I move with precision and speed and swoop down to block Ben's view. The elevator takes forever.

And I stare at those sailboats too, thinking my father had not one but six golden chances of a lifetime. I'm scared, more scared than I've ever been. I want nothing more than just to be there for Ben. And with Ben. Instead, New York State will decide if I'm fit to raise this child. If not, we'll start new and separate lives. They'll call it *joint custody*, but of course there's no such thing. It's a fraction of a childhood. A decimal.

Soon I may be joining that vilest subspecies of *Assholus Americanus*: a weekend dad. Silent trips to salad bars in chain restaurants. Awkward Sunday night drop-offs. Quick exchanges at the door about checks. Floating as I utter unreal lines to him.

We won on the karate, but I'm with her on this tattoo thing, buddy. Well, it's cool with me if you're getting sick of the place— next time we'll do Epcot. This is Cheryl—I've been telling her all about you.

You haven't said a word for more than an hour, buddy.

*　　　*　　　*　　　*

I'm on the New Jersey Turnpike, at the Molly Pitcher rest stop, the *CHECK ENGINE* light glowing since Staten Island. As instructed, I've brought $500 in small bills. And I've also purchased one plain cheeseburger, large fries, and a Fanta. I wait.

Someone I implicitly trust suggested I contact this person. He's supposedly an expert on custody issues, and he only offers advice off the record, for cash. And now here he is sitting across from me, in jeans and a ripped sweatshirt.

He counts the bills. "Cheese, nothing else, right?"

I nod. "I'm Mike Mullen."

He digs in. "I know."

As per the instructions, I update him on the law guardian and court-appointed shrink. Then I ask for guidance.

"Eeyore, huh?" He swallows more fries. "See…they're the underbelly of this corrupt system. Custody's an industry. A trillion dollar industry. Even if all the judges were honest—which they're *not*. All these parasites…lawyers, investigators, psychologists, accountants. They make money off misery. And they're corrupt to boot."

He asks if her attorney is from Queens; I say yes. What about my lawyer? She's Manhattan-based. He frowns. "This guardian of Ben's? And this Eeyore? They're probably bought and paid for. If I were you…I'd play it dumb with them. Don't reveal too much. Act like a bumpkin."

I ask him what else I should do.

"You've got a long-term problem." Now he shakes his head, gobbling his fries nine or ten at a time, like a video of a potato running through a grater backward. "Queens County. That's the most corrupt custody court I know. Queens sucks."

Finally, he stops eating. "You better prepare for the worst…"

I want to throw up.

* * * *

Acting like a bumpkin with Eeyore doesn't help. For a shrink, he's quite aggressive. Of course, he doesn't cultivate patients of his own since the county courts hand them to him. He's obsessed with the supervised visitation period—why did I go along with eavesdropping on her with Ben in public places?

Eavesdropping? Um…Judge Westphal decreed visitations were to be supervised. You know…um…because of that abduction business?

Yes, but truthfully—did I *enjoy* seeing her humiliated?

Later he mumbles something about the child's best interests, the secret password among those sucking at courthouse teats. And I note that *I* also want what's best for Ben. He stares and says, well, she's married and having a baby and they're buying—not *renting*—a house and she'll be home with the children. Doesn't that sound like a more stable life for Benjamin?

No, I say.

And why not?

It's not about mortgages, I say. Or babysitting. It's about who puts Ben's best interests first. *Always.*

He mumbles we're out of time. And Leon the parrot finally speaks: "Time!"

* * * *

"Don't forget! This guy Hugo. He's got a reach advantage. You've gotta stay the fuck inside on that bastard. Work the body."

This advice is not from Archie. It's from Paco.

* * * *

It's a Friday evening at Ring of Fire, and once more I'm facing off in a three-round battle with Hugo Concepcion. We're the last of four fights again. The small place is packed, and the hot lights have me lightly sweating as soon as the robe comes off. Archie's strong knuckles rub my shoulders and she continually whispers, even when I'm not listening. It feels like she put too much Vaseline on my face.

Ever since the Jersey Turnpike Man, I'm mad at the universe. Tonight I fight back.

"In the black trunks…from South Beach, Florida…Hu-go Con-cep-ci-on!"

I move continuously, as if standing still makes me a target.

"In the green trunks…from Queens, New York—" At this the crowd erupts, but of course they'd do the same for anyone from this borough, including hometown heroes like Donald Trump, Carl Icahn, Bernie Madoff, John Gotti. "—Mi-chael Mul-len!"

Hugo and I stare at each other in the center of the ring. At first glance, he looks the same. But while I've lost weight and toned up quite a bit since our last dance, I notice he's gone in the other direction and packed on more pounds. His arms and legs are no longer as defined, and there's a soft roll spilling over the waistband of his trunks. The ref finishes his bit and we both smack gloves a little hard-

331 · WILLIAM J. McGEE

er than necessary. In the seconds before the bell, I look around and see lots of strangers, including the odd presence of women other than Archie within these dirty walls. For some reason, many of these strangers are yelling at me, though I have no idea what they're conveying. As much as anything, they're probably reacting—positively and negatively—to the large shamrock Archie had them sew on the left leg of my emerald trunks.

Now we're off, and both of us come out quickly and aggressively. We're head hunting with jabs, though very few land on either side. I'm waiting, waiting, waiting. I want revenge for that head shot last year, and I'm determined to patiently get it. At this point, it's all straight rights and lefts. He cuffs me on the shoulder and I do the same, and then we get in close, and I drive a short, hard right into his navel and I hear him grunt. All those hours cranking out bicep curls with old-school metal dumbbells have sharpened my punches. The round seems to drag on forever—I jab, jab, jab his nose—and then finally I feel it coming. His entire body dips to the left as he winds up, and I move in quickly and land a hard right to the side of his head. Cold or hot, revenge is mine and it's sweet, as I watch Hugo stagger backwards and for a moment I think he may even drop. But those heavy legs keep him up, even moving in reverse.

Now it's my turn. I feel it. I know it. I stalk him back to the ropes, fake another right to the head, and both his hands foolishly come up high for protection. It's exactly what I want, so perfect it's almost scary, and I drive four unanswered punches—left, right, left, right—into his gut, my elbows moving like pistons. Hugo emits an animalistic sound, but it's not the *oof* cartoonists love to invoke. *Chuff! Chuff! Chuff!* Somehow through all the noise I hear Archie yelling, "Dat's it, boy!!" The bell clangs and I watch Hugo walk to his corner with his right forearm pressed against his lower abdomen.

Those strong dark hands rub my shoulders, back, upper arms as I drink and spit. There's more noise than ever, but I'm focused—like on a busy Thursday at LGA—so all those bleating voices fade away as I listen only to Archie. But for once, I disagree.

"He don't like dose wallops upside da nose. Keep doing dat, boy. Same spot."

"Uh uh." I accept the newly rinsed mouthpiece. "He don't...like body shots. Hitting him...in the belly."

Surprisingly, Archie doesn't argue, and now it's moot because she's pushing me off the stool even as the bell rings. I come out more cautiously this time, and so does Hugo. But there's a difference—I'm hunting. And he's prey. We've never exchanged a word in the ring, but it's uncanny how two fighters can read each other's minds. We both know this brawl is entirely different than Concepcion-Mullen 2015.

It's my fight to lose. And I'm sick of losing.

As we close in, I start snapping jabs at his head, partly to throw him off balance and partly to bring those arms up high again. He's throwing jabs as well, though most miss and the ones that don't have lost some sting; I'm already wearing him down. But once again, hubris makes an appearance. Just as I launch a right jab, my left drops ever so slightly, enough for him to send a sharp right cross to my eyebrow. It stings like hell, and I backpedal, concerned he may have opened a cut. Later I will see that the skin opened and folded back onto itself, like a tightly rolled empanada. I swat at my left eye with the back of my glove and see no blood, so I'm ready to resume. And here comes Hugo.

It's what I've been waiting for—he's coming in at me too quickly and far too awkwardly, almost tripping over his own feet. I step to the side and fake a left to his head and sure enough not just one but both arms come up again, and clearly he's lost his timing. My opening is here and I take it, planting my front foot and using my upper body, driving that Connecticut energy all the way up from my hip to my torso to my shoulder to my gloved fist. I drive a hard right hook deep into his navel, perhaps the hardest punch I've ever thrown at someone, so hard he spits his mouthpiece clear over my shoulder so it skips across the ring. I don't know how I can hear skipping above all the shouting; perhaps I imagined it. But then all my senses have never been so acute—I hear Hugo's moan, smell his sweat, see his eyes narrow. His mouth forms an oval, but I'm already following up, pivoting inside to plow another hook, this one a left, hard and fast into his liver. Actually—it's in the *area* of where his liver *should* be. But from the pain instantly registering on Hugo's face, I'm almost certain my gloved knuckles are compressing that delicate organ. My last punch—the last punch of the fight—is a right uppercut I bury in the same spot at his waistband. *Chuffff!!* I'm ready to throw a fourth punch in this combination, but as I draw back my left, I feel hands on my shoulder, and I turn and suddenly remember there's a ref in here with us as well. I look to Hugo, but he's fallen onto his right knee, and amidst the noise we all watch as he slowly slumps face down, his forehead barely touching the canvas, both arms wrapped around his middle. Archie is screaming—*screaming*—for me to hit the neutral corner, even though we know this ref can count to ten or even 20. Still, I move.

Already I realize that was the best series of punches I've ever thrown in the ring. The best I ever will throw. Every torque and twist and turn executed perfectly. And even as it was happening, somehow I knew this was a once-only moment, the type that recedes even as it occurs. I only wish it was Eeyore sucking that canvas.

And it's over. Hugo has stumbled to his shaky feet, his breathing labored. I approach him as we awkwardly throw our arms around each other's shoulders, and the crowd cheers even louder than during the knockout, which is saying something. The Borough of Queens: Home of Good Sportsmanship. Ha. He manages a tight smile and shakes his head while muttering something about *intestino*. Then the ref holds up my arm and I hear, "Michael *Mul*-len!!"

Victory. Elusive and long overdue. I'll take it. And I'll arise from this fiery basement a winner.

Now I'm sitting on the training table in Archie's office, sans shoes and socks and that irritating cup, in just the shamrocked shorts, waiting for her to return with fresh towels. The gloves and wraps are off and I feel a trickle of sweat on my forehead, and when I touch it I recoil. The adrenaline completely masked the pain of the bruise forming over my left eyebrow. But I feel it now.

The door opens and Archie tosses me the towels but doesn't step in; instead, she barks, "Pretty lady out dere. What da hell she wants wit you!"

So through the door steps Gina. And pretty isn't even the word. Compared to me, she's bundled up: jeans and pink sneakers and a top under a hoodie. For some odd reason it occurs to me that when we first met I was fully dressed and most of her torso was exposed. Now it's reversed.

"Hey, champ! I'm a day early for the big date. I came for an autograph…"

I'm thrilled to see her, more thrilled than I ever thought I could be. I know I'm smiling, because my lips—slightly swollen from the mouthpiece and a few straight rights courtesy of Mr. Concepcion—sting as those many tiny muscles express joy. Other emotions run alongside in an effort to keep up. Surprise. Confusion. Awkwardness over my bare torso. "Get it quick. Hanging up the gloves. Going out on top."

She moves to the table, leaning in next to me. "I never saw a boxing fight before."

I'm still smiling. *Boxing fight.* God, she's cute. "You saw the whole thing?"

"You bet. You looked pretty good out there." Her eyebrows rise. "Didn't know you were so built there, Mullen. Not bad. Cute too-chis in those green shorts…"

"How'd you hear about this?"

"Duh! I googled your name the other night. I get this weird…Ring of Fire site. With those lame-ass flames. I figure it's the wrong Mullen. But then it's like, The Pride of LaGuardia!"

She googled me? "Oh. Well…I wish I'd known you were…I mean, I'm really glad you came. I hope…hope, you know. Well, I'm glad I won. Anyway." I suddenly stare at her. "What would you have done if I'd lost?"

"Seriously? I'd be over at Hugo's room right now!" She shakes her head, but she's laughing. "Are you really this screwed up? I mean, really? You're not doing some bumbling act?"

I laugh too. "No. I'm the real deal. A genuine shithead."

Gina sighs. "God. I've gotta do everything myself." And she reaches over and gently touches my bruised eyebrow; involuntarily, I pull back slightly. "That hurt?"

"Nah. Well…a little."

She rummages through her bag, the only refuge of femininity in this place.

"I didn't see you out there. You have a good seat?"

"Good enough. Saw every damn punch. I liked it a lot more when you punched him than the other way around. I was sitting with Brendan O'Malley. A big fan of yours."

"Jesus!" I cry. She dabs at my bruise with a soft towel, and the sensation is the very definition of bittersweet. "He's like a hundred years old. Did he tell ya he fought in Sunnyside Gardens? Same card as Sugar Ray Robinson?"

She's holding what she wanted in that bag, but isn't showing it. "Yep. I didn't know what the heck a *card* was. Or who Ray Sugar was. He was very patient with me. I told him we're old friends and I came to see you. Then—right before you got hit. He says, 'He'll be socking your man in the left eye now.' And *bam*—that's what happened. Then later he says, right be*fore* it, he turns to me. 'Your man'll be socking him in the bread basket right about now.' And then, *boom*! You hit the guy in the stomach. I said to Brendan, 'How'd you *know* that?' He said he's been watching you. He said you're not much of a fighter, really. But you're a hell of a nice guy." And there's that smile. "I told him I knew that part."

"He said it just like I rehearsed him…"

Gina slides closer to me than ever; I can feel her hoodie against my bare torso as she looks over the bruise and keeps chatting.

"See how many tats he's got? More than Pink. I asked him if he had so much ink cause he's a millennial. But he didn't get the joke. He said one was his Navy ship."

She stops and looks into my eyes, but from a closer distance than we've ever shared. "Wanna hear something funny?"

I nod.

"After you won, he said to me, 'Your boyfriend did it, love.' And I said you weren't my boyfriend. And he started laughing and coughing. You know. With the missing teeth and everything. He's a cute old guy. He should be selling Lucky Charms."

"Yeah..."

"So anyway...know what he said? He said...'He's your boyfriend, love. No doubt about that.' And so I asked why, and he said it was from the way I looked at you during the fight. And I asked him, you mean because I cheered? When Mike hit the other guy? And he said, 'No, love, the way you looked when the other guy hit *him*...'"

And I wonder. I wonder how can it be my heart is beating harder now—sitting on a massage table, with no danger in sight? A half hour ago a large, strong man was trying everything he could to beat me senseless, and I was calling on fight or flight reflexes assembly-lined to me across millennia from cavemen. But at no time when Hugo stared at me over his gloves did my heart beat like it's beating now. Once more, words fail.

She dabs again at my eyebrow with a fresh towel, and finally I ask what she's applying to the wound. Gina seems hesitant, but she says, "I know it's the macho boxing place. But it's best for a bruise. So don't give me a hard time...it's diaper cream."

I laugh and shake my head. "Jesus!" She laughs too. "You trying to get me killed? Those guys out there—you have any idea? They see diaper cream on a ring wound? You'll find me in the dumpster."

"It's good stuff!"

I gently steady her wrist as she applies more cream. "One question. A and D?"

She seems startled. "What?"

"You know. I think it's called A *Plus* D. The *brand*. I've always used A and D."

Gina sort of slumps against the desk I'm facing. "Wow..."

"What?" I ask.

She's doing that thing again of staring at me. Seconds pass...

"You have no idea, do you? You really are clueless." She takes a deep intake of oxygen. "You are the hottest man I've ever met in my *life*. Because of this damn cream!" Gina holds up the tube and I see the brand. "It's freaking A and D. And you have no clue how hot you are. *None*. A guy who knows from diaper creams. I have dreamed and *dreamed* about a man like you. Someone Ashley..." She abruptly stops. "Well..."

I decide maybe words failing is not the worst thing, and slide down off the table. My arms are around her at last, and as we kiss I feel various parts of our bodies touching—jeans to bare thighs, hoodie to chest hair—the way waves lap at countless dunes before regrouping, only to come in and lap again, and again. I don't want the kiss to end. For the second time tonight, I'm close enough to hear someone moan, only this time I moan in response. Finally we separate and I stare into those eyes.

Gina smiles and shakes her brown hair. "It's about time..."

Romantical indeed.

I kiss her again, and her hand moves across my bare chest as she breathes deeply. "I came by subway. You know I don't have a car, right?"

"I believe you've ridden in my beat-up wagon? It's very loved. We call it Lovey."

She nods and brushes a sweaty lock of hair away from my eyebrow. "Why, yes. I'd be happy to accept a ride, Michael. Thank you for offering."

My wheels are spinning. "Where's Ashley tonight?"

"My mom, she took her to my sister's for the weekend. Out in Jersey. They've got little kids. It's a play date." She pauses. "Where's Benjy?"

I smile. "With my sister Katie. In the city. They're having a play date too."

Gina laughs, only this time it's a low and sensuous laugh I've never heard before, and now I'm concerned my reaction might be visible in the vicinity of the shamrock. Her smile is downright lecherous as she says, "Ya know...I'm gonna let you drive me home. And then...if you work it right. You could maybe have a play date too..."

"An *adult* play date!"

She grabs me by my bicep and pulls me to her as she bites her lip and then whispers: "Don't shower now. Just get dressed. I wanna smell you like this..."

It may very well be less than a minute later that we open the door to leave. I grab my oversized gym bag and lead the way as we hustle to the stairway. And then I pull up short. Because we're blocked by Archie and Brendan O'Malley, who obviously have been waiting for us. They stare at me, and Brendan breaks into crude laughter.

"Told ya!" He slaps Archie's muscular yet feminine arm.

My manager-slash-trainer shakes her head. "She'd do *hell* of a lot better'n him. *Hell* of a lot. Damn thick-headed boy. Tell him to hit 'em in da beak, not da gizzard. *Thick*-headed..."

As we climb out of the Ring of Fire, Gina says, "Come on, guys. You know he's not really a fighter."

*   *   *   *

The court-appointed shrink, Eeyore, focuses exclusively on Ben now. I take my son for an appointment and ask if I should join them. I'm told no, the door closing in my face. I scroll texts in the lobby, as Ben's session lasts a half hour longer than scheduled.

In the car, I tentatively ask how it went. Ben smiles. "He's got a parrot. Leon."

"I know."

"Maybe we'll get a parrot."

I sigh while changing lanes on Queens Boulevard. "I dunno, buddy. It's hard. I've gotta go to work and—"

Ben shakes his head. "No. I mean...*us*. Me and Mommy and Kasper. And the new baby. Maybe we'll get a parrot. For *our* house."

*   *   *   *

"So you won't tell me about the sex?" demands Paco. "I'm fucking licensed!"

I say no, but my smile speaks volumes.

He nods. "My friend, if you've got the head, the heart, and the fun zone—then in the relationship game, you won first prize."

About that night we left Ring of Fire and went to Gina's place: It was like something out of a 1970s movie. We tore off clothes and threw them where they landed. No need for details, other than to acknowledge it was a more than memorable 36 hours.

It was one of those weekends when you forget to eat. In fact, at one point Gina said she forgot how to walk, and joked about being bowlegged. The only time we interrupted the festivities was to call our kids on Saturday morning. By that evening I finally realized I hadn't consumed anything since Friday afternoon and then had engaged in intense and vigorous athletic activity—as well as winning a boxing match—and so we called her local pizza joint and they delivered. I would soon come to learn just how much food Gina could pack into that curvy little frame of hers. We ate standing up in the kitchen, savagely tearing out sections of the triangular slices in odd trapezoidal fashion, sauce dripping onto our chins and chests as we giggled and wiped at each other. Then we finally decided to scrub up and took a shower together. Before it was over we were back in bed, still damp.

We worshipped each other's bodies, heaping praise and complimenting every nuance and quirk. When she first unbuckled my jeans and got past those stupid green trunks, she pretended she was davening like a rabbi and whispered praise, "Todah, Lord!" And when I finally beheld her in her glorious natural state I channeled a Texas evangelist and cried out, "Oh, thank you, dear sweet baby Jesus!" But beneath the joking was the oh-so-sweet recognition we truly appreciated each other, and we both know what it's like not to be appreciated.

In between, we shared our life stories. Besides her mom, she has an older sister Sharon with a husband and two kids in New Jersey, and a younger sister Rachel who's in graduate school in Boston, studying Interior Design. Gina grew up in Forest Hills, but spent two years at Tulane University, not because she loved the school, but because she always wanted to live in New Orleans and at 18 figured now was the time. She dropped out at 20 when her father was killed—in an airplane crash of all things.

I had my arm wrapped tightly around her, staring at the ceiling, and she was speaking softly into my chest when she told me this. I gently asked a few particulars, and was surprised it rang no bells, but later I looked up the accident in the National Transportation Safety Board database. He had connected on a regional airline in Detroit to attend a medical supply convention in Rochester, Minnesota and they went down in thick fog; pilot error. Gina was devastated, and spent a year at her mom's, smoking pot and watching TV. It wasn't until later, while researching her father's death, that it hit me: This is the same woman who wanted to take me to *Charlie Victor Romeo*, the play about fatal plane crashes? She has a way of surprising me.

Afterwards, she spent a year in Maryland, where she discovered she loved teaching when she volunteered with AmeriCorps. ("Thank you for your service," I said, and she punched me in the arm.) Eventually she enrolled in Queens College and began working for the cruise line. Then she married a friend of a friend, and along came Ashley.

Gina plays folk guitar—really well. She loves Indian food, but not lamb and never goat. Her right eye is just slightly larger than her left; in fact, this type of asymmetry is duplicated in another area of her anatomy. Like me, she loves the Beatles, but unlike me, she also listens to Kanye. And, yeah, I learned she's one hell of a pole dancer; the girls at the club taught her during breaks. That tattoo near her navel is her only one. She's afraid of clowns, and plans to write in Bernie Sanders in November. When I make her laugh very, very hard, a snot bubble will grow right out of her nostril. Her favorite novel is *The Unbearable Lightness of Being.* Like me, she recently started bike riding again. And like me, she never uses Uber or visits Walmart. Unfortunately, Gina occasionally roots tepidly for the Yankees, but I'll address that. Her pinky toes are extra small, a trait the Internet claims indicates playfulness. She's a terrible driver and not much of a cook.

Now I'm more deeply in love with her than I've ever been with anyone in my life, though I haven't told her. But I did tell Paco.

A funny thing happened early on Sunday morning. We were sleeping—finally—and suddenly I jolted upright because I thought I heard Ben. For a moment I envisioned us waking up to see Ben and Ashley entering our bedroom. This is the life I want to give Ben: roots and stability and consistency. As for me, without my son, there is no family.

By the time I left to get Ben later that morning, the world had shifted. Yet again. Only this time it wasn't due to Eli Lilly and Company's most famous anti-depressant.

One week later, I came for dinner and met Ashley—along with Gina's mother, who told me to be thankful she cooked. After we dug into the strudels I'd brought from Junior's (both apple *and* cheese), Gina told her daughter I talk to airplanes and they talk to me. Ashley shook her head and told us we're silly, since airplanes can't talk. Later, she let me read to her from one of her favorite books,

Priscilla McDoodlenutDoodleMcMae Asks Why? (I felt a twinge when I saw the author was bestowed the "Mom's Choice Award," but I let it go—later I showed it to Gina and told her there are too many battles and not enough resources to fight every single fight.) Within weeks I met both sisters, although Rachel will always be my favorite since she turned to Gina and said, "You're right—he does have cute blue eyes." Days later, Gina met Ben at the park, and together the two of them beat me at Wiffle ball when both runs scored while I pretended to stare at a 747 approaching JFK. After Ben fell asleep, I watched her gently brush his hair from his eyes. Gina met various other Mullens in short order, even my father, whose behavior was exemplary. Later it was my mother who shocked me; after calling Ashley a little doll and Gina a very sweet girl, she added, "And she's got some cute little figure on her."

"Yeah?" I responded nonchalantly. "I guess so."

"Oh come on!" said Eileen Mullen. "She could be one of those...exotic dancers." Katie laughed a little too hard, until she caught my death glare.

Surprisingly, it was Katie who came around last—there's no doubt she's vicariously gun-shy on my behalf. But to her credit, the first meeting between Ben and Ashley took place when Katie invited us for brunch, which went so well Gina and I laughed in relief. Ben was quite solicitous of "the baby," and even helped her poke a straw into her juice box. Afterwards, he and I aligned chairs in the living room to play our favorite game, Airplane. Ben is always captain and I'm always on his right as first officer. But this time I suggested Ashley be captain and Ben be first officer; I could be the flight attendant serving Chris, the passenger. Ben considered this and asked, "Can you *do* that? Isn't that a *lady?*" I explained both boys and girls can be flight attendants—as well as captains. My shoulders tensed as I feared the worst. But Ben just nodded and sat to Ashley's right, showing her how the nonexistent controls work.

I heard later—from both parties—what Katie and Gina discussed during all this. My sister brought her another mimosa and they chatted about Katie doing voice-over on a video for Gina's students, then joked about the movie trope that two women can't discuss any topic other than a man. Finally Katie said, "Can I ask you something?"

Gina nodded.

"Mike sort of told me...about warning you. I mean, his life being a mess. The thing is...it's all true."

"I know."

"Yeah. Well...he's in such a bad place. It's not just the Psychotic Bitch From Hell. But all of it—his job, the debt, the depression. I mean, five years ago, five years from now—who knows. But right now this guy's in the worst place in his life."

Gina nodded. "I know. But in a weird way that's good, no?"

"How's that?"

"Well, relationships—they're sort of like job interviews. In the beginning, you know? You never really know about someone. Until stuff happens." Gina watched me pouring imaginary orange juice. "I've seen this man at his absolute worst."

Katie watched too. "See...I'm Mikey's biggest fan. Even though he can be a pain in my ass. So I get him. But...he *is* in the middle of a shitshow now, Gina. He's broke, and he's...battered. Hurting. Who knows what that judge is gonna do...how he'll take it.

So I'm gonna ask you. No offense and all. But I mean…why him? I mean, why now?"

Gina laughed and pointed at me, as the game transitioned from Airplane to a new game Chris invented, Air Rage. She pretended to throw imaginary juice on my imaginary uniform, while I called on the imaginary intercom for Captain Ashley and First Officer Benjy to turn this plane around at once and begged Katie to be an air marshal.

"Are you kidding?" Gina asked. "Just look. You can look at that man with those two kids? And ask me why I'm freaking crazy about him?"

Apparently, that's when Katie hugged her. Then ran off to be an air marshal.

*   *   *   *

It's been a year since I've gotten another missive in my mailbox from the cowardly, illiterate cretin. I've almost missed them.

What I don't know is Bob M. spotted the individual in the act and promptly told this person if it happens again, he would personally sign the transfer to Minot, North Dakota. In January.

*   *   *   *

Once again, I need to deliver a certified check to Hillary, or once again my attorneys will cease working my case. Ben joins me for the subway ride into Manhattan. In the elevator on Lexington Avenue, I lift him so he can press the button for the 19th floor. Then we discuss—at length—why there's no 13th floor. A young woman turns and thanks us, saying she's always wondered about it.

Ben and I chat with the receptionist as we wait for Hillary. And now it hits me. My attorney and I have been at war together across four years, fighting on three continents and logging endless emails and phone calls and court appearances, recording defeats and victories and more defeats, all to the tune of about $400,000. But, ironically enough, Hillary has never even met Ben.

The MacGuffin. The Holy Grail. The Pot o' Gold. The infant issue. The brass ring.

Hillary emerges and says hello, then realizes I'm not alone. Her face breaks into a smile as she leans down. "And who is *this*?"

I pat his head. "The Fruit of the Marriage."

*   *   *   *

It's our second play date this week. On Wednesday, my off day, I sent Gina a dozen red roses using a new credit card and when she called in shock, I quietly explained I knew it was the anniversary of her dad's crash; she seemed speechless, and quickly hung up. Then an hour later she called from the park. While the kids napped in the back seat, I tried teaching her parallel parking for her upcoming road test and we promptly had our first spat—I shouted she was gonna take off the damn fender! And she shouted I should chill the hell out! For several seconds I thought, well, that's that—another doomed relationship. Then we stared at each other and burst out laughing. Later I helped her devise essay questions for *To Kill a Mockingbird*.

Now it's Saturday and we're at Gina's apartment. We had such a great day; the sprinklers, followed by dinner and a themed evening: frozen yogurt coupled with a viewing of *Frozen*. Ben was told it was a girl's movie by Jeffrey in daycare, so we had a chat about movies not having genders. It's late and both kids have stayed up past their bedtimes. With Ben, that means heavy eyelids and gradually nodding off. But apparently with Ashley it means a total meltdown. Gina gets her into pajamas, but she cries and cries, and nothing—not a *Caillou* DVD, not rocking—nothing can ease those tears. Ben catches my eye and shrugs, as if to say: "Kids! What can you do?" Gina apologizes and I tell her don't be silly.

"Let me have a try," I say, picking up Ashley and holding her in a cradle lift while gently preventing her legs from kicking. She grows limp. And then I sing, but at first it's so soft it's more like whispering.

I sing *Jersey Girl*.

Initially she fights me. But eventually those small eyes flicker and then close, and I walk slowly toward her bedroom. Gina and Ben follow us. As I continue singing.

I know from small kids faking sleep, and she's out for good now, but still I won't chance it. Better to finish the job. I keep singing.

I'm rocking where I stand, while Gina tries to slow dance with Ben, softly so as not to wake the baby. But he bores quickly, and scoots back into the living room.

Gina joins me on the *Sha-la-la-la la-la-la*. Then ever so gently she lowers the safety bar and I ease myself onto the tiny toddler bed beside Ashley. I move her into place and pull the covers up to her chin and smooth her hair. Now I can stop singing.

But I turn and see Ashley's mom is kneeling beside the bed, her face just inches from mine. I smile at her and suddenly notice she's crying big wet tears. Before I can react, she grabs my face with both hands and pulls it toward her own, resting her forehead on mine. "You have no idea how much I love you," she whispers.

"Hey!" I whisper back. "That's against the rules. The dude's supposed to drop the L-word first."

She vigorously shakes her head, spraying tears on both of us. "Uh uh. There's a loophole. If the dude is a geeky dork who talks to airplanes…and sends red roses for the sweetest reason…then the chick gets to say it first."

I smile and kiss a tear. "Well, good to know. Cause I really, *real*ly love you…"

And I realize even now that just as *Molly Malone* belongs to Ben, from here on in *Jersey Girl* will belong to Ashley. Though never, of course, will I include the verse about dropping that little brat of yours off at your mom's. But I'll sing this song forever.

And I'll whisper it into the ear of a sweet young woman at her wedding, after she's asked to dance with her father.

*   *   *   *

I'm at work when I receive the email from Hillary, advising me the State of New York is ready to decide the fate—yet again—of one Benjamin Cohen Mullen. I'm to be in court Thursday afternoon for the decision.

On my break, I spot Moe on the 14th floor and tell him. He says he hopes I win. I thank him, but add that since the beginning I've always fought for *Ben* to win, so he could have *both* parents in his life.

Moe says, "I understand." Then he winks. "May the best man win."

      *   *   *   *

I'll admit the sudden emergence of such happy times with Ben and Gina and Ashley has me dreaming in ways I haven't allowed myself to dream in a very long time. The words of the Jersey Turnpike Man chill me, yet I nurse hope that somehow—*somehow*—Ben and I will be together, and not just every other weekend, or two out of every 14 nights, raising a seventh of a child. But I've learned dreaming can be dangerous.

      *   *   *   *

And now it's just my son and me.

It's a summer of concepts, but this is a difficult concept for us to work out together—what will our future be? I've played it absolutely high road, and never once did I discuss with Ben where he might want to live. Or suggest what he might want to say to the lawyers and shrinks. Now it's time to ask.

"Buddy, we need to talk."

He's had his bath and is in fresh summer pajamas. We've moved the Thomas the Tank Engine train board into his room, and he's on his knees sorting tracks. I sit on the edge of the bed, looking down at his back.

"We gotta talk…"

"Okay." Ben doesn't look up.

I cough. "Tomorrow…well, Mommy and I are going to court. The judge is gonna tell us about where you'll live."

"I know."

"You know?"

"Yep. My lawyer said so."

I regroup. "Okay…well, they're gonna want to know what *you* want. And—"

"I know. I told them." He turns to me. "Daddy, how come the bridge isn't glued?"

"You got the bridge later. After Christmas."

"Oh!" He turns back to the board.

Again, I cough. "So…you told them. What you want?"

"Yep. Daddy, we can move the bridge. Near the tunnel. See?"

"Maybe. If you move the Sodor crane…"

"Yeah!"

I watch him deftly rearrange his little world. "So, buddy…you already decided. I mean…what you want? Where you want to live."

He continues working while speaking. "I told the man with Leon the parrot. And my lawyer. I have to live with Mommy."

Time passes, but I don't know how much. Outside it's late evening in late summer, my favorite time as a kid, and birds are still chatting. I remain seated, perfectly still. Ben slips in new tracks, continually testing configurations. Finally I summon my livelihood—my voice. "You *have* to…live with…Mommy?"

"Uh huh. She said so. I have to help with the baby. She said she can't have the baby without me. I have to help her."

I move both hands to my face, unnecessarily since Ben remains rapt. My own breathing sounds amplified. I prepare to speak again. "So...that's what—..." I pause. "That's what...you told them. You wanna...live with...Mommy?"

"Uh huh." He attempts to squeeze both tunnel and bridge into place, but something will have to give, and it won't be the laws of physics.

"Buddy...are you okay? I mean...did it make you...*sad*? Having to...*choose*?"

And now Ben turns to me, all blue eyes and blond hair and baby teeth that will fall out and grow back in again. He smiles at me. "I told them it's okay."

I can't speak any longer, so I nod instead.

"I told them. I said my daddy always comes to see me. Everywhere. So I'll live with my mommy 'cause you'll come see us. No matter where we live. So you'll be happy. *Every*body'll be happy. You'll come see me, Daddy. Right?"

All I can do is nod again, vigorously.

"Daddy?" I open my eyes wider as a form of response. "Will you help me with the bridge?"

Most of the time the thing we fear more than anything never appears. Thankfully. The 18-wheeler doesn't jackknife in the rain, the missiles remain in their silos, the mole turns out to be just a mole. But sometimes our very worst fear takes shape and breathes and appears right before us, staring in defiance. My fear of fears—that my son and

I won't share his childhood on a daily basis—well, here it is. In full force. Just as I always knew. The only emotion I don't feel is surprise.

My voice is a sort of gurgle from a poorly dubbed movie as I blurt out, "Be right back!"

Now I'm running toward the bathroom, and I do what I never do when Ben is in the house: I not only close the door, but even lock it. I flush the toilet, then run water into the sink at full volume. Finally I bury my face into the nearest bath towel. Somehow I slump onto the side of the tub, undoubtedly causing the bruise on my lower back I don't feel now but will discover tomorrow. I sob and I sob and I sob, screaming in pain into the wet towel, smelling Toy Story 3 bubble bath even as I suffocate as many emotions as I can. I hear tapping on the door and mumble *I'll be right out.* All the other pains up until now—it's as if they were just preparation, like the jabs and crosses setting up that knockout of a hook.

And I have to make a decision. Not at my leisure, and not after consultation and reflection. I need to decide—*right now.* I need to decide what kind of man I am going to be. Immediately.

Ever since I was six years old I've wondered if I was capable of charging into a blazing room to save a child I never met. But courage takes so many, many forms and extracts so many, many tolls. I'll probably never know. But I do know this child. And I'm determined to do all I can to save his sanity and nurture his robust little soul.

Later Annabelle will explain I was battling seven million years of Oedipal complexes, but that's too simplistic. Ben has proven to be the wisest of the many allegedly wise people considering his fate; he is offering judgment by serving as his own Solomon. And he is handing the sword to me, not his mother.

Soon, Paco will observe I've received the greatest compliment a child can bestow—the gift of complete and utter trust.

You'll come see me, Daddy. Right?

And so now the court battle is over. It doesn't matter what those in power will tell us tomorrow, and it doesn't matter whether they're honest or corrupt. I've stopped fighting. Because as always I'm squarely on Ben's side.

Fathers and sons.

"Daddy…"

I rub my face raw with the Minions bath towel, and see my eyes are red and my hair is rumpled. "Yeah!" I yell.

"Daddy!"

I unlatch the door and see him standing before me.

"Daddy…are you *sad*?"

"*NO!*" I croak. "Tired…"

He smiles and pulls me by the hand. It's late, but we spend five minutes tending to the train board. Then while Ben brushes his teeth I scan his bookshelf. He returns and casually leans against me, his arm around my back.

"Can I pick tonight?" I ask. Ben nods. And I hold up: *We're Very Good Friends, My Father and I.*

Ben is asleep before we finish. I don't sleep at all.

*　　　　*　　　　*　　　　*

I put on my Court Suit, which is a little baggy now. But the process is much less formal than I envisioned; the judge and even her assistant are absent, and the law guardian simply hands out typed copies of the decision to both parties, right in the hallway outside the restrooms. I flip to the final page:

> *Therefore the duly-appointed Law Guardian, in accordance with the wishes of the Child, recommends the Court award Joint Custody, with the Mother as Custodial Parent.*

I pull Hillary into an empty conference room and tell her I won't appeal. She registers complete shock, and begins citing mitigating factors. I shake my head; she tells me to sleep on it. I tell her *not* to reveal this to the other side, and instead bluff for now.

We step outside, confronted by the defendant. To my complete surprise, she speaks to me: "Don't forget Benjamin is with me tonight. We'll pick him up at six."

*   *   *   *

I've kept communication to a minimum. I called my mother from the lobby, and asked her to please pass along the verdict to the family. Then I texted Gina and Paco, but decided to speak to all others tomorrow. Instead, I drove straight from the courthouse and supervised Ben's hand-off to Rabbi Cohen at my mother's place. Then I walked home. There were multiple voicemails and I started with Paco: *Courage, my friend. We can't control the fucking universe. But we can control what it does to us—*

I shut off the phone and stretched out on the living room sofa.

That's where I've been for hours. In fact, I have no idea what time it is, though judging by the opacity of the curtains the summer sun has all but set. Now the doorbell rings and I jump up fast. The lights are off, so I quickly consider sitting quietly in the dark. Instead, I open the door and find Gina standing on the stoop wearing shorts. And the Mets T-shirt I bought her last week.

I realize now that Gina and I are through; I simply don't have the energy to continue.

A Chevy from Four Ones Car Service pulls away from the fire hydrant. *We do this for a living,* the driver noted when Ben was born.

"Hey," Gina says.

"Hi…"

She tries a partial smile. "Sure. I'd love to come in. Thanks."

I follow her in and we both sit on the sofa. If it weren't for the refrigerator in the next room, I might think I was deaf. She moves closer and takes both my hands in hers.

"Don't be pissed at me. For doing the drop-in. I *had* to…"

"Uh huh."

"I mean…I called. Texted. Emailed. DMed. I was gonna try smoke signals…"

"Uh huh."

She squeezes those hands. "I know…your heart…it's *aching.* It's in pieces. I know. It's the worst day of your life. My heart hurts too. Cause I love you, honey. I want only for things to get better."

I shake my head. "Things ain't getting better…"

Gina tries hugging me, but my posture is too rigid. "I wasn't gonna leave you here alone. I don't know exactly…where we are. What phase…*plateau.* What it's called, the name. If it has a name. I just know…I should be with you. And I know you should be with me. And I can't let you…*cocoon* like this. Alone in the dark. Like Boo Radley."

I shrug. "I would've called you. Tomorrow, Saturday…"

"I wanna be with you *now*. When you need it most."

"I'm okay…"

"Honey…people in love—they're there for each other. In real time. They don't go off for a few days and come back. That's the whole point—it's good *and* bad. You don't do it solo."

It takes a tremendous effort to speak, and to speak clearly. Soon my voice—my instrument, my calling—this voice will fail me yet again. "You shouldn't…see me like this. I mean…tonight. Let's talk…the weekend."

Gina shakes her head. "No, honey. It doesn't work like that. If I were hurting…wouldn't you be with me?"

I quickly nod. "*Sure…*"

"So why can't I be here?"

My eyes are closed. "Gina…"

"Yes?"

"Gina, cause...you're not gonna like…what you see."

She moves my head with both hands, almost a wrestling takedown, and rests my face on her chest. Then she whispers. "I love you, Mike. I'm not leaving. I'm here, honey. You can't get rid of me." She pauses, then says it again: "I'm *here…*"

I'm starting to shake, and I almost pull away. But I find I've finally lost all my strength. The tidal forces overtake me, and I use my last reserves of energy to fall against her, and wrap my arms around her. I give in to her, and I give in to what I've been carrying for the last day. And now it's all coming out. My entire body lurches in her arms. Gina strokes my hair, kisses the top of my head, whispers of love and devotion. Promising she'll stay with me forever.

I have no choice, and even though my eyes are shut tight I hold her even tighter. Blindly, I trust her.

*   *   *   *

Now I've finally had sleep to digest the court's decision, and Ben's decision as well. I step outside with Gina, still wearing her new Mets shirt, and we behold a beautiful morning as I prepare to drive her home. Just as it did on the night Ben was born, amazingly the world is functioning pretty much the way it had yesterday.

*   *   *   *

The papers are signed and notarized, and we've finally reached the point I thought we might never reach. We're done. I take a last look at the Honorable Rhonda Westphal.

In my *courtroom, unless the mother is a prostitute or on crack, she is always awarded custody.*

We step into the hall, as both attorneys excuse themselves for restroom breaks simultaneously. I can't recall the last time the defendant and I were alone together. But I find I have nothing left to say.

*   *   *   *

It's a year of changes—for me, my son, all of us. And not just the summer. As 2016 slides into 2017 it's all about change, from the Chicago Cubs to Donald Trump.

I'm served with papers again—hopefully for the last time—and start paying 17% of my salary in child support. This on top of Ben's medical and educational expenses and maintaining a second home for him—an additional bedroom, food, clothes, books. And on top of raising my newly adopted child.

Some things I know. After these four summers, my life could never return to that particular hellishness of 2013 through 2016. A cooling process occurs, and I'll attempt to broker peace through Gina, Kasper, lawyers, psychologists, rabbis. As much as I can, I'll make a conscious effort to live outside her sphere. At times she'll flare up in small and petty ways, like inserting the hyphen. Occasionally I'll need to fight anger, particularly so it doesn't spill over to my wife and son and daughter. But I'll learn to disengage. Paco will say, "She's a walking anger management seminar. You should pay her." And I'll reply, "I do."

Often I'll feel pity for her, and wonder what was really churning so deep inside her when I had no idea. I can do nothing to assume my son's burdens, so I'll watch him struggle. But Paco's words bring comfort: She too loves Ben and he'll always find means to broker peace. We'll call upon the village, and the results will be mixed. We'll encounter dishonest pediatricians, weak teachers, and cowardly rabbis who won't always align with Ben. But we'll also encounter caring people who intuit my son's specific needs and assist him in finding his way. And I'll be forever grateful.

Back in court, we insist they live no more than 100 miles from Queens. Yet even as we negotiate, they're in escrow on a house in Cherry Hill, New Jersey, close to the small college where Kasper teaches. And 97 miles from Queens.

*   *   *   *

As usual, Wayne was dead wrong: *I* went home with the waitress. We'd both done big weddings, so this time we exchanged vows barefoot in the sand on Long Beach Island at sunset. My best man was considerably shorter than me, but the maid of honor was even shorter. We were married by a justice, though my cousin Desmond gave her high praise, and Moe and Eliot even booked her to officiate for them. Then the photographer lined up all my mother's grandchildren for a beautiful photo at the water's edge; Tommy and I exchanged bittersweet glances, knowing what a Christmas present it would have made.

There was dancing by torchlight under tents Tommy and Terry erected in front of the rented house. Katie and Moe twisted, while Paco—who did indeed wear that ascot I knew was in his closet—tangoed with Annabelle and Gina's mother; thankfully the bride talked her friend Sheri out of pole dancing. Archie was invited but wouldn't come. Sam took over for the DJ and spun *Rock the Casbah*.

Late in the evening—after several kids and my father had fallen asleep—my two brothers poured three shots of Jameson; being a secular humanist is one thing, but even I'd never drink Protestant swill like Bushmills. Kevin smiled at Gina, her dress hiked to her thighs as she danced with Ben. Tommy indicated Ashley, stretched out across two chairs with flowers still in her hair. My brothers toasted me and my family, reminding me just how lucky I truly am.

And then a surprise. Gina produced her guitar and sang to me. I learned later she consulted with Ben, and he made the suggestion.

The one about the people. *In My Life.*

Soon after, Ashley really did become a Jersey girl.

Now it's a Friday night and I'm scheduled—as per Queens County, which retains jurisdiction even in another state—to meet Kasper for a drop-off on the turnpike. At work I noted cold fall weather arriving, so I brought Ben's winter coat.

My bankruptcy filing prevented us from securing even a Veterans Affairs mortgage, at least for now, so instead we leased a three-bedroom condo in Freehold. The rent is high—thus continuing the great American tradition of punishing the working poor by increasing their monthly expenses—and I've got child support and those student loans and debts to my family, but we're managing. We selected Freehold not because it's Springsteen's hometown, but because Gina secured a job teaching seventh grade English at an excellent middle school there. Together, my new family and I chose to be closer to Ben in Cherry Hill. I see more of Sam but less of Moe, while Gina sees more of her sister in Montclair and less of her mother in Forest Hills. Ultimately, it seems, *everything* comes with caveats both good and bad. My son will be a teenager before I stop worrying his mother will move him yet again. Gina says I've muttered *Hague* in my sleep.

It's a later pick-up than usual. A truck jackknifed near the Molly Pitcher stop, where the Jersey Turnpike Man undoubtedly was gobbling fries and dispensing legal advice. Ben was barely awake when I strapped him in at the halfway point Kasper and I long ago calculated via Google Maps. Kasper's a lot grumpier these days, apparently because the Garden State wasn't in his long-term planning and somehow *I* am to blame for him not seeing his kids in Israel. Imagine that logic. I've found insanity often bubbles beneath fragile surfaces.

I drive and steal glances at Ben in the mirror. As we pass the turnoff I take for work, I conclude our weekends really begin Saturday mornings, not Friday nights.

My new boss at Trenton-Mercer Airport also served in Keflavik *and* said Bob M. raved about me, so we bonded in the lobby. Initially I thought her unaware of my LGA mishap, but she shrugged: "They call 'em near-misses, not near-hits." After I explained joint custody, she allowed me off during Ben's visits, so I'm free until meeting Kasper on Sunday. And I've decided to give back, by joining the union's mentoring program.

It's dark and cold and the muted dashboard lights lull me into thinking—once again—about recent history. We pass the river but the windows are sealed and the water only pantomimes motion. The wheels beneath us churn up the miles that separate.

On our honeymoon, Gina revealed something's bugged her. Back in Kew Gardens, I said my favorite subject was English; so why study Psychology? I didn't have an answer, though I considered it for days. Finally it hit me. My desire to analyze my fellow air traffic controllers is not nearly as acute as my desire to write about them.

So Gina registered me for a Creative Nonfiction Workshop at Rutgers, one of the best gifts I've ever received, and I shared pages from this journal. Then we read *The Things They Carried* and spent an hour discussing *metafiction*; during the break the instructor and I took another ten minutes deciding if these pages are fiction or nonfiction. It's hard even for me to say. Just who is this Michael Mullen? Does he even exist? And will people reading this very page flip to the author's photo on the jacket and look at that Irish-American face and ask the same thing? Am I trying to convey truth? Or Truth? How much does it matter now? Years from now? "Fiction is often the best fact," stated William Faulkner. Of course, he also stated: "The past is never dead. It's not even past."

And credit where it's due to my wife on curbing aggression; Gina suggests we modify Punch Buggy to earn points rather than punches for Volkswagens, and the one with the most points picks Saturday's movie. On the other hand, we strongly encourage Ashley at their karate dojo, not to be the cutest warrior but to be the fiercest. Also, I listened to Kanye and although I'm no fan, Gina's right about some lyrics. Like the one about the friend's daughter getting a brand new report card, and all he got was a brand new sports car.

"Daddy?"

I'm startled. I had not even noticed the boy was awake. I look at him sitting behind me on the seat. I feel quite alone but this boy has been with me. I wonder for how long.

"Hey, buddy."

I can see in the mirror his eyes are still closed; he's groggy and fighting sleep. He'll be out again soon.

"Daddy…"

"Yeah?"

"We gonna see the baby?"

I turn on the heat since fall is definitely here. "You mean, mommy's baby? You saw him today…"

"The *other* baby."

"Ashley? She's at our house."

He shakes his head.

"You mean Henry? At Sam's?"

"*No.*"

"Oh! Baby Charlotte. Aunt Chris and Aunt Katie's baby!"

"Uh uh. The...*new* baby."

Finally I nod. "You mean Uncle Kevin and Aunt Nicole's baby. It's not here yet, buddy. It'll be here soon."

"Okay..."

I adjust the heat. Lovey finally gave out and we donated her to charity, that orange *CHECK ENGINE* light glowing till the end. We've leased an azure Ford Escape, with ample room for a booster seat and a car seat, and named her Blue. One day while I showered, Gina and the kids pasted stick figures onto the tailgate: a daddy, mommy, small boy, smaller girl. Late that night I asked Gina why she didn't slice the boy into a seventh, and she gently stroked my cheek.

"How's second grade, buddy?"

Ben sighs, his eyes still closed. "We're gonna learn violins..."

"Really? Sounds like fun! Will you teach me?"

"Okay. Daddy? Can we go to the graves?"

There's nothing like a child's segues, and I deftly keep up. In addition to all the over-the-top drama in his short life, this year Ben suffered his first loss of someone close—a grandparent. "Yes. We could go."

"Grandpa Tom?"

I nod. "Yeah. We could bring him to see Grandma Eileen. And Aunt Lizzie."

It all happened so quickly earlier this year, Katie shouting about chest pains and me running five doors down and both of us driving my mother to Long Island Jewish, as per her doctor. In the car, I tried singing *Love Me Do*. We'd only been there an hour, my sister and I scribbling paperwork in the lobby, assuming we'd hear about a stent or possibly bypass, when the cardiologist called us in and said she was gone. *Gone?* We just got here! Katie and Chris picked up the infant Charlotte one week after the funeral.

"I miss Grandma too, buddy. We'll go before it gets cold."

A growing list of chores. Registering for another workshop at Rutgers. Painting Ashley's new dresser. Bidding on that *Beloved* first edition for Gina's birthday. Finding a boxing club as dingy as Archie's Ring of Fire. Scheduling Paco since I'm down to calling him just once a month; even by phone, his wisdom never ceases.

Your son has taught you at least as fucking much as you've taught him.

And Ben is asleep again. I know when we get home, Ashley will be asleep as well. But Gina will be up, wearing shorts and one of my oversized FAA T-shirts, and her dark brown glasses because her contacts will be out. She'll be drinking coffee and grading papers, to free up the weekend for the four of us. After I back into our condo's one-car driveway I'll carry the sleeping boy and his schoolbag in my arms and tap softly at our door. She'll open it and kiss me on the lips. Then she'll gently push Ben's hair from his forehead and kiss him as well; she'll take him from me and put him to bed. In the kitchen, food will be warming on the stove. Gina will sit sideways on my lap while I eat, and she'll pick at my supper and I'll tell her to get herself a plate and she'll say no, she already ate—and then she'll pick at my food again. Then I'll ask her to read the better essay answers on *1984*. We might have one of our weekly spats—the one where I mention finding lint in the clothes dryer, noting it's a fire hazard. Or the one where she traces carpet stains directly to my dirty boots. Eventually she'll wrap both arms around my neck, and the room will become quieter. I'll move my hand to her bare tummy and she'll frown and say it's getting too soft and I'll say, are you kidding, most women ten years younger would kill to have half—and she'll kiss me. Then my hand will continue moving, and she'll whisper into my scalp, *Whatcha doing, Mullen?* When she kisses me again I'll mock pretend her coffee breath has dampened my enthusiasm, but our roaming hands will belie this and in retaliation she'll mock pretend her feelings were hurt and she'll breathe coffee all over my face and I'll tickle her in the one place where I know the reaction will be immediate and she'll yelp just a decibel too loud and we'll freeze and listen for stirring from the bedrooms. Then we'll both laugh. Soon I'll check the windows and locks and together we'll make two stops—in the first room, Ashley will be curled into a tight ball with only her dark hair showing, while in the second room Ben will have partially thrashed off the covers, so Gina will tuck in a bare leg. Then we'll move to our bathroom, knowing on Saturday morning four little feet will bounce on our mattress until we groggily agree to make my legendary blueberry pancakes or ride our bikes to the creek or go pumpkin picking and hay riding. But that's still hours away, I'll whisper from behind as Gina brushes her teeth. Then her glasses will come off, and I'll kill the lights.

Our lives are as rich as I could ever have hoped for on all days, but they're richer still on those two days when Ben joins us. Yes, he shares weeks in the summer and at Christmas. And yes, we attend the momentous events; we're present for Little League trophies, recorder concerts, awards nights. And of course I call every day. But Ben is simply growing up without me. It's not fair and it's not right and it's certainly not justice that our time is so parceled. But we take what we are given. I know all this.

And what of Ben? And New York State's oft-repeated goal of serving the best interests of the child? I consider it every single day, yet I find it difficult to determine. He bounces back and forth, back and forth, between two beds and two toothbrushes and two sets of books, toys, DVDs, clothes. Are the six average days he spends with her and Kasper and the baby superior to the one average day he spends with Gina and Ashley and me? I truly can't say. My deepest hope is all his days are filled with love and nurturing.

In the end Ben was right to choose her and retain both parents. And I'll always believe he was right. All it cost was a part of my heart—the one we give to someone on February 14th. But even though the state has decreed I'm to be one-seventh of a parent, I'll spend my life assuring Ben there are absolutely no limits to his father's love. I'm determined that he never regrets his decision.

Of course, there's still so much I don't know. Yet there's much I do know.

And what I do know—yes, I do know it—I know this sweet boy will grow into a fine and strong and kind man. But just as I sat by his bed on so many long nights until he finally fell off to sleep, what I don't know is one day it will be Ben who sits by my bed, holding my weathered hand and stroking my thin hair, when I finally fall off on the longest of all nights. And this strong man will be humming to me. And then he will lean in close and sing to his father.

> *In Dublin's fair city,*
> *Where the girls are so pretty,*
> *I first set my eyes on sweet Molly Malone,*
> *As she wheeled her wheelbarrow,*
> *Through streets broad and narrow,*

Crying, "Cockles and mussels, alive, alive, oh!"

I will smile, or I will tell myself I'm smiling. Somehow there will be tears—I won't know whose—as my boy keeps singing.

"Alive, alive, oh,

"Alive, alive, oh,"

Crying, "Cockles and mussels, alive, alive, oh!"

And suddenly I have the answer to his question from years ago. Where did the love go? That love I felt for her and she felt for me. It was real, and it was here, and now it isn't. I know it existed, and nothing that's happened since—none of it—can change that. It was touchable, tangible, truthful. And physics has its laws, one of which is matter can't just disappear, not without taking another form.

I loved her and she loved me.

We laughed at things that weren't at all funny, smiled while sitting alone, broke into tuneless song while crossing a parking lot. All that happened and more, and nothing can change how I felt, or how she felt.

I remember us lying together. And I remember the love as she stared into my eyes. "Sing for me, Mikey!"

"Sing? Sing what?"

It was a summer night in Newburgh and we lay intertwined and spent. We had only recently met, and yet I felt I always knew her. My fingers danced along vital organs.

"Sing to me, Mikey," she breathed into my neck.

"But what?" I held her tighter. "C'mon, Sarah..."

Her eyes closed. "Anything..."

And so I began. I caressed her red hair, and her knee rose higher as the embrace tightened. I smiled too, and my eyes closed as well. I sang of Dublin. And I sang of her.

In Dublin's fair city,

Where the girls are so pretty,

She smiled so beatifically I truly believed my heart would never ache again.

I first set my eyes on...sweet Sarah of mine...

So where did it go, Ben had asked me. A fair and valid question. And now, finally, as I glance at him sleeping in reverse from the rearview mirror, I know. Love can be transferred, but it cannot be erased, and it cannot be denied.

So where did it go?

Ah, buddy.

You.

That's where it went. All that love—it all went into you, buddy.

ACKNOWLEDGMENTS

I am indebted—in every sense—to my family. The siblings as well as all those in-laws, nieces, nephews, cousins. Then there's Andy Postman, providing more support than seems possible. My faith in this book was bolstered by Alex Postman, Stephani Cook, and the legendary Joni Evans. Encouragement came from Tom De Haven, Lis Harris, Judy Stone, Katherine Taylor, Nick Galifianakis, Pat Navarra, Jan Elizabeth Watson, Ruth Andrew Ellenson, Victor LaValle, and Tova Mirvis. Navigating publishing was eased by W.M. Bunche, Lizz Dinnigan, Thomas Porky McDonald, Matthew Romano, Gary Ward, and Dawn Barclay. Dan Kirschen at ICM provided early assistance.

I've been lucky to have Lynne Bernstein's careful copyediting of every word and (Oxford!) comma; Eric Hoffsten's artistry; Les Luchter's promotion; and Mary Wyatt's sharp eye. Elaine Grant's counsel was invaluable. Sharon Devivo at Vaughn College was so generous, as was colleague Loretta Alkalay and the helpful folks in the LGA tower.

Many thanks to Tom Wojtaszek, David Cogswell, Debra D'Agostino, Pam Fehl, Rhonda Hack, Sue Juliano, Phyllis Fine, Maria Gil, Mike Milligan, Stacy Small, Shelley Postman, Beau Brendler, Barbara Peterson, Jackie Sullivan, Jenni Shettleworth, Lynne Ann Schwarzenberg, Tommie Howell, Delmar Ramirez, and of course Wes Gill. And all the devoted fathers, like Tommy Wilson, Paul Navarra, Jukka Paasonen, Mike Juliano, and Brian Major.

Mario Santamaria began this journey with me, and I still feel his presence. Then Lisa Albin arrived, bringing so many sparkles.

And Nick.

ABOUT THE AUTHOR

WILLIAM J. McGEE was born in New York City and received an MFA in Fiction from Columbia University. Among other pursuits, he teaches undergraduate and graduate Creative Writing; represents travelers as a consumer advocate in Washington; and is an award-winning investigative journalist and columnist. McGee is the former Editor-in-Chief of *Consumer Reports Travel Letter* and also worked in airline flight operations management and served in the U.S. Air Force Auxiliary. He is the author of *Attention All Passengers*, a nonfiction exposé of the airline industry, and is developing *AirFear*, a scripted television drama. McGee lives in Connecticut and is, of course, at work on another novel. He is also a father.

Made in the USA
Columbia, SC
19 July 2018